THE GRAVEWOOD

ALSO BY KELLY ANDREW

The Whispering Dark
Your Blood, My Bones
I Am Made of Death

THE GRAVEWOOD

KELLY ANDREW

TRANSWORLD PUBLISHERS

UK | USA | Canada | Ireland | Australia
India | New Zealand | South Africa

Transworld is part of the Penguin Random House group of companies whose addresses can be found at global.penguinrandomhouse.com.

Penguin Random House UK,
One Embassy Gardens, 8 Viaduct Gardens, London SW11 7BW

penguin.co.uk

First published in Great Britain in 2026 by Transworld TxF
an imprint of Transworld Publishers

001

Copyright © 2026 by Kelly Andrew

The moral right of the author has been asserted.

This book is a work of fiction and, except in the case of historical fact, any resemblance to actual persons, living or dead, is purely coincidental.

Every effort has been made to obtain the necessary permissions with reference to copyright material, both illustrative and quoted. We apologize for any omissions in this respect and will be pleased to make the appropriate acknowledgements in any future edition.

Penguin Random House values and supports copyright. Copyright fuels creativity, encourages diverse voices, promotes freedom of expression and supports a vibrant culture. Thank you for purchasing an authorized edition of this book and for respecting intellectual property laws by not reproducing, scanning or distributing any part of it by any means without permission. You are supporting authors and enabling Penguin Random House to continue to publish books for everyone. No part of this book may be used or reproduced in any manner for the purpose of training artificial intelligence technologies or systems. In accordance with Article 4(3) of the DSM Directive 2019/790, Penguin Random House expressly reserves this work from the text and data mining exception.

Book design by Maeve Norton
Printed and bound in Great Britain by Clays Ltd, Elcograf S.p.A.

The authorized representative in the EEA is Penguin Random House Ireland, Morrison Chambers, 32 Nassau Street, Dublin D02 YH68.

A CIP catalogue record for this book is available from the British Library.

ISBNs
9781911751588 hb
9781911751595 tpb

Penguin Random House is committed to a sustainable future for our business, our readers and our planet. This book is made from Forest Stewardship Council® certified paper.

FOR THE SQUARE PEGS IN A ROUND HOLE. SOMEDAY YOU'LL FIND A SPACE WHERE YOU FIT JUST AS YOU ARE.

AND FOR J, S, AND O, WHO MAKE ALL OF THIS WORTHWHILE.

ACT I
THE DEVIL

I know a bank where the wild thyme blows,
Where oxlips and the nodding violet grows,
Quite over-canopied with luscious woodbine,
With sweet musk-roses and with eglantine.

Shakespeare's *A Midsummer Night's Dream*

MAY
SIX MONTHS AGO

THE BEGINNING...

Initiation nights are always a bore.

The great hall of Mercy Ridge floods with runaways, led in from the cold like pigs to a slaughter. They stand in a silent line, backs against the wall and faces downturned. Hungry. Cold. Not a single one of them is impressive. They rarely are. This far north, the valley towns churn out nothing but errant schoolboys and bored pubescents, wayward youths sick of life in the rural hinterlands. Boys, not men, cowering in fear each time a wolf howls.

It isn't the wolves that scare them.

Not really.

It's the boy on the hearth, thin as a rail and quiet as a wraith. Oliver Lysander doesn't need a mirror to know what it is they see when they look at him: heavily inked hands and an unsmiling face, his features uncanny, like a baroque artist's rendering of a human. A little too pretty. A little too pale.

A little too hungry.

The boy directly before him is the last of tonight's hopefuls. He isn't privy to the bloody thoughts that pulse in Lysander's head, or the way Lysander imagines sinking his teeth into his throat. If he was—if he had any idea at all—the boy would turn and run.

He'd take his chance with the wolves.

Like the previous initiate, there is nothing about *this* particular boy that Lysander likes. This one is from Little Hill—a tiny, dull-as-dirt town just south of the mountain. Lysander can tell because he's dressed in the hideous uniform of Little Hill's stuffy Hornbeam Hall, the bare oak crest silver against a jacket the color of mud.

His name is Tristan, like fair Iseult's ill-fated knight. Last name Choi. His face is bloodless, pale. His hands open and close in trembling fists. At Lysander's back, his own fingers twitch in a subconscious imitation.

He has never been able to help himself from mimicking his prey.

"You're afraid of me." He doesn't pose it as a question, and so maybe that's why Tristan doesn't answer. The silence irks him anyway. "Don't stand there and stare. *Say* something."

"I'm not," gasps Tristan, and he sounds nothing at all like a knight. "I'm not afraid."

Lysander peers down at him, unconvinced. "I don't need liars in my crew. I need people I can trust."

Nearby, Lysander's lieutenant makes a sound that is very nearly a groan. Cyrus Talbot stands propped against the adjacent wall, his face bloodless and his eyes dull. Desiccated, the way Lysander is desiccating. Starved, the way Lysander is starving. Neither of them has fed tonight, and it's making them both tetchy.

"There's no need to drag this out," Cyrus says. "Either he's in or he's not."

The silent implication hangs between them: Either he lives or he dies. Cyrus is clearly hoping for the latter. His mouth is already full of teeth.

In the room's carpeted quiet, Tristan's heart beats faster. "I think

I'd make a valuable part of the crew," he says. It comes out in a rush, words bumping one into the other.

Lysander drags his gaze back toward this boy-who-is-not-a-knight, considering him anew. "Valuable." He mulls it over, pinning Tristan in his stare. "The Spartans were considered to have the strongest army in ancient Greece. Their battles were fought in a phalanx. Have you covered that in school?"

Tristan glances between him and Cyrus. "No."

"No, of course not," says Lysander. "God forbid they teach you history. It's a tactical formation. Heavily armed infantry would stand shoulder to shoulder, several ranks deep. Linked together, they became a single entity. They moved as one. They killed as one. When the enemy pushed, they'd push back. Can you stand?"

Tristan swallows. "Yes."

"Can you *push*?"

"Yes."

"Then you're valuable. That's not the question I'm asking. What I want to know is whether you're loyal."

"I am," says Tristan, without missing a beat.

"Maybe to someone," agrees Lysander. "But will you be loyal to me?"

Cyrus grins, teeth sharp. "He has trust issues."

Lysander ignores his lieutenant, watching Tristan fidget under his gaze. "Here's what I think—you're here tonight because you're running from something."

"Who isn't?" asks Tristan.

"Me," he counters, though this is a lie.

Oliver Lysander had run so far, he ran all the way here—to

damp, dull New Hampshire. To the belly of Mercy Mountain, perennially frozen and perpetually dark. He dug out a home for himself in the shell of the old ski lodge and then assembled his crew from the ground up. Cyrus first, and then the rest. The Mercy Boys, his very own army. Ragtag and runaway and impossible to call to heel, but loyal to the bone. He *needs* them loyal. He needs them united—a single defensive entity. One day, the thing that chased him so far north will come looking. If it finds him alone, it'll destroy him.

He doesn't plan to let it.

"Tell me what you're running from and maybe we'll keep you around."

Tristan's throat bobs in a swallow. Whatever it is, he doesn't want to say. Lysander can just make out the wild flutter of the boy's pulse in the soft curve of his neck. He can *hear* it, palpitating through his veins in frantic ticks. He can *smell* it, ambrosia sweet.

His mouth waters.

"I graduate this year," says Tristan. "My brother went to university, but my grades—my family expects me to enlist."

"And you're afraid to be on the front lines," guesses Lysander.

Tristan balks. "That's not—"

"You think this is the easy way out. Sleeping all day. Feeding all night. No responsibility to anything, or anyone."

"I didn't say that."

"You don't have to. I've seen it before. No one wants to hunt us and die. Not when they could *be* us and live. You're not special, you're—"

"I don't want to die for something I don't believe in," snaps Tristan, cutting him off.

It's a pretty answer. A *noble* answer, full of conviction. Still, Lysander can hear the avoidance in it. The way Tristan skirts around admitting the whole truth. There's something else. Something he's too ashamed to admit. Here, now, is what he's been looking for. *These* are the sorts of recruits Lysander needs.

The ones who have already shut the door behind them.

"Not everyone survives," Lysander says. "Sometimes the Rot gets into your head instead of your blood. Sometimes it breaks you."

Tristan's eyes dart to Cyrus. "What does— Does this mean I'm in?"

Decisions, decisions. In or out. Live or die. Mercy Boy or carrion. The Rot is in everything. The beasts. The trees. The boys. They drink it up from the groundwater, let the hunger take hold.

If Tristan is in, he'll live here at Mercy Ridge. If he's not, they'll cast him out and let the wolves have his body, let the forest gnaw on his bones. Either way, Tristan Choi won't be leaving the forest again.

"Your membership is conditional."

He watches as some of Tristan's courage flags. "Conditional on what?"

"On what happens when you drink from the well."

"*Finally,*" crows Cyrus, springing from the wall. "I can take him there."

The well, as it were, is more of a pump. It sits in the courtyard, rusted and ugly and girded in lichen. Its pipes run deep, pulling from the same water that feeds the forest. The same spring-fed poison that gave the trees teeth. It gives them teeth, too—those who call the forest home. It makes them hungry. Sharp. Cold. Or else it consumes them.

Like he told Tristan, not everyone Turns.

"Thank you," says Tristan as Cyrus ushers him toward the exit. He sounds a little regretful, the full weight of what he's asked for dropping down on him like an axe. Cyrus tosses a knowing smirk at Lysander as he slings an arm over Tristan's shoulder. There's no undoing what's about to be done, and both of them know it.

"I love an initiation." Cyrus crooks his elbow, hooking Tristan in close. "It's always a good time. Come on, kid, let's go see how gods are made."

The door skids slowly shut in their wake. Cold creeps in through the crack.

Outside, the hall is empty. Through peels of paint along the blacked-out windows, Lysander can just see the first few tinges of dawn. A pale, ashy light he's never felt upon his skin. He sinks into an empty chair by the hearth, kicking out his boots. Letting the fatigue crawl into him. He's only eighteen, but he feels a thousand years old. Like he carries the forest in his chest.

He shuts his eyes. Jabs a finger at his temple. He wishes for a sleep that won't come. He's not immortal—not in the storybook sense—but the possibility of eons stretches tauntingly before him regardless. A lifetime in the dark.

Alone.

"Hello?"

He jolts immediately to his feet.

A girl is there, standing in the doorway where there should have been no one. Silent, when he should have heard her approach. She looks very small between the room's wide white columns. The lights of the chandelier emblazon her features, turning her elfin in the gloom.

He knows he ought to say something. Something clever. Something cutting. Instead, he holds himself still and charts her in silence. Her hair is a mousy blonde, cut just beneath her chin. She's dressed similarly to Tristan Choi—in Hornbeam colors. A brown jacket. A pleated skirt. A regimental tie and scuffed leather shoes.

The hunger within him comes screaming to the surface. Not because he didn't expect to see her here—there have been girls at initiation before—but because of her hand, held out like an offering between them. A deep gash runs across her palm. Blood gathers in the shallow creases, red and tempting.

He stares, and she stares back. He knows what it is she sees. There's a hard pulse of hunger behind his eyes, an ache that chips at his control. When he gets like this—ravenous—his appetite leaves him bruised all over.

He knows what they call him, down in the valley towns—knows why they cross themselves when they pass too close to the trees, why they whisper his name in the midnight dark.

If the Gravewood is hell on earth, then he is its devil.

"That's quite an entrance," he says, doing what he can to ignore the trickle of blood along her fingers. "I'm curious to hear how you made it to the lodge in one piece."

"I walked." Her voice is low and sweet, an unplaceable accent softening its edges. His intrigue intensifies.

"Alone?"

"Do *you* see anyone else?"

It comes out combative—more so, perhaps, than she meant it to. Her face betrays nothing, but he can hear her heart hammering against her rib cage. His gives a single, hard thump in reply. A wordless call-and-response that leaves him rattled.

"You should never have made it here on your own. The trees in this part of the woods are carnivorous. They whisper all kinds of things when the wind blows."

The girl's shoulder lifts in a shrug. "I must not have heard them."

Ridiculously, he finds himself biting back a smile. He shouldn't be *smiling* at her impertinence—he should be throwing her to the wolves.

"I'm impressed," he says instead. He means it. "I've seen hardened forest rangers follow the voice of a loved one into the pines."

There's a beat, during which he can see her fitting his words together. Then, "Maybe I have a secret weapon."

This time, his smile breaks loose of its own volition. "Maybe you do."

Silence falls again. She doesn't rush to fill it, and so neither does he. He listens to the hard beat of her heart in the quiet. He tries to imagine her in the woods all alone, ignoring the beckoning of the birch trees, the hungry pleading of the ancient hemlocks—faces of the devoured grafted into their trunks. She stares back at him all the while, her blood gathering at her fingertips. He clears his throat.

"Unfortunately, you're too late. I've filled all available slots."

She blinks, surprised. "I'm not here to Turn."

His curiosity is so deep, it's tectonic. He wonders what her blood would taste like against the flat of his tongue. He wonders if Achilles knew, upon meeting Patroclus, that it would end in tragedy. If he went in with both eyes open anyway.

"I assume you have a name," he says.

"It's Shea."

He likes how it sounds. One syllable, soft as a gasp.

"And you know who I am."

"I do. You're the Gravewood D—"

"Lys." One syllable. Sharp as a knife. He angles his head to the side—watches her swallow his name the way he swallowed hers. The whole room smells like blood. It makes him feel stark raving mad.

"If you're not here to Turn, then you must have a death wish."

"I don't want to die."

The slight quiver in her voice narrows his focus. Suddenly, all he can see is her. All he can *hear* is her. The too-fast clip of her heart. The frantic rush of her pulse. The soft *plink* of her blood dripping to the floor. In that moment—her eyes shining with a resolve he feels all the way down in his gut—she doesn't look like an obstinate girl from Little Hill. She looks like ruination.

If he were smart, he'd send her away.

"If you're not here to die and you're not here to Turn, then why come at all?"

"Isn't it obvious?" She holds her hand flat between them. Her palm is red all over. "I'm here to make you a deal."

NOVEMBER
PRESENT

ONE

Shea

Camellia Thorley's missing poster doesn't stand out.

It's one of a dozen overlapping sheets, each one pinned to the wall outside the grocer's. It's misting today, the whole of Little Hill swallowed up in a cloud. The paper is wet—nearly translucent. It curls in on itself every time the wind blows.

The girl in the photograph is small and willowy, her smile gapped with missing teeth and her golden hair pulled back in bows. The photo is outdated. At least six years old. The last time anyone at Hornbeam saw Camellia Thorley—two weeks ago, to be exact—she was half a foot taller and in possession of all her teeth. She hadn't worn bows in years.

No one will find Camellia Thorley.

Just like no one ever found the others.

When the Gravewood swallows someone, it doesn't spit them back out.

The bell rattles over the door when Shea slips out of the November chill and into Brer's Corner Mart. The sound is muffled—nearly nonexistent—the way it always is on days when she's forgone her hearing aids. The air inside the shop is warm and thick. It condenses in a cloud along the wide glass windows. She scuffs her boots against the mat, letting the heat chase the cold from her bones. She tries not to think about Camellia at all.

"Two students at a time," shouts Silas Brer. The rest of his gripe is incomprehensible. Something about mud, she's sure. He hates mopping the floors.

Shea's come in alone, but Silas wouldn't know that. The elderly grocer is perched precariously atop his stepladder, thoroughly preoccupied by stacking boiled fruits along the topmost shelf. She's always thought his shop looked less like a grocer's and more like a root cellar, canning jars arranged haphazardly in every direction. It's the only way to eat anything grown from the ground—pickled or fermented, boiled and canned, the Rot cooked out of them.

She's sick to the teeth of cured vegetables and freeze-dried fruits, but food is food, and the pantry back home has been almost empty for weeks. She plucks several jars of canned peaches from the shelf as she heads for the candy counter, weighing them in her palm before easing them into the battered shell of her knapsack.

Silas doesn't notice. He never does. It isn't that he's inattentive, it's only that Shea Parker is a creature of silence. It's a benefit of being born in it—she knows how to come and go without making a sound. It's why she leaves her hearing aids in her pockets whenever she's sneaking. It hones the world to a point, lets her slink along the tip of it, quiet as a mouse.

The candy counter is picked over, as usual. Scant, the way

everything in Little Hill is scant. She can't remember a time when life wasn't this way. When she was small, she'd fall asleep with her mother's secondhand memories looping like a film reel through her head—Christmases in Manhattan, the windows of Saks Fifth Avenue glittering with lights. Summers on the Cape, catamaran sails puffed up with wind. Octobers in Salem, the stores packed with witchy trinkets and cheap souvenirs.

The Rot sprang up overnight, but the end of the world came in increments. Gradual—slow—so that no one noticed it happening until it was over. Once it was done, they carried on as best they could. Even as the stores shuttered. Even as the phone lines went down. Even when Washington went dark. *Adaptive as rats*, her father used to say—a comparison her mother detested. Unlike Shea's well-traveled mother, her father never left home until the Rot arrived. The first time he set foot on a train, it was as a soldier of the newly established wood watch. Ready to fight and die to preserve the final echoes of a life he'd never tasted.

These days, there are no tinsel-clad holidays, no jaunts to the city, and no summertime excursions. Food is carefully rationed. Medicine, more so. The only way to get anything extra this far north is through the Mercy Boys, and fraternization with the Gravewood Devil isn't just prohibited, it's a death sentence. If something doesn't snatch you off the path on the way to Mercy Ridge, the watch will gun you down on the return journey home.

No one comes back from the Gravewood.

Not when a single sip of spring-fed water is enough to Rot the blood. Everyone in Little Hill knows what happened in the neighboring town of Highbush—how the Rot swept through overnight.

It's a ghost town now, bordered in barbed-wire fencing. A cautionary tale, used to frighten children away from the trees.

They don't take chances anymore.

If you step outside the bounds, you don't come back.

Fishing through an assortment of old penny candy, Shea pockets a lollipop, cherry red and flat as a coin. It's hardly substantial, as far as snacks go, but the sugar will stave off the pounding in her head, at least. It's always like this the day after a feed—her throat dry, her skin aching, a percussive beat at her temples—but today it's particularly bad. She was barely able to focus in school. She's positive she failed Mrs. Appledorn's latest pop quiz—she left the last three pages blank. At the rate she's going, she won't be surprised if she's forced to repeat her senior year.

Not that it matters.

Rounding the shelves, she finds Silas stepping off the bottom rung of his ladder.

"Oh." He draws up short. "It's *you*."

She watches his mouth shape the words, wariness tightening the corners. It's the unfortunate side effect of being Calhoun Parker's daughter. She drags her dead father's reputation behind her like a ball and chain. She rattles his memory like a Dickensian ghost.

"I brought you something," she says, before Silas can ask her to turn out her pockets. She twists her backpack forward to better rifle through its side pouch, careful not to shift the stolen contents as she tugs loose several shoots of white cohosh. Silas's eyes thin in immediate suspicion.

"Baneberry like that grows out by the Gravewood."

"*By* the Gravewood," agrees Shea. "Not in it."

Silas doesn't budge. "At the rate the Mercy Boys have been picking off your classmates, I'd think you'd be a bit smarter than that."

She thinks of Lys. She can't help it. It's a knee-jerk reaction. His dark, inhuman eyes. That sharp, inhuman smile. The scrape of his voice against the shell of her ear: *That's a boring rumor. I don't take anyone who doesn't beg to be taken.*

"There was a patch of it growing out by Fletcher's," she says quickly, shoving all thoughts of the Mercy Boy in the dark where they belong. "I passed it on my walk to school this morning."

"It doesn't matter if you dug it up right in your backyard. You know I can't sell that here."

"You can if you boil it," says Shea. "My mom likes to make it into tea."

Liked. She *liked* to make tea.

The correction is a knife. It lodges in her chest.

"It's not half bad with honey," she adds, though her voice comes out pinched. "And it's good for a cough."

"*Cough medicine* is good for a cough," says Silas, but both of them know there's no cough medicine left. Still wary, he takes the wilting cohosh from Shea's outstretched hand. The mention of her mother has softened his suspicion, just a little.

Ivy Parker—formerly Everly, and the only surviving member of Little Hill's founding family—is Little Hill's fallen angel. Pretty, popular Ivy, who disappointed everyone when she married a poor boy from Highbush and moved to the outskirts of town. Pitiable, innocent Ivy, who had a baby four short months later. A sickly little thing, too still, too small, too silent.

Lovely, golden-haired Ivy, who went gray in the weeks after

Calhoun Parker left home in the dead of night and didn't return.

"Is she all right?" Silas asks. "Your mother? Haven't seen her around."

"She's fine," says Shea, and *this* is a lie. Her very worst one. "She sends her best."

Silas looks unconvinced. "Maybe I should have Marla stop over one of these days. She can bring her famous casserole. Check in on things."

"No." Her voice is too sharp to be mistaken for anything but panic. She tries again, softer this time. "Thank you, it's just that she's not up for visitors."

"Right, of course."

There's no denying how thin the excuse has worn. It's been seven years since Shea's father disappeared. Eleven whole months since anyone has seen her mother outside the house. Shea can't keep up the ruse forever.

Thankfully, Silas doesn't pry any further. His head kicks up, angling toward the door. The bell has rung again, too far off for Shea to hear it. She feels, in the soles of her feet, the subtle creak of floorboards, the telltale shift of another customer arriving.

"You'd better get on home." Silas reaches for his pushcart, his eyes on the sky. "Sun's due to set within the hour. If Constable Foster catches you out of the house after curfew, that stolen candy in your pocket will be the least of your troubles."

"It's not stolen," she argues. "I bartered for it. Don't forget to add honey to the tea."

"I'm throwing that poison right in the garbage," Silas calls after her, but she knows he won't. He's far too frugal. The last shipment was late in the summer. No trucks have come through since then.

It's those Mercy Boys, say the rumors. *They're smoking us out.*

But Shea's not so sure she believes it. The Mercy Boys weren't around when her father got sick, and there wasn't medicine then, either. It's why he left—to take the burden of watching him wither and die off her mother's shoulders. No debt. No doubt. No slow, painful demise.

Only the forest and its teeth, the lesser of two evils.

She's so lost in thoughts of her father, she doesn't notice Asher Thorley standing on the mat until she collides directly into him. Her backpack—still clutched protectively before her—jams between them. The stolen cans bite into her belly through the fabric. From the look on his face, he's felt it, too. His brows lift in quiet amusement. His hand closes over the strap before she can wrench herself safely out of reach.

"Fourteen months away and nothing has changed. You're still a little kleptomaniac."

"Let go."

He doesn't. "What do you have in there, Parker?"

"It doesn't matter, it's mine."

His smile is faint but familiar. "Somehow I doubt that."

He's dressed in a sherpa jacket, his hair buzzed short. The last time she saw him, he was leaving for boot camp. She and Camellia watched the scene unfold from across the street—crouched behind the curtains of Poppy Zahar's bedroom window as he'd argued with his father, his duffel bag banding his chest.

He didn't want to enlist, Camellia said, watching her brother through the steam of their breath on the glass, *but we need the stipend. Dad's been out of work for months.*

The Asher standing before her is incongruous with the way she remembers him. His face is more harshly defined, his shoulders broad. Even the way he carries himself is unfamiliar—at attention, his shoulders thrown back instead of rounded against the mountain cold. He looks unyielding as a wall, the playfulness drilled out of him. Only his eyes are the same—a rich golden brown. The color of Fletcher's field in late summer. In his free hand, he grips his sister's poster. Shea's heart plummets to her feet.

"I didn't know you were home," she says, eager to get the focus off her backpack.

"I'm on leave."

"Oh."

It's not that she's been counting the days since he left, it's only that she knows he's not due back for several more months, which means he's been granted special permission. *Emergency* permission. The happy, gap-toothed smile of Camellia Thorley is a bulwark between them. This time, when she tugs at her backpack, he lets it go.

"I'm sorry," she manages. "About Camellia."

His face closes up like a fist. "Everyone's sorry. Her teachers. Constable Foster. My parents. *Sorry* doesn't bring her back."

Shea thinks of how her mother retreated into herself after her father left. How she visibly recoiled each time someone offered up their empty condolences, their shallow sympathies. *Sorry* was a poison. It tainted everything it touched.

"I know." She hopes her tone conveys just how deeply she means it. "I know it doesn't."

"*Sorry* is what people say when someone dies."

There's a worrying determination in his eyes. It's the same conviction she saw etched into her mother's face, in the days and then months after her father disappeared. The same resolve that drew Ivy Parker to the forest's edge night after night, barefoot and shivering, chasing the sound of Calhoun Parker's voice on the wind—ignoring her daughter as she pled with her to come home: *Mom, it's the trees. It's just the trees, it isn't Dad.*

"Ellie's not dead," says Asher. "She's missing. And missing people can be found."

Still on the floor, Shea's heart forms a single, deep fissure. "She's not missing," she tells him as gently as she can. "She's in the Gravewood."

She shouldn't *have* to say it. She shouldn't *need* to remind him. It's been beaten into them from the moment they were born: Don't go into the forest. Don't answer if it calls. Don't bleed where the trees can taste it.

No one comes back from the Gravewood alive.

She ghosts a thumb over the bite at her wrist and thinks: *Not without the devil's permission.*

"I thought you weren't afraid of the trees." His teasing falls flat, their rapport rubbed thin by his time away, by his missing sister, by the awful things she's done in the months since he left. Her guilt is a wild, clawing thing.

She tugs the sleeves of her blazer lower just as he says, "You look different."

"*You* look different." It's a feeble comeback, and both of them know it. A band of worry runs through her. She wonders if he can tell. If he can see it on her—the pale skin, the glassy eyes, the tremor in her hands. If he knows, after months of training, how to recognize signs of a bite.

"Combat training will do that to you." The look on his face invites no further inquiry. "Did you talk to my sister? Before she left? Did she say anything strange?"

The question is like being doused in ice water. Every answer she could possibly give feels like the exact wrong one. In the end, she settles on a partial truth.

"I've already told Constable Foster everything I know."

"Well, he's not asking," says Asher. "I am."

He says it like it ought to count for something, and maybe it should. She thinks of six years past—when she'd been eleven years old and perpetually angry, every part of her itchy and ill-fitting. Earlier that day, Mr. Belrose had pulled her aside and chastised her for disrupting the lesson—made her stand and write lines on the board while the rest of the class read silently from the textbook: *I won't talk back to my elders. I won't talk back to my elders. I won't talk back to my elders.*

When school was done, she'd raced home with tears in her eyes and wrath in her throat, furious at the terrible injustice of it all. It wasn't that she'd misbehaved on purpose, it was only that she hadn't heard Mr. Foster call for order. The harder she'd tried to explain it to him, the less he'd listened, until she'd finally accused him of being the one with non-working ears.

Still bristling from the encounter, she'd wedged herself into the top of an old dogwood tree at the forest's edge. She sat and watched the trees undulate in the wind, wishing she could hear the promises swaying in their branches.

Camellia and Poppy found her there a short while later, her palms abraded and her stockings torn. When she refused to come down, they left to get help. Reinforcements arrived fifteen minutes later in the form of Asher Thorley—thirteen years old and fed up with her antics.

"I'm not afraid of the Gravewood," she'd insisted as he coaxed her down. "There's nothing to do in Little Hill but wait to die. Why not do it where the trees can see?"

She'd dropped to the ground to find Asher's expression a careful blank. She'd known right away that he was thinking of her father—of the way Calhoun Parker left his family without a word. She'd braced herself for yet another empty platitude. Another meaningless scrap of sympathy.

Instead, he'd said, "That's the stupidest thing I've ever heard."

"It isn't stupid. It's true. Which would you rather? A slow, horrible death, or a quick, painless one?"

"You're not dying a slow, horrible death."

"That's what you think."

Feeling mulish, she'd thrown out her arms and collapsed into a patch of auburn overdam, sending several woolly aphids skyward. Directly overhead was a marmalade sky and a dozen feathered seed heads and Asher Thorley's lopsided frown.

"Get up," he'd ordered. "Sun's almost down."

"So what? Are you afraid?"

His face tightened and she counted twelve whole heartbeats before he eased himself down beside her, muttering under his breath as he went. They lay that way for a long time without speaking, watching a dragonfly drift from stalk to stalk. Beneath the earthen musk of the meadow, she'd been able to smell the sharp turpentine of the trees. Cold. Crisp. Inviting. It said nothing at all to her. It never did.

"See," she'd said, "it's not so bad."

"That's because you can't hear it."

She'd turned to face him, each of them mottled in shadows like bruises. "Can you?"

He'd nodded, quiet, his arms crooked behind his head. He'd looked riveted—uneasy—focused on something faraway. A strange sort of jealousy gripped her like a fever.

"What's it saying?"

Asher didn't answer. Not for a long time. Not until dusk fell, and a nearby bullfrog began to croak. Slowly, he rolled on his side to mirror her. They lay face-to-face, the shadow of the forest looming over them.

"I'm not going to die in Little Hill," he said. "I refuse."

The wind picked up, clicking the branches. He met her eyes across the swollen dark.

"I won't let you die here, either."

It wasn't a promise from the forest, but it *was* a promise.

For years, she'd clung to it like a life raft.

"It's almost curfew," she says now. "I should get home."

She doesn't tell him what he wants to hear—she doesn't say a word about his sister, or about the horrible way they fought the day before she disappeared. She doesn't mention how Camellia found her in the third-floor lavatory, changing her bloody dressings between classes, or how she'd gasped when she spotted the half-moon lesions scored into Shea's wrist.

"Asher is risking his life to keep those things away," Camellia had hissed, the color going out of her face, "and you're letting one of them feed on you."

"Quiet. Someone will hear."

"Do you know what they'll do to us? If you bring the Rot home to Little Hill?"

"Stop talking."

"It won't just be your life on the line, Shea. It'll be everyone. Do you remember Highbush? What they did to all those people?"

The way Asher is watching her is too intense. Like he's searching her. Like he knows everything already, without her even having to admit it. She wishes he'd never come home. She's not the same girl she was when he left. She stopped waiting for him to save her a long time ago.

She's grateful when the bell jingles and two more students slip inside the store. Silas barks something incomprehensible from somewhere out of sight. *Two at a time*, most likely.

"I'll see you around," says Shea.

Asher's gaze turns unreadable. "Parker, wait—"

She doesn't. She escapes out into the cold before the door can drift shut. Before her guilt can consume her. Off in the distance, the vast goliath of Mercy Mountain rises out from above the shadowed tree line. The town of Little Hill is gray and cold, but the mountain's craggy face is awash in brilliant gold. The gilded peak feels like a lit beacon, beckoning her back.

A reminder that she belongs to the Gravewood.

To the boy who lives at the heart of it.

It's the deal she struck. It's the reason Camellia is gone. It's the damage she did, the path she chose, and she can never tell Asher any of it. She can never tell him that she had no choice, that she was out of options—that there'd been no more deliveries in months, and she badly needed hearing aid batteries to keep the quiet at bay.

In seven months, she'll be done with high school. Everyone in her graduating class at Hornbeam will go off and find their place. They'll further their studies. They'll join the watch. They'll settle down. They'll make something meaningful of themselves, keep the wheels of Little Hill slowly turning.

Not her. Shea Parker is a liability. A sunk cost. A *burden*.

Poor Ivy, she once overheard Marla Brer say to Silas. *She'll be stuck caring for that one all her life.*

In the end, the trees didn't need to offer up promises to lure Shea into the Gravewood—she'd gone in all on her own.

Asher won't understand. Just like Camellia hadn't understood. *Their* parents still live at home, unscathed by the Rot, their pantry full. Their people haven't left. Their bodies haven't betrayed them. They don't *need*. They're not desperate. Not like her.

She can feel Asher watching her all the way to the end of the road. The weight of his stare is unbearable. She breaks into a run the moment she turns the corner out of sight, where the cluttered main street gives way to farmland, the roads to crumbling stone walls and flattened cattle paths. The air is heavy and wet. The cows lift their heads to watch her pass.

Though nothing is chasing her, she doesn't stop running until she reaches home.

TWO

Shea

When Shea was young, she and her parents spoke with their hands. In the mornings, she'd grudgingly don her hearing aids and trundle the two-mile walk to Hornbeam. She'd spend the next eight hours wading through the stream of inscrutable schoolyard noises and indecipherable classroom cross talk—speaking out of turn, or else not speaking enough.

She'd race back home with her head ringing, her molars ground to dust, and find immediate reprieve waiting there to greet her. She'd cross the threshold and drop her hearing aids onto the hall tree, let the tension rush out of her as the quiet rushed in.

It was like having a secret language. At first, her parents created their own signs—a cupped hand for milk, pinched fingers for food. As she grew older and her language evolved, her father found a battered old American Sign Language dictionary stuffed into the back shelves of the Little Hill library. He brought it home with him, rolled up in his coat.

Calhoun Parker was always like that.

If his family needed something, he got it.

She remembers her father with dark, twinkling eyes. A smile that shone, even when the rest of him began to waste away. He'd lie propped in the living room recliner, a blanket in his lap, his body thin as a matchstick. With hands calloused from years of hard labor, he'd tell Shea stories about Highbush. Her grandmother's cooking. Her grandfather's love of carpentry. The little beach on Rattlesnake Island where he used to row with her uncles—spend the endless summers fishing for walleye and white bass.

He'd been away when the Rot came to Highbush—stationed on a watchtower out in western New York, where the Gravewood bled down from the Adirondacks. He'd come home on leave to find the entire town empty, as if all of Highbush had blinked out of existence overnight. The plates his mother had set out for dinner were still on the table. A basketball lay punctured in the grass. The car in the driveway sat askew. Doors open, key in the ignition.

Sometimes, after he'd gone, Shea wondered if her father had given any thought to that day when he left. If he'd cared, even a little, that his only daughter would come home from school to the exact same reality: an empty house, a mug of tea cooling on the kitchen counter.

She wonders if he knew he was taking the very last leftovers of her language with him when he went. That she'd have no one to talk to once he left. That without him around, she'd spend the next several years watching the pantry empty. Watching her batteries dwindle. Watching her mother disappear.

She wonders if he knew she'd grow to loathe coming home.

Poppy Zahar is seated on the front porch when Shea arrives. Even in the twilight, Poppy is impossible to miss. Out of uniform, she's dressed in her usual array of colors, from the mulberry-and-green stripe of her sweater to the lumpy fleece of her bucket hat, beneath which a brown, heart-shaped face and a slim, straight nose peek out. Her cargo pants are just a little too short, and a pair of boldly patterned socks stick out from the cuffed ends. She looks wildly incongruous against the dilapidated face of the Parkers' lonely Victorian.

There's a possum in her arms. It's a significant improvement from the previous week, when she took to carrying around an injured milk snake. At least this one has fur. It looks vaguely distressed and more than a little bit mangy, and it bares its teeth at Shea as she approaches, fitting on her hearing aids. There's a beep, and sound wheezes into her head in a dizzying rush.

"Are you sure that's not rabid?" she asks, ripping into her lollipop.

Poppy's expression is scandalized. "Possums don't carry rabies."

"Oh, okay." The taste of cherry chases away the dry-cotton feel of her mouth. "It's just that it looks a little bit like roadkill."

"Kit," says Poppy pithily, "is the picture of health."

As if to punctuate her point, the possum goes suddenly limp in her arms. It looks halfway dead, its tongue lolling, its legs jutting stiffly skyward.

"You've scared him."

"I didn't mean to."

The silence that widens between them feels like a chasm. In it echoes thoughts of Camellia—a half dozen secrets Shea can't bring herself to say. Poppy is the first to breach the gulf.

"He's home, isn't he?"

Shea doesn't need clarification—she knows Poppy means Asher. Her lollipop clicks against the backs of her teeth. "He is."

"I knew it. I saw his bike outside on my walk home from school."

Asher Thorley had gotten that dirt bike the summer he turned sixteen. Against his mother's wishes, he'd hauled it home from the junkyard and then spent the next twelve months slowly fixing it up in his garage. Shea had seen him there every day after school—an oiled rag slung over one shoulder as he nursed the heap of rust back to life. She'd wave at him from the road and keep going, his promise thrumming between her ears: *I won't let you die here.*

She hadn't realized how quickly things would change once he left.

On the stairs, Poppy rises to her feet. "We should go by the house tomorrow after school. We'll tell him everything we know."

Her insistence startles Shea. "And what is it we know, exactly?"

"That Ellie didn't leave on her own," says Poppy, indignant. "She wouldn't have. You know she wouldn't have. Something *lured* her. She could be at Mercy Ridge."

Thoughts of Lys pop back into her head, unbidden. She pictures the crumbling grandeur of Mercy Ridge, the fires in the hearth and the chatter in the rooms and the cold, mercurial boy at the helm of it all. A veritable prince, holding court in the shadow of the mountain. Camellia isn't at Mercy Ridge and Shea knows it, but she can't tell Poppy that.

"Maybe she got sick of Little Hill," Shea says instead. The truth sits on the tip of her tongue: *We fought. She ran. And now she's gone.*

"We're *all* sick of Little Hill," says Poppy. "That doesn't mean you just wake up one day and leave without warning. Without even saying goodbye."

And suddenly, they're both thinking of Shea's father. How he did exactly that.

"Shea, I'm sorry," says Poppy, backpedaling. "You know that's not what I meant."

"I should get inside." The taste of cherry sours in her throat. "My mom will be expecting me for dinner."

Over Poppy's shoulder, the house is dark. There's no hint of movement behind the curtains. Shea hopes Poppy doesn't notice. She hopes she doesn't see the way her stories never quite make sense. The way the lies are piling up.

The way she hasn't invited her inside in months.

"I shouldn't have said that," Poppy adds as Shea edges past. "I wasn't thinking. But Shea, we *have* to go talk to Asher. Tomorrow. He deserves to know whatever we know."

Shea pauses on the threshold. She feels as though guilt might split her apart.

"We don't know anything," she says coldly, and pulls the door shut.

Alone, she breathes in deep. The foyer is empty. The air smells wet—there's a leak in the kitchen she hasn't gotten around to patching. On the stairs, several balusters have popped loose. The wallpaper has been gashed open in places. It ribbons down the wall in thin, floral ravels, a stark reminder of the violent secrets she keeps.

Some days, she thinks she is entirely composed of secrets. They live within her, chewing at her bones like beetles. One day soon, there will be nothing of her left. She gives herself thirty seconds to feel sorry for herself. Thirty seconds, and then she shrugs out of her blazer and heads for the basement.

A dark shape darts out from underfoot the moment she takes her first step. She yelps, leaping to the side to avoid stepping on Hemlock, the old tortoiseshell her father found under the porch nine long winters ago. Her mother's cat, through and through. A pair of yellow eyes peer sulkily out at her from beneath the hall tree. At her feet curls a small, dead mouse.

"Good thinking," Shea tells the cat, pushing up her sleeves. With only the smallest amount of disgust, she leans down and pinches the mouse by the tail. It dangles in front of her as she walks, its little body curling on itself. Still warm. Still fresh.

Just the way she likes it.

It takes Shea nearly a minute to unlock the basement door. She's installed extra security in the past few months. A rusted padlock. A thick barrel bolt. A sliding steel chain. Prying it open, she's met with a cool, ubiquitous dark. The stairs are steep, wood worn smooth.

"Mom?" If her voice has an echo, she doesn't hear it. "Mom, I'm coming down."

In the quiet, there comes a sound. The pull of chains dragging over concrete. The shift of something waking. Holding the mouse at arm's reach, Shea descends.

The basement is mostly empty. They never used it for much. A boiler sits in one corner, valves rusted. In the other, a set of empty industrial shelves has been anchored to the wall. There—in front of the shelves—sits her mother. Silvered beneath a fall of moonlight, she is white-haired and emaciated, her wrists cuffed in a set of chains Shea found in her father's workshop. When she lifts her head to watch Shea approach, there's nothing in her eyes.

"I brought dinner." Her voice has an echo. Gingerly, she holds up the mouse by the tail. It spins between them in a slow pivot. On the floor, her mother's head quirks ever so slightly to the side. She's scenting blood, Shea knows, but she likes to think her mother recognizes her voice. It's a little lie she tells herself.

"I guess it's more like a snack. I didn't have time to stop by the butcher's after school. I had to stay late, and then I ran into Asher at the shop. Asher Thorley. Do you remember him? He used to come over and walk Camellia home. He always ate all the leftovers."

She used to be unnerved by the way her mother stared. By the way her jaw hung slack. By the way she never bothered to push her hair back from her eyes, when she used to hate having it in anything but a braid. She's not unnerved anymore. She's used to it.

When Shea tosses the mouse, her mother lunges. The chains rattle as she drags herself across the floor on all fours, snatching the rodent with birdlike fingers and then ripping into it with completely unbirdlike grace. Shea takes a seat on the bottom step and tries not to watch, unbothered—after months of the same—by the snap, crackle of bone, the wet tear of flesh.

"I'm sure you want to know why I'm home so late. I *politely* suggested to Owen Davies where he could stick his pencil, and Mrs.

Lennox was standing right behind me. She slapped me with a detention, which I personally think was an overreaction."

There's not much meat on the mouse. Her mother will be done soon. Still starving. Still silent. Still squatting there, listless, her hair in her eyes. At the top step, Hemlock has settled in to watch, tail flicking.

"Dad would have laughed," Shea adds, watching the moonlight drag along the floor. "If he were here, I mean. He would have tried not to, but he's always had a terrible poker face. And I know you're disappointed—you've told me a *million* times to keep my cool—but I'm telling you, Davies deserved it. He was saying these horrible things about Dad." Her voice sticks in her throat. "About him leaving."

The mouse drops to the floor. Slowly, her mother's face lifts. There's blood on her chin. A blank, hungry look in her eyes. For a fraction of a second, she looks at Shea.

Right at her.

A wick of impossible hope alights in Shea's chest. "Mom?"

There's a loud *meow* from the top of the stairs. A single warning caterwaul. And then her mother lunges. Like so many times before, the chains clatter noisily behind her. Unlike the other times, there's no resounding *clank* at the end. No violent rattling of the shelves. The couplings come loose in a horrible trill, and her mother is still advancing. Rocketing upright, Shea staggers backward up the stairs.

"Mom—*Mommy*, it's me."

The woman before her—this being, this creature, this *almost-mother*—doesn't stop her pursuit. She lurches onward, tangled in the chains, her arms outstretched. Shea's boot catches on a step and she lands hard on her tailbone, scrabbling on all fours.

"It's Shea. Mom, it's *Shea*."

A hand cuffs her collar just as her mother lunges. She's hefted unceremoniously onto her feet, the basement door careening shut with a slam that rattles the floorboards. Asher is there, his patrol-issued shotgun strapped to his chest, listening as her mother beats her body against the wooden partition.

"She won't get out," she manages. "She's too weak."

He cuts her a look. "So all those locks are just for decoration, then?"

Her heart gives an ugly squeeze. "I can explain."

She's not given the chance. Asher pries his shotgun loose, loading the chamber with his jaw wired tight. The slugs are wooden. White oak, hewn by hand. Horror grips her like a fist.

"What are you doing?"

He doesn't answer, but then he doesn't need to. They both know exactly what he's doing—what he's been trained to do in his eighteen months away. Assess a threat. Put it down. On the other side of the door comes the muffled sound of Ivy Parker's fingernails scrabbling over wood.

"Asher, you can't."

He racks the bolt with a click she feels in her spine.

"Asher, *please*. Let's just slow down for a second and—"

"Open the door." His order slams into her gut like a punch.

She doesn't budge. "No."

"*Parker*."

"She's not like the others. She's not a predator. I swear to you,

Asher. I know this seems bad, but she's different. She's *sick*. She can't help herself."

A soft chitter comes from under the door. A guttural clicking that sounds nothing and everything like her mother. Asher's response is instinctive. All reflex, he swings the shotgun into position, finding his mark through the wood.

"Open the door," he says again, pinching one eye shut. "And then get out of the way."

She, too, is all reflex. She flings out a hand, unthinking, folding it over the barrel and pressing the muzzle toward the floor.

"Asher, look at me."

He does. Not at her face, the way she'd intended, but at her wrist. With the cuffs of her blouse gathered at her elbows, Lys's bite is painfully visible. It sits in a dozen raw half-moons along her forearm.

The mark of the devil, incisor deep.

She wrenches her hand to her chest, tugging the sleeve back into place. It's too little, too late. He's already seen. For the next several seconds, neither of them says a word. On the other side of the door, her mother has gone quiet. The only sound is the faint rattle of chains, the *plink* of couplings dragged over wood.

Uselessly, Shea says, "It's not what it looks like."

"It looks," he says, in a voice flat enough to be dead, "like you let him feed on you."

Him, not *one of them*. *Him*, like he already knew. He looks unfairly resigned, like he's always known they'd end up here. For a moment she's sixteen again, standing outside the Thorley garage with her shoulders singed red by the sun, her voice a whisper: "There's a rumor he's recruiting."

Asher's astonishment had been decimating. "You want me to pledge fealty to the devil?"

"If it keeps you from dying in a watchtower, yes."

"I'm not planning to die, Parker. How many times do I have to tell you? We have a plan. You and me. Yeah? We get out of here together—that hasn't changed, it's just delayed a little."

"I guess I shouldn't be surprised," he says now, as if he's been remembering the same.

The resignation in his voice makes her hackles rise. "What's that supposed to mean?"

"You know exactly what it means."

"Spell it out for me anyway."

"Come on, Parker. You've always had one foot in the Gravewood."

Shame threatens to saw her open. She refuses to let it. Once, she used to wish for Asher Thorley to come back home from the watch. She tallied the days, keeping careful track in the leaded margins of her math notebook. Now she tallies nights. She counts supplies and she watches them dwindle. The only promises she cares about are the ones she makes herself.

She won't let anyone make her feel sorry about it.

"I think you should leave."

He doesn't. He says, "My sister is in the Gravewood."

There's no need for him to elaborate—she understands exactly what it is he's implying. She shuts it down quickly. "Lys already told me he had nothing to do with Camellia's disappearance."

A thunderous silence follows. In a voice that has gone dangerously subdued, Asher says, "Well, if *Lys* says so."

"He's never given me any reason not to trust him."

"No, of course not. Aside from the fact that he's a bloodsucking predator."

She bristles, biting back a retort. She doesn't need to stand here and spar with him, she needs to get him out of her house. She needs to figure out what to do next, now that her cover is blown. Shoving past him, she wrenches open the door. The cold night air spills into the foyer.

"Leave."

He doesn't. He remains firmly planted, his jaw set. "I want to meet him."

She's positive she's misheard. "What?"

"You know exactly what I said. I want to meet the infamous Lys."

"He'll kill you before you even get in the door."

"I don't think so." Asher yields a step toward her, flicking the brim of his cap out of his eyes. His stare is a wall, hard and unrelenting. "I think he'll make time for me. There's been rumors circulating the garrison for weeks. The northern rangers are saying there's a girl from Little Hill who has the devil wrapped around her finger. He'll do anything she says."

Understanding hits her like a brick. He already knew.

Their encounter at Silas Brer's wasn't an accident. He'd been looking for her.

"The rumors are wrong," she says. "Lys doesn't answer to anyone."

"Maybe." Something inscrutable has crawled into Asher's features, making him impossible to read. "But you're wearing his mark, and that's good enough for me. I came back to find my sister. I plan to do whatever it takes to bring her home. You want me to look the other way? You want me to pretend I didn't see what you're keeping down in the cellar? Fine. Get me in front of Oliver Lysander."

Anger bursts into flames inside her chest, smoking out whatever shame she might have felt.

"You're threatening me."

"I'm bargaining with you."

"No, you're telling me that if I don't take you to see Lys, you'll kill my mom."

He has the decency, at least, to flinch. He recovers quickly, doubling down. "That thing in the basement isn't your mother, Parker. Not anymore."

"I already told you. She's *sick*."

"She's a contagion risk, and you know it."

As if she needed reminding. As if the fear of her mother escaping the confines of the cellar hasn't haunted her since she first woke to find Ivy Parker standing over her bed, the light gone out of her eyes. As if she doesn't spend every hour, every minute looking over her shoulder. Triple-checking the latches. Lying through her teeth. Letting her secrets consume her from the inside out.

"What you're doing is selfish," says Asher. "If anyone finds out you're keeping her here, we're dead. Not you and me—everyone in Little Hill."

"I may be selfish, but at least I'm not cruel. This is *blackmail*."

"Call it whatever you want." The look in his eyes is impassive. She can feel the trust between them drawing its last, rattling breath. "You're going to get me an audience with the devil, and you're going to do it tonight."

THREE

Lysander

Oliver Lysander has been called a lot of things in his time on this earth.

When he was small, he was rotten. Disobedient when he refused to cooperate and spineless when he did. Later—once he'd grown—he was volatile. Unpredictable, impossible, *frightening*. Too grasping, too obsessive, too stubborn for his own good.

No one has ever accused him of being patient.

At present, he is trapped in a meeting that has managed to grind what little forbearance he possesses down to nothing. He can think of a dozen things he'd rather do than sit here and be unduly lectured. Swallow a hot coal. Walk across glass. Scoop out his eyes with a spoon.

To name just a few.

In the chair beside him, his lieutenant clears his throat. With a slowness that borders on impertinence, Lysander tears his eyes away from the arched windows of the Mercy Ridge conservatory. He finds Cyrus Talbot staring over at him, his head tipped toward their visitor. The look on his face says: *At least act like you're paying attention.*

The room they occupy is a half circle, cluttered with round tables and spindled chairs. It was a tearoom once. It's a war room now. A vast gallery of painted wildebeests leers down at him from the opposing wall. Directly before it sits an emissary of the southern Flatwood's reigning kingpin, sent north to reprimand him.

To *scold* him, like he's a child and not a god.

"Maybe after this is over you can give me a lobotomy," Lysander says pleasantly. "I think it'd really round out the evening."

"We have a drill in the utility closet," supplies Cyrus.

"You're thinking of trepanation. What we need is an ice pick—"

"I suppose you think you're funny," the emissary cuts in.

Lysander blinks across the table at him. "Do you see me laughing?"

This delegate is older than the others. In his early forties, maybe, his hair salted gray. It's probably why Paris Keeling has sent him— he thinks this one can't be cowed.

"Joke all you want, Oliver," says the emissary, turning a garish sigil ring over on his pinkie. A family heirloom, most likely, and offensively tacky. "You know what Paris requires of you. The hunter's moon is two weeks out. Your attendance at the revel is nonnegotiable."

Lysander sniffs. "Every year, Paris sends someone north to tell me the same thing. 'The revel is mandatory, Oliver.' 'Attendance is compulsory, Oliver.' 'This is nonnegotiable, Oliver.' I haven't gone yet. I won't be going this year, either, so it looks like he's wasted both our time. Feel free to see yourself out."

The emissary's expression tightens. "You and I aren't done here."

"We are," says Lysander. "As much as I'd love to hear what else you've come all this way to tell me, you're boring Cy, and I can't have that."

Cyrus takes his cue, straightening in his chair. "It's inexcusable."

"Inexcusable," Lysander echoes. "One might even say impolite. You didn't bring gifts. The last envoy brought little chocolates. Cy is partial to the strawberry cordials."

"My favorite," drawls Cyrus.

Languid as a tiger, the emissary rises to his feet. "You think just because you've made a name for yourself up north, that you're above reproach—that you can carry on however you like."

"I am," agrees Lysander. "And I can."

"Insolent as always." The emissary's ring winks preposterously in the light. "That arrogance of yours is going to destroy you."

Insolent. Arrogant. It's nothing Lysander hasn't heard before. He smiles with teeth.

"Another message from Paris, I assume."

"No." The emissary reaches for his coat. "That one's from me. And it's not a message, it's a warning. You'd be smart to heed it. Paris has eyes and ears everywhere. He's been keeping very close tabs on you."

The first hint of wariness licks up Lysander's spine. "What's that supposed to mean?"

"It means," says the emissary, "that you've been given a remarkably long leash, but you're still his creature. One day soon, you'll be brought to heel."

Lysander's hands curl into fists. "I'd like to see him try."

"Ah, there it is." The emissary smiles. "A crack in the armor. Very good. Is it safe to assume I finally have your attention? Because you may think you're untouchable, but I can assure you, you're anything but. Paris knows exactly where to push to make you break. And you *will* break, Oliver. You'll break beautifully. I can promise you that."

When he leaves, the door falls shut with a slam. It rattles the room, knocking a faded painting of a hunting lynx askew. Lysander tips his head to the side to meet the creature's yellow eyes.

Leaning back in his chair, Cyrus kicks his boots up onto the table. "I think that went well."

Lysander doesn't lift his eyes from the painting. He contemplates it in silence, tapping two fingers against the table in a silent rhythm. "Where would you push if you wanted me to break?"

Cyrus thinks it over. "I'd push you off a cliff."

"You know what I mean." He tips back against the wooden sheaf of his chair, braiding his knuckles until the bones crack. "That was a loaded threat. Paris knows something."

"Who cares?" Cyrus crooks his elbows behind his head. "Paris Keeling is always sending his lackeys up north to threaten you. And can you blame him? He wants you to stop being a rebellious little shit and fall in line."

Lysander considers his lieutenant sideways. "You think he's right."

Some of the playful light goes out of Cyrus's eyes. He's edging into dangerous territory, and he knows it. "I think," he says carefully, "it won't kill you to make an appearance at the revel."

"That's exactly what he wants."

"It's one party, Lysander. How bad can it be? You're beating yourself bloody, fighting Paris over every little thing. And for what? To prove yourself?"

"To preserve myself."

The correction makes Cyrus wince. He knows the significance of the hunter's revel—knows why Paris Keeling wants Lysander there at his side when the moon is at its pinnacle. He's the only Mercy Boy who understands the truth—the only one who has been there since the humble beginning, working side by side with Lysander to clear debris from the old ski lodge at the base of Mercy Mountain: *I'm going to build something here, Cy. Something that's mine.*

Cyrus alone understands how dangerous it would be to comply.

It's why Lysander came north—why he built his own kingdom from the ground up, instead of kneeling at the throne of another. Down in the southern Flatwood, Paris Keeling rules as though he's a king. His word is law. His followers are steadfast. But here in the frozen hush of Mercy Mountain, they bend the knee to the Gravewood Devil.

"I'm not telling you to hand over all control," Cyrus says, backtracking. "I'm just saying—maybe send an olive branch. Something to get him off our backs, you know?"

"An olive branch," Lysander echoes thoughtfully.

Outside, the night drags ever on. The air in the conservatory seems to thin. Distantly, he hears the sound of music. The pulse of a party, raging deep in the stony bowels of the old hotel. Underneath it all, muffled by the bass, is the sound of an engine turning over.

"Go after him."

Cyrus's head whips around. "The envoy? What for?"

"You're right—we should send him home with a message. A strong one. Something that lets Paris know I'm done with all the endless pontificating. I say you cut off that tacky costume jewelry on our emissary's finger. We can send it back in a box. Tie it nice, with ribbon."

Cyrus gapes openly at him. "That's not an olive branch. That's an act of war."

Lysander ignores him, rising to stand by the window. Outside, the night is clear and dark. The ground sparkles with frost, hard and glittering as a diamond. Beneath the pale yellow lamplight, there's a girl coming up the walk. His heart trips into his ribs.

"Take Choi with you," he says, distracted. "Show him how Mercy Boys handle business."

"Lysander, come on. I don't think—"

"Do it now."

A pause follows. Then, "You're the boss."

The door skids shut at his back. He waits for the space of a single erratic heartbeat. Two. Three. A fourth—just to test himself—and then he's off, heading out into the cold of the terrace. Far below and with her face downturned, Shea Parker doesn't see him. He moves along at a parallel, tracking her advance from above. He thinks, as he often does, how easy it would be to hunt her like this. How simple, to pin and disarm her.

How satiating, to drain her of blood.

His thirst is a whip, quick and unforgiving. The sting of it snaps his spine straight. He blinks his head clear and presses on. At the back of the covered veranda there's a set of stairs ribbed in vines. He descends quickly, stepping out in front of Shea before she can pass.

"I didn't think I'd see you again so soon."

She startles violently, her hand flying to her throat. "God!"

"Close," he says, grinning.

"Announce yourself next time."

He tips his head to the side, regarding her from a new angle. "I thought I did."

"What are you doing out here, anyway?"

"I could ask you the same question. We don't have a date until next week."

Her heartbeat stutters between his ears. Her eyes dart from shadow to shadow as though she expects to find something leering out at her.

"Don't call it that," she says sharply.

"Why not?"

"Because it isn't."

"A date," he clarifies, and she nods. "What else should I call it?"

She thinks it over, her gaze still pinging between the trees. "An arrangement."

"That's an ugly word."

Her eyes snap to his and stay there. "We're doing an ugly thing."

"Do you really think so?"

She nods again. So close to her, he can see the blood fluttering in the curve of her neck. The back of his throat prickles. Sometimes, he thinks there are two of him. The boy and the hunger. He draws nearer to her as his two selves battle for control.

"That hurts my feelings," he tells her.

"You'll get over it."

It comes out contentious, the way it always does—like she's primed for a fight. Maybe that's why he likes her so much. He knows what it's like to move through life with his fists up.

She's still in uniform, same as the first day she came to Mercy Lodge. Plain brown coat. Hideous pleated skirt. Her stockings ripped. He lifts her tie and lets it ribbon through his fingers. A thrill shoots through him when she shivers.

"I thought I told you not to come here in Hornbeam colors."

He hears her heart kick into a trot. "I left in a hurry."

She's nervous. He can smell it on her, pheromone thick. Her gaze has drifted back to the trees. He closes her tie in his fist and gives it a single firm tug. Caught off-balance, she teeters a step toward him.

"You're distracted," he accuses her.

"I'm cold. It's freezing out here."

He clocks the lie instantly. She's prettiest when she's lying. All her tells come screaming to the surface. Her toes twist in. She worries at her fingers. Sometimes—if it's a particularly terrible lie—the tips of her ears turn pink. It's so perfectly human of her it makes his whole chest hurt. Makes him think about carving open a vein and drinking the color from her cheeks.

"Invite me inside," she says. "You're being rude."

He can't help grinning. "Am I?"

"Yes."

She's an eternal paradox, her heart thundering even as she doles out orders. Pushing him so he'll push back. Provoking him the way he provokes her.

They've been doing this dance for months.

Knowing it'll infuriate her, he makes a deliberate show of offering her his arm, like they're members of the English ton. Dallying in the gardens. Flirting with scandal. Tempting fate. All he does is tempt fate whenever she's around.

"Would you do me the honor of accompanying me indoors?"

"Is that supposed to be a British accent?"

"There's no pleasing you," he says, dropping the affect. "Come inside. There's dancing."

She makes a face. "I can't picture you dancing."

He likes that—the idea that she pictures him. Back home in Little Hill. Under a broad yellow sun. Dragging thoughts of him around like her own personal thundercloud.

"You should," he says. "I'm very good at it."

A quiet *snap* draws his attention away. The sound came from the woods. He listens, and there it is again—not the quiet pad of a wolf, nor the heavy snuff of a bear, but the crack of a twig giving way beneath a boot.

There's someone else out there.

"You were followed."

Or she brought someone, says a voice in his head. But she wouldn't. The rules are clear, and neither one of them has ever crossed the lines.

"You're right," says Shea, and her voice has gone thin. "Dancing sounds perfect."

She pivots on a dime, making her way toward a wide-open door on the lower level. His hand snaps out and he captures her by the elbow, halting her escape.

"Not yet."

His eyes remain trained on the woods. He'd been sure—*so sure*—that something in the trees had been staring back at him just then. But the heartbeat is gone. He's not worried. Whoever it is, the Gravewood will take care of them. Slowly, he slides his gaze toward Shea. The slow-healing arch of his most recent bite peeks out from beneath her sleeve. His hunger salivates inside him. He chokes it down.

"You're shaking."

"It's cold," she lies. Her ears are crimson.

He releases her, lifting his chin toward the door. "After you, then."

The lower level of Mercy Lodge is thronged in bodies. Lysander and Shea enter through the pool room, enveloped at once in the thump of bass and the smack of chlorine. The air is thick and warm. It gathers in drips along the stone as they weave out into the exterior hall, past the old pinball arcade and through the crowded salon. As usual, some of tonight's attendees are Mercy, some aren't. The smell of blood stings the air, freely given. Mercy hopefuls, paying due, or else blood bunnies, offering up a vein.

He doesn't like it down here. He can't tolerate the lights, the crowd, the noise. He allows it because it keeps his inferiors happy, and he needs them happy. Needs them loyal. Needs them true. Still, it was better outside, when it was just the two of them.

Just the two of them, and the watcher in the woods.

With his thoughts on the Gravewood, he veers out into the

smoke-stung hall. Shea tails after him, sticking close. The hallway is low and thin, the stone archway pressing low as a dungeon. Shea ducks in nearer as they head up the stairs and back out into the great hall, veering toward the ballroom.

Here, the walls are lined in vast Grecian columns. The tables have been pushed out to the sides, chairs stacked alongside them. A set of wide double doors hang open, letting the night air slip in off the veranda. Leaves scuttle across the carpet, nudged on by the wind. Once, the room was used for weddings. Now it sits empty. A husk, like everything else in the Gravewood.

"You liar," Shea accuses him the moment they're alone. "You didn't even want to dance."

"I did." He makes a show of looking all around. "I do. A ballroom is the perfect place."

"We can't even hear the music."

It isn't true—he can hear it just fine. A heavy rock song thuds in the air like a heartbeat. Directly in front of him, Shea's nervousness hasn't gone away. She toys with the edge of her sleeve, the scabbed-over mark of an incisor peeking out at him. That hard whip of hunger lashes him anew. He does what he can to ignore it.

"Something happened today," he says. "You're upset."

She blinks up at him, surprised. This isn't a part of their game. They don't ask personal questions. They don't *dig*. It's a business transaction, this thing between them. Quid pro quo. Something for something. They're not supposed to think of each other after. In the daylight.

He thinks about Shea Parker all the time.

"What do you care?" she asks, wary.

"You're no fun when you're distracted."

"And you're not nice when you're hungry."

He regards her through a watery slant of moonlight. She stares back, her toes turned in. Off in the distance, the music stops. The crowd jeers. The sound is muted, punched through by the wind.

When they speak, they do so at the same time.

"Dance with me—"

"You should feed."

An abrupt silence follows, interrupted only by the far-off call of an owl. He feels, curiously, as if he's been pierced with a dart. The sting sets in as Shea presses on, her face all the way red.

"It's just that we're going to waste hours beating around the bush like this."

"Like *this*," he echoes.

"Pretending like we don't both know what I'm here for."

He stuffs his fists into his pockets and traces a slow arc around her. She turns with him, her heart hammering hard. He knows better than to give in to his more basic urges. It makes something inside him coil up tight, pacing like this. It wakens something predatory. Something fanged.

It would be *so* easy to lunge.

"I have no batteries for you tonight," he says. "You weren't due back until next weekend. Our supply runner doesn't come through until Friday."

"That's okay." The sound of her swallow is devastating. "I don't need anything from you."

"That's not the game we play."

"We can play a new one." She pushes up her sleeve, letting the moonlight slip over her wrist. An unbroken patch of skin gleams up at him. "Just for tonight."

"Don't push me," he growls.

"I'm not pushing you, Lys. I'm offering."

Deep inside his head, he feels a door click shut. He's all instinct—primal and on edge, hunger lancing through him. He moves without thinking, pinning her until her wrist is the only thing left between them.

"Don't," he repeats through gritted teeth, *"push me."*

She ignores him. "Drink."

"I don't want to." He wanted to dance. He wanted starlight and moonglow. He wanted a single fucking moment of make-believe. What good is she if she won't play along? What purpose does she serve, if all she does is make a monster out of him? She's no better than Paris, pushing and pushing and pushing until he snaps.

"Screw your twisted rules, Oliver," she whispers. "Bite me."

Oliver. He hates it when she calls him that. It's not the name he gave her. It's a *family* name. It brings up things he'd rather it didn't. The smell of blood, the smack of a backhand, the bite of rings into his cheek. *Get back up, Oliver. Stop sniveling and fight.*

This, in the end, is what snaps his resolve. There's a blackout rush. A final, brutal lash of hunger. Her skin breaks so beautifully beneath his bite. Her blood is nectar in his throat. The night hums. He is drunk on the taste of her, inebriated by the sounds she makes. Her fractured breathing. Her racing heart. Her soft, dreamlike sigh.

He pulls away before he's ready, exerting control. Pretending he had any to begin with. Pressing his tongue to a last trickle of blood at his lip, he lifts his eyes to Shea's. The change in her is palpable. It guts him every time, though he'd never admit it. Not even under pain of torture.

Her eyes are liquid, pupils blown. Beneath her ribs, her heart beats languorously. She looks as though she's underwater—out of reach. She is always just out of reach. He wonders if that's what makes the poets write. If they're all composing sonnets to the things they can't touch.

She's watching him, too, riveted.

"You're beautiful," she whispers, reaching for his cheek.

He catches her wrist before she can touch him, holding her at bay. He knows what she sees right after a feed. He knows what he looks like to her. A boy, clear-eyed and rosy-cheeked, all traces of atrocity chased away by the fleeting succor of her blood.

It won't last.

By the time she comes to her senses, he'll be a monster again.

Sometimes, in his worst moments, he wishes she'd stop coming to see him—wishes she'd vanish without a trace. Nothing at all would be easier than this. Having her in parasitic swallows, in desperate half measures. Thinking of her in the daytime.

"It's so pretty in here," she murmurs, unblinking. "You were right, this is the perfect place to dance."

"I don't want to dance anymore."

"Why not?"

"I changed my mind."

Down in the belly of the hotel, there's a disturbance. A ripple in the current. The chaos ebbs. The music cuts out, replaced by shouting. Shea doesn't take any notice of it, and so neither does he. Fights break out all the time at Mercy Ridge. Cyrus will handle it.

"You're no fun like this," Shea tells him.

"Fed?"

"All moral and overthink-y."

"*Overthink-y.*"

"Yes, see?" She reaches for him with her free hand, blood still trickling red and wet down her wrist. Gently, she presses a thumb between his brow. "You've got thunderclouds, right here."

"I don't know what that means."

She lets her hand drop. "It's something my mom used to tell my dad."

She looks sad, suddenly, and he doesn't know how to undo it. Gently—like he's catching a butterfly—he crooks a finger under her chin. Her breath hitches as he draws her face up to his. Not for the first time, he thinks about kissing her.

He's not given the chance.

"Would you do something for me," she whispers, "if I asked you a favor?"

It's a dangerous question. Not because she's asking—not because it's a violation of their agreement—but because of the answer, already on his tongue. *Anything.*

"Lysander!" Cyrus appears in the doorway, looking harassed. His eyes flick disapprovingly over Shea. "Well, that's one mystery solved. No one knew where you went."

"You're a regular detective," Lysander snaps. "Leave."

"Wish I could. Choi and I took care of your envoy issue, but we caught a watchdog snooping around the property on our way back in."

Lysander is still looking at Shea as Cyrus says it, which is the only reason he sees the flicker of guilt on her face. It's gone as soon as it appeared.

The problem isn't that *he* sees it—the problem is Cyrus does, too.

"It's her," he says. "She brought a soldier to Mercy Ridge."

FOUR

Shea

Growing up, Shea's mother used to tell her to always leave a light burning, even in the dead of night. It was one of her many rituals, same as most other families in Little Hill. Tiny, meaningless sacraments to give children the illusion of safety. A wreath of hawthorn on the door. A shallow bowl of purified water on the front steps. A silver cross around the neck.

A light, to kept the dark things at bay.

Sometimes, keeping a light on was easier said than done. So far north, it never took much to knock the power out. Ice on the wires. Wind from the mountain. A thick fall of snow. During a blackout, it usually took days for a lineman to reach them. Weeks, in deep winter.

Before Shea's father left, they'd make an event of the power outages. Her mother would start a fire in the hearth. She'd light a candle in every window. She sang the old hymns as she went— humming canticles she'd learned back when the Everly family still filled a pew at church. Before she became a Parker, and the congregation shut their doors.

Shea's father would sit awake all night and tend to the flames, feeding kindling to the fire whenever it burned low. Unable to sleep with the wind rattling her windows, Shea would creep downstairs and coax her father into telling her a story.

Her memory of these nights is such a visceral thing, it's difficult to remember if it's one blackout in particular or an amalgamation of many. She remembers her father in his chair, the lit embers setting him aglow. A shotgun across his lap, the dark pressing its face against the frosted panes as he wove her a story with his hands.

When dawn crept in and the candles were extinguished, Shea would creep sleepily to the sill and stick her fingers into the melted wax. This memory is visceral, too. First came the sear of heat, then the feel of it congealing against her skin.

That's what a bite feels like—a blinding locus of pain, followed by a hot-honey warmth. Wax in her veins. A hard, smooth clot that chases out all other sensation. Fear. Worry. Hurt. Each time she comes to Mercy Ridge, she's left perfectly, pleasantly numb. No thoughts at all of Little Hill to haunt her. Not even the good ones.

Tonight is no different. Tonight, the bliss sinks so deep into her bones that she can't even recall why she came. Can't remember what it was that made her race all the way here, rushing along the narrow switchbacks with her heart in her throat and a stitch in her side.

All she can think about is Lys. The way his eyes after a feed are cool and gray, the color of the sky in winter. Tonight, he looked—for a moment, at least—like he might lean in and kiss her. He'd been inches away, his breath shallow, when something at the door caught his attention. His head snapped up. His grip on her turned vulturine. Slowly, she became aware of a conversation taking place, snatches of it floating past her like flotsam.

"I didn't ask for your opinion," Lys says coldly.

"You didn't have to." Cyrus Talbot stands in the open door, steely-eyed. "It's my job to be your eyes and ears."

"I have eyes and ears of my own. Leave her out of it."

"Lysander, think this through. If she brought him—"

Cyrus falls quiet, silenced by a look. A single bone-inked finger taps the underside of Shea's chin, guiding her focus. She's met with the pale ice of Lys's stare. There's no trace of the devil in him at all.

"Stay," he says.

"Okay."

She says it to make him happy—to let him know she can cooperate. He doesn't *look* happy. His face falls, his disappointment apparent. His eyes cut away before she can try to fix it.

"Cy."

"Yeah?"

"Make sure she doesn't leave this room."

A tepid pause follows. Then, "You've got to be kidding me."

"Do I look like I'm kidding?" Lys tugs a clean shop towel from his back pocket, knotting it around Shea's wrist. His gaze finds hers, but this time his face is carefully shuttered. "Put some pressure on that. I'll come find you when it's done."

And then he's gone.

She stands there, unmoving, twin pinpricks of red widening along the white cloth at her wrist. She's determined to do as she's told. To prove that she can. That's what she wants to do, isn't it? To make Lys happy? She can't remember. She can't *think*. Her thoughts curdle, mushy and colorless. She can't shake the feeling that she's forgotten something. Something important.

She shuts her eyes and tries to recall the journey here. She pictures the marked road to Mercy, trunks blackened where they'd been burned back from the path. The shift of unheard whispers in the faraway branches. And there, muffled by the fading miasma of her euphoria, is a question, familiar: *You're sure you know the way?*

She hadn't been alone. There'd been someone else. But who?

She thinks harder, wax crackling as she applies pressure.

"Some of the boys have started a rumor that you've got blood like honey."

She startles, glancing toward the door. Cyrus stares unabashedly back at her.

"Honey," she echoes thickly.

"Yeah." Cyrus's pale skin is pink from a feed. His eyes shine in the dark. "They think that's why Lysander won't share you with the rest of them."

The mere suggestion curdles something deep within her. It's not like she hasn't seen the communal way they live at Mercy Ridge—like snakes in a nest, roping themselves into a ball in the dead of winter. That isn't her. She's not one of them. She's not a blood bunny, far from home, or a runaway, desperate to Turn. They're here because they have nothing left. Because they've given up. She hasn't. She still lights her mother's candles at night.

The thought of her mother brings another memory careening into the forefront: Ivy Parker scrabbling up the stairs, the door slamming shut on her face. The hard pump of a shotgun. She flicks her gaze to Cyrus. He's watching her struggle to regain control, a smile creeping slowly across his face. *Blood like honey*, he'd said.

"And what do you think?" she asks.

"I think you're nothing special. Just a passing fixation."

"Nice."

"It's not meant to be nice," he assures her, drawing nearer. "It's honest. That's what Lysander does. He hyperfixates. He *obsesses*."

The word thrums through her. "He's not obsessed."

"You don't think so?"

"I know so. He and I have a deal, that's all."

Cyrus's smile widens. "A deal is something struck between equals. You're not even close to playing on Lysander's level. *You* are small and weak, and one day soon, you'll lose your shine." His eyes glimmer as he throws in a hopeful, "Maybe even tonight."

Some of her bravura finds her through the haze. "Are you *threatening* me?"

"Oh, I don't need to threaten you," says Cyrus. "You've done a beautiful job screwing yourself over already. I told you—Lysander doesn't like to share. Thoughtless move, bringing someone else."

His words bring clarity pummeling into her. Asher. The shotgun full of wooden bullets. Their fight in the foyer. The long trek here, his ears stuffed with cotton, the forest preening around them like a living thing.

"Where is he?"

"Lysander?" asks Cyrus. "Or your boyfriend?"

She doesn't bother correcting him. "Never mind. I'll find them myself."

Shoving past him, she makes it all the way to the door before he cuts her off. He sidles out from the shadows as if he'd been one step ahead of her all along.

"Get out of my way."

He doesn't. "Do you ever wonder why you feel so numb after a feed?"

"No. Move."

She can't hear anything out in the great hall. No music. No chatter. No sounds of a struggle. That doesn't mean there isn't one.

Asher, you idiot, she thinks. *I told you to wait.*

"Everything in you slows," says Cyrus, planting himself squarely before her. "Your heart. Your pulse. Your brain. You forget to panic. You forget why you were even afraid in the first place. After a while, you even start to like it. It's why you keep coming back. Over and over. Night after night."

She takes a step back, uneasy. "If you're trying to make a point, then make it."

"He doesn't *like* you, Parker. This is just how he hunts."

There's a crash out in the hall. She feels it in the pads of her feet. This time, when she tries to shove past Cyrus, he grabs hold of her throat. With a firm shove, she's slammed hard into the wall. The back of her head hits brick as she scrabbles at his forearm, blinking away stars.

"Let *go*."

"Can't. I have orders to keep you here."

"I doubt he told you to hurt me."

"I'm improvising," drawls Cyrus.

Ignoring every instinct inside her that tells her to fight back, she forces herself to go perfectly slack. His eyes narrow, fingers tightening. Not enough to cut off her oxygen, but enough to let her know he could if he wanted to.

"Go ahead," she challenges him. "Squeeze."

"So brave. You think I won't?"

"I think Lys will gut you when he finds out."

Her voice comes out strangled, and Cyrus's mouth curls into a sneer. She's drawn up onto the tips of her toes as his fingers constrict. Her airway pinches shut, black spots scudding across her vision. For a terrible moment, she thinks he means to call her bluff. To kill her and hope Lys forgives him for it. Instead, he releases her with a hard shove. She staggers out from under him, taking several big swallows of air.

"One day, Parker," he promises. "One day soon, he'll come to his senses. When that happens, I'll be right there waiting."

There's no time to let the full weight of his threat sink in. There's another resounding crash out in the great hall—a thud that judders the floorboards underfoot.

She takes off running, her legs like lead. Cyrus keeps pace beside her, taking one long stride for every two of hers. They skid to a stop in the great hall, jostled together by the hungry throng of bodies. Drawn from their party by the promise of a show, the crowd has gathered in a tight knot around the room's lit hearth. Shea elbows her way through the mass, Cyrus on her heels.

She emerges into the heart of the circle to find Asher Thorley on his knees.

He cuts an imposing figure against the firelight, his shoulders squared and his jaw defiant. His wrists have been restrained in the small of his back and he looks as if he's already taken a few hits. His left eye boasts a red, ugly weal. A thin line of blood trickles down his chin, gathers in the beating hollow of his throat.

Directly in front of him stands the Gravewood Devil.

Lit by the embers of a dying fire, Lys looks just like a boy—cheeks pinked and eyes clear, the predator driven out of him by the rush of Shea's blood to his head. Just how she wanted him. Just how she planned. She's learned, in the past six months in his company, that he's always his sweetest after a feed. She'd planned to ask him then—to negotiate a new deal, one that didn't end up with Asher dead. It won't be enough. Not like this, with an audience leering in at them.

Not when he's putting on a show.

"I can't decide," he muses, "if you're very brave or very stupid."

"I guess we'll find out." One eye swelling steadily shut, Asher peers up at Lys. "*You're* the guy who has everyone around here so scared? You're a little scrawny for a devil."

A rustle goes through the crowd. Lys's smile isn't friendly.

"You're funny."

Asher doesn't smile back. "I can be."

"We'll see how long that lasts." Lys drops into a squat, elbows braced over his knees. With his hands inked in blackwork bones, he looks positively skeletal in the firelight. A nightmare from the forest deep. "Let's try this one more time. Tell me who sent you."

"No one." Asher shifts as best he can, restrained by his bindings. "I'm not acting on anyone's orders, I came on my own."

Lys's head tips to the side. "That makes you a fugitive."

"It does."

"I've seen what the watch does to deserters. It's not pretty."

"It isn't."

"You won't survive being caught."

"I won't."

"And yet here you are anyway." Lys rises to his feet, cuffing the sleeves of his jacket. "Highly unusual behavior for a watchdog. You can't blame me for not believing you. Hit him again."

A figure breaks away from the crowd. A Mercy Boy, his eyes overeager. He makes his way toward Asher, popping already bloodied knuckles against the flat of his palm. On his knees, Asher braces himself for another blow.

Shea knows better than to intervene. She knows Asher is only in this situation because of his own obstinance. He'd threatened her to bring him here. He'd ignored her instructions to wait out of sight. But the way Lys is looking down at him makes her feel accountable.

And so, she steps out into the circle, breaking from the crowd.

"He's telling the truth." Her voice draws every glittering eye in the room. Lys's stare is hard enough to pit her stomach. "Don't hurt him."

The ensuing silence rings like a struck bell. Nobody moves. Nobody breathes. Lit from behind, Lys looks less like a boy and more like a god. Ageless and imposing, the lines of him sharp enough to impale. He says nothing. Does nothing. He only stares right at her, haughty and cold.

She can't look away, even now, when she wants to be furious with him. She's drawn to him—so thoroughly captivated that she can no longer discern what's natural and what's chemical. Which feelings are a byproduct of her own brain, and which are a lingering effect of the feed.

She thinks of Cyrus's sneering face, his threat in the ballroom: *He doesn't* like *you, Parker. This is just how he hunts.*

Upon the hearth, the last of the embers cool to black.

There's no light left in Lys at all.

"Everyone out," he orders. "I'd prefer to continue this meeting in private."

FIVE

Shea

It never fails to astound Shea just how perfectly Oliver Lysander holds the whole of Mercy Ridge in the palm of his hand. The exact moment he gives the order, the hard clot of bodies begins to break apart. Mercy Boys and their guests disperse as though released from a thrall. No one grumbles. No one dissents.

With the venom of Lys's bite slowly metabolizing, Shea's head has begun to clear. With it comes pain. A headache builds behind her eyes. There's a sharpness to the pain at her wrist. Her veins feel as though they've been packed with sand.

Lys's eyes remain fixed to Shea's as the room empties out. As her own euphoria fades, so does his. Already, the color has begun to bleed out of him. Shadows gather in the hollows of his cheeks, turning him gaunt.

"You stay," he says.

A terrible anticipation zippers up her spine as the last few stragglers trickle out. Only Cyrus remains. He stands beside her, his hands in his pockets and his eyes bright with elation. It's going to get ugly, and he knows it.

"You too, Cy," says Lys. "Out."

Cyrus's shoulders drop. "But I—"

"Case the grounds. Take Sully and Boyce. Make sure this one didn't bring any friends."

"There's no one else," says Asher. "I'm on my own."

"All the same." Lys sinks into a wide leather chair beside the hearth. Even with shoulders slouched and limbs splayed wide, he still looks like a king. Haughty. Untouchable. The slightest trickle of red darkens one corner of his frown. Her blood, staining his mouth like rouge.

"This is why you were so desperate for me to feed," he accuses her, the moment Cyrus is gone. "You wanted me amenable."

She balks. "That's not why."

"Don't lie to me. I don't have the patience for it tonight." There's a terrible energy in him—it twitches just beneath his skin. "Do you like him?"

The sudden pivot hits her like a slap. "What?"

"You heard me."

On his knees, Asher grits his jaw and says nothing.

"Tell me what you like about him," goads Lys.

Shea blinks and sees Asher in the failing light of Fletcher's field. Asher in her doorway, his helmet under his elbow. Asher in deep summer, the sun in his eyes: *We get out of here together—that hasn't changed.*

"I don't want to do that."

"Come on." Lys's eyes are bright and clear. She has never resented his humanity more than in this moment. "There must be something. He's pretty. He's strong. He's *human*."

"Lys, *stop*."

His smile fades and Shea has the horrible sense she's done the exact wrong thing. Usually, he likes it when she's pushy. It amuses him when she's bold. Tonight, his stare is flinted. He turns to Asher, as full of disdain as she's ever seen him.

"On your feet, puppy."

Asher obliges, his balance thrown off by the coarse rope binding his hands. The weal around his eye has begun to purple and his eyelid has swollen all the way shut. He doesn't look at Shea. Not once. *He asked for this*, she reminds herself. *He insisted.*

It doesn't make her feel any better.

"Let's start with your name," says Lys.

"Asher Thorley."

"Thorley." Lys studies Asher across the lamplit dark. "Here's how we run things at Mercy Ridge, Thorley—either you have something to offer or you *are* the offering. If you want to live to see the sunrise, I'd make yourself important."

Asher doesn't hesitate. "I've spent the last two months stationed at a watchtower out by the New York garrison. Last week, one of our rangers picked up some of Keeling's guys outside Black River. They were pretty chatty."

"I'll bet they were," says Lys.

"According to them, you and Paris Keeling are on the outs."

Lys's mouth twitches. "That's not news."

"I'm not talking about a small territory dispute," says Asher. "They told us you want him dead."

Paris Keeling. The name is familiar, but only just. Shea's heard it before, whispered like a curse in the halls of Mercy Ridge. Whoever he is, it's clear that the mention has struck a nerve. Lys scowls down at Asher, a deep groove pinched between his brows.

"You have my attention."

"I can kill him," says Asher.

His declaration is followed by a single stroke of quiet. And then Lys laughs.

And laughs.

"It's a compelling offer. You'll never get close enough."

"I don't need to be close," says Asher. "I'm a sure shot."

"Confident," notes Lys. "Unfortunately, I can't stake my legacy on arrogance."

Asher doesn't back down. "It's not arrogance if it's true."

"Maybe. I'd rather not take your word on it." Lys casts a glance toward the wide bay windows. The glass is ferned in moonlit whorls of ice. "It's cold out tonight. Frost like that will lock up a scent, make you harder to track. If you're quick, you might survive a hunt."

Shea's stomach drops. "Lys, you can't—"

"Can't I?" His voice knifes through the hall, silencing her. Some of the darkness has bled back into his eyes. His pupils dilate, thinning the iris to a single thread of gray. Eventually, even the white of his sclera will be gone. He'll be a terror again, with a demon's eyes.

"Put your fists away," he says. "You're not in this fight."

"The hell I'm not."

"The guys in my garrison have a name for me," says Asher,

rushing to speak before Shea can dig them both deeper. "They call me Sunshine."

Shea half expects Lys to laugh in his face a second time. Instead, he goes still, fixing Asher in a flat, circumspect stare. "Bullshit."

"I promise you, it's not."

"The sunshine sniper has a confirmed kill count of over a hundred."

"I use wooden slugs," says Asher with a shrug.

"Handmade?"

"It's old-school but efficient."

The words ring hollow in Shea's ears. *Confirmed kill count. Over a hundred.* She is struck, once again, by how severe this new Asher seems—how formidable, even bound.

He's nothing like the boy from down the road, who liked her mother's shortbread and who made her promises by the woods and who once helped his sister and her friends make a splint for an injured rabbit. That boy has been scraped away and replaced with someone new. It dawns on her that she doesn't know *this* Asher at all.

But then, he doesn't know her anymore, either.

"I don't buy it." Lys's voice is just a touch too loud, and Shea realizes he's been watching her. "It takes stealth and precision to be a marksman. You look like you'd trip over your own two feet."

"I can take out Keeling," insists Asher. "He'll never see it coming."

Lys sniffs. "If I wanted Keeling dead, I'd have already done it myself."

"I don't think so. You're smarter than that."

Amusement crosses Lys's face. "Am I?"

"You are. Keeling controls the southern Flatwood—that's a significant territory. Most of your kind are loyal to him, and no one wants to fall in line behind an insurrectionist. You kill him, you make yourself the enemy. It has to be someone else."

"I don't need you to explain the stakes to me," says Lys, but he looks intrigued. "I'm assuming there's something you want in return."

"My sister," says Asher. "Camellia Thorley."

"Doesn't ring a bell."

"It should. She disappeared into the Gravewood two weeks ago."

"The Gravewood spans over four thousand acres," says Lys dryly.

"Four thousand acres that are under *your* control."

Lys's smile is thin. "While I appreciate the insinuation that I'm some sort of all-seeing god, I don't actually possess the omnipresence to be everywhere at once. Your sister isn't here at Mercy Ridge, which means that wherever else she is, she's dead."

"*Lys,*" hisses Shea.

"Well, it's true."

"It doesn't matter if she is or isn't," says Asher. "I promised my mom I'd find her."

"That's quite the sacrifice," says Lys. "I'm curious to hear what it is you plan to do with her, once you're successful. You can't carry her bones back home, it's a breach of quarantine. Not to mention, you're a fugitive. If the watch doesn't kill you, the woods will. You're a part of the Gravewood now, same as your sister."

Shea flinches, but Asher looks unfazed. "It's what you do for family."

"Noble." Lys ticks the superlatives off on his fingers. "Loyal. Brave. Selfless. You're a veritable fount of good qualities."

"So, you'll help me find her?"

"I'm still undecided." Lys sinks deeper into his chair, kicking out his feet. "How does Shea factor into this?"

"Shea is going home," says Shea. "She has a math test today."

There's a short pause. Then, "You're not going back."

He says it like it's an undisputed fact. The sky is blue. The ocean is wet. You're never going home again.

Her voice tight, she says, "I think I must have misheard you."

"Hornbeam is a dead end." He doesn't bother repeating himself. "I'm getting tired of waiting for you to realize it."

"I *have* to go home. I— We have *a deal*."

"We *had* a deal." Lys sits forward, rippling with energy. "Bringing a watchdog here tonight was a breach of contract, which means our agreement is null. I'm negotiating a new one."

"It's not her fault," cuts in Asher. "I'm the one who pushed her into coming."

"Protective." Lys looks less than impressed. "Another worthy attribute. No wonder she likes you so much; I'm halfway in love with you already."

Heat flames Shea's cheeks. "You're being unreasonable. I can't just never go home again. I have family that depends on me."

Lys's gaze snaps to hers. "You said there was no one else."

She backpedals as best she can. "Did I say that? I don't remember."

"You told me you were alone." Lys rises from his chair, his shadow tapering to a point beneath the rapidly diminishing dark. "You said your parents were dead."

"I *am* alone, I'm—"

"She's keeping her mother in the cellar," says Asher, and Shea whips around to face him, horrified. He doesn't spare her so much as a glance. "It looks like she ingested something from the Gravewood."

"Looks like," echoes Lys.

"The change didn't take."

"Understood."

"Don't talk about my personal business like I'm not in the room," she snaps.

"Don't keep things from me," says Lys, "and I won't have to."

"That's not part of our *arrangement*." She spits out the word like it's acid. Mangling it on purpose, so it comes out ugly. It *is* ugly, this thing between them. The hunger. The secrecy. The way she likes how he looks with her blood on his teeth. If she was smart, she'd end it now.

"That was an oversight," says Lys, nonchalant. "We'll add in a clause during negotiations."

He hasn't looked away from her. Not once. Not even to blink. Black overtakes the whites of his eyes, spilling into his stare like ink. Beneath her skin, the first hint of malaise skitters down her bones. They're crashing, both of them, her sense of self-preservation crawling back into her as the humanity crawls out of him.

And then—just when looking at him begins to hurt—he smiles. "What a unique situation we've found ourselves in."

The room feels like a powder keg. Like a single lit match will detonate the whole of Mercy Ridge, and them with it.

"Thorley needs to find his sister," muses Lys, "which is a service only I can provide. I need Keeling dead—a service that Thorley *claims* only he can provide. And Shea—" His jaw ticks. "Shea Parker needs a cure for what ails her mother."

Asher gives immediate voice to the doubt inside her head. "There *is* no cure."

"There *is*," says Lys. "And as luck would have it, that's a service I can provide."

Hope, feeble and floundering, finds purchase inside Shea's chest. "You're not lying?"

"Cross my heart," says Lys. "I can get it for you."

"For a price, I'm sure."

She'd meant to sound derisive. Instead, her voice is brittle as glass. A cure. A *cure*. She thinks of her mother, the sun in her eyes and her braid coming loose, her head thrown back in a laugh. Shea has nearly forgotten the sound of it. Her father's disappearance was quick. He'd gone overnight, slipping away without a word, and before anyone could do anything about it. Her mother is disappearing slowly. Shea will do whatever it takes to make it stop.

"What do I have to do?"

"It's simple." Lys is watching her too closely again, with a look that slices clean through her. "Paris Keeling is hosting a party at the end of the month. He's insisting that I be there. Personally, I'd rather gouge my eyes out, but I'll admit it gives Thorley the perfect window to get close to Keeling undetected."

"The hunter's revel," says Asher. "I've heard of it. It's an annual bloodbath."

"And I avoid it annually. What a nice surprise it will be for everyone to see me there."

"What does the hunter's revel have to do with me?" asks Shea.

Lys looks scandalized. "I'd never show up to a party without a date."

Her stomach hooks, though it shouldn't. Cyrus's warning runs through her in a loop: *He doesn't like you. He doesn't like you.* This is a negotiation. A new game, with a new set of rules. This is a chance to save her mother. That's it. Nothing else.

Across the hotel, several doors slam shut as the sun breaks over the mountaintop. Mercy Boys, hunkering down someplace dark. Curling themselves away in the shadows like bats. The first fans of sunlight widen along the floor. Stray beams catch in the chandeliers, throwing errant diamonds against the wall.

"Say yes," urges Lys.

She swallows around her heartbeat, gathering her mettle. "All I have to do is go to this party with you, and you'll get me a cure?"

"It's that easy." He moves, and the shadows move with him, as though he effuses the darkest depths of hell. "Although, it's a very exclusive party. Keeling is particular about who he lets in."

His voice is weighted with implication. Sleep-deprived and still aching from the feed, it takes her too long to piece it together. Not Asher. He gets there right away.

"Don't do it, Parker. It's *sick*, what he's suggesting."

Lys doesn't spare him a glance. "She can make up her own mind, Sunshine."

"You want me to Turn," says Shea.

"I'm renegotiating the terms of our deal."

The light filtering through the window has almost reached him. He doesn't flinch back from it. His stare is black as a void. Cold and expectant, like he knows he has her cornered.

She thinks about Turning—the permanency of it. If she agrees, she'll spend the rest of her life bound to the dark. Beholden to the Gravewood. She'd never see another sunrise. Never feel the heat of summer on her skin. She thinks of how—when she was very small—she used to believe she could carry sunlight home in the folds of her skirt. She remembers her mother kneeling in the kitchen, scooping great handfuls of nothing from the crumpled pleats, cupping her hands around the empty air like it was liquid gold: *You brought all this? For me? Oh, let's go quick and show your father.*

Her father is gone. Her mother is disappearing.

There's no one waiting for her to carry the sunshine back home.

"When would we leave?"

Lys knows a yes when he sees one. "A week from tomorrow."

That's seven days at Mercy Ridge, in the company of killers.

Seven days in the dark with the devil.

When the Gravewood swallows someone, it doesn't spit them out.

"How can I be sure nothing will happen to my mom while I'm away?"

"I'll put a watch on the house. No one in or out."

"What if she starves?"

"She's already starving," says Lys, and she knows that he's right.

She knows this is all there is—this is the singular path forward.

His path. The devil's road. The only way to get something important is through a Mercy Boy, and a cure for her mother is the most important thing of all. If it truly exists—if Lys is the one who can get it for her—she'll do whatever it takes.

"I'll do it," she says. "You get my mom a cure, and I'll Turn."

Lys's smile is all teeth. His eyes swallow the light. In a voice that sinks into her stomach, he says, "Looks like the three of us are going to a party."

ACT II
THE MOUNTAIN

I'll follow thee and
make a heaven of hell,
To die upon the hand I love so well.

Shakespeare's *A Midsummer Night's Dream*

SIX

Lysander

Cyrus is waiting for Lysander when he arrives back at his room.

He's sprawled across the armchair by the window, a smear of blood darkening his chin. Remnants of his most recent feed. Lysander doesn't see him there until the door swings shut. Immediately, he tugs it back open.

"Get out."

Cyrus doesn't move. Not a muscle.

"You let the watchdog live," he says.

"He made me a compelling offer."

"That's not the reason. If you killed him, she wouldn't forgive you."

His room is sparsely decorated. A bed. A trunk. A table. It lacks character, the way hotel rooms do. It was never meant to be anything more than temporary lodging for out-of-town tourists—a scenic stopover for travelers hoping to catch a ride on the old cog railway. There's a view outside the window, but he doesn't see it.

The glass has been blacked out. Sunlight gathers on the other side of the paint. A tantalizing bit of brilliance in a room dark as pitch.

"When I want your opinion," says Lysander, "I'll ask."

Cyrus's laugh is dry. "That's the benefit of having me as your right hand. You don't have to ask. I anticipate your needs, and I take care of them. It's why you keep me around."

Lysander follows his lieutenant's gaze toward the rounded tea table before the hearth. It's bare, save a single absinthe glass, a shallow pool of blood slowly coagulating within.

"You think I haven't noticed?" asks Cyrus. "You think I haven't seen how little you're taking from her each time?"

"I take enough."

"You're rationing blood like a peasant, when you should be feasting like a king. Do you think Keeling lives like this? I'll answer that for you—he doesn't. He has his pick of veins, and you're here surviving on the same old scraps."

Lysander props a shoulder against the high wooden post of his bed. He feels unduly exhausted, like he's gone twelve rounds in a boxing ring.

"This is starting to feel like a lecture."

"It *is* a lecture. You want to send a strong message to Keeling? You want to let him know you're not his whipping boy? Start by getting rid of the watchdog. Make it public. Bloody. Show everyone what happens to trespassers when they—"

"He's staying," says Lysander. "The soldier."

Cyrus blinks a slow, owlish blink. "Here? At Mercy Ridge?"

"For now."

"Great." Cyrus unfolds himself slowly from the chair, squaring off against Lysander across the cluttered dark. "Okay, no, that's fine, it's just—are you *insane*?"

"Careful," warns Lysander.

"He's wood watch. His job—his *sole* job, by the way—is to exterminate anything that comes out of the woods. And who lives in the woods? I do. *I* live in the woods."

"He's the sunshine sniper," adds Lysander.

Cyrus drops back against the bedpost, bewildered. "That's not a point in his favor. You do see that, right? Have you given any thought at all to what kind of message this sends to the rest of the crew? To *Keeling*?"

Lysander doesn't waste his time answering Cyrus's questions. "Put Boyce on the watchdog," he says instead. "I want Thorley monitored at all times. He doesn't even take a piss alone."

"Boyce is a baby."

"Boyce is a Mercy Boy. He'll do what he's told. And so will you."

He can *feel* Cyrus biting back his criticism. "Anything else?"

"Yes. Send Sully to the eastern outpost. Have Nkosi put eyes on the Parker house. Anyone goes in or out, I want to hear about it right away."

Cyrus sucks air through his teeth. "I assume that means Shea's staying, too."

"She is. She's up in the presidential wing. I put Choi outside her room. They were in the same year at Hornbeam, so they have history. I don't want her going anywhere without an escort."

Lit by a single bar of light from the hall, Cyrus looks as skeptical as Lysander has ever seen him. "So that's it, then? You're so wrapped around her finger that you'll give her whatever she asks for? Free food and accommodation here at Mercy Ridge. A private suite for her boyfriend. I bet she didn't even need to open a vein."

There's a tic in Lysander's left eye. He stifles the urge to rub at it. "It's temporary. They're only staying until the revel."

"The revel you're not attending."

"Did I say that? I've changed my mind."

"You mean *she* changed your mind."

A loaded silence follows. "Actually, Asher Thorley did," quips Lysander, because now he wants to get under Cyrus's skin. To irritate him, the way he's been irritated all evening.

He thinks of finding Cyrus dying in a shallow roadside ditch. He'd been bleeding out in a patch of dead nettle, his voice a scrape against the wind: *Help. Please help me.*

They'd hobbled together to the spring at the Gravewood's center—drank from its waters, cold and transmutative. While dawn approached, they huddled on the frozen bank and let the Rot take hold—let the forest knit Cyrus back together. It was the beginning of a brotherhood. A blood bond, forged in deep winter. Lysander learned early on in life that every beginning has an end. He has no problem cutting the cord if it comes down to it.

"Since you don't seem to need me for anything," says Cyrus, "I guess I'll see myself out."

"I wish you would."

With a muttered *"asshole,"* Cyrus stalks toward the door. He doesn't make it far. Lysander cuffs him hard by the shoulder, stopping him dead in his tracks.

"There's bruising on her throat."

"Are you surprised? She's always struck me as the kind of girl who goes looking for trouble. Guess she found some."

"Guess she did." Lysander smiles his most chilling smile—a menacing sneer he learned from his father. "Mark her like that again, and I'll kill you."

He lets go, and Cyrus staggers forward. His stare is closed-off, but Lysander can smell the fear on him. He knows he's replaceable.

"You kill me, and you'll be giving Keeling exactly what he wants."

"*Anticipate my needs*, then. Don't put me in a position where I'm forced to choose."

Cyrus tugs the rumpled leather of his jacket flat. "If you're not careful, your little obsession with Shea Parker is going to destroy everything you've built. And that's not an opinion, Lysander, that's a fact."

He slams the door shut behind him when he goes. Lysander stares at the place where he'd been, blinking away swimmers.

His eyes catch on the glass of absinthe. A single starburst of light illuminates the blood within, making it glitter like a ruby. He ought to bolt it down. Swallow it, quick, before it clots. Cyrus is right—he's starving. It isn't enough, to survive on sporadic swallows of blood. To take what little Shea offers, when she sees fit to offer it. To be *careful* with her, while he desiccates a little more each passing day.

He *ought* to drink it, but he doesn't. He is, as always, a creature of impulsivity. At the mercy of his most intrusive thoughts. Crossing the room in three swift steps, he picks up the glass and hefts it hard at the wall over the fireplace. It shatters, sending blood running along the wallpaper in thin rivers of red.

It doesn't make him feel better, although he hadn't expected it to. With a sigh, he sinks onto the trunk at the foot of his bed. He feels like a petulant child. He feels several eons old. The paradox of it threatens to tear him asunder.

When the door opens again, the light finds him there, his head in his hands.

"The door was shut for a reason," he says to the floor.

He's met with silence. Slowly, he lifts his head and peers out through the messy curtain of his hair. Viola stands in the open door, frail as ever. Mercy Ridge's resident matron is wraithlike as a ghost. Lysander's own personal nightmare. She wears her raven-black hair pulled back in a chignon, exposing the angry lattice of scars disfiguring her moon-pale face. One eye is strangely off-color, its pupil blown. The other is webbed in white glaucoma.

He should be used to the sight of her by now.

"I didn't send for you."

Her smile is patient. *Placating.* As if he's still a child. "There's a girl in my wing."

"It's impermanent," he assures her, rising to his feet. Everything in him feels ground to dust. The smell of blood clings to the wall. Even his teeth ache. "She'll be gone within the week. Leave her alone."

"She's pretty."

"She isn't." The lie sticks in his throat. "How would you know, anyway?"

"I peeked out my door when she went past. She's human."

Like me comes the unspoken afterthought.

"She is."

"Do you like her?"

The question is as unexpected as it is ridiculous. He fixes Viola in a look.

"You're angry." Her smile quivers. "Don't be angry."

"Don't ask ridiculous questions, and I won't be."

"It's just that I want you to find someone. Someone you care about. I don't like thinking of you alone." She wrings her hands together like she's washing them clean. She'd scrub them raw, if she could. She has before. He used to tape oven mitts to her wrists, back when they first came north. He thinks maybe he should start again.

Her knuckles are knotted, cheeks concave. He tries not to notice the subtle little ways she's changed. The way it feels like time is taking her from him in pieces. As though one day, he'll wake and find her transformed into a laurel tree, like some sort of Hellenistic nymph. Destroying herself to escape the long arm of Zeus.

"I'm not alone," he tells her, forcing a smile. "I have you."

"You never come to see me."

The pang of guilt in his chest is impossible to ignore. He does his best. "That's because every time I do, you beat me at chess."

"You *are* a very sore loser," she says fondly.

"I am."

"Just like your father."

The smile slips off his face. She didn't say it to hurt him. She never does. Deep inside his chest, a familiar red ember of anger ignites. He shuts his eyes and takes a single, steadying breath.

When he opens them again, Viola is still there, hovering on the threshold. He recognizes the slack set of her jaw. The glass of her eyes. She's caught in a flashback. He knows, from experience, that there's no reeling her back in, once she's adrift. It doesn't stop him trying.

"Mom," he says.

Her eyes snap to his. She looks clean through him. "You're doing so well," she says softly. "You're being so brave. My little boy blue."

Sometimes it takes considerable effort to remind himself it's not his mother he's upset with. Some days he can't even stand to look at her face—at the damage he did.

There's a reason he's alone. A reason he's exiled himself to the north.

He can't afford an attachment. No distractions. No weaknesses.

No small-town girls with defiant eyes and gold-spun hair.

He very nearly kissed Shea Parker tonight, and that would have been a mistake.

Quietly, he tells Viola, "I'll get someone to walk you back to your room."

When she's gone, he sends for Boyce. The younger Mercy Boy appears not long after, skidding into the doorway. He's tall and gangly, black skin shining from a feed and his hair in twists. Aiken Boyce was one of the earliest recruits, back when Lysander first opened the doors of Mercy Ridge. He'd been eleven years old—too small to pledge—but he'd come north with his older brother. *There's no one left. If I join the watch, there won't be anyone to look after my kid brother. This way, we stay together.*

"What's up?" Boyce asks. He's not eleven anymore, but he's still too young. His arms and legs are growing faster than his brain. He nearly elbows a lamp off the dresser as he ambles into the room, bristling with his usual energy.

"Cy gave you your assignment?" asks Lysander.

"Yeah," says Boyce, setting the lamp back onto its base. "I have to babysit the watchdog."

"Sniper," Lysander corrects him, and Boyce's eyes go wide.

"Are you bullshitting me?"

"I am not."

The first glimmer of interest appears in his eyes. "So, he's deadly?"

"Not as deadly as you," says Lysander. "He's staying in the guest rooms. Go down and get him. Tell him I'd like to talk."

Asher Thorley is slow to arrive. Lysander waits, prying loose the baseball card he keeps in his jacket. Mickey Mantle. 1952. There's a bit of blood in one corner, so faint it could be mud. A fingerprint, smeared. He fits his thumb against it and feels a careful sort of nothing.

He hears the watchdog well before he appears. It's impossible not to—Asher Thorley walks like an elephant. He stomps in through the open door at a pace suitable for a death march, his left eye swollen shut. Lysander tucks the card out of sight and waits for him to say something. He does.

"I guess you're too important to come get me yourself."

Lysander tips a smile in his direction. "Are you impressed?"

"No."

His tone is blunt. Unapologetic. It doesn't escape Lysander's notice, how startlingly like Shea Asher is.

"Do you really have a hundred kills?"

Asher's good eye narrows to a slit. "Something like that, yeah."

"Does it eat at you?"

"I sleep just fine at night. How about you?"

Lysander's smile broadens to a grin. "I'm more of a day sleeper."

"Right."

The conversation flags. The smell of blood scrapes at the back of Lysander's throat. In the quiet, Asher shifts his weight from one ungainly boot to the other.

"Did you call me up here just to compare kills?"

"No," says Lysander. "I have a job for you."

The steady current of Asher's pulse is loud in the quiet. "I don't work for you."

"True," agrees Lysander. "But I can't ask anyone else."

"You don't trust your own crew?"

"Not with Shea."

A pause follows. Shea's name hangs untouched between them in the silence. Lysander is met with the faint sense that Asher Thorley will do anything for Shea Parker. The understanding twists something ugly inside him, though it shouldn't. It's a good thing. He can use that sort of allegiance. He can bend it to his will.

And he'll have to. He thinks of what the emissary told him—that Paris Keeling is watching his every move. Assessing him for weak spots, inspecting him for cracks. Waiting for the chance to hit him where it hurts. If they're going to get close enough to Paris to kill him, Lysander will need to be untouchable. And there's no denying that Shea has become an exposed nerve.

"What do you need?" Asher asks.

"You and Shea have history. You grew up in the same town. You went to the same school. And now here you are, braving the dangers of the Gravewood together. The love story practically writes itself."

There's an incredulous pause, and then Asher barks out a laugh. He sobers the instant he realizes Lysander is serious. "There's not a chance in hell."

"You asked me what I need. This is it."

"You want me to seduce her."

Seduce. He hates the way it sounds, the way it coils in his gut like a snake.

"What's the matter, Thorley?" he asks. "Not a closer?"

"You—" Asher gapes at him. "That's not the problem. I don't want a part in whatever sick head game the two of you are playing."

"You inserted yourself in the middle of our sick head game," Lysander reminds him. "And now, thanks to your enterprising mind, the three of us are about to walk into the lion's den. I'm trying to keep her out of harm's way."

"If you really cared about keeping her safe, you and I could have done this alone. Parker could have gone home. She *should* have gone home. The road to the Flatwood is going to be dangerous, and she's never even left Little Hill. There was zero reason for you to drag her into—"

"I need her."

He hadn't meant to say it like that. *Desperately.* The admission pings off the walls of his room. *I need her. I need her.* The smell of blood is making him twitch. He drags the flat of his hand along the nape of his neck, feeling half mad. He thinks of the envoy: He knows exactly where to push to make you break.

"Here's a scenario for you—you're Paris Keeling. You want me to submit. How would you make me do it?"

Asher is too quiet, sighting him like a hunter. "I'd go after something important."

"Exactly."

Lysander has him by the throat. He can *feel* it. It isn't just that Asher Thorley will do anything for Shea, it's that he'll do whatever it takes to keep her out of the hands of the devil. Lysander tips back against the mantel, cool as ice. Inside, he's coiled tight enough to snap.

"From here on out," he says, "assume we're being watched. Keep close to her. Be seen with her. It doesn't have to be real, it just has to be believable."

SEVEN

Shea

The great irony of Shea Parker's existence is that she prefers the silence.

If it were up to her, she'd live in it forever. She's learned—out of necessity, or else over time—to slot the noises into place. The brain is a funny thing. It adapts. It attributes meaning to dissonance, makes sense of the clicks and creaks and scrapes. It forgets what things used to sound like, before the sound went away.

When she was young, there was a clinic in town. Her parents upended the last of their savings to get her fitted for silicone molds. It took months after that for the hearing aids to arrive. In that time, she and her parents subsisted on boiled root vegetables and watery broth. It felt like a cruel joke, that she had to starve for sound, when she didn't even want it. Crueler still that her parents starved with her, when she'd have been perfectly happy in the quiet.

Silence hadn't been an option. The rest of the world wasn't as hospitable as home. No one at school spoke with their hands. No one in town knew what to do with her. As she grew, so did the stakes, until her looming graduation began to feel like an expiration date. There was no place in Little Hill for the childless, the unemployed, and the unenlisted. Those who ate up resources without giving something back tended to disappear. They became just another face on a poster. Missing. Lost. Gone.

Useless.

For a long time, her parents did whatever they could to shield her from the truth. When the clinic shut its doors, her father left town in search of batteries. He went to the city to pawn what he could—his father's favorite watch, his mother's wedding ring. Carving up the remains of his family. Shea paid him back for his sacrifice with tantrums. Slammed doors and angry tears, her hearing aids off and her eyes shut. *I hate it, I hate it, I hate it!*

Sometimes, when he first left, she thought maybe he'd done so because he was sick of bleeding himself dry for her sake. She thought maybe if she'd been more grateful, more tolerably behaved, he'd have stayed.

That maybe if she hadn't squandered everything he'd worked for, he wouldn't be gone.

She bleeds herself dry now.

She microdoses silence in the space between.

If she Turns, the rest of the world will be at her mercy. She won't be forced to capitulate to its whims. She won't have to play by its rules—to cut herself down to size. She won't have to empty out her veins over and over for a life she never even wanted.

She spends the day thinking it over, shut away in a room with a view of the mountain. There's a little balcony on the other side of the glass, the prim white railing sponged in moss. The bed is broad and plush and piled in pillows. The walls are plaid, pastoral and charming.

Perhaps most surprisingly, the room comes with an attached bath. It's small and neat, containing a single, deep tub and a pedestal sink. An old painting of Mercy Mountain hangs on the wall, slopes demarcated in colored runs. Several clean, dry towels have been left atop the toilet seat.

She can't remember the last time someone left towels out for her. It makes her think of her mother—of being wrapped up after a bath, her fingers pruning. She used to wriggle and writhe and gnash her teeth whenever her mother brushed her hair. *You're a great wild thing*, her mother would laugh, combing loose the tangles one by one, *and so you have great wild hair.*

The memory has ground sharp, over the years. It hurts to try to hold it.

By the time the red haze of a dusk settles over the mountain, she's made up her mind. When she tugs open the door to track down Lys, it's to find Asher standing on the other side, his fist poised to knock. For several seconds, they blink at each other in surprise.

Finally, he asks, "Can I come in?"

The question jars her into action. She shuts the door so hard she feels it in her teeth.

"Parker, come on" drifts Asher's voice through the wood. "Open the door."

She doesn't.

"Look," he says, muffled, "I know you're upset—"

She wrenches the door wide with a vehemence that ruffles her skirt. He stands with both hands braced against the frame, his left eye swollen shut.

"Hi."

"*Upset?*"

He flinches. "Well—"

"You think I'm *upset?*"

"You seem upset."

"You tried to unload a shotgun into my mom."

Gingerly, he says, "I think you and I can both agree that there were extenuating circumstances."

"You told Lys about her. That she's sick."

"I did. I did do that, and I'm sorry." He searches her face, his own crumpling when he finds only steely resolve. "Give me a little grace here, Parker. I'm just trying to find Ellie."

"I want to find Ellie, too," she snaps. "You have no idea—I'd do anything to get her back. But not like this. You cornered me last night. You *threatened* me."

"If we're going to fight, let's do it in the room, at least."

"I don't want to fight. I want you to leave me alone."

He cuts her a plaintive look. "I can't do that."

"You can. I'll help."

She moves to slam the door in his face again, but this time he anticipates. He shoves it back open with ease, bringing them face-to-face in the newly fallen dusk.

"Five minutes," he says. "That's all I need."

"I'll give you two."

"Four."

"Three."

"Done." He steps inside and lets the door fall shut behind him with a click. She scuttles back several steps, out of arm's reach. It's for his safety, not hers. She's furious enough to strike at him.

"Where's Tristan? He was supposed to be standing guard."

"I sent him away."

"How?"

"What do you mean, how? I've known Choi since he was eating crayons in preschool. I told him to beat it for a few minutes, and he did."

She glowers up at him. "Get him back."

"I still have three minutes."

"It's two now," she says. "Not that it matters. There's seven days until we leave for the Flatwood. Until then, I have nothing to say to you."

"You have every right to be mad," he tells her. "I didn't come here to talk you into forgiving me. I came to tell you that Lysander is posting a watch on your house. I asked if I could go with the first patrol."

Her anger deepens. "I hope he told you no."

"I'm heading out as soon as we're done here," he says, and flinches back from the expression on her face. "Look, I think it's safe to say that neither of us could predict how things would play out last night. I came to Mercy Ridge with a Hail Mary, and I had no idea you'd get swept up in it with me. So, as a peace offering, I told Lysander I'd go get your things. I came by to ask if there was anything you'd like me to grab while I'm there."

"I don't want you going through my stuff."

Through the red haze of her anger, she is starkly aware of how mortifying it would be to have Asher Thorley poking through her belongings. Her brain fires off a series of scenarios, each one worse than the one before: Asher rifling through her underwear drawer. Asher flipping through her math notebooks and finding entire pages doodled with his name. Or—perhaps worst of all—Asher uncovering her cookie tin stuffed with unsent letters, every last one addressed to his garrison. Promises made and then broken, before they ever saw the light of day.

"Are you sure?" he asks. "What about your rabbit?"

Her stomach flips at the casual mention of her old stuffed rabbit. "Don't touch Bugs."

"You still sleep with him?"

The memory is a whip, quick and stinging. She's fifteen years old again, spending the night at the Thorley house. Camellia and Poppy were fast asleep upstairs, but she'd tossed and turned for hours, sick with jealousy over the fact that Asher had gone out riding with Alameda Morales. It was after midnight, and he still hadn't come home.

Restless, she'd tiptoed downstairs for a glass of water, her sleep shorts sticking to her skin. She'd stumbled upon Asher sneaking in through the open window, his neck dark with several hickeys. They'd frozen at the sight of each other, her with Bugs held before her like a shield and him with one foot in the wide farmhouse sink. *How about you don't tell my parents you saw me*, he'd finally whispered, *and I won't tell anyone at school you still sleep with a stuffy?*

"That's none of your business," she says now.

He grins. "So, then yes."

"Your three minutes are up." It comes out abruptly.

Compliant, he pries open the door, watching her too keenly as he does. She studies a spot on the wall and waits for him to leave. He doesn't. He lingers.

"Are we still friends?"

Her chest gives an awful pinch. "Were we ever?"

"No," he admits, though now he sounds careful. "That's not the word I'd pick."

Her eyes jolt to his, surprised. His stare is honey dark. Lit by a silver wedge of moonlight, he looks almost regretful.

"I'll grab Bugs," he says, and pulls the door shut before she can argue.

When he's gone, she waits just long enough for him to be out of sight before heading out after him, her residual anger driving her at a full tilt. She finds Tristan standing outside as if he'd never left.

"Thanks for nothing," she bites at him, and takes off down the hall.

He falls in after her, looking penitent. "Where are we going?"

"To talk to Lys."

She arrives outside Lys's bedroom to find it shut. A hazy yellow light leaks out from the gap beneath. She shoves inside without bothering to knock, her nerves a hard knot in her belly.

"If the plan is to Turn me, then let's get it over with— *Oh.*"

It isn't Lys inside the room at all. It's a woman, her raven-dark hair curtaining a face gone ropy with scarring. She's seated by the unlit hearth, contemplating a chessboard. Reaching for a white pawn, she smiles up at Shea.

"Do you play?"

"No," Shea admits, too surprised to say anything else.

The woman's left eye glimmers curiously. The other is clouded white. A pale, opaline stare that seems to gaze clean through her. "It's Oliver's favorite. Although he's going to lose this game. He went with the Sicilian Defense tonight. Aggressive, but he's left himself full of holes. He must be in a bad mood."

As if he'd been waiting for his cue, the door swings wide with just enough force to send it dinging off the drywall. Lys appears, looking treacherous. In the hall behind him, Tristan peers nervously over his shoulder.

"Leave," Lys tells the woman.

She sets the pawn into a space, unhurried. "But it's your move."

"And I'll let you know when I've made it. Get out."

"There's no need for histrionics," she tells him, rising out of her chair. "I'm being perfectly well-behaved."

Lys doesn't answer as the woman glides between them, light on her feet. She pats his cheek, and then she's gone, the door swinging shut in her wake. Alone, the silence bristles.

"That was rude of you," notes Shea.

On a normal night, the casual condemnation of his character might amuse him. On a normal night, he might laugh. Tonight, he stares dead ahead, unsmiling. He looks as tired as she feels, his eyes bruised and his cheeks hollow, his hair a messy fall of black.

"You shouldn't have come here." His voice is tumbled stone. It scrapes clean through her.

"I needed to talk to you."

He still hasn't looked at her. "I didn't send for you."

"Well, that's too bad. I'm not one of your lackeys, I'm your—"

She falters and he pounces, quick as a cat. "My what?"

"Never mind."

"Don't stop now," he goads, fixing her in the full-black of his stare. "I'm dying to know what it is you were planning to say."

"Nothing. It doesn't matter."

"It does to me." He stalks nearer, predatory in the gloom. "What are you, Shea? My iron supplier? My human blood bag? How many more ugly phrases can we think up to give this thing a name?"

"You *are* in a bad mood."

His smile is humorless. "What gave it away?"

He looks as waspish as she's ever seen him, and she suddenly regrets coming at all. Everything feels different, now that the rules have changed. Like she and Lys have been stuffed into an airless box and then rattled. His agitation drones in the air between them—a palpable buzz that sets her blood humming.

"I wanted to talk to you about Turning, but clearly I came at a bad time."

She manages to get the door partway open before he pushes it shut, his hand splayed against the grain. Pinned, she can smell the clean, cold scent of him. Smoke and pine, like the forest in deep winter. Without a fire, a chill has crept into the room. The knob is ice-cold beneath her palm.

"I've changed my mind," he says. "Let's talk."

Pulse fluttering, she turns to face him. A half inch away, Lys is a study in shadow. Hunger threads along his throat in pale blue rivers. It takes her several heartbeats to gather her courage.

"I've thought it over, and I think I'm ready."

"You think?" His voice is hard as glass. "Or you are?"

"I am."

He contemplates her for a long moment. "Your toes are turned in."

"What?"

"You go pigeon-toed when you lie."

"I do not."

"Do too."

The careful way he's studying her makes her cheeks heat. Her heart gives a single hard thump. He hears it, the hunger in his skin splitting into tributaries of dark. She resists the urge to reach out and trace the lines with a finger.

"You're starving."

He makes a face. "I'm always starving."

"Lysander!" There's pounding at her back. "Open up!"

They step away from the door just as Conall Sullivan bursts through it. He's gangly and thin, his head a mess of ginger curls, his pale skin freckled with remnants of a former life lived in sunlight. He takes silent note of their proximity in the dark—no signs of a feed to mark what they'd been doing.

"Sullivan," says Lys, suddenly sober. "You're not where you're supposed to be."

"It's Nkosi," says Sullivan. "He and the others caught someone breaking into the Parker house."

At the news, everything in Shea shuts up tight. *Mom*, she thinks, going cold. Her vision tunnels, ears ringing. She shouldn't have left her mother there alone. She shouldn't have thought she could get away with it, straddling the thin line between night and day. Lys's voice swims toward her in the narrow channel of her panic.

"Where is he now?"

"He has the suspect in custody," says Sullivan. "He and Cyrus are out there with a small recon crew. The watchdog is with them. They're waiting for your orders."

Lys is already shrugging on his jacket. "I'll deal with it myself."

"Lys, wait." Shea moves with him as he presses past her. "Wait, I want to come."

He doesn't slow. "Absolutely not."

"It's *my* house." She tails after him, undeterred. "I'm coming."

His response is reflex-quick. A half step, and then she's pinned beneath him, her jaw cupped in the hard cradle of his palm and her cheek pressed flat against the wall. Bracing himself, he leans in until his mouth is at her ear. Every part of him is cool and controlled, save his heart. It slams against her chest, thrashing like a wildebeest at the bars of its cage.

Sometimes she thinks that when it finally gets free it'll tear her apart.

"Keep pushing me like that where anyone can see," he hisses into her ear. "You'll get both of us destroyed."

He's gone before she can ask him what he means, the door to his bedroom slamming shut in his wake.

EIGHT

Shea

Here is a memory: summer, two years prior. The Thorley house in late August, rosy milkweed growing in tangles along the front walk. Shea remembers lying on her belly in the grass, her textbook open, unread pages ruffling in the wind. She'd spent the better part of the afternoon chewing on the metal end of her pencil—watching Asher as he helped his father haul wood.

Beside her sat Poppy, humming a cheery, tuneless hum and weaving loose dogwood blooms into her braid. She wasn't reading, either. She was watching Camellia diligently transcribe a section of notes. The weather was perfect—the trees in bloom and the sky a bold, blistering blue. The exact sort of day that was meant for daydreaming. Only Camellia seemed intent on studying.

Out by the fence, Asher stacked firewood into the shed. There was a smudge of dirt under his eye, the first hint of a sunburn on the bridge of his nose. The hickeys on his throat had nearly faded. Every so often, he'd cast a furtive glance in Shea's direction. She'd avert her gaze, her heart in her mouth—pretend to be engrossed in her reading. After about an hour of this, Camellia shut her book with a slam.

"He's not even doing anything interesting."

Shea dropped her pencil, startled. "Who?"

"Asher. If you stare at him any harder, your eyes will fall out."

"I'm not staring at him."

"Well, you're definitely not staring at your book," said Camellia as Poppy hummed a little louder. "If you don't pay attention, you're going to fail Mrs. Lennox's test tomorrow."

"Poppy's not studying, either," Shea pointed out.

"Poppy doesn't need to study. She has top marks in all our classes."

Shea rolled from her stomach to her back, throwing her arms wide in the grass. "I don't see what the point is. I already know I'm not going to Humboldt."

Only the top-performing students were sent on scholarship to the last surviving college—Humboldt University, down in Boston proper. They returned home with medical and engineering degrees, just enough practical knowledge to treat a cold and set a broken arm. Enough understanding of infrastructure to keep Little Hill up and running. The rest joined the watch—to serve at whatever wooded garrison needed bodies—or else stayed home and married young, popped out the next generation of soldiers and scientists.

Shea would do none of these things.

Her hearing made it so she couldn't keep up academically, and the watch didn't take anyone with a preexisting condition. Furthermore, she was a Parker, and no one wanted anything to do with the Highbush boy's wild daughter. She was doomed, it seemed, to a life between the cracks.

She'd made her peace with it. Mostly. There were some days the fear of the unknown gripped her. Some days, she worried that she'd be labeled useless and disappeared—shipped off to the stone halls of Gridley's Sanatorium to be forgotten. On those days, she sat by the forest and willed it to entice her—to make her a promise she couldn't resist. On those days, she thought maybe it wouldn't be so bad, to give herself over to the Gravewood's dark embrace.

On those days, she'd think of Asher. *I won't let you die here.*

When she peered back at the shed, he was watching her.

"Pop quiz," sang Camellia, poking Shea with her foot. "What sweet-smelling chemical is found in both plants and decomposing animals?"

"Oh," said Poppy, dropping the last of her dogwood. "I know."

Camellia frowned down at Shea. "Shea?"

Feeling peevish, she said, "I don't see how I'm supposed to know that."

"It's trimethylamine," said Asher, appearing directly in Shea's line of vision. His T-shirt was dark with sweat, the sun streaming in behind him. Shea scrabbled upright, embarrassed by the grass stains in her stockings, the wild bramble of her hair. "It's a natural-acting deterrent. Things that feed on blood won't go after something that smells dead. And don't worry, that question isn't even on the test."

"Leave," demanded Camellia, flinging her pen. "This is our study circle."

Asher dodged the pen with a laugh, adjusting the bundle of firewood under his arm. "Don't work too hard. None of it matters anyway. They're just keeping you busy so you stay out of trouble."

"I'm never trouble," Shea told him.

His smile stretched wide. "Parker," he said, "you're trouble to your bones."

There's no way in hell Shea is staying behind. Not with her mother home alone. Not when anyone at all could have stumbled upon her, chained and forgotten in the basement. Certainly not when Asher Thorley was part of the unit sent to canvass her house. Every time she shuts her eyes, she sees him standing in her foyer, his finger on the trigger. The boy who stayed out past curfew and who made her promises is gone. This new Asher has been custom-built into someone who kills without a thought.

How can she forgive him if she doesn't even trust him?

She waits until she's certain Lys is gone before she follows. Outside his room, the hall is empty—Tristan nowhere to be seen. The entire lodge seems to have emptied, and she slips into the dead of night without running into another soul. It's drizzling out—a slow, icy rain that turns the ground to gloss. The sky overhead is veiled in clouds, the moon cast in a funny halo of silver. It bathes the whole of Mercy Ridge in a feeble glow.

She hurries down the front walk, teeth chattering. Her fingers are numb by the time she reaches the end of the larch-lined drive. Switching off her hearing aids, she slips out from beneath the mountain's shadow and into the wood. She's met with the silence of her head and the deceptive serenity of the trees. Everything hangs perfectly, precariously still. Even the rain slows, caught in the canopy's evergreen tangle.

The trail is marked by a painted cross. White, the sign for mercy. The trees along the path have been burned back, their trunks hollowed out and full of ash. It gives the forest a sinister coloring, as though she's waded out of the waking world and into some sort of lightless hell dimension.

At least here, the trees are voiceless. She keeps her hearing aids off regardless, at ease in the silence. It hones her eyes to a point, brings the night veering into razor-sharp focus. She sees everything. She *feels* everything. The white-tailed flit of a deer. The hunting swoop of an owl. The leathery flutter of a bat leaving its roost.

It's near midnight by the time she reaches the old logging tracks. The sky here is a river of dark, and the rain falls freely onto the tracks. There's no moon left at all. She makes her way hurriedly along the rain-slick sleepers, driven onward by thoughts of her mother.

A head lifts from the mushroomed fall of a tree as she hops between ballasts, her arms thrown out to the sides for stability. She braces herself on one leg, expecting fangs, and finds only a doe, its black eyes dewy with suspicion. There's a moment of pristine stillness—of mutually held breath. And then the doe takes flight, disappearing with the white wave of a flag. It's heard something. Something Shea didn't. The moment she realizes it, the hair rises on the back of her neck.

There's someone behind her.

She doesn't run, though instinct tells her to flee. To run is to invite a chase, and she's come this way often enough to know there's no outrunning a Mercy Boy. Heart in her throat, she keeps moving, her arms pinwheeling against the dark. Hop. Stop. Balance. Hop. Stop. Balance.

Now that she's aware of the presence, she can feel him—his footfalls on the ground and the scrape of his boot over stone, the snap of a twig under his heel. The night gives way to his body, crackling around him in nearly undetectable ways. Ways she feels in her skin. Ways she catches, spotting flickers out of the corners of her eyes.

She walks a little faster.

She makes it all the way to the covered bridge before she slips. A patch of black ice, invisible in the dark, is all it takes. Her feet go out from under her and she pitches forward, catching herself on the heels of her hands. It's not enough to keep her from gashing the tip of her chin open against a ballast.

Her teeth crack together, and her curse sends a nearby nightjar fluttering skyward. She lies there for a moment, her ego bruised and the wind knocked out of her. Eventually, the nightjar returns. It hops to-and-fro along the railing, its beak open. Unleashing a soundless warble.

She thinks, unbidden, of her father in late summer, the grass undulating around his waist. She'd sat atop his shoulders, feeling tall as a giant. His voice rumbled against the back of her legs: *Listen. Can you hear that? It's a meadowlark. There's a predator nearby.*

Clambering back onto her feet, she takes stock of the damage. Her palms are bloody with gravel. Her chin burns, the skin scraped raw. She wipes the grit on a pleat of her skirt and keeps going.

She doesn't make it far.

There's a boy waiting at the far end of the bridge.

She slows, wary—unable to make out his features in the dark. He doesn't announce himself as she approaches. Instead, he stands perfectly still, his arms hanging slack. Down in the ravine, a narrow river runs hard and fast, broken sheaves of ice bottlenecking along the shore. She clicks on her hearing aids and is immediately met with the rush of running water, loud enough to drown out the murmuring forest.

"Busted," she says, striving for levity. "How long have you been following me?"

He doesn't answer. The rain has slowed, and the moon slips out from beneath the clouds. Its light catches in the red curl of the boy's hair. *Sullivan.*

"You're bleeding." His voice is garbled, muted by the river.

Instinctively, Shea tugs her hands into her sleeves. "It's just a scrape." She edges past him, heading for the path as quickly as she can. "You can go. I don't need help."

"Do you know what I've just realized?" He does a hard about-face and falls into step alongside her, his gait heavy. "I haven't fed tonight. I've been too busy running errands."

"Take it up with Lys," she says. "I didn't ask you to do anything for me."

"Not so fast, Princess." His hand snaps out, closing tight around her elbow. She's veered sideways into the railing, the wild river frothing just below. The icy spray kisses her cheek.

Horrified, she coughs out, *"Princess?"*

"That's what they're calling you." He leans in close, his smile sharp. "The Gravewood Princess. That makes me your knight. And do you know what princesses do to show knights their appreciation? They bestow a favor on them."

"I'll scream," she says, tugging at his grip.

The tip of his nose runs along her carotid artery. "I'm depending on it."

When his teeth sink into her throat, the pain is punishing. Her scream comes out throttled, cut off by the appearance of a shadowy figure standing in the dark just over Sullivan's shoulder. A bipedal creature, the lines of it disfigured by the trees. With liquid grace, the shadow brings a finger to its lips. *Quiet.* She obeys as if compelled, her breath sawing against her ear. She feels the pull of a swallow, the rush of blood—the first surge of liquid venom into her veins. The world goes gray at the edges, the pain dulling with morphine quickness. She blinks, and the creature is gone.

A half second later, so is Sullivan.

He's ripped away with a shout—a garbled scream that cuts off in a yelp. Over the rush of water, she hears the wet tear of flesh. The brutal sever of bone snapping in two. She staggers away, one hand pressed to her throat to staunch the bleeding. Blood ribbons, hot and sticking, through her fingers as she peers into the covered dark of the bridge.

Sullivan lies unmoving on the ground, his chest gorged open.

The shadowed figure hunches over him, his still-beating heart clutched in its hand. More beast than boy, the creature hunches oddly, the seams of its shirt strained to breaking along the protrusive ridge of its spine. Moonlight gleams through the curve of two fluted horns. The bloodied tips of its talons puncture the organ in its grasp.

She scrabbles backward, intending to run. A twig snaps beneath the heel of her boot, and the creature's head kicks up. She's met with a familiar face. A thin, bowed mouth. A thin, straight nose. A dark fall of hair, rainwater dripping into eyes as black as brimstone.

A startled breath shudders out of her. "Lys?"

The heart drops to the ground with a wet squelch. The creature takes a single step toward her. A second. Blood falls from its fingertips in blue-black drips. A shout in the distance draws its focus. Light streams through the trees, splicing the dark into strips of silver. Shea is momentarily blinded as the beam of a flashlight sweeps over her face.

When it moves on, the creature is gone.

"Over here!" someone shouts.

Several Mercy Boys appear one after the other, wedging themselves hurriedly through the trees. They shove and jostle, their shadows tapering along the mirror-slick path. One by one, they catch sight of Sullivan lying there beneath the covered bridge.

"There's a body," someone calls out.

"I can't see," gripes another. "Move your big block head."

"Hey, dickwad, you're on my toes."

"Shit, is that Sully—"

"It's Sully!"

An uneasy silence crawls over them as they notice Shea standing nearby. They keep their distance, drawn like sharks by the scent of blood. A familiar face elbows his way to the front. It's Tristan, the wide beam of his flashlight sweeping over Sullivan's heart. The organ sits, steaming, atop the ice. Rotted through and ruined.

"Holy shit," he breathes.

"Out of the way!"

The group parts and Cyrus appears, his hair matted flat by the rain. He takes quick stock of the scene, his eyes lifting toward Shea. Disgust curdles his mouth into a sneer.

"He attacked me." The cold has set in, or else the shock. Her teeth won't stop chattering. "I didn't— I was— I fell. My hands were bleeding. Lys—"

"Stop talking," orders Cyrus, and she does. "The rest of you, go back to the lodge."

No one moves. A ripple of unease moves through their ranks.

"You're not in charge," someone mutters.

Cyrus's scowl deepens and he rounds on the rest of them. "Unless you want to spend the next few hours digging a grave in this rain, I'd suggest you do what I say."

This time, they listen. They disperse one by grumbling one, dissipating like shadows between the trees.

"You too, Choi," says Cyrus.

"Me?" Tristan's gaze lifts toward Shea. "But I thought—"

"I'll handle Parker. Go."

Shea watches the broad beam of Tristan's light diminish until it disappears. And then it's only her and Cyrus. And the body. The rain has picked up, turning to ice. It ricochets off the roof.

"If you care about Lysander at all," says Cyrus, "you'll keep your mouth shut."

"Who would I tell?"

As if in answer to her question, a final figure emerges from between the trees. Not a Mercy Boy, but Asher, a drawstring bag over one shoulder. *Her* bag, a single velveteen ear flopping out from the cinched enclosure. He looks as stoic as she's ever seen him, shotgun in hand and a bandolier strapped across his chest. The slots have been fitted with wooden bullets, whittled sharp. He surveys Sullivan warily as he steps onto the bridge, prying loose a set of earplugs.

"What the hell is this?"

"An accident," says Cyrus, before Shea can answer.

"Doesn't look like an accident." Asher ventures nearer to the body, prodding its shoulder with the butt of his shotgun. "He's one of yours?"

"Not anymore," says Cyrus wryly. "He's been demoted."

"Interesting choice of words," notes Asher.

"Would you call it something else?"

"I would. This was a slaughter, plain and simple. From the way the wounds run parallel to the skin, I'd say it was an animal that did it."

Cyrus's eyes glimmer. "You're the expert."

A sudden scream rends the night in two. The sound is bestial. An eerie, tortured howl that unspools through the forest. Asher jolts to attention, readying his gun with unrecognizable speed.

"What the hell was that?"

"One of the Gravewood's great mysteries," says Cyrus with a shrug. Hunger has begun to crawl into his throat in spider-thin bruises. "If you don't mind, I'm going to leave you to escort Parker back. She's a little too bloody for my liking. Don't be long."

He's gone before either Shea or Asher can protest, abandoning them beneath the covered bridge. On the ground, the freezing rain begins to build into a wet slush. It reflects the light of the moon, turning the forest a polished gray.

"Are you okay?" asks Asher, shouldering his gun.

She swipes at her throat with her sleeve. "I'm fine."

"Let me see it."

"I said *I'm fine*."

She tries to duck away from him, but he's faster. He takes hold of her chin, angling her face to the side. The night air kisses the wound, drawing out a wince. Her head is full of Asher at sixteen, his voice cracked in laughter: *You're trouble to your bones.*

"Shit." He's not laughing now. "That looks deep."

"It'll heal." She wriggles out of his hold. "We should get back. Are you coming?"

He doesn't answer. He's staring down at Sullivan, his expression darkly contemplative. "Did you see what attacked him?"

"No."

Asher's eyes flick up to hers. "What do you mean, no? You were standing right here."

"It was dark."

"Not that dark. You saw *something*."

"I didn't—" She falters, blinking away the image of Lys, a heart in his fist. "I don't know what I saw. I would tell you if I did."

His brows pinch together. He searches her face for far too long. "You're lying," he finally says. "And I don't know why you're lying, but I'll figure it out. Until then, we have a bigger problem."

"What is it?"

"The intruder Nkosi found at your house? She's been brought to Mercy Ridge."

Shea's heart gives a horrible crack. "She?"

"It's Zahar," says Asher. "Poppy is here in the Gravewood."

NINE

Lysander

The first thing Oliver Lysander is cognizant of is the sound of birds.

One bird, to be exact. A wood thrush, perched just outside his window. He can't see it, but he can hear it. The flutelike *ee-oh-lay* pervades the air. Stops. Starts again.

Ee-oh-lay. His head snaps up. *Ee-oh-lay, ee-oh-lay.*

His brain feels as if it's been pared open with a knife. His wrists are cuffed in leather bands, ankles similarly strapped. His chest, bare save the intricate workings of a rib cage done in grayscale ink, is belted tight. He's on the ground level of Mercy Ridge, in a cold, cluttered room, restrained against the unyielding steel of a standing cot. The bed is walled in thin, clinical rails. The walls are stone, thick enough to swallow a scream.

He swore he'd never need to use this room for its intended purpose.

Up until now, he hasn't.

It's become a gallery of sorts, in its years of dereliction. A shrine to his fixations, or else a dumping ground for oddments. Bones on shelves and beetles in shadowboxes, a hex jar full of dried dianthus and butterflies of all shapes and sizes, each one housed in an elegant glass cloche. He names them one by one. *Grayling. Green hairstreak.* He tries not to think about the previous night. *Painted lady. Viceroy.*

When he last saw Shea, she'd been bleeding.

Ee-oh-lay, goes the wood thrush.

His head pulses. His hand closes in around nothing. He never knew bones could snap so easily. He never knew how satisfied he would feel. How like a god, ripping up a life by the root. *Common brimstone. Holly blue.* Something is different. Something new is among his things. Something that doesn't belong. He can *feel* it, like a sour note. It takes him a moment to spot it—a jar that hadn't been there before. Someone has filled it to the brim with pickling brine. In it floats a heart, dark with Rot.

"Do you like it?"

He cranes his head around and finds Viola seated at the far side of the room, hard at work on a cross-stitch. The needle is threaded with red, the fiber thin and dark as sinew. On the sill, the thrush lets out another tremulous *ee-oh-lay*.

"Did you put that there to mock me?"

"Mock? Never." She tugs the needle skyward, thread pulling taut. "I thought it would make a nice addition to your collection."

"My collection," he echoes flatly. It sounds so trite. So childish—like he's still a little boy with his bin of old Matchbox cars. "I killed him. Do you understand that? The boy who belonged to that heart is dead."

Viola sets her embroidery hoop into her lap and looks up at him, blinking oddly. The faraway gleam in her eyes makes him feel as though he's swallowed battery acid.

"I killed him," he says again, and this time his voice cracks. "I killed him with my bare hands, and you're not even angry."

She gives a single owlish blink. "Do you want me to be angry?"

"Yes." It feels like there are a thousand lifetimes packed into that little word. A thousand hurts. A thousand nights spent curled inward, his hands over his ears, a shout rattling through the dark: *Get up, Oliver. Get up and face what you've done.*

Viola's mouth curves into a smile. "You were just a little boy. Such a lovely, sweet little boy. How could I ever be angry with you?"

He watches, saying nothing, as she resumes her cross-stitch, pushing the needle methodically through the linen. Stab. Push. Pull. Stab. Push. Pull.

"Do you want to keep her?" she asks without preamble. "Shea?"

"No." The lie is a sharp stone in his throat.

"I like her. I like having her here. I like her for you. I want you to have someone you'd put a heart in a jar for. It means you're alive."

The guilt that cracks open within him is sharp as glass. Suddenly, he can't bear to look at her. Like a coward, he turns his face away.

"The stars have gone red again," she says. "I don't like it when they watch us so closely."

"It's day," he reminds her tiredly. "There are no stars."

When Viola finally departs, she goes without a word—without offering to untie him. She leaves her hoop behind. It sits unfinished on her chair, the thread hanging loose. Cyrus appears moments later, slinking round the corner as though he'd been waiting.

"Took you long enough," gripes Lysander. "Let me out."

"I have something to say to you first."

"While I'm strapped to a bed? How intrepid of you—"

"We need to consider the possibility that Mercy Ridge has been compromised."

Lysander's molars grind hard enough to hurt. "It hasn't."

"And you're basing that on what, exactly? Ego? Pride? Willful ignorance?"

"Enough."

It comes out a register too low, remnants of last night still coiled in his chest. Cyrus takes a step back. He schools his expression into a careful blank.

"There's a reason Sullivan went after Shea last night."

"There was blood," says Lysander. "He lost control."

"And the rest of us didn't?" asks Cyrus. *"You* didn't?"

Lysander thinks of Shea in the rain, her throat gleaming red, the smell of blood sticking to everything. The memory leaves an ache in his gut. A gnawing sense of hunger that isn't entirely his own. He takes a deep swallow of air and slides his gaze toward the shelves. *Adonis blue. Mountain ringlet. Swallowtail.* Across the room, Cyrus is watching him too closely.

"That girl has you so turned around, you can't think straight. You've been tripping over your own two feet since the night she turned up, and everyone sees it."

Luna moth. Lulworth skipper.

He feels like he's been dropped from some great height, the Rot seeping out of his cracks.

"The other day, you asked me where I'd push you if I wanted to make you break," says Cyrus. "I told you I'd push you off a cliff. What I should have said was this—if I really wanted to mess you up, I'd go after Shea. We need to face the facts—Paris Keeling tugged at your leash last night, and he used Sullivan to do it."

"Last night was an accident. It had nothing to do with Paris."

"What about what Paris did to your mom? Was that an accident, too?"

The air in the room seems to fold in on him. He regards his lieutenant coldly, his lungs constricting.

"Careful."

Cyrus doesn't heed the warning. "All I'm saying is, he's forced you to fall in line before."

"And I've taken the necessary precautions to make sure he never does it again. We're done with this conversation. Untie me."

This time, Cyrus obliges. Loosening the first strap, he stands aside and lets Lysander do the rest himself. Every muscle in his body aches, and it slows his progress considerably. He's annoyed all over again by the time he finally steps free.

"It's not just you anymore," says Cyrus, the moment he's loose. "You owe it to the rest of them to get your head on straight."

"My head is fine." Lysander locates his T-shirt and tugs it on, snatching up Viola's embroidery as he does. The cross-stitch is aimless. Disordered. Just an errant cluster of red snarls on white linen. Reaching for his hoodie, he tosses the hoop on a shelf with the others. A half dozen linens stitched in similar, frenzied fashion. Nonsense, all of it.

Do you want to keep her?

And what if he did? What if he tried? It would ruin him, that's what. Here, on his shelf, sits the raw and bloody proof. His best intentions, rotting in a jar.

He zips his hoodie and reaches for his jacket, shrugging it on as he heads out into the hall. Cyrus follows.

"Speaking of your head, you might want to take a look in the mirror."

Lysander doesn't slow his pace. "What's that supposed to mean?"

"Ah." Cyrus sucks air through his teeth. "I don't want to say."

"Five minutes ago, I couldn't get you to shut up. What's changed?"

"What's *changed*," says Cyrus as they turn a corner, "is that now you and your shitty attitude are within striking distance."

Lysander skids to a stop. "*Say it*, Cy."

"You have horns." It echoes horribly.

"Horns," Lysander repeats.

"Very small ones," Cyrus amends, as if it's any better.

Cautious, Lysander probes at his temples. What he'd thought was the worst headache of his life is, in fact, a coarse bit of bone, piercing his flesh on either side. The skin is tender around the base, gored open and fevered to the touch. He drops his hands. His stomach roils.

"I'll shave them down."

Cyrus lifts a brow. "And what about the next time?"

"There won't be a next time."

"Sure," says Cyrus. "Unless my theory is correct, which would mean Paris convinced Conall Sullivan to go after Parker. And if he got to Sully, he'll get to someone else. You showed your hand last night. It's only a matter of time before it happens again."

The ache in Lysander's gut has become a Gordian knot. The only way to handle it is to slice it clean in half. It might not dull the hurt, but it would simplify it. He takes off down the hall, pulling his hood over his head.

"Get me Poppy Zahar. I'll meet you in the boardroom in twenty minutes."

"Where are *you* going?" calls Cyrus after him.

"To make sure what happened last night doesn't happen again."

Asher Thorley's room is a glorified custodial closet. Lysander's doing—he'd been feeling petty the night the soldier arrived. He's not too proud to admit it. The narrow space boasts a cinder block floor and a single egress window, a mop in one corner. Boyce sits just outside, whittling some sort of indefinable creature out of wood. A bear, maybe. Or a wolf. He tosses it down as Lysander rounds the corner, flicking shut his knife and rising to his feet.

"Take a break," says Lysander. "Go find something to eat."

He waits for Boyce to be out of sight before he shoves inside, not bothering to knock. The door falls shut and he finds himself at the end of a shotgun. Watery daylight spills in through the egress, haloing Asher Thorley in a dusky white. Lysander keeps to the shadowed fringes, his hood up and his hands in his pockets, the light burning through him like an unholy fire.

"Hawthorn?" he asks, eyeing the gun.

"Oak," says Asher.

"Superstitious?"

"Practical. White oak splinters on contact."

"Ouch."

A beat passes. Asher lowers the gun. "You look like dog shit."

"I *feel* like dog shit. But I'm here with good news."

"Oh yeah?"

"We're upgrading your accommodations. Presidential wing. Third floor. There's a great view of the mountain."

"You want me to keep an eye on Shea," guesses Asher, setting the gun against the wall.

"I want you to do a better job winning her over."

"It's been one day. I'm working on it."

Lysander bites back a retort. "She came to see me in my room last night. Sullivan saw, and he attacked her within the hour. My lieutenant is under the impression the two things are connected."

"And what do you think?"

"I think you've got an arsenal of white oak bullets and a hundred notches in your belt. We can both agree you're no Casanova, but I'd still feel safer if you were closer."

"I'll bet you would." Asher's smile doesn't touch his eyes. "I'm glad you brought up Conall Sullivan, actually. I asked Shea what attacked him. She said she didn't see it. You want to hear my theory?"

"It was very dark, and she was disoriented?"

"I think she's protecting the attacker."

Somewhere in his head, Lysander hears the snap of bone. Sullivan's scream.

"That's an interesting theory."

"It is, isn't it?" The way Asher studies him makes Lysander want to ask if he grew up hunting. He tracks each tic like he's searching him for weak spots. The light falls between them in a chalky barrier. It makes Lysander's blood bubble up, hot and sick in his veins. He grinds his teeth until they ache.

"The question is," says Asher, "*why* would she do that?"

"Couldn't tell you." Lysander tempers the urge to swipe his hood lower.

"I've been doing this for a little over a year now," says Asher. "I've never seen something kill like that before. In basic, they teach you that wolves go in as a pack, usually targeting the flank. My first week out, I saw a bear bite clean through someone's femur. Your kind goes for the throat. I've never heard of anything ripping out the victim's heart."

Lysander stares at him and says nothing. He stares back.

"We brought a girl in last night," says Lysander, when the pain becomes unbearable.

"I know," says Asher. "Poppy Zahar. Don't change the subject."

"But this is relevant to your interests. I thought you wanted to find your sister. Isn't that what you asked me to do?"

"It is." Asher's expression tightens. "Zahar has no idea where Camellia is."

"But she saw her last," says Lysander. "And so that's where we'll start."

Poppy Zahar is waiting for them in the boardroom when they arrive. It's impossible to miss her—if a color exists, she's wearing it. It's like a rainbow vomited and she waded right through the mess. She looks perfectly at ease atop the table, her legs swinging, shoelaces trailing. A possum lies beside her as though dead, belly up on the varnish.

There's a round metal tin in her lap, a line of butter cookies printed along the rim. She grips it tight, like it's full of gold bricks.

Cyrus sits at the head of the table, feet up and looking grim. "Is it dead?"

"Kit? No. That's just how he sleeps."

"Like he's dead?"

She fixes him with a look. "How do *you* sleep?"

Spotting Lysander, Cyrus launches to his feet. His relief fades the moment he catches sight of Asher sidling in after him. "What's he doing here?"

"He's with me," says Lysander. "Leave."

Cyrus blinks over at him. "You're joking."

"Do I look like I'm joking?"

The pause that follows is heavily weighted. In it, Lysander can practically hear his patience fraying. He's had enough of Cyrus for one day. Enough of his sideways comments. Enough of his paranoia. With a last glance at Asher, Cyrus wedges himself past Lysander and disappears out into the hall.

The moment he's gone, Poppy places a protective hand over the cookie tin. "You're going to ask me to show you what's inside here, but I'm not going to do that."

Lysander slants his gaze toward her. "Are you psychic?"

"No. Your friend already asked."

"And what'd you tell him?"

"Same thing I told you. It's not important."

"But you were at Shea Parker's house looking for it," hedges Lysander. "Nkosi found you searching her room."

"Hypothetically," says Poppy.

Lysander frowns. "You were wedged under her bed—"

"*Allegedly.*"

"—looking for *that* tin."

They all look down at the cookie tin. Poppy sighs.

"Camellia and Shea passed notes in school," she says. "Incessantly. One time, in fourth grade, Mr. Belrose caught them and made them read their notes aloud to the whole class. They started writing in code after that, swapping out their letters in a reverse alphabet. They got pretty good at it."

"That's what's in there?" asks Asher. "Coded notes from my sister?"

Poppy's grip tightens around the tin. "I'm only telling you this because I want to find Camellia."

"I know," says Asher, his voice gentling. "I want to find her, too."

Poppy squeezes her eyes shut. It's several seconds before she opens them again. "You have to understand, Shea is—well, she gets really attached, doesn't she? She's been that way since her dad left. It was so sudden, remember? He didn't leave a letter or anything."

"I remember."

Lysander feels Asher's answer like a knife to the chest. Here is another piece of Shea he doesn't possess. Another sliver of her psyche he's never seen—Shea Parker in the daylight, holding tight to the shattered fragments of her family.

"She started keeping letters or cards or anything similar," says Poppy. "I think maybe it was a way for her to hold on to people. I thought if I found something from Camellia—a note, or something—I could find a clue."

"Ellie's been gone for weeks," says Asher. "Why didn't you ask Shea earlier?"

Now, Poppy is deliberately avoiding Asher's gaze. Lysander can see her looking anywhere but at the watchdog, her eyes darting along the wall's peeling varnish. "I couldn't," she finally says. "I mean, I could, but she's— Well, it's complicated. She and Camellia fought. Badly."

"When?" asks Asher.

Poppy stares down into her lap. "The day before she disappeared."

TEN

Shea

The shower water washes away most of the blood.

Shea stands in the tub with her forehead against the tile and watches the drain turn red, then brown, then eventually clear. When it's done, she towels dry and dresses slowly. Her school uniform is soaked through, the stockings ripped, and she fishes through the bag of clothes from home in search of something dry.

She pulls on a wash-shrunk top and her father's old flannel, a shredded pair of jeans gone soft with wear. The water was kettle hot, and a gray condensation has collected along the mirror. Rising up onto her toes to wipe the glass clear, she catches sight of her neck. Two deep punctures gorge the soft underside of her throat, the bite red and angry and careless.

Her first thought is this: If Lys had Turned her, last night wouldn't have gone the way it did.

Gingerly, she presses a clean bit of gauze to the wound, taping it in place. She feels strangely arthritic, her joints ground down and her knuckles throbbing, and it makes every task take twice as long. When it's done, she braids her hair into two messy plaits and slips on the pendant necklace she'd found nestled among her things.

It isn't anything special—just her grandmother's cross and a flat, silver ring slung on a chain.

Just another piece of home Asher knew well enough to bring along.

As if she summoned him just by thinking of him, she finds Asher waiting when she exits the bathroom. He's seated on the edge of her bed, his injured eye the exact color of a boysenberry. An immediate and immolating panic consumes her as she realizes what he holds in his hands.

A cookie tin. *Her* cookie tin. The lid is off and paper juts out in every direction. Pink stationery and serrated notebook shreds. Sticky notes and torn-out pages and even a napkin or two. Most damning of all are the letters. There's a half dozen at least, neatly folded and tucked into unsealed envelopes, the same name neatly penned on every last one: *PVT Thorley, Asher.*

Her mouth goes dry. "Where did you get that?"

"Zahar," he says plainly.

Panic wars with relief. "You've seen her? She's okay? I haven't been able to find Lys anywhere and Cyrus said—"

He cuts her off. "Why didn't you tell me you and Ellie fought?"

The question plunks like a stone between them. Every last answer seems like the exact wrong one. She watches from somewhere outside herself as he pries loose a ripped bit of paper from the tin. Camellia's curling handwriting stares up at her, scribbled in code: *I don't think I can be friends with someone who makes blood pacts with the devil.*

"You can understand that?"

"Zahar gave me the cipher," says Asher. "But it's not exactly advanced encryption."

The look on his face wrenches an admission out of her. "I didn't want you to hate me."

"I don't—" Asher's face falls. "Parker, I don't hate you. It's not like you had a road map to Ellie hidden away. It's just that—" He seems to be considering his next words carefully. "I *asked* you if anything happened with Ellie before she disappeared. You could have told me then. It would have been nice to know."

"She saw the bites on my wrist." Her voice comes out thin, chewed up by guilt. "She wouldn't talk to me all day. I went by your house after school, and your mom said she never came home. I figured she must be with Poppy—that maybe they wouldn't want to be friends with me anymore. The next morning in school, they told us she was gone."

"That's not your fault," says Asher.

"How do you know?"

He's quiet. He *doesn't* know, and neither does she. Clearing his throat, he places the note back into the tin. "We leave in four days. In the meantime, Lysander has sent scouts ahead to see if they can find any trace of Ellie. They're going to ask around some of the other nests in the area."

He says it with disdain. *Nests*. Like the thought of his sister being holed away with something less than human disturbs him beyond words. Like she'd be better off dead. And maybe she would. Maybe death, to him, is better than being like this. Like Shea, yoked to the devil and waiting to Turn.

She wonders what he'll think of her after she goes through with it. If he'll even think of her at all.

Setting the tin onto the bed, he rises to go. He makes it nearly to the door before she asks the question battering at her chest.

"Are you mad at me? About Ellie?"

He turns back to face her. "Are *you* mad at me?"

"I don't want to be."

"Then let's start over."

Relief blooms, petal thin, in her belly. "How do we do that?"

His eyes drop to the cross around her neck—to the ring beside it, plated silver hammered over a mandrel. Another promise unmet. Another bridge uncrossed.

It feels as if she's set a torch to it.

"We could go back to how things used to be." He's being too nice. Too similar to the old Asher, before the garrison carved away everything that made him familiar. It feels like a front. "You can pretend like you're annoyed with me, and I can pretend I don't notice."

When she only stares, reluctant, he adds, "You can make a hurtful joke about my feet."

"That was one time. And you've grown into them very nicely."

His smile is too easy. She doesn't trust it. Not really. It doesn't stop her from smiling back. She's lost too many people already. She doesn't think her heart can handle losing anyone else. Even this new, alien version of Asher.

"Where's Poppy?" she asks, desperate to change the subject.

"Three doors down. I'm pretty sure she's asleep."

"Sleep sounds nice."

"It's been a long twenty-four hours," he agrees. She expects him to leave it there, but he doesn't. He lingers, restless, rapping the back of a knuckle against the doorframe. Finally—quietly—he says, "I wrote you letters, too."

"Oh." Everything inside her shuts up tight. "Why didn't you send them?"

His honey-dark gaze kicks to hers. "Why didn't you?"

He leaves her there to ponder the question alone, the tin full of letters leering up at her. Door shut, she stares at the wood veneer until her eyes blur. For the third time that night, she thinks about Turning. About swallowing the Rot and letting it case her heart like solid Teflon.

Maybe then everything would stop feeling so sharp. Maybe she'd stop nicking herself on the edges of all that she's broken. Shoving the tin under a heap of pillows, she tiptoes out into the hall.

Tristan is there, dozing in a windowless nook, his head tucked into the curve of his elbow. She creeps past as quietly as she knows how, stopping at the third door down and rapping lightly against the frame. If there's movement on the other side, she doesn't hear it. She knocks again, a little more urgently than before, casting a furtive glance toward Tristan's sleeping form.

She's about to give up and leave when the door pulls wide to reveal a bleary-eyed Poppy. She takes one look at Shea standing there and pads silently back toward her bed, climbing in and lifting the sheets in invitation. With a swell of relief, Shea clambers in after her. The room is bathed in a cranberry glow, the sky outside the window awash in color. Her feet are ice, Poppy's warm. There's a lump at the foot of the bed she's almost certain is some sort of creature. She doesn't investigate. Instead, she pulls the sheets over her head and lies flat, breathing in the smell of cotton.

Beneath, the lighting is Thulian pink—like they're wrapped inside a cocoon. It makes her think of the blanket forts they'd make whenever Mari Thorley hung the laundry out to dry. They'd spend their afternoons playing at being witches, mashing rose petals into paste and brewing love potions out of twigs and grass and pale white bunchberry, squabbling until the fireflies winked awake and Camellia's father came out to gripe about the mess and send them home.

The pang in her chest is strong enough to make her want to weep.

"I'm sorry you got dragged into this," she whispers.

"That's okay." Poppy's voice is thick with sleep. "I don't mind."

"But—" Shea rolls to face her. "What do you mean? How can you not? You were accepted to Humboldt. Just a few more months, and then you were finally going to get out of Little Hill. You were going to do something important."

"I *am* doing something important," says Poppy. "I'm looking for Ellie."

Another pang follows, more painful than the first. Shea thinks of the long walk to Mercy Ridge, roots grown over bone. The forest is full of the dead. Rib cages pried apart by pines, pale white femurs wedged between the branches. Human skulls, their jaws gaped open, peering out from the hollows of the old oaks. Picked clean by birds, or else offal for wolves.

She wants to find Camellia alive, she does.

Her doubt doesn't make her cruel, it only makes her a realist.

"We kissed," Poppy blurts out, invading her thoughts. "Me and Ellie."

Shea blinks, startled. "Oh."

"Well, she kissed me." Poppy rolls onto her back, folding down the blanket. The air outside their cocoon is cold. The light has gone mauve. "Or, I don't know, I kissed her. The whole thing was kind of a blur. And I should have told you. I really *wanted* to tell you, but Ellie said not to. Not yet. She wanted it to be just for us a little while longer. I think she was worried you'd feel like our friendship would change. Like it'd be me and her, with you on the outskirts."

"It's okay," says Shea, sitting up. "It's fine that you didn't tell me. We all—"

We all have secrets, she'd been about to say. But Poppy and Ellie's secret hadn't hurt anyone. Hers had. She swipes a finger over a raised half-moon at her wrist. It doesn't feel remotely the same.

"It's just that everyone keeps saying she ran away," says Poppy. "They said she was unhappy, and she left. That maybe the trees promised her something better, and she followed where it led."

Outside the window, the sun has nearly set. The last dregs of daylight gild the heavy bottoms of the clouds. Poppy's eyes glitter in the fading light.

"She wasn't unhappy. And she didn't run. Something *took* her."

Silence blankets the room. Shea isn't sure how to fill it, and so she doesn't try. Eventually, Poppy drifts off to sleep.

Shea watches the sky sink into black and tries to do the same, but sleep doesn't come. Neither does hope. She tosses this way and that, restless and bitter and overheating, until the creature wriggles free to hiss at her. It's Kit, his eyes glowing and his fur spiked.

"Sorry." She slips out of bed, yielding the blankets to the sharp-toothed terror.

For the fourth time that night, she thinks about it.

Turning.

Out in the hall, Tristan has abandoned his post. To hunt, most likely. She can feel Mercy Ridge coming slowly alive in the pads of her feet. Floors creak. Doors slam. The rhythmic thud of bass settles into the stone. It gives the lodge a heartbeat, like it's a living, breathing thing. Another insatiable part of the Gravewood. Another mouth waiting to swallow her whole.

Her mind made up, she heads downstairs.

Outside, the weather has turned. The air smells cold, like wind over ice. She picks her way along the path, heading for the rose-engulfed gazebo on the western lawn. She's never come this way before, but she knows what's out here. What it's used for.

Up close, the gazebo is so thoroughly encased in canes of winter-dormant vines that only the steepled cupola is visible. Several whippy shoots of green curl off the handrails, reaching for her as she ducks beneath the matted roof. Inside is still and dark, both the wind and the moon snuffed out by the leaves. An old hand pump rises out from the pebbled earth. Strange, she'd expected more opulence—a well with a pulley and bucket, or else a gleaming fountain, water frothing out into the basin. Instead, the pump is ugly and plain, its cast-iron spigot orange with rust. There's nothing to hold the water but her own two hands, already stiff with cold.

Sometimes it keeps her up at night—wondering if her mother drank from the Gravewood's waters willingly, or if she was tricked by something in the trees. If she'd been too brokenhearted to go on, or if she'd fought with everything she had to come back home to her only daughter. Sometimes, in Shea's very worst moments, she thinks maybe her mother has done something she can't forgive.

Sometimes, she feels like all that's left of her are the bitter bits.

It takes several pumps of the handle before water sluices out. She cups her hands beneath the flow, letting it pool like quicksilver in her palm. Her fingers shake as she lifts it to her lips.

"I wouldn't."

She glances up, startled, to find Lys standing just outside the pavilion. With his hood obscuring his features, he looks like some sort of ineffable winter god. A midnight Boreas, approaching on the wind.

"Why not?" She dries her hands against her pants, teeth chattering. "It was part of our deal."

"But it's windy tonight."

"What does the wind have to do with anything?"

"You might blow away." His voice is light, but his gaze is heavy. It sinks into her.

"That's a bullshit answer."

He doesn't walk it back. He watches her shiver, hunger banding his skin like striae in marble. She thinks of the creature on the bridge—monstrous, clawed, a heart pulsing in its hand. She knows it was him. She's never been more sure of anything. Before she can tell him so, he beckons for her to follow.

"Come on. I want to show you something."

He heads back toward the lodge, confident she'll follow. And she does. She always does. She falls in after him, every cell in her body compelling her in his wake.

It's begun to snow. The wind ferries the flakes in sideways, twisting them round in a white-out squall. Shea tails after Lys as he slips through a battered fire exit. The heavy door grinds shut. The wind snuffs out. The silence here is all-encompassing, like some great Goliath has placed a bell jar over the whole of Mercy Ridge.

They stand in a circular room with soaring rafters, windows fanged in broken glass. Snow spills in through the gaps, falling in slow motion over a carefully preserved greensward. Lush. Alive. The floor is carpeted in evening primrose. Ivy rains from the ceiling in lavish vines. Most striking of all are the orange jack-o'-lantern mushrooms that cluster along the rotted beams, gills glowing blue-green. It pits the whole of the room in an ethereal cast, like she's stepped into a ring of fairy stones and found herself whisked somewhere new.

She does a slow turn, taking it all in. When she stops, she finds Lys propped against a nearby column, a folded letter in one hand. All sense of awe flees her body. Her heart plummets to the floor with an icy crack.

"There were no letters to me in your little tin," he says.

"That was private."

"Can you blame me for looking? It really paints a picture of your life back in Little Hill."

"Don't be a jerk."

"I'm not. I'm fascinated. Although maybe you can solve a mystery for me." He unfolds the paper with needless aplomb, scanning the date scrawled along the top. "This is the last one. May eleventh. That's six months ago."

The heat of his gaze cuts through the cold. She thinks of the previous spring—the trees in bloom and the long trek to Mercy Ridge, her palm stinging. The wild way he'd looked with her blood painting his chin, his eyes gray all the way through.

"I hate a cliffhanger," he says. "Why'd you stop writing?"

"Why'd you kill Sullivan?"

The letter crumples in his fist. Hunger forks into his skin in cyanotic brooks.

"Don't push me," she says when he only stares. "I'll push you back."

He stalks nearer, casting the balled-up letter aside. He doesn't stop his advance until they're nose to nose in the dark, their foreheads kissing. Not like lovers, but like boxers in a ring, staring each other down before a match—fists at the ready, both of them breathing just a little bit too hard.

Cutting herself on the edge of Oliver Lysander is better than falling on the blade of her worst mistakes. Fighting him is easier than taking swings at her ghosts. At least, with Lys, she manages to land a blow every now and again.

His voice is sandpapered when he says, "Push me again."

"I'd never write you a letter. We have nothing to say to each other."

His smile is soulless. Reaching into his jacket, he procures a narrow blister packet. The alkaline batteries gleam oddly in the light. Without a word, he slips them into the front pocket of her flannel. It's cold. It's ugly. It's familiar ground. Everything in her steadies as she rushes to cuff her sleeve. Lys peers thoughtfully down at the shape of his bite, his features limned in a blue-green cast.

He looks like a creature of the forest, more myth than boy.

With a touch that borders on delicate, he closes his fingers over her wrist and guides her into a turn. Her back collides against the flat wall of his chest. Breath held, she allows him to coax her into position. The flat of his thumb digs into her pulse. His breath fans along her skin.

"You know why I killed Sullivan," he says. "It's the same reason you stopped writing letters to Thorley."

She stifles a cry when he bites down. There's a rush of blood, a white-hot locus of pain, and her head tips back against his shoulder. The bioluminescence seems to ebb and then flare as he pulls deep from her veins. The click of his swallow is loud in the quiet.

So, too, is the sound of a door careening open.

She looks, and there's Asher. He stands frozen a few feet away, the light from the interior hall falling in around him. Lys sees him, too. He sinks his teeth in deeper, biting down until Shea sees stars. His hand finds her waist, fingertips digging into bone. Every nerve ending in her body gathers beneath his touch and she lets out a single, mortifying gasp.

Asher takes it all in with an unflinching stare, his expression remote. Some deeply buried instinct tells her to push Lys away. To wriggle free. To *explain*. She doesn't. The soporific effect of the bite culls her panic. Her heart slows. The world grinds to a halt. Even the snow hangs motionless, shimmering.

Inhibitions banished, she reaches for Lys, her fingers skimming the contours of his cheek. There, just above his temple, her touch snags on the hard rind of bone ground flat.

The change in Lys is immediate. He works his bite free, shoving himself away from her in the same fluid movement. She sways around, dizzy, and finds him wiping the blood from his mouth with the back of his hand. His cheeks are pink and full. His eyes are the color of a lake in deep winter. For a tremulous instant, she can see panic thrashing just beneath the surface. And then his gaze ices over and he turns his attention to the door.

"Thorley. Nice of you to join us."

Asher's voice is tight. "What the hell did you do to her?"

"Nothing she didn't ask me to do," returns Lys smoothly.

"You're *sick*."

"Incurably," agrees Lys. "What are you still doing awake? Isn't it past your bedtime?"

"You asked me to keep a closer eye on her. Choi said her room was empty." Asher's lip curls in thinly veiled disgust. "Clearly the two of you are occupied. I'll see myself out."

"Stay."

Shea hears her voice from far away, drifting down with the snow. Asher and Lys turn to look at her in unison. Everything feels slow, slow, slow, like they're all underwater. Afloat, her heart thuds dully between her ears. Lys is the first to recover.

"You heard her," he says, smiling affably at Asher. "She wants you to stay."

"You have to do what I tell you." She can hear how ridiculous she sounds, even buried in the fog of a feed. It doesn't stop a snicker from bursting out of her. She drops into a mock curtsy, ankles crossed. "Didn't you hear? Conall Sullivan says I'm a princess."

Asher's face is stony. "Conall Sullivan is dead."

"Well, he wasn't being very nice."

Another snicker. Asher looks at her as though he's seeing her for the first time. The blood at her wrist. The glaze in her eyes. The way she inches nearer to Lys without even trying. She's a moon in his orbit, winking through the black infinity of his pull.

"Is this good for you?" he asks Lys. "Having her like this?"

"Not at all," says Lys, with complete sincerity.

"And yet here you are anyway."

Lys smiles and shrugs. "We all have our crosses to bear."

Asher's eyes land on the crumpled letter, his name still partially visible. He stares at it for a long time without speaking. Darkly, he says, "You asked me for a favor."

"Did I?" Lys swipes his hood from his head. "Or did I suggest a plan that would be mutually beneficial to the three of us?"

"It's not benefiting anyone," bites out Asher. "You're screwing it up."

The quiet stretches out and resettles. Off in the distance comes the faint call of a whippoorwill. A winged herald of death, alerting to the presence of a predator.

"No wonder Sullivan went after her," says Asher.

Lys's jaw clicks. "Sullivan made a mistake."

"And you're delusional if you think so." Asher huffs out a disbelieving laugh. "My sister's life might just hinge on your ability to maintain control of the Gravewood, and right now you don't even have control over yourself."

"That's what this is about?" asks Lys. "Your sister?"

Asher's scowl deepens. "You want me to see this through? You want me to put on a show for Paris Keeling? You're going to stay out of my way. Do you understand?"

"I'm not sure I do." Lys isn't smiling anymore. "Why don't you spell it out for me, Sunshine?"

"Find somewhere else to get your sick little kicks," orders Asher. "From this point on, you and Parker are done."

ELEVEN

Shea

Here is another memory—an earlier one: Hornbeam Academy in March, the air thick and wet. Not quite winter, not yet spring, only the hardiest of daffodils pushing through the granulated slush. Yellow on white. Gray on everything. She'd been ten years old, sitting on the swings at recess and watching the forest through the chain-link fence. Every memory of that day is a somatic pulse: the rattle of the swing, the creak of old chains, the stream of her ribbons in the leonine wind.

Nearby, Poppy Zahar and Heather Borkowski jumped rope and sang a skipping rhyme. Between them, Camellia Thorley executed a perfect double Dutch, her voice cutting loud and clear across the blacktop:

Better light a candle, better light two.
The trees are watching closely, and they might snatch you.

Shea stayed on the swings and looked on from a distance. She imagined—as she so often did—that she was a part of the forest.

Quiet and overlooked. Alone on the fringes. She'd kicked her feet into the air and tried to feel like the branches felt, scrabbling at the sky.

The mist had turned to rain by the time old Mr. Bosch blew his whistle, summoning the students back inside. In the mad dash across the glistening blacktop, Shea accidentally trod right atop Owen Davies's shoe.

"Didn't you hear me?" he'd asked, catching her in the rib with an elbow.

Next to him, River Albero wrinkled his nose. "She probably didn't."

"She didn't see me, either. I said 'move it,' Helen Keller."

She'd scurried out of the way, embarrassed and angry, the cold in her lungs. The forest at her back felt like a wildebeest. A physical embodiment of her anger, wind snarling through its branches. Like Daphne, she sent the forest a silent plea for protection. Only, instead of transformation, she asked the trees for something with teeth. She didn't want to be hidden away. She didn't want to fit herself in.

She wanted to bite back.

Poppy is knitting. In the middle of the day, in the heart of the Gravewood, in the house of the devil, Poppy Zahar is knitting a scarf. She's made quick work of it. Already, the fabric spills over her lap in wefts of brilliant pink and royal blue. She looks perfectly at ease, and Shea is met with the sense that Poppy could make herself feel at home anywhere.

Her serenity is the exact antithesis to Shea's current state of being.

"I'm going to die," she announces, falling back onto the bed.

Poppy doesn't look up from her knitting. "You're not going to die."

"You don't know that." She shuts her eyes. She feels as though her bones have been wrenched out through her mouth and then shoved back in, out of order. Everything hurts. Everything throbs. She pulls a pillow over her head and screams into it. Falling slack, she adds, "I need something with sugar."

Poppy plucks the pillow off her face and lobs it onto the floor. "Maybe it's a good thing."

"What is?"

"The fact that Lysander won't be feeding on you anymore. You're making each other sick."

She told Poppy everything as soon as she'd arrived back at the room, crawling into bed with blood still drying on her wrist. Conall Sullivan. What happened on the bridge. The unsent letters and the pump out in the gazebo and the strange encounter between Lys and Asher in the snowy room. She left out the details about Lys in the rain, the heart throbbing in his hand.

She skipped over the bit where she reached for him and felt bone.

"Lys isn't sick," she counters. "He's perfectly fine."

"Are we sure?" Poppy's needles click soothingly. "He didn't look fine when I saw him."

Shea flops onto her stomach, burying her face into the quilt. "It's not even Asher's decision to make." Her voice is muffled by the mattress. "It's mine."

"It is," agrees Poppy.

"He has no right to stick his big, stupid nose in my personal business."

"He doesn't."

Shea picks up her face, aghast. "You agree with him."

"I didn't say that."

"But you're doing that thing you do."

"What thing?"

"You know exactly what. Whenever Ellie and I used to fight, you'd agree with both of us to keep from picking sides."

Poppy doesn't deny it. "Sometimes it was the only way to keep the peace."

Her smile is faint, her eyes sad. The mention of Camellia has shifted the mood. Subdued, Shea rolls onto her side and watches Poppy pick at a snit in the fabric.

"Who's that for, anyway?"

"Ellie. The temperature is dropping a little bit every day. She must be freezing."

Outside, the snow has stopped, but frost still clings to the glass in feathery whorls. No one could survive in this sort of cold for long. She doesn't say it. It feels too cruel to point it out, even if it's true. She owes it to Camellia to believe she's still alive.

"We'll find her," says Poppy, pulling the snarl loose.

"I know," says Shea.

But it tastes like a lie.

She doesn't know when she drifts off, but she must, because she's woken by Poppy shaking her awake. It's dark, moonlight silvering the ice on the windows. Blanketed in sleep, Shea fumbles under her pillow until she finds her hearing aids. Sound hammers into her skull, loud and obtrusive.

Someone is knocking on the door.

"You're being summoned," mumbles Poppy, and draws the blanket over her head.

With a groan, Shea rolls out of bed, snatching up a knitting needle as she goes. When she wrenches the door wide, Tristan is there. His hair sticks out every which way, exhaustion shadowing his features. His eyes drop to the needle, wary.

"What's that for?"

"I thought you were Asher."

"You were going to stab him with a knitting needle?"

"I haven't ruled it out. What's happening?"

"There's a package," says Tristan.

She blinks, unsure she's heard him correctly. "Okay. And?"

"It's for you," he clarifies. "Someone has sent a delivery to Mercy Ridge with your name on it."

Tristan leads her to the basement, where the ceilings dip low over salons full of bar-height tables and backless stools. A felted pool table sits in one corner, surrounded by bodies. Lys is among them, his face lit from beneath as he racks the balls in starting position. Cyrus watches, chalking his ferrule. A few feet away stands Asher, looking out of place. Of the three of them, he's the only one to acknowledge Shea's sudden appearance. He gives her a grim nod, and nothing else.

She finds the package in question right away. It's a sleek black garment box, longer than it is wide. Someone has opened it already. The crimson ribbon trails loose over the edge of the table, and from out of the interior puffs black wrapping tissue. Inside is a dress. She lifts it out by the shoulder straps, letting the rich red silk spill away and away from her. The gown is cut like a slip, overlaid with sheer black lace. There's a note on the inside, handwritten. She sets the dress aside and plucks it off the tissue, her heart in her throat.

For the revel. I think red is your color.
XO an admirer

"Our cover is blown," says Lys as she sets the note back into the box. "Keeling knows we're coming."

Cyrus shoves the pool cue into his hand. "Are you going to make us go over it again, or are you going to break?"

"I'd rather play without him," grumbles Tristan. "He's too good. It takes all the fun out."

Shea runs the silk between her thumb and forefinger and reads the letter again. *An admirer.*

"I think we're getting ahead of ourselves," puts in Asher. "We don't know for sure that the dress came from Keeling."

"Who else would it be?" demands Lys, irate. "Getting you close required the element of surprise. How do you plan to drive a stake through his heart when he's watching you approach?"

"Like I told you, I'm an excellent shot."

"Arrogance killed the cat," quips Lys.

Asher lifts a brow. "I think it was curiosity, actually."

"Well, it shouldn't be."

"*I'm* going to break," announces Cyrus, to no one in particular.

"If it was Keeling," says Asher, ignoring him, "then why didn't he sign his name? Why the secrecy? If I was trying to rattle you, I'd want you to know it was me."

Lys contemplates Asher narrowly. "You want to rattle me, Thorley?"

"I think you're rattled enough. You don't need my help."

"I'll wear it," says Shea.

The balls scatter, pinging dully off the felted rail. "Choi," barks Cyrus, "you and Sunshine take solids. We'll play Little Hill versus Mercy."

"*I'm* Mercy," gripes Tristan.

"I'll wear the dress," says Shea, a little louder this time.

The only answer is a soft *thud* as Lys sinks his ball in the corner pocket. He looks more devil than boy in this lighting, his pupils distending as the monster resurfaces. She feels the same resurfacing deep inside her chest, the sucking gasp of sense breaking through the shell of her euphoria. They are doomed to be forever each other's inverse, the two of them teetering wildly between extremes.

You're making each other sick.

He sinks a second ball. A third.

"This is what I'm talking about," mutters Tristan. "It's a break and run every time."

"I say we burn the dress," suggests Cyrus. "We can send the ashes back to the Flatwood."

"That's a bad idea," says Asher. "Feels like poking a bear."

Cyrus tosses him a look. "Good thing you're here for your muscle, not your brains."

"Let's assume, for a second, that the dress did come from Keeling," says Asher, ignoring the jab. "If you send him a box full of ashes, you'll be making a statement. The wrong one. What we need to do is—"

Shea snatches the white cue off the table. Four sets of eyes lift to hers. Three of them human. One of them black as the River Styx.

"I want to wear the dress, Lys."

His mouth corkscrews into a scowl. "No."

"Why not?"

"Because I said so."

"It was sent *to me*," she reminds him.

"In *my* house."

His eyes are inky in the dark, his stare uncompromising. She's met with the sudden compulsion to snap his cue stick over his head.

"I'm getting pretty sick of everyone telling me what I can and can't do," she says, and drops the ball into the nearest pocket. "Oh no. Looks like you scratched."

She stalks toward the door, snatching up the dress as she goes.

"Wait for me," calls Asher, setting his stick against the wall. "I'll walk you back."

"Don't bother," she snaps. "I know the way."

She slams the door behind her before anyone can chime in otherwise, her anger blistering beneath her skin. With the dress draped over one arm, she heads back toward Poppy's room. She doesn't make it far. Rounding the corner toward the main stairs, she finds Tristan there waiting. He looks apologetic.

"Seriously?"

He lifts his shoulder in a tired shrug. "Orders are orders."

She sniffs and takes off, veering out from the narrow conduit of stone and heading up the stairs, quick as she can. Tristan follows at a brisk walk, his hands stuffed into his pockets. For a while, he leaves well enough alone, letting her stew in silence. He doesn't speak at all until they've nearly reached her room.

"I'm sick," he says, from somewhere behind her. "That's why I pledged."

She stutters to a stop, peering back at him. He hovers by a narrow cantilever window, staring out at the trees.

"You didn't ask," he says, when he feels her looking. "But that's the reason. I'm not just a runaway, I'm—"

He falters, his voice sticking in his throat, and she wonders what kinds of promises the forest made him. If it dangled a cure in front of him like a carrot, or if he went looking for forever his own. She keeps quiet and waits to see if he'll say anything more. He does, his knuckles white against the sill.

"We found out over winter break last year. It was my leg—I woke up one day and I could barely put weight on it. My parents brought me to see this bone doctor down in New York. Turns out, it was a sarcoma. The doctor recommended some hospital down south."

"Gridley's," she says, and his eyes pull to hers. "It's not a hospital, it's a halfway house. It's where they put people like us when they're waiting for them to die."

"Not for free," says Tristan ruefully.

"Nothing is."

He nods, grim. "I saw the bill. The cost alone would have broken my parents. Do you know what they do to debtors? When they can't pay?"

She does. She remembers hiding in the cupboard in the dead of night, watching her parents roll change at the kitchen table. Losing sleep. Missing meals. Prying themselves to pieces for her sake. For her ears. For her ingratitude.

"We can take out a loan," she remembers her father saying.

"And if we can't pay it back?" Her mother's reply had been voiceless, the words shaped by her lips. "I can't lose you. Not like that. We'll find the money. We'll talk to my father if we have to. We'll figure it out."

In the window, Tristan has fallen to tracing the mullions, staring down ghosts of his own.

"I'm sorry," she says. "I had no idea."

His breath blooms along the glass. But Tristan doesn't appear to have heard her. "He promised me that this was the better alternative. Turning, I mean. Instead of being slowly killed from the inside out, I'd become the killer. He made it sound like there were no strings attached, and I believed him."

The hairs rise on the back of her neck. "What do you mean? What strings?"

He turns to face her, apologetic. "I just wanted to tell you, because we've known each other our whole lives, and I don't want to hurt you."

Too late, she realizes she's cornered. The stairs are behind him. The door to the presidential wing is a few feet ahead, shut tight. They're in a narrow alcove, with nowhere to run.

"We're not talking about Lys," she asks, "are we?"

"Lysander?" Tristan frowns over at her, hunger twisting into his skin in a grid of deep blue. "I'm talking about Paris Keeling. He's the one who told me to pledge. He told me to get close to Lysander.

To wait. Tonight, a package was delivered to you. I accepted it. The courier who delivered it had orders for me."

"Orders to kill me," confirms Shea.

"I don't want to hurt you," he says again. "I just need you to scream."

Shea ducks just as he lunges, feinting out from the wallpapered recess. She's fast, but Tristan is faster. Jutting out his palm, he slams Shea hard into the wall. Poppy's knitting needle snaps in her back pocket just as her head knocks against the plaster. Starlight glimmers along her periphery.

"Come on, Parker," implores Tristan. "Please don't make me hurt you. *Scream*."

Reaching into her back pocket, Shea withdraws the jagged needle, splinter sharp. She jabs wildly, feeling the soft puncture of flesh as she plunges deep. Tristan falls back with a howl, sulfur-dark blood widening in a circle beneath his ribs.

"I'm sorry," she cries, taking off at run. "I'm sorry!"

Behind her, Tristan has abandoned all sense. He lunges after Shea with a snarl, gaining on her, even wounded. She rounds the corner at a clip, skidding along the carpet with enough force to cause it to ribbon in on itself. The movement sends her tripping into a narrow console table. She tugs it down behind her, sending a decorative vase crashing to the floor. Glass shatters like shrapnel as she flings herself out onto the landing, racing down the wide staircase.

She's so intent on watching behind her, she doesn't see Asher ascending the steps until she slams directly into him.

"Move," he barks.

He's got his right eye trained along the bridge of a crossbow, a wooden stake notched in the stirrup. Tristan hurtles around the corner just as Asher lets the cable fly. There's the whistle of a projectile through the dark. The smack of a palisade finding its mark. Tristan drops to his knees upon the steps, sucking in a breath. The stake protrudes from his abdomen, inches below his heart.

"You missed," he wheezes.

Asher drops his crossbow, his expression grim. "I never miss."

A door bangs open somewhere unseen. Cyrus appears, his expression guarded as he takes silent stock of Tristan on the stairs.

"Do you believe me now?" he asks.

For a moment, Shea isn't sure who he's speaking to. Slowly, she becomes aware of a lone figure standing atop the landing. It's Lys, quiet as a specter. Dark as a void. A single strip of moonlight bridges his nose as he peers wordlessly down at Tristan Choi.

"Mercy Ridge is compromised," says Cyrus. "Keep acting like you don't see it, and you'll bring the rest of us down with you."

Slowly, Lys lifts his eyes to Shea's. His stare is onyx, glittering bright.

"Change of plans," he says coldly. "Go upstairs and pack your things. We leave within the hour."

TWELVE

Lysander

There's a bottle waiting for Lysander when he arrives back to his room.

An old whiskey decanter on ice, its contents red. Red, like blood. Red, like that ridiculous fucking dress. A note has been fastened to the neck, the message tied with twine. Unlike the last note, he recognizes the handwriting on this one—he knows it cold.

The queen is valuable, but a hobbled king is powerless.
x Paris

Chess. Of course, it's chess. It always is. He snatches the bottle off the table, uncorking the crystal finial with a pop of his thumb. Tipping the carafe to the side, he lets the contents trickle onto the rug at his feet.

He's still standing there when Asher Thorley brightens his doorway.

"Hello, Sunshine," he says as the liquid thins to a stop. "You've caught me at a bad time."

"I've seen your kind kill before," says Asher, without preamble.

"Oh, good. We're skipping the small talk." Pinching one eye shut, Lysander peers into the empty carafe. Asher appears on the other side, large and upside down. "Tell me more."

"If Tristan Choi wanted Shea dead, she'd be dead. Same with Conall Sullivan."

Lysander lowers the glass. "An interesting theory."

"It's not a theory. They were toying with her."

"In your expert opinion, of course."

Lysander sniffs at the lip of the glass. Pig's blood. His stomach curdles.

"I know it was you who killed Sullivan," says Asher.

The snap of bone pings across his hindbrain. He sets the decanter onto the table with more force than he'd intended. "You're full of conspiracies tonight."

"Drop the act. You knew this would be Keeling's play. It's why you dragged me into it. You said he'd go after something important, and he has. Only he's not cutting you off at the knees, he's drawing you out. He's baiting you, and he's using Shea to do it. I just can't figure out why."

"Don't hurt yourself," says Lysander. "You're not here to play detective. You're here because of your ability to put a stake through Paris Keeling's heart from a hundred meters away."

"I'm here because you told me you could help find my sister."

"Your sister's body," Lysander corrects him.

Asher is quick for someone so colossal. Cuffing Lysander's collar, he rounds him hard into the bedpost. They're brought nose to nose, the canopy shuddering overhead.

"Say that again."

"Gladly," says Lysander. "In just under an hour, you and I are going to head into the Gravewood to track down your very definitely *dead* sister. Recovering what's left of her was already going to be a chore, but now it looks like we're also going to be saddled with the herculean task of keeping Shea Parker alive along the way."

"So, you admit I'm right."

"I'm not oblivious," says Lysander. "Why do you think I asked you to step in? I'm not handing her over to you on a silver platter out of the goodness of my own heart. There's nothing selfless happening here. I'm doing it for me. To protect myself."

"From what?"

"Does it matter? This is your chance to be the hero. Get the girl. Save the day. Speaking of—you did a very okay job out there tonight. I'm impressed. A little more to the right, and you might have even managed to kill our traitorous little knight."

"I wasn't *trying* to kill Choi."

"No?"

"*No.*" Asher releases him with a shove. "If I'd been trying, he'd be dead."

"Let's hope so," says Lysander, smoothing the wrinkles out of his shirt. "I'd hate to get all the way to the Flatwood and find out you couldn't even hit the outside of a target."

Asher's expression is murderous in the gloom. "That won't be a problem."

"Good," says Lysander. "Because Keeling is pissing me off, and I don't like to lose. Can you ride a bike?"

"I can."

"I don't mean one with a little bell on the front."

"I can ride," repeats Asher. "Why?"

"Because we'll need to be fast, and bikes are our best option."

Asher casts a glance toward the blacked-out windows of Lysander's room. A frozen rain patters dully against the glass. "It's not exactly backpack weather," he says. "It's freezing out there."

"It'll be warmer where we're going."

"And where is that, exactly?"

"I have a contact in Pennsylvania," says Lysander as coolly as he can. The thought of going back to that secluded house of horrors deep in the heart of Lancaster County has his stomach in a free fall. "We can stay with him until it's time to head south for the revel."

"And you trust him?" asks Asher. "This contact of yours?"

"As much as I trust anybody."

Ushering Asher out of his way, Lysander pries open the trunk at the foot of his bed. He sets to rummaging through his things, conscious of Asher still standing in his room. Still eating up his air. Still intruding on his space. *Find somewhere else to get your sick little kicks.*

He wonders what Asher Thorley would say if he knew Lysander counted Shea's heartbeats even when she wasn't in the room. If he knew he'd memorized the cadence of her pulse, the rush of blood through her veins. If he knew how hungry he is—how unsatiated—his mind all in pieces.

Lysander thinks of Viola, a rocking chair beneath her and a book in her lap. *I'll read a verse; you recite it back.* His head is stuffed with his mother's doggerel. Words and words and words, all of it meaningless fucking drivel. He thinks of John Donne, an elegy for jealousy: *His soul out of one hell into a new.*

Someday he will lose his grip on himself completely.

Someday, but not tonight.

"We'd get lone wolf rangers sometimes," says Asher, intruding on his thoughts. "Down in the garrison. They'd come in from the forest and spend the night—restock on food and supplies. If they came from up north, they'd tell us stories about the Gravewood Devil."

"I hope they mentioned my good looks."

The quip is half-hearted. He's not thinking about rangers. He's thinking about Shea in the pavilion, water running down her fingers. Shea in the garden, the curve of her hip under his hand and the slick of her blood against his tongue. The divine wrongness of Asher watching them, color in his cheeks. Her voice soft in the blue-green quiet: *Stay.*

He wonders if Asher has replayed it as many times as he has.

Distantly, he's aware that Asher is still speaking. He zips his bag shut and rises to his feet.

"They all say you're not like the others," says Asher. "Like you weren't built right or something. Like you're some sort of mythical harbinger of the end times."

Lysander turns to face him. "Who's to say I'm not?"

"Me," snaps Asher. "*I* say. I'm looking right at you, and all I see is a kid with too much power and a crush, and no idea what to do with either."

He recovers just a beat too late. "A crush implies it's unrequited."

A rap at the door brings their heads up. Cyrus is there, propped lazily against the frame. His eyes glimmer as they slide from Asher to Lysander before pausing over the blood-soaked floor. His gaze lingers there for a long time.

"The revel is another week out," he finally says. "Where will you go until then?"

Lysander shoulders his bag. "It's better if you don't know."

"You don't trust me."

"Mercy Ridge is compromised," says Lysander. "Just like you said. Per your advice, it'd be shortsighted of me to trust anyone."

"You trust *him*."

He means Asher. The object of his ire stands idle between them, taking up entirely too much space. Not physically—not here, in Lysander's bedroom—but subliminally. He's inside Lysander's head, dragging all his flaws kicking and screaming into the light. Grabbing the monster by the cuff and shaking it, making Lysander look it in the eye. *Is this good for you? Having her like this?*

"Thorley and I are playing a game," he says mildly.

He doesn't say more. He doesn't owe anyone an explanation. Certainly not Cyrus. He veers around his lieutenant, heading out into the hall. He doesn't need to look back to know Asher is following—he can feel each ungainly thud of the soldier's boots against the floor.

"We built this place together," calls Cyrus when he's halfway down the hall. "It's as much my home as it is yours. You think I want to see Keeling bring it down around our ears?"

"It's not Mercy Ridge I'm worried about," says Lysander, without turning back. They both hear what he doesn't say. *It's Shea.* It's always Shea, even when he pretends it isn't. He thinks of slamming back into awareness in a sunless cellar, Sullivan's heart in a jar.

Do you want to keep her? his mother asked.

It doesn't matter if he wants to or not. The truth is, he can't.

Not until Paris Keeling is dead.

Over his shoulder, he says, "Tell Viola we'll finish our match when I get back."

"You're making a mistake," calls Cyrus.

"We'll find out."

It's as much of a goodbye as either of them is likely to have. If things go wrong at the revel, he'll never come back to New Hampshire again. Not as he is.

A harbinger, Asher called him. A sign of things to come.

"Go pack your things," he tells the watchdog. "We move while it's dark."

He finds Shea in her room, solemnly considering an old stuffed rabbit. He stands in the open door until she notices him, his hood up and his hair in his eyes—hoping against hope that his horns aren't visible. He's shorn them down twice already, filing them to studs until the sink was full of pale white shavings.

"I tried on the dress," she says when she spots him. "It looks fantastic on me."

His gut gives a violent kick. "Let me see."

She fixes him in a cold stare, as though she can't believe he had the gall to ask. And maybe she's right.

"You'll have to wait for our date."

He doesn't tell her that he can't stand the thought of her getting anywhere near the revel. Not after what happened with Tristan. Not with Sullivan's blood on his hands. Not now that Paris Keeling knows her name. He doesn't tell her he shouldn't be in here, or that he's not quite sure how to make himself stay away. He crosses, instead, to where she stands, plucking the rabbit off the bed for a closer examination.

"Hey! Give him back."

"Who is he?"

"He's Bugs. And he's mine."

He lifts the rabbit out of her reach. "Hello, Bugs."

"Don't *talk* to him," she says, horrified.

"But I like him." He raises the rabbit higher, turning it this way and that. "He reminds me of a book I read once. Everyone went walking around with their soul outside their body, right there next to them for anyone to see."

She drops back onto her heels, scowling up at him. "I can't picture you reading."

"I am *very* literate," he assures her, and hands the rabbit back to her. "And this is what your soul would look like."

"A rabbit," she guesses, shoving it deep into her bag.

"Threadbare."

She pulls the drawstring shut with a snap. "Did you come up here just to antagonize me?"

"No. I brought you candy." He reaches into his pocket and digs out a handful of anise drops, each of them twisted in red cellophane. "It's for the drop. I know the sugar helps."

She looks surprised, then touched, then endearingly disgruntled.

"No, thank you."

"Suit yourself."

He slips all but one back into his pocket. That one, he tucks into his cheek. There's the briefest twinge of licorice, earthy-sweet, before the taste turns to ash on his tongue.

He thinks that maybe he is cursed to forever grasp at scraps. Scraps of daylight. Scraps of flavor. Scraps of boyhood, sucked from the veins of a girl who will only ever give him scraps of her affection. When he pockets the wrapper, she's watching him sideways.

"What would yours be?"

The candy cracks between his molars. "What, my soul?"

"Yeah. If you took it out and looked at it."

If, if, if. If he gave in to his impulses and kissed her right this moment, he wonders if she'd taste the licorice at his lips. He feels like King Midas, doomed to defile everything with his touch.

"I don't have a soul to take out."

"What are you talking about? Everyone has a soul."

"Not me," he assures her. "I've looked."

She fixes him with a glare. "That's ridiculous. You *haven't* looked."

"Says who?" He wrestles her bag from her, engaging in a brief but fervent tugging match over the strap before she relents. "Let's go. Thorley's outside, and I've noticed his temple starts to throb when he's mad. It's not good for him. He'll give himself a coronary."

. . .

They find Asher waiting with Poppy Zahar alongside the bikes. The cold has slapped pink into his cheeks, pinched the tip of his nose red. He watches them approach, his gaze too assessing. He's looking, Lysander knows, for signs of a feed. Lysander stares back at him, hard and unblinking, daring him to ask. Itching for a fight.

Your sick little kicks.

In the end, he doesn't ask. He glances skyward and says, "Two hours until dawn."

"More or less." Lysander stuffs Shea's things into his tail bag. "If we take the Gravewood roads, we can make it to Killington before then."

"Killington? That's a bad idea. We'd be better off sticking to the coastal highway. There's easier access to working gas stations. Rations. Places to stay."

"The Gravewood is safer."

"For you, maybe," counters Asher, handing off a helmet to Poppy. "Not for me. Not for Zahar. Not for *Parker*."

Next to Lysander, Shea bristles. "Don't say my name like that."

"Like what?"

"Like you're provoking him."

"Yeah," says Lysander, lifting his chin to fasten his helmet. "Don't provoke me."

Asher flips down his visor, but not before Lysander catches the beginnings of something uncouth. Flicking Asher two thumbs-up, he hands off a helmet to Shea and climbs onto the bike.

On the bike beside him, Asher tugs on his gloves. Poppy settles in just behind him. Her oversized rat has been stuffed into a knitted sling, and it bares its teeth at anyone unlucky enough to look at it.

"Did you need to bring the roadkill?" Lysander calls over to her as Shea swings her leg into place at his back.

"His name is Kit," says Poppy. "And he's essential to the mission."

Whatever he might have said in reply is lost as Shea's arms wrap around his middle. He feels like Aglauros, turned to stone and set on the steps of purgatory. Because if there's a hell, surely it is this—holding himself still while Shea Parker's hands lace across his stomach.

The feeling that courses into his blood isn't hunger. It's something else. Something too sharp to name, too dangerous to examine. He squeezes the clutch and the bike leaps to life beneath him. Shea's grip goes tight enough to cut off his oxygen, her helmet pressing into his spine.

He grins like a fool into the lining of his lid.

With the lodge lit like a votive at his back, he pulls out onto the main drive and signals for Asher to follow. They knife in and out of the rubble, headlights carving bars of yellow along the bore-dark trees as they descend the mountain switchbacks, the river-black roads carrying them away from Mercy Ridge.

He came to New Hampshire to carve out a kingdom. To make a name for himself—Oliver Lysander, devil of Mercy Ridge. Leader of his own pack. Keeper of his own fate. Paris Keeling is chipping away at his defenses, which means it's time to go on the offense.

He won't lose. Not this fight. Not with Shea holding tight to his middle, her heartbeat in his spine. Not when he finally has something worth carving out. All those years biting his tongue bloody, reciting words with no meaning and waiting for the dawn.

He's not a frightened little boy anymore, gutless and disobedient. He's a god.

This time he'll take the fight directly to Paris Keeling's doorstep.

This time, he'll finish it.

ACT III
THE ROAD

Over hill, over dale,
Thorough bush, thorough brier,
Over park, over pale,
Thorough flood, thorough fire

Shakespeare's *A Midsummer Night's Dream*

THIRTEEN

Shea

Shea startles awake to silence, a pit in her stomach.

She'd been dreaming of Christmas. Snow in the window and her mother on the couch, humming as she threaded a needle along a cranberry garland. Her father in his chair, his legs thin beneath a woolen blanket. No fire in the fireplace. No food in the pantry. Sound in her ears, grating enough to make her weep. Bing Crosby on the turntable, his baritone indecipherable.

The room she's awoken in looks nothing like home. A faint yellow film clings to everything. The ceiling is dark with water rings. On the narrow console sits an old television, the screen fractured. It takes her a single, panicked moment to remember where she is—a roadside motel, the curtains drawn, sunlight falling in at a slant. The bed is lumpy, the comforter covered in yellow-gold carnations. Everything smells cold and wet. There's a stain on the floor that looks like blood.

They'd come upon the motel in the final moments before dawn, pulling into the abandoned lot just as the first bit of sun broke over the trees. After Asher cased the building and found only raccoons in the lobby, they'd stashed the bikes and headed inside. Wind-whipped and motion-sick and cold to her bones, she'd fallen asleep before her head hit the pillow.

Awake, she stretches out a cramp in her thigh. She feels curiously battered, her body fatigued from the ride. Poppy lies curled on the bed beside her, breathing deeply. The chair where Asher kept watch, his shotgun across his lap, is empty. Lys is nowhere to be seen. Sliding out of bed, Shea slips on her hearing aids and pads toward the bathroom, pulling the door shut partway behind her. The mirror over the sink is hackled, disfiguring her likeness in the glass. She tests the faucet and finds it dry. Only a single, fat droplet plops into the sink.

She doesn't notice Lys until she turns to leave. He lounges in the empty bathtub, his knees bent and his head tipped back against the tile. She gives a violent start at the sight of him, her elbow catching on the towel rack.

"Shit!"

"Hi," he says.

"What are you doing in there?"

He flicks a baseball card between his fingers, considering her with one eye pinched shut. The corner of the card taps against the yellowed fiberglass in a restless *rat-tat, rat-tat, rat-tat.*

"It's too bright out there."

"Oh. *Oh.* Sorry." She pushes the door all the way shut. The last of the daylight snuffs out with a click. "Better?"

"Infinitely."

Another drop of water plops into the sink.

In the near-total dark, she asks, "Can I sit with you?"

Lys is quiet. She hears the rustle of the curtain and the slide of a shoe, his heel stuttering as he shifts to make space. It's as much of an invite as she's going to get. Fumbling along the tile, she feels her way to the tub, climbing in across from him and tugging the curtain closed.

By what little light slips in beneath the door, she can just make out the angular lines of his face. Her knees slot into place between his. Her heart stutters against her ribs. She wonders if he can hear it. *Rat-tat-tat*, goes the card against the tub.

"I used to imagine it was a wolf," he says. "My soul, I mean."

The declaration feels immense, though she can't say why. She scoots back against the tile and wills her eyes to adjust. "Why did you stop?"

"Because make-believe is for children."

She can't make out his expression in the dark, but she can feel the hard impact of his stare. Quietly, she says, "I used to be jealous that everyone else could hear the Gravewood except for me."

There's a brief pause as he considers her admission. "That's ridiculous."

"I know." She suppresses a smile. "Logically, I knew that it was because I couldn't hear as well as everyone else. But when I was younger, it felt like maybe I wasn't worthy. Like maybe everyone else could hear the trees whispering to them because they'd done something right. I used to sit at the edge of the Gravewood and make wishes. I'd ask the forest to send me a protector."

"What did you need protection from?"

"Nothing, really. Nothing that matters anymore, anyway. Kids can be mean, and hurts feel bigger when you're small."

"That's bullshit," says Lys.

She frowns. "It's something my mom used to say."

"Well, your mom is wrong. Sometimes they're just big hurts, no matter what size you are."

She peers up at him and finds him focused on the card, turning it over and over like a talisman. He sees her looking and tucks it out of sight, scooting up just enough to slide it into his back pocket.

"You and your mom are close?"

"We are," she says. "Or, we were."

She thinks of waking to find Hemlock on her chest, yowling futilely in the dark. Beside the bed stood her mother. She'd been oddly hunched, jaw slack and eyes dull. She hadn't responded when Shea called out to her. She'd only lunged. It should have rattled Shea more than it did. Instead, it felt like a natural progression. The next logical step in her mother's slow disappearance into herself.

"It was hard for her, after my dad left," she explains. "She started spending more and more time out by the Gravewood. She used to say she could hear him in the wind."

"She was lured?"

"Maybe." It hurts to admit it—that there's a chance she hadn't been. "Sometimes I think she would have gone into the woods either way. She and my dad married so young, and I don't think she ever learned how to be alone."

"She wasn't alone," says Lys. "She had you."

"I guess." Shea draws her knees into her chest. "I wasn't the easiest kid."

He's quiet for a long time after that. She can feel him watching her, unapologetic in his focus—not bothering to pretend he's doing anything else. She focuses on the fraying seam of her sock, plucking the thread until it unravels.

"Why a wolf?" she asks, when the quiet starts to eat at her.

"Maybe I like wolves."

"Or maybe there was something you needed protection from, too."

His mouth tips into an almost-smile. "Do I look like I need protection?"

"Not now. Not like this. But maybe before."

He says nothing. Without the card, he falls to tapping his finger against the fiberglass. The drumming keeps time with her heartbeat. He seems on edge. Restless and overstrung. Had he been that way when he was small? She tries to imagine him before. It isn't hard. She's seen him after a feed—quicksilver stare and an easy smile, no fangs in sight. She tries to picture him in a school like Hornbeam. In a tie and sport coat, a stack of books under one arm. He must have gone to school somewhere. He must have had a home.

He must have had something terrible enough to run from.

"Stop thinking about it," he says.

"About what?"

"About me."

"I'm always thinking about you," she admits, and watches his smile die. She hadn't meant to say it like that. She hadn't meant to say it at all. She knows better. She knows this feeling in her chest isn't real. She knows these thoughts were put there by the venom in her blood. By this poisonous thing that compels her to him, makes her docile and unafraid.

He knows it, too.

"You can't help yourself," he says, his voice acidic.

She'd been thinking the exact same thing, but hearing him say it out loud turns her mortification to hostility.

"I can, too."

Lys's brow lifts. "Yeah?"

It's a push. A small one. She pushes back.

"*Yeah.*"

He moves before she can react, shifting so she's pinned beneath him, his mouth at her throat. Her chin kicks up, granting him access. She's all reflex, lightning crackling in her blood.

"The neck is the most vulnerable part of the body," he murmurs into her skin. "Every single animal on this earth is born with the instinct to defend the throat, and then look at you. I could sink my teeth into you right now, and you wouldn't even try to stop me."

"I would," she says into the tiled dark.

"Prove it, then. Fight me."

The ensuing quiet is a held breath. She wedges her hands flat against his chest and feels him brace for the shove. His heart is a jackhammer. It drills into her palm.

"You can't do it," he says bitterly. "I'm in your blood."

He says it like it's the worst possible thing he can think of.

"I don't need to prove anything, and neither do you. We both know you won't hurt me."

He pulls back just far enough to meet her eyes. "Your trust in me is synthetic."

"Is it?"

He doesn't answer. There's a hint of panic in his expression, like he's not so sure. Like he wants to believe the opposite is true.

"You didn't come after me that night on the bridge," she reminds him. "And I know you don't want to talk about it, but I *saw* you, Lys. You were barely in control, and you still didn't hurt me. Just like you're not going to hurt me now."

The panic in his eyes sharpens into revulsion. Leaning in, he licks a brazen stripe along her throat. Her surprise comes out in a gasp.

"Maybe you think about me all the time," he says, "but I think about *this* all the time. This spot—*right here*. I can see your pulse. I can *hear* your pulse. It's in my head, even when you're not in the room. It's making me fucking crazy."

"So, bite me."

"No."

"Then Turn me."

He goes still as Perseus, the air shutting up around them like a box.

"Turn me," she says again, emboldened by his silence. "And then it won't be like this."

He shuts his eyes, brow furrowed. Slowly—reverently—he leans in and presses a kiss to the flutter in her throat. So fleeting, she doesn't even realize what he's done until it's over.

And then—in a voice so low she's not entirely certain she heard it—he says, "Not yet."

The quiet is ruptured by the sound of the bathroom door flying open with enough force to crack tile. The curtain wrenches back and Lys sails off her with a yelp, the base of his spine slamming hard into the sink. He crows out a laugh, righting himself.

"That was a very exciting entrance, Sunshine."

In the open door, Asher stands with his shotgun slung over one shoulder. He's in an orange ball cap and a fleece-lined jacket, the cold wafting off him in waves. Shea scrabbles to her feet, humiliated—an explanation at the ready—but Asher isn't looking at her.

"You need to feed on someone, feed on me."

"Tempting," says Lys. "Although I'm not so sure you'd be appetizing."

"Then starve. I told you, Parker's off-limits."

Anger drives away the sting of embarrassment. She clambers out of the tub, her socks slipping over tile. "Don't talk about me like I'm not in the room."

Asher rounds on her, primed for a fight. "You want to be included in the conversation? Great. Let's talk about it."

"Let's," she hisses.

"What happens if he forgets to stop, huh? I bet you haven't even thought about that. If he loses control during a feed, you die."

"Ease off, Asher. Nothing happened. We were just talking."

"Oh yeah?" Asher flips the brim of his cap around, driving nearer. "You were just talking?"

She doesn't trust the look in his eyes. "Yes."

"While straddling? In a bathtub?"

"God, how old *are* you? We weren't straddling."

"Looked like it to me."

"Get your eyes checked then," she snaps.

He doesn't back down. "You ever see one of them rip out someone's carotid artery? Because I have. It isn't pretty, and it isn't quick."

"Are you trying to intimidate me?"

"I'm trying to wake you up!" His shout cascades along the tile. All the air rushes out of the room. "You're acting like you're in control, but you're as lost to the Gravewood as Camellia."

Her voice is icy. "I'm not lost."

"To me, you are."

He looks immediately regretful, as if he hadn't meant to say something quite so vulnerable. For several seconds afterward, neither of them can think of a single thing to say. It's Lys who breaks the silence, a smile creeping in at the corner of his mouth.

"That was thrilling." He stands against the sink, his eyes gleaming. "For the record, Sunshine, I'm rooting for you."

Asher's expression is murderous. "Don't start."

"No, I mean it." Lys's smile widens, and for a moment he looks truly monstrous. A grinning devil, his stare black all the way through. "It must be hard. You shipped out to basic and spent the next year doing the sorts of things that would break a lesser man's spirit. I'll bet some days, the only thing that got you through was the thought of coming home. Am I right?"

"Go to hell," says Asher.

"Did you think she'd be waiting for you? You did, didn't you? What a fucking cliché, going after your kid sister's friend. You must have thought it was a done deal."

Asher takes a steadying breath, but Lys isn't done.

"I'll bet it really pissed you off when you found out she hadn't waited for you after all."

The silence blisters. Asher's eyes jump to Shea's. Seventeen years of serendipity passes between them. Fletcher's field in the spring, his face turned to hers. The Thorley kitchen in the dead of night, his fingers grazing hers as he handed her a glass of water. Her foyer in the late fall, mistletoe in her hair and her stomach in knots: *You can stay, if you want.*

And then, though she doesn't want to, she thinks of Camellia with her head thrown back beneath a winter sky, catching snowflakes on her tongue: *Do you think we'll be sisters someday?*

"I brought food," Asher says flatly. He's not looking at her anymore. He's staring at the floor, the tile webbed in cracks. "I'd eat and get some sleep. We're back on the road by sunset."

The door shuts soundlessly behind him. Shea rounds on Lys the moment he's gone.

"What's wrong with you? Why would you say that to him?"

"Because it's true," he says, digging his thumb into a crack in the tile.

"It's *mean*."

He looks right at her, his expression cold. In the bathroom's sordid dark, he really does look like a wolf—carnivorous and cruel, no light in his eyes. A predator, down to his core. He contemplates her for a long time before speaking.

"It's kind of funny, isn't it?"

"What is?"

"Just a few minutes ago, you were so sure I wouldn't hurt you."

She exhales sharply. "Asher's right. You can go to hell."

"You say that now," he points out, "but you'd still let me feed on you if I asked."

He anticipates her slap, tugging her effortlessly into him. They collide inelegantly, her wrist shackled in his grasp.

"I guess you have a little fight in you, after all."

"Screw you."

He smiles. "Maybe someday."

She thinks of his voice in the bath, the edges hard and wanting: *It's making me fucking crazy.*

"You're feeling it right now," he guesses. "A rush of blood to your head. An ache in your stomach. Your brain has tricked you into thinking it's an infatuation, but it isn't. It's your body telling you to run."

Her heart beats off-kilter. "How the hell do you know what I'm feeling?"

"Because I feel it, too. I feel it every time I'm around you. Every time you get close." He swallows up her space, his head ducking low. "But it's not telling me to run. It's telling me to sink myself into you until the aching stops."

FOURTEEN

Shea

Shea doesn't speak to either Lys or Asher the following night.

Not even when they stop to refuel, the wind tunneling beneath the sagging steel-frame awning. At Lys's direction, they pull off the main road just before dawn. The early-morning sun burgeons on the horizon by the time they find what Lys is looking for—an old bed-and-breakfast, forgotten in the trees.

The wooden sign out front hangs loose on its chain. *Nutmeg Nook. 1898.* Several steepled roofs of alternating height sit wedged in an overgrown snarl of juniper. The white stucco is engulfed in a wall of bloodred sweet spire, windows embellished in a thick diamond lattice. Lys spends the day holed up somewhere dark. Asher, in stark contrast, sits out on the porch, the sun on his face and his ears plugged with wax. Watching the road.

"They're not very chatty," notes Poppy, picking snarls out of her scarf. She's sitting cross-legged on a lumpy old love seat, her green turtleneck and appliqué overalls at odds with the puce-colored cushions. "Do we think they'll ignore each other all the way to the Flatwood?"

"Hopefully," says Shea, who has been drafted into untangling a hank of yarn. Thus far, her efforts have proven futile. "How did you tangle this so badly?"

"It wasn't me, it was Kit. He keeps batting at them." Poppy pokes despondently at the scarf with the tip of a needle. It's a few minutes more before she speaks. "I heard the argument. Yesterday, I mean. At the motel."

Shea feigns nonchalance. "Did you?"

"It isn't like the three of you were very quiet. Do you want to talk about it?"

"Not really, no."

"You can, if you want. I'll keep my opinions to myself."

"Don't bother, I'm sure I can guess."

Poppy hums. "You might be surprised."

Shea glances across the room and finds Poppy laser focused on a knot, dissecting each individual strand with surgical precision. When Poppy doesn't offer up anything further, Shea sags back against the couch. The cushions are upholstered in dizzying floral. *Everything* in Nutmeg Nook is floral. The wallpaper. The glassware. The pillows. Even the artwork. It gives the house a charming sort of ugliness.

Outside the window—framed in hideous floral drapes—Shea can just make out Asher's profile set against the sun. She tosses down the yarn and sits up in a stretch, her patience frayed.

"I quit."

"Maybe I will, too." Poppy holds up the scarf between them, peering glumly at Shea through the misshapen holes. "This is turning out to be the ugliest thing anyone has ever made."

"It's not that bad."

Poppy drops the mess of fabric into her lap. "You don't have to lie."

Later, when the sun hangs in the sky's midpoint, Shea removes her hearing aids and slinks outside to gather juniper berries off the trees. The lowest-hanging fruit has been gnawed away by deer, and so she climbs up onto the porch railing, clutching a woven basket she found in the kitchen.

It's sticky work, but the silence is comfortable. Familiar, like slipping into better-fitting skin. In the quiet, everything else sharpens. The kiss of sun on her skin and the thick smell of pine. The rustle in the air as a bird takes flight. The world breathes out as she breathes in, letting her mind play through memories like a click reel—her mother in the yard, gathering dark blue juniper berries into her apron. Her mother on the porch, laying her yield out to dry in the hot summer sun. Her mother in the kitchen, bare feet on the floor and mortar in hand, pestle blue with pulp.

Shea's not sure if it's one single afternoon, or several of them overlapping. They've all blended one into the other, separating her life out into Before Calhoun Parker Left and After. These days, the clearest memories she has of her mother are this—Ivy clawing at the walls. Ivy lunging up the stairs. Ivy digging into offal like a wolf.

Ivy, her mind lost to the Gravewood.

Lost, like Camellia.

Like Shea.

"I'm not lost," she says to a nearby waxwing. The bird startles and takes flight, dropping a berry as it goes. She watches it disappear into the nearby trees, feeling unspeakably lonely. Nearby, the branches sway, dark and inviting. She thinks maybe it doesn't matter that she can't hear their entreaties. Her head is already full of Lys. She feels drawn to him, always. Wound tight with thoughts of him, restless in a way that makes her want to crawl out of her own skin and set it on fire.

Anything to burn him out of her bones.

I feel it, too.

Basket in hand, she heads back around to the front of the house. Asher is still outside on the porch. He's whittling a bit of wood, his knife throwing slivers of light with each pass. She slows to a stop a few feet away, watching the bark curl off in ribbons. Sensing her presence, he casts her a fleeting glance and continues without a word.

"Will you teach me how to use that?"

He pries a plug loose from his ear. "What?"

"I want to learn how to fight with a stake."

"That's what I thought you said. And it's a bad idea."

"I've been attacked twice already. Shouldn't I know how to defend myself?"

His gaze slides to the trees. Frowning at whatever he hears clicking through the branches, he rummages through his rucksack and pulls out a small, hand-cranked radio. Winding it up, he turns the dial. An orange light flicks on, and the little clearing is flooded in static.

"What if something happens and you're not there to step in?" she asks, the moment his attention is back on her.

"Lysander will be there."

"And what if it *is* Lys?"

He pins her in a searching gaze. Looking, again, for signs of a feed. For evidence of fever, of malaise, of a bite, fresh and red.

"Teach me," she repeats.

He flips the stake, inspecting its whittled tip. "The first thing they tell you in training is that if you're close enough to use this, you're already dead."

"Then what are you doing sharpening it?"

"I'm feeling pretty close," he says, with a glance back at the house.

There's no sign of life in any of the windows. No snap of a curtain. No shuttering of blinds. Lys's presence lingers anyway, as palpable as if he's standing right there with them. With a sigh, Asher holsters the stake and rises to his feet.

"Yeah, okay. I'll teach you. But not with this."

Five minutes later, he's assembled a firing range of sorts—setting a collection of floral vases atop a split-rail fence. Shea stands where he's indicated and clutches his pistol crossbow, her eyes squinted shut against the sunbeams that stripe vertically between the trees.

"It's easier to hold on to than I thought it would be," she says as he jogs to meet her. The radio is clipped to his bandolier, emitting static. "Have you killed anyone with it?"

"It's definitely the lighter of my arsenal," he says, avoiding her question. "Sorry, this isn't the best spot, the sun's in the way. Can you see anything?"

She squeezes one eye shut. "Sort of."

"Here." He tugs off his cap, flattening down a cowlick as he plops it onto her head. It's too big, and the brim slips into her eyes, but it does the trick. The worst of the glare extinguishes, leaving the glade a flat, hazy gold. "Better?"

"Uh, yeah." She lifts her chin. Her cheeks burn. "Thanks."

"It's all right." He keeps his distance, looking uneasy. "You'll, uh, want to stand with your feet shoulder-width apart. Point your left foot where you plan to aim."

She follows his instructions, lifting the pistol the way she'd seen him do. "Like this?"

"Sort of." He palms his chin, considering her. "Can I make some adjustments?"

"Please."

He hesitates and then steps closer, folding his hand over hers. Her fingers curl against the foregrip as he guides her higher. Even this—this unbearable proximity, this sunlit scene—is familiar. She's twelve years old again, sighting a stag down the barrel of his father's rifle, his voice at her ear: *Don't tell Ellie. She'll tell my dad, and he'll tell your mom.*

And then she'll kill you and plant you in her garden.

His laugh had been loud. The stag, hearing him, took off like a shot. *Exactly.*

"Look through the scope," he says now, coaxing her into position. His free hand skims her hip, angling her until her spine lines up against his chest. She can feel the heat coming off him, like he's swallowed the sun. His cheek grazes hers as he asks, "Do you see the first vase?"

The radio static thrums through her. "Yeah."

"Okay, good." He clears his throat and steps back. "Fire when ready."

She swallows a breath and pulls the trigger. With a ping, the wooden bolt goes wide, arcing past the vase and lodging itself neatly in a nearby patch of hobblebush. There's a moment of silence. Asher stands with his hands in his jacket pockets, a muscle working in his jaw.

"That was—"

"*Don't* laugh," she orders, rounding the unloaded crossbow on him.

He puts his hands up in surrender. "I would never."

"That was horrible. I didn't even come close."

"It's okay," he says. "I missed my first time, too."

She glowers at him. "No, you didn't."

"You're right, I didn't." He peers out at her from beneath the shade of his palm, and she can see him biting back a smile. "Come on. We'll go again."

It takes four more tries for her to get anywhere close to a target. On the fifth, she manages to explode a vase into pieces. It wasn't the one she was aiming for, but she takes the win. She turns, elated, unable to hold back a grin.

"I did it!"

"You killed it dead," agrees Asher. "Think you can do that again?"

"Let's hope."

She notches the wooden bolt, feeling it click firmly into place. Her arms ache. There's a crick in her neck. All around them, dusk begins to settle, color bleeding out of everything. She sights the next vase, her finger on the trigger.

A flicker of movement draws her concentration too late. The

whistle of her projectile is cut short just as Lys snatches the stake out of midair. It hovers, point sharp, an inch from his chest. Unfazed, he tosses the stake to the ground. His cheeks are sunken, his eyes bruised.

"Am I interrupting?"

"You are," says Asher. "You look terrible, by the way."

"I *feel* terrible. How about you help me out and open up a vein?"

The ensuing silence thickens with the dark, deepening to a gulf as the stars blink awake. A screech owl trills, emerging from a nearby roost to hunt. Asher unzips his jacket and Shea realizes he means to go through with it—to offer himself up as her proxy. Her stomach sinks to the dirt.

"Asher—"

"It's fine," says Asher, cuffing the sleeves of his flannel. If Lys is surprised, he doesn't show it. "Go ahead. I meant what I said."

"You think you're stronger than her?" goads Lys. "You think you wouldn't start to crave it, after a while?"

Asher's throat bobs in a swallow. "Better me than her."

Lys's smile is slow. It doesn't touch his eyes. "What a fucking hero."

There's a commotion behind them—the sound of running feet. They turn in time to see Poppy skid into the open front door. She looks out of breath, Kit cradled in her arms. "I was up in the attic looking for Kit. He likes to wedge himself into the eaves when he naps—any small space, really, I think it's the burrowing instinct—"

"Get there faster," says Lys.

"I saw a light out the window." It comes out all as one word. She expunges a heavy breath and adds, "I think there's someone in the woods."

Asher tugs his sleeve back into place. "Rangers."

Far off in the distance, a gun fires. A dozen starlings take, screaming, to the sky.

"They're hunting something," says Asher. He and Lys share a meaningful glance.

"We should have left five minutes ago," says Lys. "Let's move. And keep quiet."

They next stop just before the dawn, the shadows of the Catskill High Peaks emerging like giants against the lightening sky. Lys leads them off the highway and into the trees, down a little dirt road ravaged by rainwater. At the end of the road is a battered old A-frame wedged deep in a grove of towering hemlock. It's loud, the murmuring forest stifled by the roar of a nearby waterfall.

"How much farther?" asks Asher after he's conducted a sweep of the cabin.

"Another night of riding." Lys pokes through the kitchen cabinets, taking out the coffee mugs one by one for inspection. "Maybe less, if we make good time."

Asher watches him, hanging up his jacket by the door. "Tell me more about this guy in Pennsylvania."

"He's human," says Lys, "if that's what you're asking."

"Do you trust him?"

"You asked me that already." Lys lets the cabinet fall shut with a slam.

"I'm asking you again."

There's a beat before Lys answers. "Keeling is after me. The watch is after you. We need someone neutral."

"And is he?" Asher asks. "Neutral?"

The twitch in Lysander's eye is nearly imperceptible. "Let's just say, the only thing he cares about is himself."

The day passes much the same as the previous one. There's a woodstove in the living room and Asher builds a fire, stoking it until it floods the cabin with heat. Shea lies curled on the couch, listening to the thundering falls and watching the sun drag across the floor in rectangles of gold. Poppy knits. Asher whittles. Lys stays shut away in the cabin's windowless loft. A nighttime creature, burrowed in the eaves with Kit.

She wakes when he stirs. With her hearing aids off, it's more of a feeling than anything. The groan of a door. The creak of a floorboard. She sits up just in time to see him descending the ladder staircase, a skeleton finger held to his lips. Poppy is asleep beside her, the knotted scarf trailing onto the floor. Asher dozes by the fire, a stake in hand. Neither of them wakes. Not when Lys slips outside.

Not when she follows.

Out in the yard, the sun has just set. Remnants of it blister, liquid gold, between the distant trees. The air here isn't as cold as up north, but there's a chill regardless. She pinches her flannel closed as she joins Lys at the railing. A dark-eyed junco clings to a nearby balsam sprig and bobs in the wind, assessing them with suspicion.

Lys waits as Shea fits her hearing aids in and turns them on. There's a telling beep. A rush of sound, indistinguishable at first, until she remembers the waterfall. Heralded by the deafening cataract, they watch the bird. Neither of them mentions the fight in the bathroom, or the way he'd looked half mad as he whispered, *I feel it, too.*

"My mom calls them snowbirds," he says, breaching the quiet. As if in answer, the white-bellied bird lets out a single, sharp *kew*. Shea glances up at him, surprised.

"Your *mom*?"

"Did you think I materialized out of thin air?"

"I don't know, actually. Cyrus says you were spat out of hell."

His face crinkles in a smile. She's amused him. Another *kew* sounds, farther than the first, and the songbird takes flight. They watch as it fades to nothing against the blackening sky. The wind picks up, tugging strands of her hair loose from its plaits. Their hands sit flat on the railing between them, their pinkies close enough to touch.

"She used to tell me that whenever I saw a snowbird, I should remember to be brave," he says. "Everything has an end. Winter. Night. Pain. None of it's permanent, and the snowbird knows."

"Is that what you're doing? Waiting for an end?"

He looks slighted by the question. "Waiting is a coward's game."

"Oh. Sorry."

"I stopped listening to my mother's advice a long time ago. If you want to be done with something, you end it yourself."

She tries to picture him as a little boy, looking for the junco. Remembering to be brave. Waiting for spring to bloom, for the sun to rise. For a wolf, sharp and snarling. She wonders if he only ran because he realized no help was coming.

She wishes he would hold her hand.

He doesn't, of course. He stuffs his hands into his jacket pockets and pivots to face her, propping an elbow atop the railing. He is deceptively casual this way, his ankles crossed and his lean lazy, his hair spilling into his eyes. His nonchalance is a ruse. His features are gaunt, his skin gray. Dark vessels pop into the wide column of his throat.

"Don't do it," he says.

"Do what?"

"You're thinking about offering up a vein. Don't."

"Why not?"

"Because I don't have the discipline to turn you down."

"So then, don't turn me down."

He catches her forearm, flattening her wrist between them. Carefully—*carefully*—he drags the pad of his thumb along the bowed gash of his bite. Teeth, sunk deep. Until the aching stops.

"Thorley won't like it."

"He's not the boss. And you're starving."

"And you want it." He drops the accusation between them like a gauntlet—like he's daring her to deny it.

"I wouldn't have followed you out here if I didn't want it, Lys."

His face is a barrage of emotions, relief warring with disappointment. He tips his forehead to hers, his eyes drifting shut. He exhales. She inhales, the knot between them slack enough to draw breath. In the quiet, she can almost pretend he's just a boy—that this is just a crush.

When he bites down, she doesn't make a sound. And when it's done, she tucks her hand into her sleeve and cleans the blood from his chin. The gesture is absurdly intimate. Both of them freeze, caught, the wind battering them from all sides.

"Sometimes you make me nervous," he says quietly.

It's so unexpectedly earnest, it startles a laugh clear out of her.

He frowns. "Don't laugh."

She can't help it. Everything feels funny. She laughs again, harder this time. He's so close she can taste the blood at his lips, metal and heat. His eyes are a pale, angelite blue. He turns his head just a fraction, his nose brushing along the length of hers. Electricity snakes up her spine, and suddenly she's not laughing anymore.

"Lys—"

"Don't say it." His breath blooms across her jaw. "Don't ask me to Turn you."

"If not now, then when?"

He's too quiet. She pulls back to get a better look at him, but he halts her in her tracks, grabbing a fistful of her flannel. His eyes are on the house, listening to something Shea can't hear. His throat cords in a swallow.

"Our chaperone is awake."

Just as he says it, the screen door swings wide. Asher is there, his cap pulled low and his eyes still heavy with sleep. He takes quick stock of the tableau before him—Lys's full cheeks and bright eyes, blood pooling in Shea's open palm.

She expects him to yell. To criticize. To get *angry*.

He doesn't.

"Let's get back on the road," he says flatly. "We've got a long night of riding ahead."

FIFTEEN

Shea

November in Pennsylvania is crisp and clear, leaves still clinging to the trees. As if the cold hasn't wrung all the color out of this part of the world just yet. They reach their destination just as the dawn breaks. The forest falls away, replaced by flat, bucolic fields dotted in decaying colonials. At their backs, the sun sits in a parhelion along the sky's eastern basin.

They've cut it too close to sunrise. Uneasy, Shea taps Lys's thigh. He nods once, the pale sliver of his throat visible, and urges the bike a little faster.

Head aching, she holds tight to his middle. Wide flaxen fields fall away on either side—sprawling farmland broken here and there by crumpled silos or flame-blackened barns. A deer flits across the road in front of them, fleet of foot.

Signaling to Asher, Lys slows into an upcoming turn. With a thump, the road narrows to a single, muddy artery. A small herd of horses stands grazing in a nearby field. The stallion whickers a warning as they pass, the whites of his eyes gleaming.

The way is slow going, and it takes several more minutes to navigate to the tunneled end of a driveway. By then, the sun is nearly all the way in the sky and Shea's heart has wedged itself neatly in her throat. She gives Lys's side a squeeze. *Faster.* He flattens his gloved palm over her hand and squeezes back. A silent affirmation. *I'm going.*

The wide, alpine acreage before them is trapped behind tensile fencing, wire swallowed in flowering bull thistle. A cluster of stables dots the nearby hills, the well-tended buildings nestled into a patchwork landscape left to grow wild. A mule lifts its head from a patch of clover as they pass, chewing crookedly on the leaves.

They come to a stop beneath an old oak, its branches flooded with ruby-crowned kinglets. Beyond the tree sits a sagging house. The white siding has gone green with moss, fretted windows cracked. It looks, at first glance, entirely unassuming—a stark contrast to the old-world grandeur of Mercy Ridge.

Shea doesn't know what she'd been expecting, but it isn't this.

Lys—infuriatingly—is slow as mud. He takes his time dismounting, inspecting the chassis of his bike like he has all the time in the world. At his back, the sun creeps steadily higher. The first of the daylight hits the farthest field, gilding the meadow gold.

"Hurry *up*," she mutters, giving him a shove. He traps her hands against his chest, pressing them flat beneath his gloves. She can't see his eyes through the dark tint of his visor, but she can feel his heart. It pummels into her open palm. With a start, she realizes he's afraid.

"You don't want to go in."

"It's not my favorite place," comes his muffled response.

"Then why did we come?"

He tips his chin up to the distant trees, where the sun escapes in brittle shoots of yellow. His throat is gridded in veins, slivers of dark already rising into his skin.

"There's only one person in the world who hates Paris Keeling more than me," he says. "And he lives in this house."

"Hey, prince of darkness," calls Asher, his eyes on the sky. "Let's hustle."

They reach the wide, wraparound porch just as the first of the kinglets begin to herald the morning sun. The door swings wide seconds before Lys manages to knock. A man stands there, thin as a spindle and bowed in the shoulders, his hair silver alloy. His spectacles are bottle thick. He peers through the lenses, his mouth going white.

"Oliver," he says. "You're far from home."

Lys flips up the visor on his helmet. "Let us in."

"Now just a minute." The man swipes off his glasses, blustering slightly. "I'm going to need a little more than that. You've never darkened my doorstep like this before. Not by choice."

"There's been a development," says Lys.

"Has there?" The man follows his gaze to Shea. He sizes her up for a long moment, his mouth moving in silent appraisal. "This is different company than you normally keep."

"Like I said," grits out Lys, "there's been a development. I need help."

"I'm afraid you won't find any here," says the man. "As you well know, I learned my lesson the hard way the last time you were—"

With a snarl, Lys lunges. There's a sound of split leather, and then the old man is pinned against the doorframe, Lys's gloved hand suspended inches from his throat. Only, the ends have been rent wide. A set of talons protrudes from the interior, tips rutilated as quartz. He looks as he did the night of the first attack, like he'd been ripped out of the shadows.

"*Oh*," says Poppy.

"Holy *shit*," breathes Asher.

Trapped beneath Lys, the man doesn't even flinch. "It's started. You should have sent word."

"And what would you have done?" grinds out Lys. "Cast me out again?"

"I never cast you out," says the man. "You left on your own. This is different, Oliver. The potential here is catastrophic. You and I both know where this story ends. Your mother fought much too hard—"

"Stop," warns Lys.

"—and for much too long to watch you unmake yourself like this."

"I said, *shut up!*" The kinglets take flight all at once. In the commotion, Lys struggles to quell his temper. "You swore an oath."

"To your mother," says the man. "Not to you."

Out in the field, the sun scrapes across the grass in a widening verdure of gold. The light is nearly at their feet. Shea's urgency fans into full-fledged alarm.

"Please," she says. "He can't be out here. Just let us in, we won't be any trouble."

Still pinned beneath Lys's grip, the man cranes his head around to face her. He looks speculative. Curious. A little bit sad, like he's just come to some sort of terrible understanding. Solemnly, he peers back at Lys.

"It's her," he says gently, "isn't it?"

"Don't look at her."

"You've handed him a victory. You do understand that, yes?"

The corner of Lys's mouth tips up in a sneer. "Not yet, I haven't."

Sunlight pushes through the wide old oak in violent pinpricks. The wind shifts, and suddenly the porch is pierced in arrows of white. Lys hisses—a sharp, pained sort of sound.

"Let us in," says Asher. "He'll die out here."

The man mops at his brow, uneasy. For a moment, it seems like he might double down and send them away. Instead—and with one last glance at Shea—he relents. "Get inside. All of you—quickly."

Lys enters first, the rest falling in behind him. The door swings shut, shrouding the foyer in a murky dark. The only spot of light streams in through a wide entryway at the far end of the hall. A curtained shaft of gold, thick with dust. The smell of cloves clings to the air.

"Do you remember where your room is?" the man asks Lys.

"How could I forget," intones Lys, peeling off his gloves with his teeth. His nails are short and neat. There's no sign that he ever sprang talons at all.

"Sun hits the house around eight," says the man. "It'll be full light in here shortly. Go on upstairs. Shut the door. I'll send for you at twilight."

Lys lingers, his gaze sliding to Shea. "She comes with me."

"Your companions will stay put. All of them, even the girl."

Lys's lip curls. "I don't want you filling her head with your inane ideas."

The man sniffs. "They tell me you call yourself a king, up there in New Hampshire. The *Gravewood Devil*. It does have a certain ring to it. To me, you're the same feckless little boy you've always been, and this isn't the Gravewood, it's my home. Under this roof, *my* word is law. Now, you've asked for my help. Either you trust me completely, or you get out."

Behind the curtains, the sun grows bolder. It turns the hall a funny olive hue. Not quite light. Not quite dark. Lys looks tense as bowstring, his knuckles white.

"Sunshine," he says.

"I've got it under control," answers Asher.

When Lys is gone, the rest of them are ushered into the living room. The space is timeworn but neat, every available surface covered in a potted plant. Fiddle-leaf and spider plants, sweet-smelling jade and a wide golden pothos. A towering monstera sits in the empty hearth, the wide fans of its leaves gone fenestrated.

"I suppose I'll go put on the kettle," says the man, when they've sat. "Please, make yourselves comfortable."

In his absence, Poppy pulls out her knitting. The coffee table before them is clad in a doily, a scalloped candy dish left out beside a planter of striped haworthia. The dish is filled with the same red-foil candies Lys offered Shea the night they left. She unwraps one and tucks it in her cheek.

Wedged on the lumpy velour cushion to her right, Asher sits as if carved from granite, his hands laced between his knees. He hasn't said a word to her. Not since he stumbled, bleary-eyed, out onto the porch and found her out there with Lys.

"Are you mad at me?" she asks.

He doesn't lift his eyes from the haworthia. "No."

"It feels like you're mad," she presses. "You haven't looked at me once today."

He turns to face her. His eyes are stone, hard and unyielding. "There. I'm looking right at you."

She should let it drop. She *knows* it. She doesn't. "Why aren't you angry?"

"Do you *want* me to be angry?"

"It's just that it feels like a giant elephant in the room. You've made your position about Lys and me perfectly clear, and I don't understand why you're suddenly okay with it."

"Because you can't help yourself." It pops out of him like he's been bottling it. "You can't help yourself, " he repeats, gentler this time. "And I'm starting to think he can't help himself, either."

His anger is one thing. His pity, another. It lodges like a knife between her ribs, makes this thing with Lys feel uglier than ever. Out in the kitchen, a kettle begins to whistle.

"It's very quaint in here," Poppy says, a little loudly. "Don't you think it's quaint in here, Shea?"

"You didn't even blink," says Asher. "He had claws, and you didn't even flinch."

The room goes quiet. She searches for something to say and finds nothing.

Needles clicking, Poppy says, "My dad always says we shouldn't judge a person by the way they look, but by the content of their—"

"You saw him," accuses Asher.

"—character," finishes Poppy, scowling over at Asher.

He doesn't notice. He's looking right at Shea now, his eyes bright with an epiphany, and she wishes he'd look anywhere else. "The night Sullivan attacked you it was Lysander who killed him. That's why you lied—you were covering for him."

"So what if I was? I'd do the same for you."

"He *killed* someone."

"You've killed hundreds."

He shakes his head. "Not like that. It's not the same."

"Oh, I'm sorry," snaps Shea, her patience frayed, "I must have missed that chapter in the handbook on *murder*. I guess it's only acceptable when it's a head shot from a hundred yards away."

Asher's eyes go wide. "Parker, he tore out someone's heart with his bare hands."

"Oliver did?"

Their host has reappeared, a wide rattan tray in hand. Instinctively, both Asher and Shea go quiet. Poppy knits faster, avoiding the man's gaze as he peers at each of them in turn.

"This is very troubling, if true."

Asher says nothing. Neither does Shea.

Frowning, the man sets the platter onto the table, shuffling the contents into order. There's a waxy truckle of cheese, a wedge cut loose. A sleeve of crackers and a handful of nuts. A large copper kettle rests on a shallow trivet, steam rising from the spout. Taking a seat in a nearby rocking chair, he regards them across the top of his spectacles.

"Please," he says, gesturing toward the tray. "Help yourselves.

And perhaps while you do you can fill me in on what happened to Oliver."

"It was a private conversation," says Asher tightly.

"Of course." The man smiles. "You're reluctant to share sensitive information with a stranger. I understand. In that case, let's begin with introductions. Perhaps, by the end, we won't be strangers anymore."

"I don't need an introduction," says Asher. "I know who you are. You're Egor van Haut."

Egor's eyes sparkle. "Oliver told you about me?"

"He didn't. But your property is pretty clearly marked on the geospatial maps back at the garrison. Anyone stationed out this way has strict orders to stay at least sixteen klicks from the border on all sides."

"And yet here you are," Egor notes.

Asher's expression tightens. "I'm on leave."

"You mean to say you're a fugitive." Egor tips back in his chair, fingers laced over his stomach. "Don't worry. As someone who has long been morally opposed to some of the more—oh, what should we call them—sadistic methods employed by the wood watch, you won't hear any criticism from me. Although I'll admit Oliver makes a strange ally for a soldier."

"We have a shared interest," says Asher.

"Do you? Intriguing." Egor's eyes drift to Shea as he reaches for the kettle. Water pours into a set of chipped porcelain cups, steam releasing into the air in thin tendrils. "Does anyone take sugar in their tea?"

"I'm set," says Asher.

"None for me, thank you," says Poppy, who has stopped knitting to pick at a handful of almonds.

"Suit yourself." Egor spoons out three lumps of sugar into his cup and sits back, his chair creaking beneath him as he stirs it in. His eyes find Shea for the second time in as many minutes. "How about you? A cup of tea is an excellent remedy for mild hypovolemia."

"Blood loss," says Poppy, in response to the look of confusion that plays across Shea's face. "You *do* look a little sweaty, Shea."

"I'm fine."

"There's no need to be ashamed," says Egor. "You wouldn't be the first human to form a symbiotic bond with one of Oliver's kind."

Symbiotic. Another ugly word for this ugly thing they've done. Her stomach turns over. She can't bring herself to look at Asher at all.

"That's not what— It isn't—" She falls off, flustered. "I'm *fine.*"

"Drink," insists Egor, gesturing to the still-steaming cups. "You'll feel better."

Sensing it would be rude to turn him down a third time, Shea leans forward and takes a cup from the tray. The porcelain is hot in her hands, and she breathes in the flowery scent of hibiscus. Several yellow shoots swim to the top. It makes her think of her mother, trimming the blossoms from the calendula out back. Pressing the petals between the pages of a book. *Good for fever.*

"Thank you."

"It's my pleasure." Egor smiles affably at her over the lip of his cup. "Now, if nobody minds, I'd like to direct the conversation back to our mutual friend. Oliver killed someone. Who?"

Shea busies herself by taking a too large sip of tea. The heat of it scalds the roof of her mouth and she coughs, sputtering.

"No one of importance," says Asher.

Egor narrows his eyes in Asher's direction. "I have to confess—I find your instinct to protect him perplexing. And perhaps misplaced. Oliver is a ticking bomb. When he detonates—and he will—the damage will be astronomical."

Silence swells. The morning sun shines directly on the glass, turning the room to an oven. Under her myriad layers, Shea begins to sweat. Wedged as she is between Poppy and Asher, there's no space for her to shed her flannel. She sets down her teacup and tugs at her collar, resolving herself to her fate.

"Is there a bathroom I could use?" asks Poppy suddenly. Every head in the room turns to face her, and she smiles, rising to her feet. "Sorry, it's just that we've been on the road for days. I'd really love to clean up."

"Me too," says Shea. "I could use a shower."

An ice-cold one. She feels like she's catching fire. The temperature in the room is slowly creeping toward unbearable. Sweat trickles in a line down her back.

"Yes, yes, of course," says Egor. "I'm sure you're eager to get the dust off." A smile appears on his face, wan and nervy. "You'll find a bathroom at the top of the stairs. Please feel free to use anything you need. Perhaps we can come back to this conversation a little later."

Asher bristles. "Unlikely— *Oof.*"

"Thanks," says Poppy, who has trod right on Asher's toe. "That's very generous."

Asher rises after her with a scowl, and Shea follows. The moment she stands, the room tips on its axis. She catches herself on a narrow console table lined in string-of-pearls, sending its leaves fluttering toward the floor in verdant helixes.

"Hey," says Asher, stabilizing her by the elbow. "You okay?"

"Fine. Just tired, I think."

"Shea," calls Egor as she reaches the door. "It's Shea, right? Would you mind staying back just a minute? I'd like to speak with you. It won't take long."

Poppy is already upstairs. Asher hesitates on the bottom step, his brow raised in a question.

"I'll be right up," she says. "You can go ahead."

"You're sure?"

"Go. I'll be fine."

She watches him leave before turning back toward the living room. Everything feels slow and diluted, like she's moving underwater. She catches her shoulder against the doorframe in a lopsided lean, wicking sweat from her brow. In his chair, Egor looks on edge. His eyes dart from her to the hall. His teacup rattles against the saucer.

"I was a young man when the Rot first appeared," he says, speaking like he's rushing to get something out. "New to my career and already jaded. Everyone likes to say it all happened so quickly, but that simply isn't true. Men like me—scholars, botanists, scientists—we'd been sounding the alarm for years.

"As a phytologist, I published several peer-reviewed articles on the melting Arctic, the rising temperatures. We had good reason to believe that certain ancient microbes were trapped in pockets of gas, miles beneath the ice. That soon, they'd escape. They'd get into the groundwater. They'd wreak havoc on our modern ecosystem. We were discredited for our writings, my colleagues and I. Even now that the worst has come true, people still feign ignorance."

The temperature in the room is stifling. Tea-water hot.

"Why are you telling me this?" asks Shea.

"You are important to Oliver," says Egor simply. "That makes you important to me. I'd like it if you knew who I was. What kind of man I am. It might make this visit a little easier."

Shea considers him through the blinding swell of a sun flare. "Back home, Father Isaac says the Rot came from hell. He says the world ripped itself open to punish us for our sins."

Egor's eyes twinkle behind his glasses. "And is that what you believe?"

"I don't go to church."

Egor smiles around another swallow of tea. "I see why he likes you. You're very similar, you and he. You both carry so much anger. I only wonder—if you strike two flint stones one against the other long enough, eventually they catch fire."

The sound of his voice winnows out. She catches herself on the back of the couch, dizzy. Sweat pours down her face. When she swipes the back of her hand across her eyes, her focus snags on the dregs of her tea. The bottom of the cup is rimed in a flat blue paste. Petals ground down to powder. Tasteless. Toxic.

"Scutellaria," says Egor, when he notices her looking. "Although you likely know it by its more common name."

Shea thinks of her mother culling weeds in the garden, pointing out the mountain whorls mixed in among the wildflowers:

Pay attention, Mouse. It's important not to mix up the petals.

"Skullcap."

"Like I told you," Egor says, "you're important to Oliver, which makes you important to me."

The air snuffs out, and the foyer—all the drab olive green of it—comes rushing toward her.

When she hits the floor, she hits head first.

SIXTEEN

Shea

This is a memory, or else a dream—the Thorley house in deep summer, in the middle of a heat wave. The air is so thick, it snaps against the pavement. Poppy and Camellia are in the hammock out back, feet tangled and eyes on the sky. Laughing themselves sick over a private joke.

Shea isn't with them. She's standing in the garage, her bare feet burning, a crown of yellow hawkweed wilting atop her head. She wandered over in search of Howard, the family beagle, and now she's here—watching Asher work. It's two days before he leaves for the garrison. For now, he's home, and things are the same as they always are. He sits on a stool by his bike, a rag over his shoulder and Howard dozing at his feet. His hands are stained with oil. Sweat adheres his T-shirt to his spine. They both know she's staring.

"Are you really going?"

"Yeah," he says. It comes out bitter as a rind. "Looks like I am."

Off in the distance, Camellia lets out a full-bodied cackle. The sound carries in on a stale breeze. Everywhere, everywhere, the air hangs hot and heavy. Shea wants to unzip her skin and crawl clear out of it.

"You don't have to do what they tell you. You could leave."

He sets the wrench down with a clatter, startling Howard awake. "And where would I go?"

"The Gravewood."

She hadn't meant to say it like that—like a reflex. Like she thinks about it all the time. Running. Leaving. The forest, cool and dark. Horrified, Asher glances quickly around—searching the garage like he's certain someone might have overheard.

Finally—stiffly—he says, "Don't joke."

"It's not a joke. I mean it."

"You want me to pledge myself to the devil? How is that any better?"

She's practiced this, at home in her mirror. At night in her bed. In the mornings, as she brushed her teeth. "Because then I could come with you."

His expression shifts to one of surprise. "Parker—"

"You promised," she says quickly. "Remember? You promised we'd leave together."

"That was years ago. We were kids."

"So what if it was? Are you saying you didn't mean it?"

"I did mean it, I just—" He falls silent as Camellia appears, dragging Poppy behind her. They stutter to an abrupt halt at the sight of Shea in the garage.

"You're not allowed to steal my friends," Camellia declares, jabbing an accusatory finger at her brother. "Shea isn't interested in your dirty old bike, anyway. Tell him, Shea."

Her cheeks heat. "I, uh—"

"We're going inside to see if there's ice pops," Poppy interjects. "Want one?"

"I'll be right there."

"Perfect." Poppy ushers Camellia hurriedly inside.

Alone again, the silence blisters. Asher tugs the rag from his shoulder and falls to cleaning his knuckles, his jaw locked, his stare crawling through her. The air smells of hibiscus. Floral. Tart. She wants to tell him she doesn't know how to watch another person leave. She wants to say that she hasn't learned how to say goodbye—that she's never even been given the chance.

She doesn't say it. And she hadn't said goodbye that day, either. The dream is all wrong—she'd gone inside with Camellia and Poppy. She'd sat on the counter and eaten an ice pop, feeding the last few licks of it to Howard. When she'd finally gathered the courage to sneak back outside, Asher had been gone, and so had his bike. It was the last time she saw him.

But what if she'd stayed?

What if she'd said goodbye? What if they'd made a new promise?

She wants to ask him now—wants to start over, to do better, to rewrite every wasted moment—but she can't. She's gripped in the coils of a slithering sort of awareness, immobilized by the feel of a presence at her back. A shadow, cool and dark. It's Lys, standing stalwart in a blaze of yellow sun. The light eats away at him, devouring him in sunlit blisters. He looks like a true skeleton this way, all bone and sinew, the hollows of his eyes as black as hell.

"This will end, too," he says in a voice like death. *"Like everything else."*

When she swallows, she tastes hibiscus.

She opens her eyes.

The moment she does, panic engulfs her. She's on a bed, her wrists and ankles strapped to the mattress and her chest belted tight. The room is basement dark, windowless and dank. The only light comes from several wall-mounted plant lamps, under which sits a row of glass terrariums. Inside each cloche blooms a poison plant—blue skullcap and white oleander, toothy larkspur and flowering nightshade and spiky castor beans, red as blood.

Someone is shouting. She can't place the noise. Can't slot the bilabials into words. It all pings, indecipherable, off the walls. The light hums, flickering at vertigo speed. Everything loses shape and regains it, focusing like a camera's aperture with each blink.

"*Look,*" says a voice, just out of her line of sight. "Oliver, look. Look, and then breathe. She's awake. She's unharmed. You're making this harder on yourself."

The shouting stops. She tries to crane her head and finds movement impossible, a thin strap belting her forehead. She feels like a butterfly, pinned to a board for examination. In the quiet, Lys's voice sharpens into coherence.

"Let her out."

"Now, Oliver." Egor sounds weary, as though they've gone several rounds already. "You're being willfully obtuse. It doesn't suit you. I know you feel it—the misalignment in your proprioception. In hers. It goes well beyond a youthful obsession, and I saw it the moment you appeared on my doorstep. How it doesn't keep you awake at night—"

"It does. Is that what you want to hear?"

"What I want," says Egor carefully, "is to take a closer look. No one has to get hurt."

Distantly, there comes a hammering sound. Another meaningless noise, no perspective to give it roots. The buzzing light makes her dizzy.

"You want me to cooperate?" Lys's voice is flat. "You want me to be a good little lab rat? Let her out."

The hammering gets louder. Shea's mouth is cotton, her thoughts mud. Her tongue feels thick and unwieldy and she can't dredge up the words to speak, to scream. Her heart thuds in time with the distant pounding. A snare against a drum.

"He'll get through the door eventually," says Lys. "How do you think that'll end?"

Not a snare, a fist. Not a drum, a door. Asher's outside. More sounds drift toward her as she struggles against her bindings. Egor appears, lit from beneath by the lamps. He's slipped into the pressed white of a lab coat, an stethoscope slung around his neck. A silver head mirror glimmers down at her like a third eye. Panic pops into fireworks and she thrashes, pulling at her straps.

"There, there," says Egor, in a voice she's sure he means to be soothing. "There's no need for alarm. I'm not going to hurt you."

He bends over her, pressing back her sweating hair. She tries to flinch away, but she's bound too tight. She feels wild and tethered—her fangless teeth bared—as he presses two fingers to her pulse and checks his watch.

"She's got a nice, strong pulse. She'll be back on her feet in no time." To Shea, he says, "I'm going to go ahead and loosen these straps. I'd like you to sit up slowly. Understood?"

She nods as best as she can, and he falls to unfastening her ties. Outside, the hammering has stopped. In the quiet, her ears ring. The lights flicker maddeningly at her peripherals. She allows Egor to help her into a sitting position. A dizzying heat crawls up her neck and she tips forward, catching her hands on her knees.

Slowly, the room around her coalesces into shape. A human skeleton hangs from a hook nearby, ivy wound along its bones. A wide curio cabinet sits flush against the wall, several wet specimen jars nestled against the shelving. Backlit, she can just make out the shapes of the creatures within. A frog, its webbed feet extended. A rabbit, its little body curled inward. A fawn, its head tucked in.

A human fetus, its full-black eyes wide and unsettling.

Shackled beside the shelf is Lys, his arms hyperextended and his wrists cuffed, inked fingers hanging loose. His expression is as murderous as she's ever seen it. The lamplight throws the lines of him into monstrous relief, accentuating the twin peaks of solid bone that curve out from beneath the messy curtain of his hair. He looks like a satyr in the dark.

A storybook monster, and not a boy at all.

"Do you hear that?" he asks Egor, with bone-chilling calm. "Thorley's stopped knocking."

"Perhaps he's come to his senses."

"Or maybe he's got a plan B. I'd work fast, if I were you."

"It's just a small sample collection, Oliver," says Egor, reaching for a metal trolley. It clatters toward him on a pair of squeaky wheels, a wide array of sharp-looking tools rattling atop the tray. "There's no need to put up such a fuss. Aren't you at all curious to know how your insides reflect the changes on the outside?"

"No," says Lys.

Egor *tch*s, reaching for a silver lancet knife. "Insolent, as always."

"It's been said." Lys eyes the blade in Egor's hand. Sweat beads along his brow. "You're not coming anywhere near me with that."

"Your mother brought you here because she thought I could help you," Egor reminds him, turning the lancet over so that it catches the light. "Let me help you."

"Last time I was here, you said I was beyond help."

"The variables have changed," says Egor. "This girl—a *human* girl, no less—has caused a violent upheaval in the natural order of your existence. She's a cataclysm, Oliver. You will not survive her. Not without my help."

Lys's gaze snaps to hers. There's panic in his eyes, wild and dark.

"She is exactly the sort of stimulus we've been looking for all this time," says Egor. "The kind of trigger your father would have—"

"Stop." Lys's voice slips out like smoke. He's not looking at Shea anymore.

A *cataclysm*, Egor called her. The word reverberates horribly between her ears.

Outside, there's a new sort of commotion. The splintering of a door giving way. It starts with a crack. A second. A third, and the door falls flat, rattling the room and everything inside it. Asher steps across the threshold, his shotgun at the ready. On his heels comes Poppy, wide-eyed and tight-lipped.

"Kill him," orders Lys.

Asher doesn't move. He stays frozen, sighting Egor down the barrel of his gun.

"What the hell are you waiting for, Thorley?" Lys demands. "An embossed invitation?"

"He's a civilian," says Asher.

"This is a terrible time to get selective. *Shoot* him."

"He's unarmed."

"I don't care."

"Lys." It's the first word Shea's managed since she woke. It comes out thick, muddled by the swelling of her tongue. Lys blinks over at her, his jaw wiring tight. "No killing."

It's a push. She's always pushing him. There's a beat—a single, deadly moment—where this could go either way. Both of them feel it—that familiar precipice, the two of them teetering on its edge. He grimaces, as if the idea of doing as he's told—of letting Egor live—repulses him. But he listens.

"Bind him," he orders.

"Happily." Shouldering his shotgun, Asher reaches for a loop of rope on the wall. "Put your hands behind your back."

Egor splutters. "This is absurd."

"His keys are on his belt," says Lys.

Asher yanks them loose and tosses them to Poppy, who snatches them out of midair. She crosses to the wall where Lys is chained, her attention caught on the numerous lit specimens suspended in embalming fluid. She lingers at the fetus, looking contemplative.

"Take your time, Zahar," snipes Lys. "I'm comfortable where I am."

She frowns as she reaches up to unlock his cuffs. "That's a baby."

"Is it?" he asks thinly, rubbing his wrists. "I hadn't noticed."

"You're making a mistake," calls Egor. "You know it as well as I do."

Lys ignores him, heading toward the cot. Shea sits on the edge, her feet swinging. She feels as though she's slowly resurfacing from some lightless depth, water in her lungs and pressure in her ears. The lights have crawled into her head. The buzzing rattles her vision, turns the ringing in her ears to a staticky hum. Sick with it, she shuts her eyes.

"Open," orders Lys, the moment she does. She finds his face an inch from hers, his gaze searching. His touch ghosts along her throat, lingering at her pulse. "Are you okay?"

"You have horns," she says.

His face closes up like a fist. "It's temporary. I'll shave them down."

"You don't have to."

Asher appears at Lys's side, looking grim. The light clings to him in a way it doesn't cling to Lys, illuminating him in a lambent cast. "What do you want to do with Van Haut?"

"Leave him here." Lys coaxes Shea down off the cot. The room wobbles, or else she does, and he catches her just before she falls. They're laced all together, her arm around his neck, his grip tight against her waist. His voice is a texture. A vibration. "If he gets out, he gets out."

"And what if he doesn't?" asks Asher. "He'll starve."

Lys's smile is flat. "Do you know what desanguination is, Thorley?"

"It's when a body is purposely removed of blood," says Poppy, answering before anyone else can. She's still standing by the shelf, her arms folded conspicuously over the bib of her overalls. The jar containing the fetus is missing, a dark ring left behind in the wood where it sat. "It's a form of bloodletting. Remove too much, the patient dies."

"Except we don't die without blood," tacks on Lys. "We desiccate."

"Living corpses," says Asher. "I've seen them, in the holding cells at the garrison."

Lys makes a face. "I'll bet you have."

"I was only trying to help you, Oliver," calls Egor. "It's what your mother asked me to do."

He sits bound on the floor, his arms behind his back and his ankles knotted. At the mention of his mother, Lys's expression contorts.

"Let him starve," he says. "We leave at dusk."

Upstairs, they gather in a lamplit room, the dormered windows blacked out with paint. The wind has blown in a storm, and the rain hisses against the roof. The air smells wet and cold.

Still coming back to herself, Shea rests her temple against the wall and takes quick stock of her surroundings. A bunk bed sits against the wall, a quilted full beneath a narrow twin. It's a child's room, the wall papered in navy stripes, the shelves cluttered with knickknacks—green soldiers and stacked comic books and action figures with the faces worn blank. A stark, homey opposition to the clinical horrors of the Van Haut basement.

"I'm going to do a sweep of the grounds," says Asher. "The rest of you should get some sleep while it's still light."

"You won't find anyone," says Lys. "No one comes out this way if they can avoid it. Van Haut isn't known for being a good host."

Poppy sniffles, rubbing at her nose. "That feels like an understatement."

"What?" asks Lys. "You're not having a nice time?"

The door drifts shut on Asher's scoff. In his absence, the room falls quiet. The only sound is the click of the radiator, the steady drill of rain against the glass. Shea feels like she is both light as a feather and heavy as an anvil. She tries to will herself to move and fails.

Poppy has no such trouble. Stifling a yawn, she climbs into the top bunk and collapses, face first, atop the pillow. Above her, a pink prehensile tail curls around the narrow wood of a ceiling joist. Kit's ghostly face appears, his eyes squinted nearly shut against the lamplight.

"Oh, there you are!" Shea hears Poppy say. "You missed all the excitement."

Within minutes, her soft snores flood the room. Shea watches, her heartbeat sticky, as Lys drops to his back on the bottom bunk. Awareness crackles between them as he settles into place, his arms crooked behind his head.

He looks like a prince of death, the white of his horns gleaming like opals. It gives him an oddly fae appearance, like he's a thousand years old. She can't stop herself staring. As if he knows it, his eyes drift to hers. His gaze is heavy, and she feels it like a physical touch. She gives an involuntary shiver, that funny underwater haze clinging to everything.

"It'll wear off," he says, like he knows just what she's thinking.

"Maybe." Her voice is thick. "What's proprioception?"

His mouth turns down at the corners. "Who knows? Come over here."

"I don't think I can. My legs feel like lead."

"Shea."

It's less a push and more of a nudge. She feels it just the same—a compulsion. A tightening, as if he's tugging on the other side of a rope. Willing herself off the wall, she makes her painstaking way onto the bed alongside him. He holds himself still as she crawls into place, staring up at the top bunk. Above them, the thin wooden splines are stuffed with baseball cards, glossy placards interspersed with vintage matte. She feels like she's crawled into a coffin alongside him. The air is tight, the space enclosed. They lie in silence and listen to each other breathe.

"The Titan of Terror," he whispers when her eyelids grow heavy. "The Colossus of Clout."

She angles her head toward his. "What?"

"Babe Ruth." He tips his chin toward the planks deckled in cards. "The Great Bambino. Twenty-two seasons, seven hundred fourteen home runs. Not the record but close."

Directly over his head is a man in blue-striped knickers. He's squinting into the sun, his wooden bat in mid-swing. The card is bent at one corner, the details sun-spoiled from years of exposure. It looks like the card he carries with him, its corner fingerprinted in blood.

"It hurts," he says, when the quiet deepens. "Desiccating, I mean. You feel everything."

A wordless anger sinks its teeth into her. "Did he do that to you? Egor? Did he drain you of blood?"

It's a while before Lys answers, his voice wry. "'There can be no progress nor achievement without sacrifice.'"

She rolls on her side to face him. "Who said that?"

"Van Haut. Although I think it's a quote from someone else."

"It sounds like bullshit."

His smile is rueful. He still hasn't looked at her. "Sometimes on the very worst days, I used to list all the baseball stats I could remember. It was a trick my mom taught me, to hold on to myself if I started to feel like I was coming apart."

She pictures him small and starving, his eyes black all the way through. It doesn't fit the image she has of him—the Gravewood Devil, spat out of hell. King of the runaways, motherless and wild. She swallows the shard of glass in her throat. She forces herself to ask the question she's been turning over since they first came upstairs.

"Is this *your* bedroom?"

"No."

"Oh. Because the way Egor talks about you—" She pauses, reconsidering, and then approaches it from a new angle. "It's just that it seems like maybe a little boy lived here."

"A little boy *did* live here," says Lys. "I occupied it for a while, but it isn't mine."

"Whose was it?"

"A miniature Van Haut," he says. "Insufferable little shit. He used to talk all night."

Poppy shifts overhead, coils creaking, and they both go quiet until she settles.

"He's dead now," adds Lys, offhand.

There's something raw in the way he says it—something open and bleeding that doesn't invite further probing. Instead, she asks, "Did you grow up near here?"

"In Pennsylvania?" he clarifies, like he's never heard anything more horrible in all his life.

"Yeah, in Pennsylvania."

"No."

She's not given the chance to investigate further. The door skids open to admit Asher, his dog tags gleaming and his hair slicked flat by the rain. He casts a hard look in their direction as he shuts the door and locks it. Silence hangs, deep and expectant.

"I call little spoon," says Lys, puncturing the quiet.

Asher's gaze shutters. "Toss me a pillow. I'll sleep on the floor."

"I can take the floor," says Shea, already sitting up. "I don't mind."

"Parker, *stay*." Asher barks the order like a commanding officer. She freezes, one leg already off the bed. With a groan, he scrubs a hand through his wet hair, turning it to spikes. "Sorry. Just—throw me a pillow, will you?"

"Put him out of his misery," says Lys. "Can't you see he's having a crisis?"

Shooting Lys as deadly a stare as she can muster, Shea tugs his pillow out from beneath him. He thumps back onto the mattress with a laugh. She tosses the pillow to Asher, who swipes it out of the air and gives it a single, firm plump before dropping it to his feet. With a grunt, he lowers himself to the hardwood. The floor creaks as he tosses first this way, then that. Finally, and with a weighted sigh, he flops flat onto his back.

The ensuing silence has a heartbeat. Three of them.

"Sweet dreams, Sunshine," says Lys.

Asher doesn't answer.

Not one of them sleeps. Not until dark.

SEVENTEEN

Shea

Shea wakes to pitch black.

She's alone in bed, the pillow beside her cold. Immediately, the hairs on her neck stand on end. She sits up, careful not to bump her head on the top bunk, and peers out in the room's dormered dark. Seeing nothing, she fishes her hearing aids out from under the pillow and fits them on. Two beeps follow in quick succession. There's a rush of white noise. Beneath it, silence.

"Thorley?"

"He left" comes Poppy's voice from above her. "He took the crossbow."

Shea slides out of bed and clicks on the lamp, squinting in the sudden glaze of light. The room is cold, like someone's left a window open. Pulling on her flannel, she hops into her boots one after the other, laces trailing as she makes her way toward the door. Poppy descends the ladder, already dressed to leave. Kit dangles in the cradle of her arms, teeth bared in a skeleton grin.

"Did you see them leave?"

"Lysander was gone when I woke up," says Poppy. "Asher went to look for him. He said to stay put."

Shea casts her a hard look. "Fat chance."

"He said you'd say something like that."

"I'll bet he did." She pulls open the door and peers out into the hall. A light is on downstairs. The air is cold as ice, and her breath blooms before her in pale sheaves of gray. "Come on—let's go see what's going on."

"I don't know, Shea," says Poppy, hanging back. "What if there's trouble? We don't have any weapons."

"They would have woken us if there was trouble."

"You really think so?"

She doesn't. Not really. But there's no way she's going to sit around and wait for trouble to find her. There's no way she's going to tell Poppy that she can feel him—Lys—wrapped around her ribs like twine. He's too far. The distance cinches tight, cutting off circulation.

"We can go see if there's anything to eat in the kitchen," she says, pleased with how casual she manages to sound. "If we still haven't found them, we'll go back up and wait. No one will know."

"*I'll* know," counters Poppy, but she tails after Shea regardless.

Downstairs, the foyer is quiet. The front door hangs open, cold spilling in in waves. The rain has stopped, but everything outside looks slick and silver in the moonlight. The horses are gone from the pasture. Nothing moves. Nothing sings.

"This feels bad," says Poppy. "Don't you think?"

A door falling shut behind them brings them both whirling about.

"Did you see anyone?" asks Shea.

"No. But I see blood."

So does Shea. Gobs of it, dark with Rot. It drags in a jagged line down the narrow hall. They creep along the trail, rounding the corner into a narrow kitchenette. A pair of heavy work boots poke out from behind a wooden island. Blood oozes, ink dark, onto the penny-round tile.

Heart in her throat, Shea reaches for the knife block on a nearby countertop. A carving knife slips loose with a slight *ping*.

There's a wet cough. Then a man's voice: "Keeling? Is that you?"

Poppy scrabbles for the knife block next, drawing out a serrated bread knife. Shea tosses her a look, which she returns, her shoulders lifting in a shrug.

"Goddamn it, Keeling," calls the man. "I know you're in here."

Shea swallows a breath and steps into view. The man on the floor is older, but only just. He looks to be in his early twenties, his sour-milk skin sheened in sweat and his hair a short crop of blond, the light going out of his lake-blue eyes. He lies slumped against the cabinets, his hands clutched to his middle. The damage is immense. His abdomen has been gorged open as if by the claws of some horrible hell-beast. A wolf, in the body of a boy.

"You," he grits out.

Shea grips her knife tight by the hilt. "You know me?"

The question makes him laugh, and the laughter devolves into a fit of coughing. Blood dribbles, dark as pitch, down his chin.

"Do I know you?" It comes out mocking. Derisive, even dying. "Everyone knows you. You're Keeling's singular obsession."

Keeling. Her heart races hard enough to hurt. "Is he here? In the house?"

There's a dull thud, somewhere beyond the kitchen. The scrape of something dragging along the wall. A palpable slackening in her chest. The man's face falls, and suddenly he isn't looking at her at all. He's staring clean through her, out into the dark of the hall.

Reverently, he whispers, "If it's the devil you want, he's just behind you."

Shea stills, the hair on her arms standing on end. Another thud sounds, closer than the last. Shea takes her first deep breath in minutes as Poppy draws in close, her grip tightening around the bread knife.

"This feels worse," she says.

Shea turns to follow her gaze. Lys is there, just as she knew he would be—just as she felt him—his frame swallowing up the exit. He looks the way he did that night on the bridge—veined beyond recognition. His teeth are fanged sharp, his claws bloody. In his right hand, he grips a wooden baseball bat, the grain dark with blood.

On the floor, the man begins to chant. Quietly, like he's reciting a prayer. "From the fount of the forest comes the age of the beast. From the fount of the forest comes the age of the—"

"Lys," Shea whispers. "Look at me."

His head quirks oddly, following the sound of her voice. Locking onto her, as though sighting prey. His eyes are flat and cold, no recognition in their depths. He takes a single step, his bat clicking over the grout. The kitchen is small. There's nowhere to run. The island's edge bites into the small of her back.

Behind her, the man is still chanting. "From the fount of the forest comes the age of the beast. From the fount—"

"Babe Ruth," blurts Shea. "The Titan of Terror."

Lys halts, going vulturine still.

"The— *Shoot*, what was it? The colossal *something*—the colossal—the *Colossus of Clout*!"

"Shea," whispers Poppy. "What are you doing?"

"He played, uh, twenty-two seasons of baseball," she goes on, raising her voice in an effort to drown out the man and his chanting. "He had seven hundred, uh, seven hundred fourteen home runs. Not the record holder but close. Who holds the record? You never said."

Lys's eyes open and close in a reptilian blink.

"Finish it," goads the man. "Kill me."

"Shut *up*," snaps Shea.

"You know you want to," says the man, ignoring her. "You want to know what my plan was? You want to know how I would have done it? I'd have crept upstairs, whisper-quiet. I'd have gutted her while she slept. Broken her right in front of you—drained her of blood and made you watch."

With a snarl, Lys lunges. He doesn't make it far. There's the twang of a string loosing, the sick *thwack* of a wooden projectile lodging itself into drywall. Lys is pinned by the shirt, blood pouring from a graze in his lower abdomen. Asher stands in the door, already reloading.

"Run," he orders, his voice even. "Now."

Lys releases an inhuman snarl, grabbing the stake with both hands and wedging it slowly free. Blood trickles down his abdomen like water from a sieve. On the floor, the man goes scrabbling back, dragging a trail of dark in his wake.

"From the fount of the forest," he gasps out, "comes the age of the beast. From the—"

"Parker, *move*!" shouts Asher.

She edges hurriedly toward the door just as Lys rips the stake free. As she passes, Asher rams the flat of the crossbow into her chest. She catches it, surprised.

"If something comes at you, shoot it," he orders.

She nods and takes off running, Poppy at her heels. There's the click of a loaded chamber, an unholy howl. A gun fires just as she and Poppy burst out into the night, their breath breaking over them in sheaves of gray. The night is overcast, the moon a pale disk in a nebulous sky.

They race toward the barn without stopping, stumbling over hilly pitches and crawling under fences. They emerge from the meadow soaking wet and shivering. An abandoned RV has been left parked alongside a tall tensile fence. All around them, the night is horribly, painfully quiet. Shea peers toward the house.

"Do you hear them? Do you— Is there anything?"

"No," says Poppy. "It's quiet. We probably shouldn't stay out in the open like this, though. If anything is scenting us, we're upwind."

"Okay." Shea palms the stitch in her side. "Okay, no—you're right. Let's keep going."

On the other side of the fence sits a barn. It's been built into a bank, the two-storied edifice jutting out of the shallow hillside like a dryad's saddle. Searching until she finds a suitable stick, Shea tosses it at the wiring. When nothing sizzles, she gestures for Poppy to follow her, slinging the strap of the crossbow over her shoulder.

The fence is high, wires taut. They climb to the top of the RV before scaling the rest of the way on their own, careful not to snare themselves in the sumac veined along the posts. The drop to the opposite side nearly steals the breath clean out of her lungs. She doesn't stop to recover. They keep moving, scrabbling one after the other over the stony pitch and slipping through a gap in the second-story door.

Inside is dark. By what little light illuminates the space, Shea can just make out the bare bones of a workshop slung with cobwebs. The air smells like dry leather and wet hay and—beneath it—something foul. Immediate unease swims into her. It isn't the room itself, which at first glance doesn't look all that different from her father's workshop back home. Tools hang suspended from the walls in every direction. Muck forks and straw brooms. Pitchforks and shovels. A hacksaw, for cutting metal. A tenon saw, for shallow incisions. A panel saw, for hewing and splitting.

It's what's in the middle of the room that turns her stomach. A hook hangs from the ceiling, tips pronged sharp. The floor beneath is stained a dark, deep brown. The color of dried blood.

"This seems like the wrong time to ask," whispers Poppy, poking at a moonlit blade, "but why do we think the watch isn't allowed onto the premises?"

Below them, something bellows. Both Shea and Poppy freeze, their eyes meeting across the dark.

"Was that a cow?"

"I don't think so," says Poppy.

Another cry reaches them, higher and keener than the first. They follow the sound down the shallow set of stairs, emerging onto the first floor to find themselves in a cluster of stalls, all dark. The only light falls in through an open Dutch door at the far end of the barn. The air hangs still, smelling of stink. Of sweat.

"Something is in here," whispers Poppy. "I can hear it moving."

Shea readies her crossbow, her heart hammering, but Poppy hangs back, dubious.

"Whatever it is, I don't think you should shoot at it."

"Poppy, not *everything* is a stray animal in need of saving."

"It's not that. It's just—what if you miss?"

Shea swallows, glancing down at the singular projectile lined along the barrel. She doesn't have any more ammunition, which means she has only one shot. One chance.

"I won't miss," she promises.

She repeats it internally, in a desperate chant: *I won't miss. I won't miss. Please, don't let me miss.* Inching forward, she peers into each stall in turn. Every last one is empty, the floors wet with straw. At the final stall, she rises up onto her toes and peers inside.

This one is different from the others. The straw is fresh and dry. The paneling looks strange, as if it's been shingled in paper. She peers a little closer, bringing her face near the bars. As her eyes adjust, she can just make out the tiny typeset of baseball cards. Dozens upon dozens of them, same as there'd been on the bottom of the bunk.

In the dark, there comes a soft trill. It's a sound she knows cold—a sound she's heard a hundred times, seated at the bottom step of her cellar. Watching what's left of her mother tear into whatever scraps she's managed to bring home from the butcher's.

"Shea," hisses Poppy, her voice urgent.

Out of the corner of her eye, she sees something shift. A humanoid shape breaks away from the dark, shoulders hunched and head hanging. It's a boy, his movements odd and quirking. His face is sunken in, his lips peeled back from his gums. With a snap of his teeth, he rushes the bars.

Shea topples back, stifling a scream.

"What is it?" demands Poppy. "What's in there?"

"It's my son."

The voice is decidedly male and unnervingly close. Shea whips around, her finger depressing the trigger without meaning to. The projectile embeds itself in the wood just beside Egor van Haut's head. He stands unbound before them, looking startlingly unperturbed.

"Well," he says, removing his glasses to clean them, "I'm certainly glad that wasn't another inch to the right."

"I wish it had been," seethes Shea.

"Do you?" Egor lifts a brow. "Whatever happened to 'no killing'?"

"I said that before I knew what you did to Lys. You're lucky he's not here. I'd let him tear you apart."

Egor replaces his glasses, his smile thin. "You really would, wouldn't you? You'd let him do anything, even if it destroys you both. And it will. Like I told him before, you're a cataclysm."

"That means nothing to me," says Shea.

"It will," Egor assures her. "Before the end. For now, I'd like to use what little remaining time we have together to tell you a story about my son."

The door to the stall rattles. Egor's smile wavers.

"Nel was taken with Oliver from the very first day he and his mother appeared on my doorstep. He'd always wanted a sibling, but his mother and I had a late start. We were already old when we had him. The world was already over. We weren't in a place to have more children, which meant Nel was a very lonely little boy. He took to following Oliver everywhere, and there wasn't much I could do to stop it. Oliver was tolerant of it but only just."

In the stall behind them, the boy trills.

"All Oliver has ever learned about love is that it hurts," Egor goes on. "He doesn't know any other way. I'm sure he thought Nel would Turn. I'm sure he thought he'd be stronger. Faster. Crueler—just like him. But the change doesn't always take."

Understanding worms its way into Shea. She blinks and sees her mother standing over her bed, her eyes lightless, her throat clicking horribly. The beginning of the end.

"What is he?" asks Poppy.

"Nel is a natural byproduct of the human body's immune system," says Egor. "It's common knowledge that not everyone Turns. What's less known is why. When the Rot is ingested, it knots itself so tightly along the human genome, it creates something entirely new. Some bodies accept the change. Some bodies fight."

"Acute rejection," Poppy cuts in. "It's what happens when the body sees a transplanted organ as foreign and attacks it."

"Precisely." Egor beams over at her. "You're a very clever young woman."

"I read," says Poppy.

"Yes, well, as you might imagine, there aren't too many books on the topic. And the critical difference in this situation is that the change takes place so quickly, by the time the body recognizes what's happening, the Rot is already coded into its DNA. It attacks itself, hollowing out until there's nothing left but a husk."

The boy slams into the stall door again. Shea thinks of her mother, scooped clean. Of the way she'd have done anything, said anything, sacrificed anything to preserve her. She's come all this way in hope of a cure. She's not all that different from Egor van Haut, clinging to hope in the dark.

"I am fond of Oliver," says Egor. He's watching her too closely, inspecting every blink and every breath. Taking note of her, like she's a specimen in a jar. "He is a marvel, yes, but he is a danger. I am not oblivious to his faults, and what he did to my son is nothing compared to what he's capable of. A cataclysm is a violent thing, you see. The damage it does is irreversible. I'm afraid I cannot, in good conscience, allow you to continue leading him down this path."

"I'm not leading him anywhere," says Shea.

"Oh, but you are," Egor disagrees. "We are, all of us, balanced on the razor-thin tightrope of equilibrium. One shove from you, and everything topples into chaos."

Push me again.

"Lys will never forgive you if you hurt me." It comes out thin, lacking bluster.

"I don't need his forgiveness," Egor assures her. "I needed my son. Oliver took something precious from me. Something I can never get back. And so now, I'll take something precious from him."

"This isn't about maintaining ecological balance," says Poppy, "this is revenge."

Egor's eyes have gone watery. He blinks them clear. "I am a man of science, and science requires sacrifice. Anyone will tell you that. I'm terribly sorry to say it, but Shea Parker will not be leaving this place alive."

The quiet night is rent in two by the squeal of tires, the honk of a horn. The barn floods with headlights as the RV comes rumbling into view. A door squeals open and then slams shut with equal force. A lone figure steps out into the light. It's Asher, his shotgun readied. He stares down the barrel at Egor, eyes burning, a streak of blood on his cheek.

If Egor is surprised to see him, he doesn't show it. "Are they dead, then?"

"Yes."

"Every last one?"

"Yes." His voice is cold, iced over in a soldier's careful detachment.

"Impressive," says Egor. "I suppose they call you the sunshine sniper for a reason."

Asher blinks, lowering the barrel. "You knew who I was?"

"I suspected," admits Egor. "Your disappearance has caused quite a stir in certain circles. There's a bounty on your head, you know. A fairly sizable one, at that. There are rumors, too. I'm afraid they don't paint you in a very favorable light."

Asher pales. "You want the money? Is that it?"

"I'm only pointing out a fact. It's a rather large bounty. It would keep my research funded for a year, at least. Maybe more."

"Go ahead and call it in," says Asher. "See if I care. Parker, Zahar—get in the RV."

They don't argue, slipping out from the barn and racing for the vehicle. In action, it looks even worse than it did as a lawn ornament. The retractable awning hangs loose. There's a crack in the windshield. The body is off-color, fiberglass yellowed with age. The inside isn't much better. The windows are shuttered in bent vinyl blinds. The furniture is torn in places. Mold seeps out from under the fridge, discoloring the floor.

"It's disgusting in here," says Shea.

"I think it's homey," says Poppy, collapsing into the dinette. "Oh, hello, Kit. I didn't even see you there."

The door slams shut, sending the possum scuttling for cover. Asher climbs the shallow staircase in three short stomps, his face bloodless. There's a hunted look in his eyes as he takes hold of Shea's chin and angles her face toward his.

"Are you okay?"

She weasels out of his grasp. "I'm fine."

"Zahar?"

"I'm not dead," says Poppy, "but I would prefer not to do that again."

Asher zeros in on Shea. "That was some horrible listening back there."

"Yeah, well." She shrugs. "My ears don't work so good."

"Don't give me that bullshit. You should have followed orders."

"I've famously never been great at that," she reminds him hotly. "God, what is that smell? It reeks in here."

"That would be the mold," says Poppy cheerlessly. "Where's all our stuff?"

"In the back room." Asher slings off his shotgun and drops into the driver's seat. "And I raided the Van Haut kitchen. We should be good on food for a few days, at least."

"What about the bikes?" asks Shea.

Asher checks his mirrors. "No longer an option. You should take a seat, the suspension on this thing is crazy loose."

"What about Lys?"

His eyes flick to hers in the rearview. "Parker, will you *please* sit?"

"Not until you tell me where he is."

As if in answer to her question, the shuttered entrance to the back bedroom rattles with the full force of a body slammed against fiberglass. She sees now that the bifold doors have been bound with the same chains that held him in Egor van Haut's sunless basement.

"He's alive," says Asher.

"Will that hold him?"

"Let's hope. Now, sit. We've got a lot of miles to eat up before morning."

EIGHTEEN

Lysander

The ride in the camper's back bedroom is the worst Lysander has ever endured in his life.

Not because the suspension rattles his teeth. Not because sunlight pokes in pestilent pinpricks through the blinds. Not because everything smells wet and sweet, like mildew.

Because the last time he was in this camper, it was with his mother.

He thinks of Viola in the dead of summer, heat wrapping everything in an infernal sweat. He can still hear her voice, imbued with a false cheeriness that made him want to shout: *We're going to go north and see a friend of mine. Would you like that? It'll be fun. A road trip, just the two of us. He has a little boy about your age. I think you'll like him.*

There's a shallow laceration in his side. He lifts his shirt and jabs a finger at it, watching as his skin knits itself slowly back together. Distantly, he is aware of the trill of chains coming loose. The door opens a crack and a thin strip of yellow appears, broken by the broad-shouldered frame of a boy in an orange cap.

Lysander can't remember his name.

He pokes around in his head, irritable, and discovers he can't remember much of anything. His head is full of synapses, misfiring in sparks. Words and words and words and words. None of them his. None of them sane. All of them meaningless drivel, forced into his brain by his mother's ceaseless recitation. *Again, Oliver. Again, the sun isn't up yet.*

"All things burn with it," he says. "As with a flame."

The watchdog's scowl is so stark, Lysander mimics it without even trying.

"What did you say to me?"

"'Nameless,'" says Lysander. "By William Montgomerie."

The answering quiet knocks at his chest. Or maybe that's his heart. Maybe it's moments away from exploding. Maybe he'll take the whole place with him when it does. He blinks and sees a girl. Straw-colored hair and a knife in her hands. Blood under her boots. *Lys, look at me.*

He can't remember her name, either. It makes him feel like something vital has been torn out of him. Something black and blue and beating. Everything hurts.

"I don't know who William Montgomerie is," says the watchdog. He sounds annoyed.

"Unsurprising. You strike me as illiterate."

The watchdog's mouth quirks. "If you're cracking jokes, you must be feeling better."

"It wasn't a joke," he mutters, and crooks his elbow over his eyes. "Close the door. The light hurts."

The soldier obliges, slamming the door shut. The light snuffs out. Lysander feels the mattress sag as the watchdog collapses onto the bed beside him. He peers out from under his elbow and watches the soldier pluck his ball cap off his head and drop it over his face. *Asher*, he thinks. *Thorley*. His name flits back into Lysander's awareness like a moth.

"Don't even think about feeding," he says. "If you come anywhere near me, I'll open the blinds."

Lysander replaces his elbow without a word. He imagines ants are crawling through his brain—digging at the cavities of his face. He wants to claw his skin clean off. Wants to howl and thrash and tear.

Instead, he says, "You shot me."

"You'll be fine," comes Asher's mumbled response. "You're not dead."

"It is easy to be dead," mutters Lysander. "None wears the face you knew."

Mouthless dead. Charles Hamilton Sorley.

One more time, my little love. It's almost dawn.

"It creeps me out when you do that," says Asher. "Shut up for a little bit, I need to sleep."

Lysander is quiet as long as he can stand it, the suspension clunking horribly, his molars grinding down to dust.

Caving, he asks, "Who's driving?"

"Parker." Asher's voice slips from beneath his cap.

Where Asher's name skimmed into his subconscious, Shea's pierces it like an arrow. He sucks in a punctured breath. "She's hitting every fucking pothole in Pennsylvania."

Asher snorts, and then he's out, breathing deeply. He sleeps on his back, his throat exposed and his pulse slow. Lysander holds himself still and wonders if this is what it feels like to be trusted. He falls asleep counting Asher Thorley's heartbeat.

They've come to a stop by the time Asher wakes. The room is dark, the light at the edge of the blinds tinged red with a sunset. Lysander stands propped against the low-lying cabinets and untangles a Slinky he found stuffed in one of the drawers. *His* Slinky, the steel wire hopelessly jumbled. He waits for Asher to notice him. It doesn't take long. From beneath the cap slips a bone-weary sigh.

"Is there *anything* else you can do to occupy your time?"

Lysander pries the coils apart like an accordion. "You know what I find interesting?"

"Whatever it is, I'm sure it's deeply disturbing—"

"You haven't asked me about your sister since we left Mercy Ridge."

The Slinky trills shut. Asher lifts his cap off his face and peers out at Lysander from beneath. "Maybe you haven't noticed, but we've been under attack at every turn."

"That's not it," says Lysander. "I think you know your sister is dead."

The pause that follows is too long. Too damning. It takes Asher a beat to recover.

"If I really thought that, then what the hell am I doing here? Why would I desert my post and get a bounty put on my head in the process? Why would I follow you into the Gravewood on a suicide mission? Why would I give up *everything*?"

"I haven't figured that out yet," admits Lysander.

"Yeah?" Asher drops his cap back onto his face. "Well, do me a favor and leave me alone until you do."

They're deep in the devil's backbone, surrounded on all sides by towering loblolly and ancient red maples. A former state park, gravel lot shot through with spurge. Through the windshield, Lysander can just make out the last of the daylight glinting off a metal slide. Shea perches on the bottom, the crossbow in her lap.

Waiting for the last of the sun to fade, Lysander drops into the dinette alongside Poppy. She shifts to the side without ever once looking up, too absorbed in her knitting. There's no discernible pattern to the garment in her lap. The colors clash. The yarn is knotted. It reminds him of his mother's cross-stitching. He watches her complete a row before he speaks.

"Tell me about Asher's sister."

Poppy glances up at him, her brow crinkled in concentration. "What do you want to know?"

"Anything," he says. "Everything. What was she like?"

Poppy considers the question before answering, "She's a lot like her brother, actually."

"A giant stick-in-the-mud?"

"No," says Poppy, stifling a smile. "Assertive."

"Ah."

"But in a protective way, you know? She'd do anything for her friends."

Lysander drums his fingers on the laminate. "And you don't think she ran?"

"I *know* she didn't." It twists out of her, sharp, and Lysander studies her anew.

"You love her."

It's not a question. He can see it in the color of her cheeks. He can hear it in the stutter of her pulse. He can sense it, pinching the air in her throat. He waits as she scrambles for something to say, her fingers knotting in the fabric.

"I haven't told her so, but yes. I think I might."

"What is that like?"

"Loving someone?" Her eyes lift to his. "That's an impossible question. I don't have an answer."

"I don't believe you," he says. "You're a know-it-all."

Her nose crinkles. "You know, some people might consider that rude."

"It isn't rude, it's true. You have an answer for everything."

"That's hyperbolic," says Poppy. "I don't know *everything*. And love isn't an exact science. There are no set parameters. It looks different for everyone."

Outside, the sun has set. Moonlight trickles down in broad, leafy shafts. From where Lysander sits, he can just make out the lines of Shea. She's on her feet, gazing up at the cosmos. Sometimes, in his very worst moments, he thinks he'd like to black out all the stars—cast the whole of the universe in darkness so there's nowhere she can go where he isn't. But whatever that is, it isn't love.

At least, he doesn't think so.

"That's a hideous scarf, by the way," he tells Poppy, heading for the door.

Her smile is small. "It is, isn't it? I've decided it's the perfect metaphor."

"For what?"

"For love, I guess."

He looks back at her, half in and half out. Cold careens in through the crack. "Love is a scarf full of holes?"

"Love is hideous."

And there they are again—thoughts of Shea, pulsing through his head. Occupying far too much space in his brain. *We're doing an ugly thing.* He hopes she never thinks about anything half as much as he thinks about her. He wouldn't wish this feeling on his enemy.

"See?" he says, smirking up at Poppy. "You did have an answer."

He finds Shea seated on a swing, its steel joists overgrown in wood sorrel. The November air is warmer this far south, but she's layered as it gets. She's stolen his hoodie and it peeks out from beneath her flannel, hood up and sleeves overlong, the cuffs engulfing her hands so only the pale buds of her fingers are visible. Her cross gleams silver at her throat.

It's meant to ward him off. A holy relic, intended to burn. It doesn't matter that it's only superstition—it could sear him to bone, and he'd still be out here, lowering his skeleton into the vacant swing beside her. Silently, he wills her to look at him. She doesn't, even when the chains grind noisily beneath him. He kicks out his feet and joins her in looking up at the stars, feeling resentful.

"Barry Bonds," he says, when the quiet begins to corrode his patience.

She blinks over at him. "What?"

"He holds the career record with seven hundred sixty-two home runs." There's a stick on the ground and he leans forward to swipe it up, poking holes in the dirt with the stunted end. "I don't really care about baseball. It was Nel's thing, but there wasn't a whole lot else to do out in the middle of nowhere, Pennsylvania."

When she's quiet, he continues.

"There was a ghost town about three miles out from the farm. Blackburgh. There'd been an outbreak a few years back, and the watch came through and cleared it out. No one was left. At night, we'd hop the fence and go through the houses. We'd find all kinds of shit, most of it useless. Nel liked baseball cards, so that's what we took."

She's looking right at him, her temple pressed up against the rusted links, and there's no light in her eyes at all. The look on her face is a fist around his guts. Her wool cap is askew beneath his hood, her nose nipped pink by the cold. She picks at a run in her stockings, her skirt ruffling in the wind.

"Did you Turn together?" she asks. "You and Nel?"

He doesn't want to answer that question. He thinks of Nel racing out of the pine thicket behind the farm—tripping over himself with excitement, his chin wet and pupils blown. All these years later, Lysander can still feel the panic in his chest: *What the hell did you do?*

That memory brings another—the uneasy quiet of Nel's dormered room, the smell of bile permeating the air as he pushed his fingers down Nel's throat. *Come on. Come on, Van Haut. Fuck. Fuck!* A rapid-fire knock on the door sent him lurching to his feet. Nel stayed down, curled in on himself in a small, dark c. He didn't get up.

On the swing next to him, Shea is still waiting for an answer. It isn't fair of him, and he knows it—the way he covets everything of hers, and offers nothing in return. But all his secrets are damaged, disfigured by a lifetime in the dark. She won't like them.

On a whim, he reaches into his pocket and pries out a set of batteries. A half dozen alkaline stars glitter in his palm. All the cosmos he can give her.

"Here," he says, more vehemently than he meant to.

She peers warily into his hand, like he's offered her a live snake. "What's this for?"

"For the feed. Back in the Catskills."

Her starless eyes flick to his. She doesn't move. Doesn't speak. That fist around his guts tightens until it hurts. He's doing everything right. He's playing by the rules. *Her* rules. *Her* game. And she's looking at him like he's struck her.

"Take the batteries, Shea."

"I don't want to."

"Why not?"

"Because you're making it feel cheap."

He searches her face, confusion rattling in his chest. "This is how we've always done things. Blood for batteries. I'm giving you this because I owe you payment—"

"Payment," she echoes, and the look on her face shuts him up immediately.

She launches to her feet and he follows, frustration radiating through him. Even his best intentions come out spoiled, withering before they can blossom into something worthwhile.

"That's not what I meant."

"*Payment,*" she says again. She spits it out like poison. "For services rendered?"

He cuts her a look. "Don't do that."

"Like I'm a *whore*?"

"No." His patience is strained to breaking. "You know that's not what— Where are you going?"

She doesn't answer. She's storming away, veering off the road and into the cluster of wide red oaks ahead. He falls into a jog after her, pocketing the batteries as he goes.

"Shea, wait."

Her voice comes from somewhere just ahead. "I don't want to talk to you anymore."

"Fine. Just stay where I can see you." He ducks under a low-hanging branch just before it snaps back in his face. "Did you hear me? Shea? You can't— *Shit*. Shea!"

She's gone, swallowed by the wood. With a curse, he tails after her. The air here is sharp and cold, and the smell of turpentine clings to everything. The trees thicken, gathering close. He wedges himself sidelong between the boles, doing what he can to scent her in the dark. Cupping his hands to his mouth, he calls for her again. His voice catapults uselessly off the trees.

"Fuck!"

He falters to a stop, tuning his ears to the forest's deadly frequency. He listens to it breathe—to the primeval pulse of it, same as the pulse through his veins. Sticky. Slow. In the quiet, he hears the murmur of wind through the trees. The snap of a branch and the flit of an animal. The far-off sound of some small thing dying.

There, beneath it, is the hammering of a human heart. One he's memorized. And she's afraid.

He takes off running at a clip, shoving through a thicket of needled balsam and bursting into a wide, open clearing. The stars have been dulled by the clouds, blown in from the east. A storm is coming. He can feel it. The moon sits behind a screen of gray, the light sucked out of it.

In the middle of the clearing stands Shea.

"I'm sorry," he hears her cry. She's not speaking to him. She's looking out into the trees, transfixed by the gaped mouths of the ancient trunks, their limbs humanoid. Old oaks, the bones of their prey tangled in their branches. Ancient leshiye, hunting for their next meal. He wonders what it is Shea hears, calling from the dark. He doesn't have to wonder for long.

"Ellie, I'm sorry," she cries. "I'm looking, I swear."

He steps out in front of her, cutting off her view of the forest. "Shea."

She stares clean through him, the vision dancing in her head. Her cheeks are wet, her eyes fractured in tears. He pinches her chin between his thumb and forefinger, lifting her face to his.

"*Shea,*" he says again, firmer than before. "Look at me."

Her stare pulls to his. Her pupils are blown, her gaze unfocused. Still caught in the forest's thrall, her expression contorts into one of fear. She moves with surprising quickness, shifting so that Asher's crossbow sits flat between them, the tip of the stake jabbing neatly into his sternum.

"Get back," she whispers. "Get away."

In the quiet of the clearing, he hears her heart give a single loud thump. *Hideous*, he thinks. He has never coveted anything so badly in his life. Reaching a hand between them, he adjusts the crossbow until the stake sits between his fourth and fifth rib.

"If you're planning to shoot, you'd better not miss."

Something in his voice calls her back. She blinks up at him, her eyes clearing. Slowly, recognition crawls into her features. She doesn't lower the crossbow.

"I saw her," she whispers. "I saw Ellie in the woods."

"It wasn't her. It was a trick of the trees."

"It *looked* like her."

"It wasn't," he repeats. "And you know it."

Each time he draws breath, the stake digs into his chest. Just a little. Just enough to make him shiver. On the other end of the weapon, Shea is his mirror. Her hands shake, and not from the cold. Her knuckles are white against the foregrip.

Quietly, she says, "Egor van Haut said you and I are going to destroy each other."

It hurts to breathe. "He's probably right."

"Doesn't that scare you?"

"It terrifies me."

It's the most he can give her—a jagged confession. He can hardly tell her the truth—that she's already destroyed him. His heart feels as though its clawing out of his chest to get to her.

It will, before the end.

"What if you Turned me?" she asks, and he should have seen the question coming. "Would we destroy each other then?"

He doesn't want to talk about this. Not here. Not now. Not when he can hear the nearby burble of a stream, its running water laced with Rot. Not when he thinks he might have changed his mind.

"Maybe," he says thinly. "Maybe not."

"So then Turn me, and let's find out."

"Not yet."

"Why?"

"Because." His voice is gruffer than he'd meant for it to be. "I'm not ready."

Whatever she sees in his face makes her drop the subject. It's a small mercy. She lowers the crossbow and he staggers forward as though he'd been leaning all his weight upon it, crowding her without thought—swallowing up her space until there's nothing left between them but a shredded breath and a sliver of dark.

"Your heart is beating so fast," she whispers.

"So is yours."

He can smell blood somewhere on her, as if she nicked something while stumbling through the forest. The heat of it—metal and salt—brings the hunger frothing to the surface, makes him feel like he's splitting at the seams. He can't tell if he wants to sink his teeth into her throat or press his mouth to her pulse—forget her name and drain her dry, or kiss her until he forgets his own.

"Do it," she says, and he realizes that he's said it all out loud, muttering his private inner monologue like one of his mother's recitations. He feels half mad, the last shreds of his composure going up in smoke as she rises onto her toes beneath him and whispers, "Kiss me."

It isn't real, the way she's looking at him, no light in her eyes at all. It's his venom in her blood. It's his teeth at her wrist. The real Shea Parker is pining after a boy named Asher Thorley. She lives in Little

Hill with her mother. Her cheeks are freckled from the sun. She doesn't spare a thought for what lives beyond the trees.

"You don't mean that," he says.

"How do you know?"

Her breath blooms over his lips, slips between his teeth. He wants to do it. He does. It would be easy to give in. He turns his head instead, screwing his eyes shut as sense prevails.

"Coward," whispers Shea.

He'll take it. He'll take cowardice over this—this awful, synthetic thing between them. This knowledge that they are doomed to fail. The snap of pine snags his focus, and he opens his eyes just in time to witness Asher barreling toward them. For once, Lysander is relieved to see him. He falls back as Asher catches himself against his knees, doubled over and breathing hard.

"Holy shit. I've been looking everywhere for the two of you."

"Your timing is impeccable as always, Sunshine." Lysander flashes him a grin he doesn't mean, ignoring the wary look Asher cuts his way. "I'll do the noble thing and take the next watch. I could use the air."

He leaves them there without another word, slinking off into the trees. Overhead, the sky is devoid of stars. Just how he wanted it. He moves beneath them, unmoored, haunted by Van Haut's final warning: *She's a cataclysm, Oliver. You will not survive her.*

NINETEEN

Shea

A storm hits midway through the following day, bringing a wall of freezing rain that drives them off the road. They shelter inside the mouth of a twin-bore tunnel, watching the sleet turn the pavement slick as glass. The mood in the RV is tense. It's as if Shea's fight with Lys has put a crack in the foundations. The very air feels tremulous. As though at any moment, this unsteady thing they've built might all come crashing down around their ears.

Shea passes the time in the corner dinette, loading and reloading the crossbow until her fingers are raw. Poppy sits in the front passenger seat, knitting her scarf and singing along to an old mixtape she found in the glove compartment. The sound of classic rock floods the little space, driving out some of the day's dreariness. Outside in the tunnel, Asher watches the road.

Lys stays shut away in the dark. He doesn't speak to anyone at all.

It's late afternoon when Shea heads out to swap places with Asher. The sound of the rain is loud against the overpass as she takes her spot against the wall. The stone is cool to the touch, the air thick and wet. For a while, Asher stays behind, cleaning the barrel of his gun with a slender boring brush. She hugs her knees to her chest and peers over at him, watching him work.

"Is this what you pictured?" she finally asks. "When you said we'd leave Little Hill someday?"

He stops scrubbing. "Not really, no."

"Me neither." She fiddles with the ring on her necklace. "Out of curiosity, what *did* you picture?"

He's quiet for too long. Longer. Eventually, he sighs. "You know how my dad is. He runs the house like a war general. It's not that he's— He's not an angry person, he just doesn't like disorder."

It feels like the understatement of the century. Whenever Shea and Poppy visited, they'd leave their shoes at the door and follow Camellia upstairs on the tips of their toes, stealing like ghosts through the halls. The Parker house may have been silent to Shea, but it never *felt* silent. It felt full. Full of her father's music, scratching on the record player. Full of her mother's singing. Full of laughter and mess and happy, warm disorder. In contrast, the Thorley house was a powder keg. Alder Thorley had very little patience for disruptions.

She thinks of an April day eight years past, when she and Camellia broke one of her mother's vases. They'd been using it as a cauldron, mixing yellow merrybell petals into a maidenhair stew. At some point, they began quarreling over the ladle. The vase went crashing to the floor.

Asher found them seconds before his father did.

He took the blame, staying behind to sweep up the scattered petals and chunks of ceramic. He'd come to school the following day with his knuckles split, the skin raw. He never said a word about it.

"Wherever I end up," he says now, "it'll be different."

"Loud," suggests Shea. "Chaotic. Messy."

He cracks a smile. "A pigsty."

She matches his smile with one of her own. "We're off to a great start, then. The RV is disgusting. Your dad would hate it."

"He'd light it on fire," Asher agrees.

"In all fairness, it *should* be lit on fire."

"I don't know." He tips his head back against the stone. "It's growing on me."

A companionable silence settles between them. She shuts her eyes and listens to the rain.

"Asher?"

"Yeah?"

"You're a good brother."

The quiet that follows stretches to the point of unbearability. She opens her eyes and finds him watching her, an unreadable look on his face.

"I'm trying to be," he says.

When he's gone, Shea passes the time stacking loose chunks of asphalt into teetering cairns, feeling the hum of the rain in the pavement beneath her. Night steals in like a thief, turning the tunnel dark as pitch. At some point, she looks up and finds Lys standing there, his hands in his pockets.

He doesn't say a word, and so neither does she. They switch places in silence, giving each other as wide a berth as they can manage. When she looks back at him, he's seated in a jagged semicircle of stone, quietly examining her handiwork.

Throat tight, she heads back into the RV. The air here is warmer, but only just. There's a chill in her bones she can't quite shake. She finds Poppy in the booth, studiously examing a jar. It takes Shea several heartbeats to comprehend what it is she's seeing—the specimen container from Van Haut's lab, a human fetus curled within.

"*Ew.* I thought I saw you nick that."

"It looks like him," says Poppy, balancing her chin on her fist. "Lysander. Don't you think?"

"This fetus looks like Lys?"

"You know what I mean. Look at its eyes."

She does. Its stare is black all the way through. It gives the fetus a vaguely cryptid appearance, like it's some sort of changeling. Like if it had lived, it might have grown into something wild.

"None of the others have eyes like that," says Poppy. "Like Lysander."

"Except for this fetus."

"*Shea.*" Poppy groans. "I'm being serious. Egor van Haut called him a marvel. There's obviously something going on. I mean, he has horns. A-and claws. Don't you think—"

There's a sound outside, and she falls silent, watching the door. It stays shut.

"I keep thinking about what that guy was chanting," says Poppy. "The one in the kitchen. Do you remember? He said something about the age of the beast."

Shea had nearly forgotten. "That was weird."

"It was more than weird. It sounded like he was praying to Lysander. Like he's some sort of god."

"Lys isn't a god."

"*I* know that," says Poppy. "But he's keeping things from us. And with everything that's happened, I'm worried not knowing the truth might get us into trouble once we get to the Flatwood. I mean, Lysander has asked Asher to kill someone for him. That's not exactly a small favor."

"It isn't a favor, it's an exchange. Lys is looking for Ellie."

"But he isn't," argues Poppy. "We've been on the road for days, and we've barely searched for her at all."

An ice-cold guilt pools in Shea's lungs. She thinks of Asher's silence in the tunnel, the cryptic expression on his face. The way it looked a little bit like resignation.

Poppy sits back and rubs at her eyes. "This isn't a search party. It's an assassination mission, and no one has stopped to ask *why* Lysander wants the mark dead."

"Paris Keeling has sent multiple people to try and kill me," points out Shea.

"Yes, but he wanted Paris dead before that. This power struggle didn't start with you, but it's nearly gotten you killed on more than one occasion. What if the next hit is successful? What if you don't survive it? What if I lose you *and* Ellie?"

It's the first time Poppy has come even remotely close to admitting what Shea has long suspected: that no one is bothering to look for Camellia because she's already dead. It feels like a light has guttered out. On the table, the fetus stares blackly up at Shea.

"I'm not saying Egor was in the right," says Poppy, "but it's clear he's intelligent. If he says we're on the cusp of causing some sort of catastrophic chain reaction, don't you think we should at least try and figure out what that is?"

Outside the RV, Shea can just make out Lys in the dark. He's seated against the stone, his hood pulled up and his knee bouncing. Restless, the way she's restless. Electric, the way she's electric. Her heart tithes a beat, and it's as if he's heard it. His knee stills. His eyes find hers through the glass. Quickly, she ducks down into the booth, tugging Poppy with her as she goes.

"God." She buries her face in her knees. "What's wrong with me?"

"Do you want me to say it," asks Poppy, "or was that rhetorical?"

"Rhetorical," Shea grumbles into her kneecaps.

Everything feels suddenly unendurable. If Camellia was here, she'd force them to grin and bear it. To dump it all out into the open, and then laugh themselves sick over how sideways everything has gone. But Camellia isn't here. Camellia is gone. And so Shea stuffs it away.

"One of us needs to talk to him," says Poppy. "You know what they say about ignorance."

Shea lifts her head from her knees. "It's bliss?"

"*Is* that what they say?" Poppy drops her head onto Shea's shoulder, nestling in close. "My mom always said it was the root of misfortune."

Eventually, Poppy climbs into the cab to sleep. Shea stays awake a while longer, loading and reloading the crossbow until it's a reflex. Until her finger callus and her knuckles ache. She's conscious, all the while, of Lys watching her through the window.

He'd promised to Turn her. That was the deal they'd struck—a cure for her mother in exchange for a lifetime in the dark. She'd resigned herself to her fate, back at Mercy Ridge. She's ready. She's willing.

And she can't figure out why he keeps yanking the offer away.

Maybe he doesn't want this anymore. Maybe he finally sees that it wasn't courage that drove her to his doorstep that first fateful night, but desperation. Maybe he'll leave her behind the very first moment he can.

Everyone else has.

She spends the better part of an hour trying to garner the courage to go out and confront him. It's near midnight when she gives up. Rising into a stretch, she heads for the bedroom. Asher is already there, fast asleep on his stomach, one arm draped off the edge. Doing her best not to wake him, she crawls tentatively into bed. He doesn't stir. She lies there, restless, staring out into the open cabin.

She's still awake when Poppy takes over the watch, sliding bleary-eyed from her perch. Lys appears a few minutes later, taking in the sleeping arrangements through a shuttered gaze.

"I hope you don't expect me to be a martyr like Thorley. I'm not built for the floor."

He collapses onto the bed before she can answer, rolling onto his back alongside her. He lies there quietly, massaging the skin around his horns like he's rubbing away a headache. She thinks of the man at Van Haut's, his dying words staining the air: *From the fount of the forest comes the age of the beast.* She watches Lys in silence, wrestling with indecision, Poppy's voice urging her on. *Ask him. Do it.*

"None of the other Mercy Boys are like this," she starts. "Like you, I mean."

His mouth sharpens into a wry smile. "Perfect?"

"No."

"Pretty?"

"Lys."

"Prodigious?"

"A pain in the ass," grunts Asher sleepily, and Lys grins into the dark. With Asher awake, the opportunity dissipates. Irritable, he mutters, "Both of you shut up and go to sleep. We have another long drive tomorrow."

Shea wakes in the predawn dark to the smell of something burning. Panicked, she tries to sit up, and finds herself trapped. In the shuttered dark of the little back bedroom, it takes her several seconds to make sense of her surroundings. She freezes, swallowing around her heartbeat. Her head is nestled against Lys's sternum, her hand splayed flat against his stomach.

It isn't this that's prevented her from rising—it's Asher. His chest is a wall at her back, warm and solid. His arm belts heavily across her middle. She's pinned in place, her legs mixed up in a jumble of four others. Her pulse kicks into an all-out gallop.

In the midst of her panic, she becomes slowly—mortifyingly—aware of their audience. Poppy stands at the end of the bed, smiling brightly down at her, a wedge of something resembling a rock cradled in her oven mitt.

"Great news," she announces. "The oven works. Bad news, I burned the scones."

The sound of her voice sends Asher rocketing upright. He takes all the heat with him, a pink flush crawling up his throat as he, too, takes horrified stock of the sleeping arrangements. Newly freed, Shea pries herself off Lys as carefully as she can. It's too little, too late. He's wide awake, his stare flat and immutable.

"What's the occasion?"

"It's November twelfth," says Poppy, as if it should have been obvious. When Lys only stares, her smile grows. "Didn't you know? Today is Shea's birthday."

What follows is a mostly silent breakfast of burned-black scones, during which Shea does her level best to make eye contact with no one while Poppy conducts an overly enthusiastic solo of the happy birthday song. After, they gather around the dinette and lay out an old road atlas. Lys hangs back in the shadow of the bedroom, his expression indecipherable.

"Here's where we are," says Asher, circling a spot with a pen. "And here's where we need to be. It's two days' drive to the Flatwood. Three, if the weather stays this bad."

From his spot in the open door, Lys makes a disapproving sound. "We're approaching Keeling territory. It won't be safe to stick to the woods for much longer."

"Which puts us on civilian roads." Asher tucks the pen behind his ear. "I don't love that."

"Why not?" asks Shea. "Back at Mercy Ridge, you were the one who wanted to stick to the coastal highways."

"That was before he knew there was a bounty on his head," guesses Lys. It's the first time he's spoken to her all morning. She peers over at him and finds him looking back, his stare enigmatic.

"That's not it." Asher sounds distracted, his focus lasered on the map. "If we hit a checkpoint, they might search the vehicle. Lysander's kind are contractually bound to the forest. If he's out, he's a containment risk. Watchmen will have orders to execute him on sight."

"Aw, Sunshine." Lys's grin is wolfish. "You *do* care."

But Shea has caught onto something else entirely. "Contractually? I thought it was sunlight that kept you bound to the Gravewood. I didn't know there was some sort of written code."

"Of course you didn't," says Lys. "Just another example of the public school system failing our young minds. When we're done here, you should write a strongly worded letter to Hornbeam."

Asher skews a look in his direction. "You're in rare form today."

"It was a hell of a way to wake up."

Suddenly, they're all thinking about it again. An uncomfortable silence swells.

"It was Paris," says Poppy, swallowing a rock-hard chunk of scone. "Wasn't it? He's the one who negotiated the contract. Is that why you want him dead?"

It seems like a stretch to Shea, but Lys doesn't deny it. "Among other things, yes."

At the table, Asher looks as grim as ever. He stares down at the map, rubbing a hand along his jaw. A light scruff has grown in during their time on the road. It's another marker of how much time they've lost. How far they've gone from home. When he left for basic, he couldn't even grow a beard.

"What about you?" asks Shea.

He doesn't look at her. "What about me?"

"What happens if we're pulled over at a checkpoint and you're recognized?"

It's a beat before he answers. "I'd be brought in before a tribunal. There's a pretty lengthy process. A lot of paperwork. I'd be okay."

"He's lying," says Lys. "I've heard what they do to deserters at the garrisons. I'd be getting the better end of the deal."

"Then we stick to the wooded roads," says Shea.

Asher makes a face. "Parker, I don't know if—"

"It's not a question." She snatches the map off the table. "We'll handle it as it comes. We've handled everything else Keeling's thrown at us so far."

He rubs at his eye, looking exhausted. "Barely."

"I don't care. I'm not losing another person."

Camellia's name throbs in the quiet. Shea thinks of her face in the forest, bitten away by Rot, her bones showing through. Already a ghost. *Did you forget me? Are you even looking? This is your fault. Yours.* Her throat tightens. She casts a quick glance toward Poppy and finds her peering back, her smile wobbly. Somehow, the acceptance in her eyes is so much worse than the false sense of hope she's been carrying around for weeks.

We'll find her, Shea wants to promise. *We'll do whatever it takes.*

But she doesn't know if it's true, and so she says nothing at all.

TWENTY

Shea

They're on the road within the hour, sticking to the mountain roads. The rain doesn't let up. It gets heavier, bringing with it a wall of fog that turns the mountain pass to soup. They make camp at dusk, stopping for the night at an old fieldstone church buried in boxwood. A soaring Gothic bell tower sits like a spindle against the sky, its turrets glazed in sleet.

"This'll work," says Asher, folding himself over the wheel in his efforts to peer out the windshield. "I don't like the idea of spending another night on the road, and it doesn't look like anyone's been here in years."

Even so, they canvass the chapel in pairs, searching from top to bottom for signs of squatters. When there's nothing to be found, they congregate in the sanctuary. Battered by the rain, moonlight falls in through the stained glass in colorful caustics. They build a fire on the carpeted altar, burning strips of paper in an offering bowl filled with sand. Once it's grown to a heat-giving blaze, they gather around it, their backs against the pews, sharing the last of the scones between them.

"You're a Scorpio," notes Lys, his arms draped over bent knees. "What a coincidence."

His tone makes Shea feel defensive, though she can't say why. "What makes it a coincidence?"

"Nothing." His eyes glimmer blackly in the firelight. "Just interesting timing."

Her belly full, Shea closes her eyes and listens to the patter of rain against the windows. She used to drive herself crazy, wondering if anyone else heard the rain the way she did—if she was missing out on something beautiful, mistaking her own stilted perception for loveliness. Now, if she holds herself very still, she can almost pretend she's back home, sitting by the fire with her parents, warm and dry while a storm rages outside. She wouldn't resent it, not ever again.

"Do you remember your thirteenth birthday?" asks Poppy suddenly. "Your mom had Ellie and me over for cake, but there was that snowstorm and we got trapped at your house."

"I remember," says Shea, glad to have something else to talk about. "Thorley had to walk a mile through the blizzard to get Ellie. He was so mad."

"I didn't come for Ellie," says Asher.

The fire pops, flinging embers skyward. The memory is a cloudy dandelion, seedlings knocked loose. Shea and Poppy had spent that snowy afternoon reenacting scenes from *A Midsummer Night's Dream*, Camellia directing the entire production with relish. Shea had been cast as lovesick Hermia and draped in spare bedsheets, a chaplet of dried mistletoe set atop her head. At Camellia's instruction, she'd gone to fetch a jar for the love potion. She'd drawn up short at the sight of Asher in the foyer.

"Your mom let me in," he'd said. "I think she's getting me a slice of cake."

"Oh. That's good. She made way too much, as usual." Her face had gone hot. She felt supremely ridiculous, wrapped in sheets, a Christmas garland slipping into her eyes. Down the hall, she could hear Camellia and Poppy giggling. "You can stay, if you want."

"That's okay. The snow's supposed to get pretty bad. My mom wants Ellie home before then." He pawed at the back of his neck, looking nervous. "I, uh—made you something."

Her chest warmed. "You did?"

"Yeah, it's here somewhere, hold on." He drew a sleek, silver ring from his pocket and dropped it into her outstretched hands. "It's nothing special—just an old spoon."

"I love it," she whispered. "Thank you."

His cheeks dimpled in a smile. "Happy birthday, Parker."

Now, she folds her fingers over the ring, feeling it clink softly against her grandmother's cross. She can feel Lys's eyes glued to her hand. Next to her, Asher pokes wordlessly at the fire, coaxing it higher.

"I think I'll try and sleep a little," says Poppy, covering a yawn. "The three of you were too busy snuggling last night to relieve me at the watch."

"Poppy," hisses Shea.

"Well, it's true." She stands, gathering Kit in her arms. "Happy birthday, Shea. Next year, you, me, and Ellie will celebrate somewhere a little less damp."

It comes out empty. A hollow platitude.

Shea's heart feels as though it's been nailed to the wall.

She tries for a smile anyway. "It's a date."

"Don't go too far," calls Asher as Poppy departs.

She hums in response, her footfalls dulled by the carpet. They're left alone, the fire dying.

"Does she always say exactly what she's thinking?" asks Lys.

"Always," say Asher and Shea in unison.

Lys's answering smile is faint. He tips his head back against the pew, his throat exposed. His skin is veined in dark, swollen tributaries forking along his jaw. Starving, like always. Asher sees it, too.

"You should feed," he says.

Lys peers at him beneath heavy lids. "Should I?"

"You took a pretty hard hit the other day—"

"When you shot me."

"—and you lost a lot of blood."

"Again," says Lys thinly, "when you *shot me*."

Asher tosses down his stick. "Will you give me a break? I'm trying to fix it."

Lys lifts a brow. "Is that what's happening?"

"You can't starve all the way to Florida," says Asher. "And I don't know why, but it's becoming increasingly clear you won't hunt."

Lys stares at him, contemplative. "Maybe I'm lazy."

"Among other things," Asher mutters, rolling up his sleeve. "Just don't make me regret this, okay?"

Slowly, Lys's eyes travel to Shea. She sits cross-legged on the other side of the fire, her skin pebbled, her scars itching. Wishing for all the wrong things.

"He's right," she says. "You have to feed. It's him or me."

Pick me, some small, twisted part of her begs. The part that craves. The part that wants him to *need* her the way she needs him. She stifles it, but it's too late. He's seen it—in her face, perhaps, or else her eyes—the hunger that poisons the well of whatever this is between them. Something akin to disgust curdles his lip and he turns away from her, craning his neck until it cracks.

"Looks like it's you, Sunshine," he says. "Hold out your wrist."

Asher proffers his forearm, skin bare and unblemished. She watches, breath held, as Lys takes hold of Asher's arm. His black eyes lift to hers as he sinks his teeth deep, breaking skin. Asher sucks in a single, pained gasp.

"Shit," he breathes. "That hurts."

Lys's grip tightens and he pulls deep, his swallow loud in the cathedral quiet. Directly in front of him, Asher is his stark converse. He gathers the dark as it leaves Lys, his chest heaving, his pupils dilating wide enough to engulf his irises entire. All the while, his focus never strays. He watches Lys, his lids heavy and his jaw slack, wincing when Lys finally pulls free. Fingers flexing, he brings his wrist close for inspection. An angry half-moon bite mars his skin. Blood seeps freely from the wound. He presses a thumb to a puncture, frowning slightly.

"One of the first things they teach us in basic is how to identify a bite," he says. "Two punctures means it was a clinical feed. Quick and dirty, no connection. It's the victims with a full impression that we flag. It means they've been marked. There's a bond."

He lifts his eyes to Lys, who has gone steadily quieter as he spoke. "You marked me?"

"You shot me," says Lys.

Asher huffs out a laugh and then winces, shutting his eyes. "God. Everything's spinning."

Lys tongues the last of the blood from his lip. "That'll stop."

"I feel like I'm going to be sick."

"That'll stop, too."

Asher thumps back against the pew, his cap shading his eyes. Lifting his chin, he peers out at Shea from beneath the brim, his skin sheened in sweat and his eyes glazed gold. She wonders if this is what she looks like to Lys—dazed and unfocused, a fever sweating out of her.

Untended, the fire burns low. It's a long time before anyone speaks.

"You looked like a goddess," says Asher.

Shea stills. "What?"

"On your birthday—the year I gave you that ring. I'd just come in from the snow, and you were standing right there, dressed in white. You had these green leaves in your hair."

"Mistletoe." Her mouth feels like cotton. "It was mistletoe."

"I know. I remember, because I panicked. I kept thinking, *You're supposed to kiss a girl if you see her standing under mistletoe.*"

"Oh." Her heart is racing. Dumbly, because she can think of nothing clever to say, she adds, "I was Hermia."

Asher's brows lift. "Hmm?"

"From *Midsummer Night's Dream*," says Lys. He's watching them too astutely, his eyes a pale, clouded blue. "It's a play, by Shakespeare. *William* Shakespeare."

"I *know* who Shakespeare is," says Asher, defensive.

"I'm only trying to help." There's a beat of quiet—as painful as any Shea has ever endured—and then Lys adds, "Hermia was in love with Lysander, incidentally."

Of all the things he could have said, this feels like the worst. Shea has never wanted so badly to curl in on herself and disappear. It worsens tenfold when Asher peers thoughtfully across the fire and asks, "Are you?"

Her heart misses several beats at once. "Am I what?"

"In love with him?"

The dark of the cathedral shuts up around her. She can feel Lys's eyes boring a hole in the side of her face. She doesn't look at him. She can't.

"It's okay if you are," says Asher. "I've decided it makes sense to me."

Her stomach tightens. "What does?"

"This."

The word throbs horribly between them, both vague enough to be meaningless and succinct enough to mean everything.

"You don't mean that," says Shea. "It's the bite."

"You think so? Because I'm not so sure. It all comes back to you. It's always been you. You're the reason I became a ranger. You're the reason I came home. It's like—it's like you're the center of my universe. No matter how far out I go, I keep looping back around to you."

Her heart squeezes painfully. Next to her, Lys looks wary. "What do you mean by that, exactly?"

Asher's gaze lifts to Lys. "By what?"

"That whole tangent." He drops his voice from a tenor to a

baritone. "'You're the reason I came home.' I thought you came home to find your sister."

"Leave him alone," says Shea. "It's just the venom talking."

"Are we sure?"

"*Yes*. Back off. He'll wish he hadn't said all of that in the morning."

"Is that what happens to you?" Lys's eyes slide to hers. "You regret everything in the morning?"

Her cheeks heat. "Sometimes."

"But you come back anyway." He seems so like a boy—all Oliver, warm and open and unguarded—that it hurts to look at him. It's harder to excuse his cruelty this way, when there's no trace of the forest in him. "Over and over, you come back. Why?"

She hears what he isn't saying—what he isn't brave enough to ask.

Is it real? Or is it the venom in her blood?

"I don't know," she whispers.

"I don't know, either," says Lys. "And it's making me sick."

Outside, the rain slows. Only a few red embers remain in the bowl. They're pitched in near-total dark. Exhausted, Shea climbs over the altar and collapses against the pew alongside Asher, letting her head drop against his shoulder. He sighs, half asleep, and rests his cheek atop her head.

"I feel horrible already," he mutters.

"You'll feel worse in the morning."

"Can't wait."

A few minutes pass, and then Lys drops down on her right. His knee bumps up against hers. He doesn't move it away. *This*, said

Asher. *This*, she thinks. They watch the last of the embers cool to black. Slowly, Asher's breathing deepens.

"I'll keep watch," says Lys. "You should get some rest."

She does. For once, her sleep is dreamless. The rain sounds like static.

She doesn't yearn for home.

TWENTY-ONE

Shea

The following day is sunless.

The whole of the church is blanketed in a murky dark, the shadows steeped in blue. Shea finds Asher in the rectory, stretching out an ache in his tricep, a cup full of sunflower seeds on the pulpit beside him. He clocks her approach, glancing quickly away.

"Look, Parker, I was out of my mind last night. I said a lot of—"

"It's okay," she rushes to say. "We don't have to talk about it."

"Okay." His throat bobs in a swallow. He looks as cautious as she's ever seen him. "Are we good? You and me?"

"We've never been better."

Her voice is saturated in false cheer, and she can tell by the way he looks at her that he doesn't quite believe it. She's not sure she does, either. Everything feels knocked out of alignment. She watches as he falls to stretching out his quadriceps, one hand pressed flat against the wall. The light—what little there is—seems to cling to him. Anointing him so that he looks silver all over. The morning is humid, the air thick. He's shed his outer layers, and Lys's bite is stark against his forearm.

"There was a tick on me when I woke up," he says when he feels her watching. "It had about nine hundred legs."

"That number seems high."

"Does it?" He casts a wary gaze skyward. "This place is overrun with bugs. I found a silverfish in the bathroom sink this morning. I don't think they want us here."

He's making light of it, or trying to. It doesn't land the way it might have, back home in Little Hill. Back before she uprooted everything. Back before he followed her into the forest.

"I was wrong," she blurts out. "I do want to talk about it."

He stops what he's doing, his eyes flicking toward her. "Oh."

"It's just—last night, you said I was the reason you became a ranger."

"I did say that, didn't I?"

"You did."

"I thought maybe I dreamed it."

"I didn't even know you *were* a ranger," she says. "All this time, I thought you were standing on the top of a watchtower somewhere, bored out of your mind."

His smile is half-hearted. "You don't rack up a kill count like mine standing watch."

Suddenly, she understands. "You were hunting."

"I was, yes." She's never seen him look so uneasy. "The other day you said you didn't believe I missed my first shot. You were right. I didn't. I hit it, dead center. I hit it the next time, too. And every time after that. You remember how my dad was—he used to drag me out before school, show me how to load a rifle without making any sound. It's hard to hunt over a scrape when you can't get close to the trees. You learn to drop a buck at two hundred, three hundred yards. Let it wander out, wounded. Hitting a static target was nothing. Easy. I was a few weeks in when I got tapped for the field program."

"Because you're a good shot," says Shea. "Not because of me."

He grits his jaw, exhaling through his nose. She can feel him skirting the edges of the truth, taking the long way around. "My mom wrote me a letter. She asked me not to do it. She wanted me to serve my four years on the watch and get out. You're right—you don't see a lot of action up in a tower. But the rangers have boots on the ground. They're out there hunting hollows."

She frowns. "Hollows?"

"It's what we call people who don't survive the Turning. There's nothing left in them but Rot. You learn how to spot them pretty quick. They've got this look in their eyes, you know?"

She does know. She knows all too well. She thinks of sitting on the cellar steps and begging her mom to look at her. To *see* her. To remember the daughter who needed her, still. Every single plea was met with that same empty stare, as if Ivy Parker had gone into the Gravewood and had her insides scooped out.

Her next breath is a wet hiccup. She hadn't even realized she'd begun to cry. Embarassed, she swipes at her cheeks with the sleeves of her flannel, but it's too late. Asher has already seen. He looks quietly stricken, as if he knows just what she's thinking.

Clearing her throat, she asks, "What does any of this have to do with me?"

His shoulder lifts in a shrug. "High risk, high reward. The watch is four years of active duty. Fieldwork gets you out in two. I'd have been home by the time you graduated."

There is no word for the feeling in Shea's chest. No adjective to describe the way it rends her open.

"If you survived it."

"I would have survived it." His smile is rueful. "I made you a promise. And I'm a good shot."

"Oh." She spent all that time thinking he'd gone back on his word—that he'd left home and forgotten her, the way everyone else had. She'd hoarded her unsent letters, looking for her own way out. In the end, he wasn't the one who broke the promise. She was. "Asher—"

"We both did what we had to do," he says, before she can apologize. "And we've ended up exactly where we need to be."

And there it is again, pulsing between them—that everything and nothing feeling. *This.*

"Here?" she asks. "In an abandoned church in Virginia?"

"Sure," he says, though they both know that isn't what he meant. "It's not so bad. Although there was a spider in my boot when I got up this morning."

"They come inside when it rains."

He shudders. "Eugh."

"You know," she says, "for a trained assassin, you're kind of a baby about bugs."

This time, the smile he flicks her way is genuine.

This time, she can almost pretend everything is exactly how it used to be.

• • •

She spends the rest of the morning outside. Alone, and grateful for it for once. The air feels like wet wool. The grass is rimed in ice. It crunches underfoot as she follows a buried footpath out to the insular courtyard. It's a tiny, gated cemetery, the headstones worn flat. At the graveyard's center stands a stony angel, her arms outstretched, her sightless eyes weeping black mildew.

It's as good of a target as any. Shea practices nocking the stake before taking aim, her fingers stiff with cold. Summoning all the confidence she can muster, she lets the palisade fly. It veers left, into the trees. Frustrated, she loads another. She thinks about Asher, hitting the mark every time. Doing what he had to do to come home to her. This time, the stake glances off the tip of a wing.

All this time, her guilt has been slowly eating away at her. Today, it feels like she's been swallowed whole. She won't let herself feel sorry for it—that she did what she needed to do to take care of herself. The third shot scrapes over the angel's abdomen before falling to the grave beneath with a clatter that makes her see red.

"It's not a direct hit," says a voice from behind her. "But who knows? Maybe you nicked something vital."

She spins, crossbow notched, and finds Lys hovering under the shade of a black locust.

"You're getting faster," he says.

"I've had five hundred miles to practice. How long have you been watching me?"

"Long enough to be moderately impressed." His eyes are black again, no trace of white. He's gripping something tight in his fist. "There's a great view up in the bell tower."

She follows his gaze to the soaring wall of fieldstone. The belfry is dark, louvers shuttered. When she looks back down at him, he's staring again. If being looked at by Asher feels like stepping out into the sun, then being looked at by Lys feels like staring in a mirror. Like whatever wild thing writhes inside her lives in him, too.

"Why do you want Paris Keeling dead so badly?" she asks.

Amusement glimmers in his eyes. "It's a little early for all these questions, don't you think?"

"It's just one question."

"Not by my count. You've been interrogating Thorley all morning."

Heat crawls into her skin as she realizes he'd been listening. "That was a private conversation."

"Relax, Hermia. It's nothing I didn't already know." He tosses the object in his hand up into the air. It's a tiny brass sprocket, plucked loose from a machine. It glimmers with a penny sheen and then drops, *smack*, into his palm. "Let's talk about something else— Did you know church bells weren't always used as a call to worship? The Celts used them to ward off evil."

She wants to press him harder—to double down and ask him again about Paris. Instead, she plays along. She always does. "So, if I rang the bells, you'd go running?"

"Maybe." He looks delighted. "Or maybe *I'll* ring the bells, and you'll come kneel at my feet."

Her heart skips a beat. "Try it and find out."

It's familiar ground, this push and pull. This precipice. The smile slips off his face and he surrenders a step, hunger banding his throat. Beneath her skin, her blood fizzes through her veins. She always comes back to this in the end—cutting herself open on Lys when the rest of the world becomes too much to hold on to. This morning's conversation with Asher felt like clutching a fistful of broken glass. There's no way to put any of it back together.

And so, maybe she'll let it all go.

"I don't want to be an escape," says Lys, the moment she reaches for her sleeve.

She draws up short, frowning over at him. "What?"

"You heard me."

"I didn't—that's not what this is."

"Isn't it?" His stare is heavy. "You're feeling guilty, and you want me to make it all better. Maybe I don't appreciate being used."

"But I'll bet you appreciate being fed," she snaps.

His mouth curls into a sneer. "And you say I'm the one making this feel cheap."

Whatever else she might have said, she's not given the chance. They're interrupted by a whistle, sharp. Asher stands at the front of the church, two fingers in his mouth, a fresh bandage at his wrist.

"I'm starting to think he does this on purpose," grumbles Lys.

"Let's move!" Asher's shout sends a nearby grackle into flight. "We're on the road in five."

They make it to midmorning before they're forced to stop for gas. They pull off the road to navigate, parking at a scenic overlook. Shea and Poppy curl in the dinette and peer out at the miles and miles of trees, peaks girdled in mist, while Asher and Lys disappear into the back bedroom to argue over the map.

"Have you talked to him?" asks Poppy, keeping her voice to a whisper. "About Paris?"

"I've tried." Shea cuts a glance toward the bedroom, where she can just see Lys's and Asher's heads bowed low. "He doesn't exactly make it easy."

Asher stalks out of the bedroom a moment later, slamming the door behind him. Shea and Poppy exchange a glance as the engine starts with a weary *chuff.*

"Reckless fucking—" He shifts into drive, punching the gas with far more force than necessary. "He's going to get us killed."

They drive another thirty minutes before Asher pulls off the main road, navigating them into an old factory town. The houses are in varying states of decay, all of them abandoned to the nearby forest. Farther out, steel mills rise from winter-pale meadows, iron shafts gone black with rust. Smokestacks sit empty against the mid-November sky. They creep along a street slung with downed wires, finally coming to a stop in the parking lot of an old gas station. Several bikes sit parked out front, gleaming bodies askew atop the asphalt.

"Stay in the car," orders Asher.

Shea launches to her feet after him. "I should come with you."

"Parker, for once—" He rounds on her, steepling his hands in front of his face in an effort to be calm. "Every single place we've gone, someone has tried to kill you."

"Not *every* place," she argues. "The Nutmeg Nook was very nice."

"I liked the little A-frame house," says Poppy. "I'd go back there."

Asher gives them both a long-suffering look. "We're five hundred miles from the Flatwood. The chance that these are Keeling's men is very high."

"No one's going to recognize me on sight," she says. "Not if Lys isn't there."

"I'm not budging on this one, Shea, I'm sorry.'"

She plants her feet, obstinate. "Who died and made you king?"

"I have seniority."

"He's pulling rank," gasps Poppy. "Oh, Ellie *hates* when he does that."

"I'll get my shoes," says Shea.

"Parker," says Asher, "read my lips. *You're not coming.*"

Five minutes later, Asher stalks out of the camper with Shea in tow. The sun is little more than a feeble mark in the sky, gridded by clouds. The air is cold and wet, and Shea finds herself rushing through puddles to keep up with Asher's elongated stride.

The shop's interior is bare, pegboard shelving picked clean and windows blacked out. A bell rings as they enter, drawing the eyes of the elderly clerk slouched behind the counter. A younger man in riding leathers stands off to the side, playing solitaire. Nearby, a peroxide-blonde woman lounges on an ice cream cooler, a cigarette toggled at her bloodred lips. The entire storefront is tobacco-stung, smoke swirling in thin gray eddies. No one says a word as Asher and Shea make their way to the counter.

Tugging the brim of his cap low, Asher fishes through his pocket and pulls out several crumpled bills. The clerk scoops the money into his hand and begins counting it out at an arthitic pace.

"What pump?"

"Three," says Asher.

"Most customers around here don't pay with cash," says the man playing solitaire. He doesn't look up from his cards. "Blood'll get you a hell of a lot farther this deep in the forest. But I'm sure I don't have to tell you that."

Asher says nothing as he pockets his change. His bandage peeks out from beneath the sleeve of his jacket, white and obvious. He tugs the cuff into place and drops his hand to the small of Shea's back.

"Come on. Let's get out of here."

"Are you Mercy?" The question comes from the woman seated on the cooler. She's watching them through a ring of smoke, her eyes heavily lined in blue pencil.

Asher freezes, his hand flat against Shea's spine. "Sorry?"

"Are you a Mercy Boy?"

He pulls his cap lower. "Uh, no."

"You look familiar." The woman slides off the cooler and draws nearer, running her nails along the pegboard shelving in a *click-click-click* that sets Shea's teeth on edge. "I'm sure I've seen you before. I wouldn't forget a pretty face like that. What about Paris? Are you one of his? A mercenary, maybe?"

"No. Sorry." With a nudge, Asher propels Shea toward the door. "Let's go."

The bell rings as they slip back out into the parking lot. The sun has burned off the remaining clouds and the day is bright. The puddles shine gold against the asphalt. There's no chance of being followed. At least not yet. Shea rounds on Asher the moment they're out of earshot, puddle water seeping into her socks.

"That woman recognized you."

"She must have been confused." His eyes are on the sky, scanning the trees. "Get back in the camper."

Uneasy, Shea complies. She keeps watch in the window while Asher fills up at the pump, and then they're back on the road. Lys appears as Asher coaxes the camper to its limit, bracing himself in the doorway.

"What's the rush?"

"They recognized him," says Shea as Asher merges onto the highway.

Lys's eyes narrow. He's looking at Asher too keenly. "Did they?"

"I'll bet you anything we pick up a tail as soon as it's dark," she adds.

"It's fine," says Asher. "It was a mistake."

Lys is quiet for too long. Shea can practically hear the gears turning in his head. She doesn't like the way he's looking at Asher—with a wariness that makes her skin crawl.

"We should get off the road," he finally says. "While it's still light."

In the end, they leave the woods behind entirely, snaking down the mountain roads and driving until they hit the sea. They camp on the beach, parking the RV beneath a patch of old oaks dripping with moss. The sky is distended with rain-swollen clouds, their bottoms emblazoned with every possible color. The road nearby is buried behind a row of flowering loquat, trunks fringed in bitter panicum. Shea sits in the shade of a palmetto and watches the tide rush out. Poppy sits beside her, wiggling her toes in the sand.

"I feel like I'm betraying Ellie," she says, after a long while. "Being here, I mean. Without her. She always used to talk about going to the beach. Do you remember when she found that old coastal living magazine on the book rack at Brer's? She brought it home and cut out all the pages. She made it into a scrapbook, I think."

"It was a vision board," says Shea.

She'd made one, too, cutting and gluing everything that caught her eye. She remembers lying on her stomach in the Thorleys' living room, her legs swishing through the air, scraps of paper fluttering every which way. She hadn't looked up until she'd felt a presence behind her. It was Asher, his mouth thin as he quietly surveyed her work. The moment he noticed her looking, he averted his attention to his sister: *You're getting paper everywhere. Dad's going to lose his mind.*

Camellia ignored him, propping herself up to see what Shea had managed to cobble together. *We're supposed to be manifesting, Shea.*

I am manifesting.

You're not. That's just the Gravewood, and it's depressing.

Shea swallows the sharp wedge of grief in her throat. Out at sea, a lone gull swoops low over the water. She watches it snatch a fish from the surf and take off with a screech.

"Do you think she's still out there? Ellie?"

"I do." Poppy tips her head into the wind. "I have to. The alternative hurts too much."

Shea thinks of sitting on the cellar steps and waiting for her mother. The way hanging on felt better than letting go. The way hope was a lifeline—something to cling to as she treaded water.

"I can *hear* you thinking." Poppy's smile is dreamy, her eyes shut. The wind teases at her curls. "I get it. I know it's not logical. And I know it's not likely. But I have to believe she's okay."

The problem with treading water, Shea's learned, is that you can't do it forever.

Eventually, you sink.

"And what if she's not? What if we're too late? What if I'm the reason she's—"

She can't bring herself to say it, but it doesn't matter. They both know what she means. The word hangs heavily between them. *Dead.* She could be dead. They could be looking for a ghost.

Poppy is quiet for a long time. Finally, she says, "Have you ever felt so tightly threaded to someone that it hurts when they're away?"

She has. She does. She is inextricably knotted, her heart pinched so tight it's gone black and blue.

"Yes," she says. "I feel it all the time."

Poppy nods sagely, as if everyone does. As if it's normal, to be bound so thoroughly to another person that it hurts to breathe without them.

"I think," she says softly, "if Ellie was gone, my soul would know it."

They lapse back into quiet, watching the waves rush in. Shea peers back in the direction of the camper and finds Asher under the lopsided overhang, his hands in his pockets and his shoulders rounded. She wonders how long he's been standing there, listening to their conversation. She wonders if he's already given up, or if he's clinging to some secret, quiet hope.

He hasn't brought up Camellia in days.

She isn't given the chance to try to parse out the look in his eyes before Poppy is on her feet, tugging Shea up after her.

"Enough of this. If Ellie were here, she'd make us all stop moping and go in."

"That doesn't mean we *have* to do it," says Shea, but she lets Poppy drag her to the water's edge, kicking off her boots and socks as she goes.

The clouds are ablaze with color, pink as pomegranates. The water is ice-cold, the last of the sun glancing off the surface in a blinding halo. A wave rinses over her ankles before rushing back out to sea. She leaps up with a yelp, the sand beneath her sucked along with the current. It sends her toppling into Poppy, who cackles and throws her arms wide.

"Thorley, c-come in here," Shea calls, teeth chattering. "The w-water is p-perfect!"

"I don't believe you," he lobs back.

The sun sinks lower, deepening the sky to a bloodred hue. A second wave follows the first, and this time, the current nearly bowls them both over. They collapse one into the other, shrieking, water soaking their clothes. With a curse, Asher shrugs out of his jacket and kicks off his shoes, balling his socks into pellets. He jogs into the surf after them, stopping short the minute the water rushes up to meet him.

"Shit, that's cold," he yelps, yanking his elbows up by his ears. "No. Absolutely not."

"Lighten *up*," goads Shea, catching his arm before he can escape back onto shore. "Where's your sense of adventure?"

He stumbles, catching himself, as a wave nearly takes him out at the knees. The sight makes them roar with laughter. Grimacing, he whips his hand through the water, dousing both of them in an icy spray. His assault has a countereffect—they laugh harder, their fingers numb.

They're still laughing when the sun extinguishes beneath the water. The sea goes dark as oil, only the faintest vestiges of gold left in the sky. With the color leached out of them, the clouds look like true storm clouds. The wind picks up. The surf slaps against their shins. Catching her breath, Shea glances up to find Asher looking down at her, his T-shirt soaked through and his expression serious.

"Your lips are blue," he says.

"It's a little c-cold."

He closes his fist in the hem of her T-shirt and pulls her to him. She trips easily over the shifting sand, sea-foam girdling her ankles. He pauses for a fraction of a second—just long enough for her to realize what's about to happen—and then he bends down and slants his mouth over hers.

It's a kiss. Chaste. Sweet. The sort she used to dream about, back home in Little Hill. Another wave hits. Her knees knock together and she braces herself against the hard plane of his chest. The heat of him cuts through the cold, ignites a flame low in her belly. He pulls back just as it begins to rain, searching her face to gauge her reaction.

"They're a little warmer now," she admits.

The skies rip open, the rain becoming torrential. The flame within her sputters out, turning her smoky with panic.

"My hearing aids," she gasps.

"Shit." Folding his arms over her head, Asher tugs her back to shore, hollering for Poppy as he goes. She comes racing after them, her pockets stuffed full of pale shark-eye shells.

Tripping out of the surf, Asher tugs his coat off the sand and holds it over Shea. It's soaked through, but dry beneath, and they scramble back toward the RV, slipping over sand gone pocked with rainwater. They find Lys waiting beneath the awning, his expression indecipherable in the gloom.

"Nice work, Sunshine," he says. "You came through. Just when I was beginning to think you were a lost cause."

Some of the color goes out of Asher's face. "Don't."

"I wouldn't dream of it." Lys smiles a close-lipped smile. "Enjoy your silver platter."

"Lys, wait." Asher's voice grits out of him just as Lys reaches for the door. He freezes, his grip tight, the dark clinging to him like a second skin.

"*Lys?*" His knuckles are white against the handle. "You think because I marked you, we're friends? You think this means something? Once a watchdog, always a watchdog. All you're good for is following orders. You take mine so well."

The door slams shut with a rattle.

"What the hell was that?" demands Shea the moment he's gone.

Asher doesn't look at her. He's watching the door, his face bloodless. "Nothing."

"Oh yeah? It didn't sound like nothing."

"It's nothing, Shea." Asher scrubs the rain from his hair. "Please, for once in your life, will you drop it?"

She balks at his tone. "What? You're mad at me now, too?"

"I'm not *mad* at you, I'm— *God.*" He groans, running a hand down the length of his face. In the rain, Lys's bite has bled through the white of his bandage. It leaves a red, watercolor grin at his wrist. A mark, same as hers. Everything feels suddenly too precarious, like she's holding together a vase that has already been shattered. Like the slightest shift will bring it all crumbling to pieces.

Poppy senses it, too. With far more cheer than the situation merits, she asks, "What if I made more scones?"

"I need a minute," says Asher to the sky. "Just—don't follow me, okay?"

He's gone before Shea can argue, slipping back out into the downpour. Shoulders rounded, he heads back toward the sea, where the tide rushes in on a white, wild surf.

He doesn't come back until dawn.

TWENTY-TWO

Shea

The drive the next day is silent.

Even Kit is quiet, dozing in a cabinet out of sight. They stop to rest at a cabin along the Gravewood's southern terminus. So far off the main roads, the forest is wet and lush. It feels like a land lost to time, like they've stumbled out of the real world and into a storybook. Everything is lovely and green, white-capped mushrooms growing in rings everywhere Shea looks.

The inside of the house is just as charming. Well-tended, as if whomever lived here kept it with a loving hand. The main room boasts towering ceilings and a pressed stone fireplace, the hearth blackened with soot. The soaring cathedral windows have been thoroughly blacked out, and the walls are paneled wood. In its abandonment, signs of neglect have crept in. The furniture is damp and moth-bitten. A careworn couch sits atop a rug gone patterned in mold.

"What is this place?" asks Asher, once he's finished his inspection.

On the couch, Lys kicks his feet onto the coffee table. "An abandoned nest."

It's the most they've spoken in hours, their voices clipped, as if they're each doing their level best not to come to blows.

Asher eyes the blacked-out windows. "We don't have to worry about guests?"

"We shouldn't," says Lys. "No one comes here anymore."

"Why not?"

"It has bad blood."

"That's not an answer," says Asher tightly.

Lys tips his head back and shuts his eyes. "It's all you're going to get, Sunshine. Be a good little soldier and build me a fire. There's wood out in the shed."

"Sure," says Asher. "And when it's done, maybe I'll shove a hot poker up your—"

"Poppy and I will bring in the firewood," says Shea, cutting him off.

In the end, the task is easier said than done. It takes them the better part of an hour to find wood dry enough to burn. With a fire sputtering in the fireplace, they scrounge together a meal from the remainder of their food supply. They eat in silence, the cabin smoky. Shea finishes first, shoving back from the table and snatching a flashlight from the top of Asher's bag.

"Where are you going?" calls Poppy, when no one else cares enough to ask.

"To find a window to fling myself out of," she says, without turning back.

"Oh," says Poppy. "Okay. Be careful."

Two sets of eyes follow her out. She finds a bedroom at the very top of the stairs, small and sparse and neat. A crib occupies the farthest corner, its wooden slats splintered. Over the top of the crib hangs a handcrafted mobile of felted stars, all of them red. A book sits on the wooden rocking chair beside it, pages deckled. She picks it up and flips through. It's a collection of old poems, none of them familiar.

It feels invasive, snooping through the room's battered contents—like she's a grave robber rifling through a tomb. She sets the book back down, careful not to knock the pages loose. When she straightens, her flashlight sweeps over the wall. Her eyes catch on the black gloss of marker, handwriting small and cramped. There's writing over the crib. A lot of it. She leans in close for a better look, her blood running cold.

From the fount of the forest comes the age of the beast.

It isn't written just the one time, or by just the one hand. It's been inscribed over and over, from floor to ceiling. Sometimes neat. Sometimes scribbled. Sometimes etched deep into the paneling, as if by a knife.

From the fount of the forest comes the age of the beast.
From the fount of the forest comes the age of the beast.
From the fount of the forest comes the age of the beast.

A soft scrape draws her upright. She whirls, her heart flying into her throat, and finds Lys standing by the crib, lit silver in the beam of her light.

"You scared me," she says. "I didn't hear you come in."

He looks as serious as she's ever seen him. "I need to talk to you."

"Oh." She lowers the flashlight to their feet. "Okay."

He pokes a finger at a red felt star. They all go wobbling, cast out of orbit by his touch. He waits for them to still before saying, "Not in here."

"What's wrong with this room?"

His gaze drifts meaningfully to the wall. To the dozens of inscriptions, repeated like a prayer over the empty crib.

"It feels like a crypt," he says, mirroring her thoughts. "Let's go across the hall."

She lets him lead her out of the nursery and into the adjacent bedroom, flashlight glancing off every oblique shape in the dark. This room is sparse and undecorated, save a modest bed and an empty dresser. A set of doors leads out onto a balcony, panels shattered and mullions snapped. He steps outside and she follows, glass crunching underfoot. The trees grow in close, red cedar pine engulfing the railing. A screech owl takes off at the sight of them, gliding into the woods with a ghostly tremolo.

"I think Thorley is hiding something," says Lys the moment it's quiet.

Shea bristles, wary. "Hiding what?"

"I don't know." He doesn't look at her. His focus is honed on the railing as he pries up a splinter with his thumbnail. "I haven't figured it out yet."

"Oh, well, obviously." It comes out sharper than she meant it to. "And you're basing this off what, exactly? Did he say something? Do something?"

"It's just a feeling I have."

She gapes at his profile, incredulous. "A feeling."

"Yes."

"A *feeling*?"

His eyes lift to hers. "Are you going to keep saying it?"

She bites back a scream. "You're unbelievable, do you know that?"

She turns her back on him, walking away before she says something she'll regret. He tails after her, undeterred, glass ground to stardust beneath his boots. Her fury finds her there, in the middle of the room. She whirls, nearly crashing headlong into him in the dark.

"This is about last night, isn't it? You're upset."

His eyes flash dangerously. "What do I have to be upset about?"

"Jealous, then."

He looks, for an instant, startled. And then he laughs right in her face. A cold, unfunny laugh that makes the hairs on her arm stand on end.

"You think I'm jealous? Of Thorley? A barely sentient jarhead?"

"Don't *call* him that."

"It's what he is," snaps Lys, swallowing up the space between them. "He's a small, little crush from your small, little town, and if I hadn't stepped in, you would have settled for him and gone on to live a small, little life."

The words hit her like a slap. She rears back, shocked. Lit from beneath by her flashlight, he looks as unassailable as ever. Not a god but a demon cut from the cloth of hell.

Tightly, she whispers, "Maybe that's what I wanted."

His jaw wires shut. "Maybe it is."

It shouldn't hurt, hearing him say it. It shouldn't feel like she's been ripped open. She's known all along that this thing between them is synthetic. Ugly and unsustainable.

But, says a voice inside her. *But.*

Directly in front of her, Lys stands as still as a living statue. His cheeks are veined like marble. His throat bobs beneath thin cobalt bruises. He's menacing in the gloom—menacing and inhuman and all his own.

And she thinks she might love him.

"I need to leave," she gasps out. "I can't be in here."

His gaze turns thunderous. "Go, then. I'm not keeping you."

She turns, her flashlight carving a wobbling arc through the hallway's inky black. The dark feels like it's going to collapse in on her. The knot around her chest cinches tight enough to cut off circulation. Spots bloom in front of her eyes. She can't breathe.

"You should know," calls out Lys, his voice as cold as she's ever heard it, "Thorley was acting on my orders."

She stutters to a stop atop the threshold. She waits for him to say more. When he doesn't, she swings around to face him. Her throat feels like she's swallowed nettles.

"What are you talking about?"

"I told him to get close to you," says Lys. "To trick you into thinking he liked you as more than just his kid sister's friend."

"What?" She searches his face, not understanding. "When?"

"His first night at Mercy Ridge."

She stands frozen, useless, the fight going out of her. She thinks of Asher on the bed, the box full of letters in his lap. He'd been too forgiving. Too eager to move on. She'd seen right through it, and she ignored her intuition. Because she was weak. Because she was afraid. Because she wanted it to be true.

"Why?" Her voice is thin as a reed. "Why would you do that?"

"Because this thing between us is a sickness," says Lys, "and you were starting to mistake it for something else."

She wants to laugh right in his face, but she can't find the air. It feels like her lungs have been punctured. Each inhale rattles like broken glass inside her chest.

"If that's true, then why did you bring me? Why talk me into coming? Why drag me along on this whole stupid road trip?"

"Come on, Shea," he goads. "You're smarter than that. You know why."

It's become a habit, reaching for her wrist—running her thumb along the raised sickles of his bite. She does so now, his eyes tracking her movements. Blue splits deeper into his skin, veins popping along his throat. Hungry, even now. Insatiable, even as he breaks her.

"You needed me," she realizes. "You needed blood. God. You let me think it was something more. You let me—"

Love you. You let me love you. She feels like she's going to be sick, right here on his shoes. Cyrus Talbot's voice plays on a loop through her head. *This is how he hunts.*

"Were you ever going to Turn me?" Her voice wobbles, unsteady. "Or was that a lie, too?"

A muscle ticks in his jaw. "I told you what you wanted to hear."

Oliver Lysander is a creature of the Gravewood, plying her with promises he never meant to keep. He's never been anything but what he is. It was never a secret. It was always right in front of her face. And she ignored it at every turn.

"What about the cure?" The question comes out brittle. Small. "What about my mom?"

"What do *you* think?" he asks, and this is all the answer she needs.

She needs space. She needs air. She needs to be anywhere but here, a thousand miles away from the only thing that mattered, staring up at the devil who lured her from her doorstep. She feels as lost as any missing person, consumed by the forest. Devoured by its dark.

She fumbles out into the hall, tripping down the stairs and into the living room, where the fire has burned itself down to nothing. Asher launches to his feet the moment he sees her.

"Hey." He ducks into her line of sight, swallowing up her exit. "Are you okay? What happened?"

"Was it all a lie?" The question punches out of her, wild and hoarse.

He scowls, confused. "What do you mean?"

"Don't play dumb," she snaps, shoving at his chest. When he doesn't budge, she shoves him again, pushing at the wall of him until he yields a step beneath her trembling hands. "You fed me this big, tragic story about everything you went through. For me. For *us*. Was it a lie? Did you make it up?"

His gaze lifts to to the stairs. Lys stands against the railing, cold as a serpent.

"You fucking brat," he bites out. "What did you say to her?"

If Lys responds, she doesn't hear it. She pushes past Asher and whips open the door, slamming it shut behind her just as Poppy calls her name. She's enveloped in a chilly quiet, the cold seeping into her socks. Propelled by her anger, she stalks down the stairs and out into the dark, hurrying along the overgrown pavers before anyone can follow.

It's stopped raining, at least. The night is black as pitch, the gaps between the treetops sugared in starlight. Her flashlight bounces off the trunks of the trees, disappearing into the infinite spaces between. She walks without aim, pressing forward at a clip. She doesn't stop until there's a stitch in her side. Until the tears begin to fall.

She's standing just outside an old turkey barn, the roof caved in. Matted doveweed froths out from the open door in a leafy spew. Collecting her senses, she casts the flashlight across her surroundings. Darkness leers back at her from every direction, no discernible landmarks in sight. She's lost and unarmed, the cold sinking into her bones, and all she's managed to do in storming out of the cabin is prove, once again, how helpless she is.

"So stupid," she hisses.

She wanders several aimless yards in the dark before frustration wins out. Loosing a wordless shriek, she kicks at the ground. Her big toe hits a rock and she shrieks again, toppling onto her backside as the stone goes skittering between the trees. Knees bent, she buries her head in her hands. Her heart pounds hard enough to hurt.

"I want to go home," she cries into the dark.

But home isn't there anymore. What she wants is her mother in the garden, culling weeds. Her father in the workshop, sanding wood. Hemlock belly up in a sunspot and the windows thrown wide, everything quiet and peaceful and still.

She'd resented it then. She'd begged the woods to take her.

And the Gravewood delivered.

She doesn't know how long she sits there before the stone comes skittering back. It rolls across the wet press of leaves, coming to an impossible stop between her heels. For several seconds, she stares down at it, confused. Slowly, her confusion gives way to fear.

She's not alone. She lurches to her feet, dragging the flashlight along the contorted faces of the trees. There, pinned in the broad yellow beam, is the woman from the gas station. She regards Shea through a too-keen stare, her head tipped to one side.

"You shouldn't cry over him. He's an awful boy."

Shea knows this game by now. She understands the rules. "I'll scream."

"There's no need to do that," says the woman, drawing nearer. "I'm not going to hurt you. I'm here with a message."

Suspicion swarms into her chest. "A message from who?"

"From Paris Keeling, of course." The woman's teeth are fanged sharp, ivory glinting in the moonlight.

"I'm not interested," says Shea.

"Are you sure?" Crooking an arm around the thin trunk of a tree, she swings herself out of sight. She appears on the other side, eyes glittering. "He's heard a rumor that your poor, sweet mother isn't feeling her best. That you've come all this way in search of a cure."

Shea stills. "There is no cure."

"Is that what Oliver told you?"

"Well, no," admits Shea. "But it was heavily implied."

The woman *tsk*s. "Oliver can be very tricky when it suits him. He tells all sorts of lies to get his way."

"And Paris doesn't?"

"Paris Keeling is a businessman. He makes decisions with his head. Oliver makes decisions with his heart. It's his fatal flaw. Surely, you see it. Otherwise, you wouldn't be out here all alone, crying in your socks."

"I wasn't crying," says Shea.

"But you're alone," notes the woman. "It isn't good to be friendless in a place like this. The dark might gobble you up."

Shea stands her ground, her toes numb with cold. "You can tell Paris I'm not interested."

The woman peers down at her, untroubled. "That's a shame. He's *very* interested in you. And he has connections. All sorts of them. He's not like Oliver, scraping and scavenging for every scrap. He's a kingmaker. A dealbroker. A *man*, not a boy. He can get you what you need with the snap of his fingers. But if you're sure . . ." She turns to go, slipping out from the circular beam of the light.

"Wait," calls Shea.

The woman reappears, her mouth curving into a bloodred smile. "Yes?"

"Is there really a cure?"

"There is," says the woman. "And they don't want us to have it. There's not enough food. Not enough supplies. It's better, if some of us die. Easier, if some of us survive on blood. Simpler, if we devour one another. But Paris—Paris can get anything. For you, he would."

"Why me?"

"You're everything to him. The linchpin in all he holds dear."

Shea's blood pumps a little faster. "What do I have to do?"

"Come to the revel," says the woman. "Alone. You and Paris can—"

There's a sickening squelch and the woman coughs—a short, shallow hack that paints her chin with blood. Stunned, Shea follows her gaze down to her abdomen. Five onyx tips protrude from her torso in arcuated points. They disappear with a sound that turns Shea's stomach. The woman drops to her knees with a wet burble.

Behind her stands Lys. Bruises burgeon across his skin in shades of violet, fracturing along his jaw. His veins are thunderhead dark, thin lines of desiccation deepening to a swollen pitch. He is as inhuman as he was the night on the bridge, his body corded beyond recognition.

Between them, the struggle runs out of the woman. Her eyes go hazy, pupils ashen.

Feebly, she whispers, "From the fount of the forest comes the—comes the—"

She topples to the ground with a thud. She doesn't move again. For several seconds afterward, there is only this—Shea and Lys standing face-to-face, the wind clicking through the branches. The forest gleams with starlight, diamond fractals dripping from the pines.

Even Lys is glazed in it, the fluted ridges of his horns gone onyx with rainwater. He holds her in the black bullion of his stare, severe and unblinking. He has never looked more beautiful to her than in this singular moment. And she loves him. She *loves him*.

She doesn't know how to make herself stop.

Even now, when she knows it's poisoning them both.

Scenting the air, he takes a single step toward her. There is no recognition in his face—no sharp smile, no knowing leer. She's cornered, nowhere to run.

"Lys," she whispers. "Lys, it's me."

He moves in closer, moving like a wolf, locking in on his prey.

"My mom loves to garden," she blurts out, unthinking. "Loved. Will love again. She kept the yard full of perennials. Purple astilbe likes full sun, although sometimes in a heat wave she'd sit out there with an umbrella, just in case it got too hot. Spiked speedwell likes well-drained soil, and it has to be cut back every year or you won't get blooms."

Lys's head quirks oddly, canting to the side.

"Coral bells like partial shade." Her back collides into the wide trunk of a tree. She takes a swallow of air and keeps going, unable to do anything but watch Lys approach. "They tend to heave out of the ground in the wintertime, so you need to mulch after the first freeze. I missed it this year, and I'm worried they'll uproot while I'm away."

He sways into her, a clawed hand braced against the flat of her stomach. The bloodied tips of five sharp talons snag in her shirt. She shuts her eyes.

"Then there's bleeding hearts," she whispers. "They're my favorite. They grow in the shade, kind of like you. My mom keeps them next to the red columbine, because they match, and because they both attract hummingbirds."

His hand closes around the hem of her shirt. Fingers—human—scrape the bare skin of her belly. Slowly—*slowly*—his forehead lowers to hers. His breath shreds the air between them.

"What are you doing?"

Relief blooms, sunshine bright, inside her chest. "I don't know any baseball facts."

A distinctly Lys smile tugs at the corner of his mouth. He sways, unsteady.

"Lys?"

She pulls away just in time to see his eyes roll back. He collapses into her, boneless. He's heavier than her by a large margin. They go down together, hitting the cold, wet ground.

"Lys?" She shoves at him, to no avail. *"Oliver."*

Something heavy crashes through the trees up ahead. She rolls as best she can, scrabbling for the flashlight just as Asher emerges. He takes in the scene before him—the body on the ground and Lys's head tipped back, his hair matted with rainwater.

"Help me," she cries. "Help me get him up. I can't—he's too heavy."

"Okay. It's okay. I've got him." Asher hauls Lys onto his feet, pulling an arm over his shoulder to prop him up. His head drops forward, eyelids fluttering.

"Get his other side," orders Asher.

Shea rushes to obey, wedging herself under his shoulder like a crutch. The stars as their audience, they make their way back to the cabin. Shea slips in the mud as she goes, struggling under Lys's weight. She feels small and weak and angry, her heart in her stomach, the woman's words beating like a drum in the hollow of her chest: *Come to the revel. Alone.*

TWENTY-THREE
Lysander

It's getting worse.

The clock, tick-tock-ticking in his head.

The bomb, tick-tock-ticking in his chest.

Nothing inside him will be quiet. Not his thoughts. Not his dreams. Not the bugs in his veins. They crawl along the empty arteries, scrape at the ventricles of his heart, boring deep, deep, deep. Sometimes he thinks that if he lay down and died, his body would get right back up again and keep going on without him in a mad little jig.

He thinks of a poem. A nursery rhyme—he detests children's rhymes. He hates the repetition. The nonsense words. The oversimplified cadence. Most of all he hates how they make him think of his mother. *Home again, home again, jiggety jig.*

He's not thinking of his mother right now.

He's thinking of *her*. It's hard not to—she's looking right at him. Her eyes are narrowed in anger. Her voice is pinched tight.

"Asher, stop. Stop it—don't touch him. He's fine. He just needs to rest."

He's conscious of a boy's voice. A low, irritable baritone. A punishing white light jackknifes along his periphery and then disappears. A door slams. There's a featherlight touch at his brow, the feel of fingers pushing back his hair. His head is on fire. His bones grind tight. Everything, everything aches.

And then, in the maelstrom, he hears her. "Catmint needs full sun and well-drained soil. It blooms in late spring and has these really pretty tubular flowers. It's not as sweet smelling as lavender, but the bees love it—"

Time stands still. Or else it passes. He comes to on his feet, in the dark of a bathroom he knows cold. Wide wood paneling. A scalloped pedestal sink. The timeline of his life threatens to collapse in on itself. For a moment, he's certain he's six years old again, cowering in the bathtub with his hands over his ears, waiting for his mother to stop wailing.

Everything ends. Everything ends.

There's no wailing now. The door is shut. The curtain has been ripped down from its rod. The mirror is shattered. He grips the edges of the sink and stares into the glass. His own reflection leers back at him in compound fragments. Not a frightened little boy at all, but a beast. Black eyes. Bruised lids. Horns dark as pitch, curving back in on him in needle-sharp points.

The Gravewood fucking Devil, breaking everything he touches.

The rattle of the knob brings him bolt upright. The door opens and Shea slips in, falling back against it until it clicks. For a long time, neither of them speaks.

"Say something," she orders. "So I know you're in there."

"You walked away." His voice is graveled.

"You told me to."

"Obviously, I didn't mean it."

"And what about everything else? Did you mean that?"

He takes a tentative step closer. When she doesn't run, he takes another. She's watching him, wary, her back pressed to the wall. He doesn't know how to tell her he regrets every word he said. He doesn't know how to say he's sorry in a way that means something. Carefully—experimentally—he fists his fingers in the hem of her T-shirt. Same as he watched Asher do, waist deep in the surf. They both look down at his hand. Neither of them moves a muscle.

"I acted badly," he whispers. "Here's what I should have said last night—I don't care if you're his, as long as you're also mine."

Her eyes snap to his. She looks surprised. Then resigned.

She presses a hand flat against his sternum. His heart thunders into her palm as hope roars into his chest. Gently—firmly—she gives him a push. It isn't like every other time, when she's pushed him over an edge. This time, she's pushing him away. His grip on her comes loose. His back hits the sink, hope extinguishing just as quickly as it ignited. She holds him there at arm's length, the apex of his heart at the tips of her fingers.

"I'm not his," she tells him. "I'm not yours, either."

Fear bolts through him in a killing strike. "You don't mean that."

"I do." Her touch is as ephemeral as a butterfly's. Her voice is flat, lacking inflection. "You were right, before. This thing between us—it's transactional. I misread the situation."

Her words are a sucker punch to the gut. "You didn't misread anything."

"Blood for batteries. That's what this is. It's what this has always been."

"Stop."

There's never any light in her eyes when she looks at him, and he hates it. The night Asher Thorley kissed her, she'd come in from the rain with eyes shining. All he knows how to do is snuff things out.

To take pretty things and break them, just like his father.

"I came in to check on you, that's all." She's eerily calm, and he can't stand it. He wants her to shout. To cry. To fight him—*push* him—until they're through to the other side of whatever this is. He wants her to kiss him the way she kissed Asher. On her toes, a tide rushing in.

She doesn't. She only asks, "Do you need to feed?"

He's never heard a viler question in all his life. *"No."*

"Then you and I are done here."

Panic sinks its fangs into his throat and he catches her wrist quick, before she can leave. His bite marks leer up at him, feed after feed stitched into her skin in raised pink scars. Everything feels fractured, sharp. Shea studies his fingers encircling her wrist, her expression closed off.

"I panicked," he says. "I said things I shouldn't have—"

"Egor van Haut said you and I have knocked each other out of alignment."

He blinks, slow. "Van Haut is a nutcase."

"Is he?" She looks up at him, her stare empty. "I asked Poppy about proprioception. She said it's your body's ability to sense where it is. Since we met, all I feel is you. All I see is you. But that's not love. I thought it was, but it's just the feed messing with our heads."

His grip turns raptorial as his panic builds. "Please."

"Let go of my wrist, Oliver."

"I can't." The voice that comes out of him doesn't even sound like his. "I need you."

Her breath catches. The sound is so quiet, it's almost imperceptible. But he hears it. He clings to it.

"It's just the feed," she repeats, and she's lying. He knows she is. She has to be. "It's not real."

"Don't—don't say that." He gapes down at her, bewildered, searching for a tell. "How can you think that? I'm so fucking gone for you, Shea Parker. Everyone sees it but you."

She blinks. Blinks again. She looks like she did that night in the devil's backbone, clearing her eyes of a thrall. Resurfacing. He can feel himself losing her, and it makes him rabid with terror.

"Tell me what I have to do," he begs. "Tell me how to fix this."

"There's nothing to fix."

"No." He shakes his head. "No, I don't accept that."

"Let go of her, Lys."

His head kicks up, and there's Asher, standing on the threshold as if he's been there all along. And maybe he has been. Lysander is off-kilter, unable to see anything—hear anything—other than the girl in front of him. Funny, he always thought the fire in her chest burned the same as the flame in his. And now he's gone and snuffed it out. She's cold as a coal in his hand.

"Did you hear me?" asks Asher. "I said, let her go."

He obeys, blood humming in his ears. Shea slinks back from him the moment she's free, gripping her wrist to her chest like he's bitten her. He feels disoriented, sick, his equilibrium thrown off. Out of alignment, his body attuned to nothing but the way she moves, the way she breathes, the way her heart beats out of lockstep.

Distantly, he hears Asher ask, "Are you okay?"

"I have nothing to say to you," snaps Shea. "Not unless it's about Ellie."

She's leaving, her bare feet thudding against the hardwood, Asher on her heels.

"Shea, come on," he calls, "we have to talk at some—"

A door slams shut somewhere out of sight. It rattles the joists, sets the old wooden cabin resettling on its haunches. Lysander tips back against the cool porcelain of the sink, striving for a calm he doesn't feel. He can sense Asher watching him, his expression grim.

"Are we fighting, too?"

"Don't start," says Asher.

"Why not? Misery loves company."

Mephistopheles. A Faustian horror. A master manipulator. A demon from the deep woods. He is what he is. What he's always been.

"Why haven't you killed me?" he asks Asher.

Asher grimaces. "What kind of question is that?"

"I've punched a hole through your life at every turn." He runs a finger along the inside of his collar, the muscles in his neck stiff. "You're just going along with it. It doesn't make sense. You're a good shot. Why haven't you taken it?"

He doesn't miss the way Asher's trigger finger twitches. "You and I have a deal."

"And I haven't held up my end of it. We're no closer to finding your sister than we were at the start. We're not even looking."

"Don't bait me," says Asher.

"It's an innocent conversation, Sunshine."

"No, you're upset, and you're looking for a fight. I'm not giving you one."

Lysander sniffs. "What kind of friend are you?"

"*Are* we friends again?" Asher's brows kick up. "I thought I was just your foot soldier."

He shoves past Asher with a snarl, refusing to dignify him with an answer as he heads swiftly for the shuttered door at the far end of the hall. Un-fucking-flappable as always, Asher falls into steady step behind him.

"Leave her alone, Lys."

He doesn't. He can't. He shoulders open the door to his childhood room and skids immediately into Poppy, standing just on the other side. In her arms, the possum hisses up at him, teeth bared. He draws up short, snatching his fingers out of reach.

"What are you," he asks, "security?"

Poppy's smile doesn't touch her eyes. "I think you should find somewhere else to be."

"I *have* nowhere else to be."

There is nothing more important than this—fixing what he broke. Mending it, before the cracks can splinter into his psyche. Before there's nothing left of him. He can see Shea just behind Poppy, her legs tucked under her in his mother's rocking chair, red starlight wobbling around her head. In her lap she cradles a little board book, a thin white rabbit on the front. The spine is creased, pages bent. He knows every line cold.

He barreled in here without a plan—without any thought in his head but her, her, her—but now that he's here he knows exactly what he wants to say.

"My mom used to read that to me," he says, speaking around Poppy. "The boy in the story loved that rabbit so much, its fur wore thin and its stitching came loose."

"Oliver," warns Poppy.

"There's a line in the book about what it takes to be real," he says, speaking like he has something to prove. "It's not about how you're made. It's about how you're loved—"

"*Oliver.*"

"—so much that it rubs you raw."

Shea's eyes are on his. He swallows around the grit in his throat. *Threadbare*, he'd called her. He'd said it all wrong, that night at Mercy Ridge. He's always saying everything wrong.

"That was very nice," says Poppy, wedging the door into his chest. "Now leave."

"Wait." He jams his boot in the gap just before it closes. Reaching into his pocket, he pries out the small brass sprocket he'd pulled from the bell strike at the old stone church, collapsing the system with a single, swift tug. "Can you give her this?"

Poppy stares down at the cog like it's live ammunition. "What is it?"

"A birthday gift."

"Her birthday is over."

"Poppy."

"Oliver."

"Just give it to her." With more defensiveness than the situation merits, he adds, "It's for her necklace."

"I'll consider it." She plucks the cog from his open hand. "Now go away."

The door snicks shut before he can argue. He's left staring at the splintering inlay of his childhood bedroom, the dark swimming around him in dusty fractals. And he's not alone. He can feel eyes on him, cool and assessing. Asher stands a few feet away, his shoulder butting up against the wide paneled wall.

"What are *you* looking at?" he asks hotly.

"You," says Asher. "It's like watching a train wreck."

He wrings both hands over the back of his neck. "Fuck."

"She'll forgive you," says Asher. "You just need to back off."

Lysander barks out a bitter laugh and sinks to the floor. Swiping his hood onto his head, he kicks out his feet and settles in to wait. After a minute, Asher joins him. He lowers himself with a grunt, forearms draped over bent knees.

"Are we going to sit here until she comes out?" asks Lysander.

Asher lets his head fall back against the wall. "Looks like it."

"Pathetic."

It's nearly night by the time the door swings wide. They both launch upright, knocking one into the other in their haste. Poppy stands on the threshold, her eyes big. Lysander braces himself to be admonished—chewed out and then chased away.

"It's Ellie," she says instead. "She was here."

"What do you mean?" Asher cuts a glance at Lysander. "What do you mean, she was here?"

"There's something on the wall behind the crib. Come look."

They pile into the room to find Shea on her knees, her flashlight trained on a section of wall along the crib. Lysander doesn't need to get close to know what the majority of the writing says. He's heard it all his life, chanted over him like an exaltation. His legacy, written in blood.

From the fount of the forest comes the age of the beast.

Shea kneels before it like a priestess at an altar. His own personal cataclysm. A cog in the chain of his psyche. Pull her loose, and what then? He can already feel it, building inside him. A reckoning. An upheaval.

"Look," says Shea. "It's right here. She wrote it in our code."

He bends in close, elbowing Asher out of the way. Among the myriad inscriptions, a single line of nonsense words has been carved into the cedar with a knife. *Hgzb zdzb uiln gsv uozgdllw.*

"What does it say?" asks Asher.

It's a minute before Shea answers, running trembling fingers over the disrupted grain as she translates the schoolyard cipher. Finally, she rises to her feet. Her flashlight arcs feebly through the room. She's a pale blade of light, knifing through the dark where he grew.

"It says 'Stay away from the Flatwood,'" she says. "And it's a message for me."

ACT IV
THE TRAITOR

O, then, what graces in
my love do dwell,
That he hath turned a heaven unto a hell!

Shakespeare's *A Midsummer Night's Dream*

TWENTY-FOUR

Shea

Camellia Thorley knew they were coming.

She'd been there, in that strange little house with the wall full of writing, and somehow—impossibly—she'd known Shea would pass through, too.

"But *how* did she know?" she demands, circling back around for the umpteenth time. "*I* didn't even know I'd be there."

"Maybe it wasn't her," says Asher, giving her the same answer he'd given her the last six times she asked. Just like the last six times, he adds, "Or maybe the note was left for anyone who might stumble on it. It's not like it was addressed to you."

It's been this way for the past hour—her questioning, and him maintaining his stance. *We don't know for sure. We don't have any answers. We keep going as planned.* If she was in possession of a sword, she'd run it clean through him.

"It's a code Ellie and I made up," she snaps, irate. "In *fourth grade.* Who else would she have left it for?"

They're just outside St. Augustine—their penultimate pit stop before the revel. It's the sunniest it's been in days: hot and bright, no shade for miles. They hunker down for the day in an empty bungalow on the bounds of the Flatwood. The house is boxed in by several narrow columns of towering longleaf, surrounded in every direction by swaths of glossy gallberry and stunted slash pine. It was built for summers, with cool tile flooring and a sun-splashed facade. Lys is forced to shelter in the windowless half bath for the duration of the day.

It's a relief, being out of his crosshairs. She's been tied up in knots since their fight, too angry to forgive him, too hurt to try. Too terrified that he might sense it on her—the fact that she's planning to leave. *Come to the revel. Alone.* The woman's advice is at odds with the warning Camellia left. She isn't quite sure how to reconcile them.

And just like that, she's circled back around again.

"Ellie must be traveling with someone," she insists. "Someone who knew where that cabin was, and how to get there without running into trouble."

The atlas sits on the kitchen table between them, the route to the revel traced in black. Asher stands over it, his jaw wired tight. She can practically hear him running out of patience.

"What if she's with one of Keeling's people?" asks Poppy. "What if Paris took her?"

"That would mean she's here, in the Flatwood." Shea tips back in her seat, tucking her legs up under her. "It's not impossible. He got to Tristan. He convinced him to Turn just so he'd be in position when Paris needed someone on the inside."

"Tristan Choi Turned because he was sick," says Asher.

"He was a pawn," Shea counters. "Paris uses people, we know that. He used Tristan. He took someone who was scared and looking for a way out and he turned that fear into leverage."

Poppy hums. "What if Paris took Ellie to try and lure Lysander away from Mercy Ridge?"

Asher presses his fists to the table, his shoulders tense. "You're both taking massive leaps of logic. My sister has never even met Lys."

"But she's important to Shea," says Poppy. "And Paris has been using Shea to manipulate Lysander at every turn. The evidence is right in front of us. It's not a leap of logic to work with what we know."

Asher pushes off the table, pacing away to the window, where the screened-in pool sits empty of all but a shallow layer of standing water, furred in algae. Lacing his hands over the top of his cap, he turns to face them. "Fine. Let's say, for argument's sake, that Ellie is here in the Flatwood. Let's say she's with Paris. We still have to find our way into the revel."

"Unless it's a trap," says Poppy.

Asher's eyes tighten. "We're not changing the plan, Poppy."

She doesn't back down. "Ellie left that note as a warning. And if Paris knows everything about Shea, you have to assume he knows everything about you, too."

"I'm not a part of it."

"Except you are, Asher," says Poppy. "This is bigger than you and your uncomfortable feelings. It's about Ellie. What if we do something wrong, and it gets her killed? What if he's playing all three of you? What if, by going to the revel, we're giving Paris exactly what he wants?"

"Then we give it to him."

Lys looms in the open door, his hood up and his hands in his pockets. His horns carve out from beneath his hair in violent points. His cheeks are sunken, eyes bruised, and Shea wonders just how long he's been standing there, listening.

"We go to the revel," he says, "and we beat him at his own game."

An hour later, they still haven't agreed on the best way in.

"We cut around south," says Asher, jabbing a finger at the map. "Approach from the flank."

Lys brushes his finger away. "There's no point in trying to surprise him if he knows we're coming."

They're in the upstairs bathroom, a pillow shoved into the egress window. The sun finds its way in anyway, turning the tiled space a funny blue color. Lys soldiers it in silence, teeth gritted and hoodie zipped, sweating through his things.

"If we go straight in, we have to take the coastal road along the old beachfront resorts," says Asher. The map is laid out in the bottom of the Jacuzzi tub, and they're perched on its edge, bumping into one another in the cramped space. "I don't like that plan, either."

"What's wrong with it?" asks Shea.

"Keeling and crew nest in the resorts," says Lys, without meeting her eyes. "Hotels like that are full of blackout curtains. It's easy to keep out of the sun. And it won't be a concern, because they'll be shut away during the day. No one will notice us driving through."

Asher makes a face. "In a giant camper?"

"It's not exactly inconspicuous," agrees Poppy.

"It's falling apart," tacks on Asher. "I say we keep away from the coast. Stick to the Flatwood. It's served us well the whole drive so far."

"Brilliant idea," says Lys dryly, dragging an inked finger along the narrow artery of a road. He stops over a patch of green terrain, finger hovering. "That brings us right past Gridley's."

Shea's knees buckle. One word, and she's seven years old again, watching her parents stack loose change at the kitchen table. Watching them argue. Watching them break.

"We're near the sanatorium?"

"It's just a detour," says Asher, casting a knowing look in her direction. "We won't get close."

Lys's jaw ticks. "I'd prefer to stay as far away as possible, actually."

"Why?" asks Poppy. "What's the risk?"

Asher snatches the map out of the tub. "There *is* no risk," he says, as Lys says, "Contagion."

A sick sort of understanding swims into Shea's stomach. "Gridley's is full of hollows."

Asher tosses a murderous look toward Lys. "What are you doing?"

"Telling her the truth," says Lys. "She doesn't need you to coddle her. And you and I both know that if you're not leaking Rot at intake, you're sure as hell full of it by the time you leave. Gridley's is a death sentence. It's run by botanists, not doctors. There's no oversight, no quarantine protocols. Nothing. They're not trying to control the spread; they're trying to study it."

"The more variables they have for their research, the better the data," says Poppy.

Shea's blood turns to lead. "They're experimenting on sick people?"

"They're not sick," says Asher. "They're gone."

"My mom isn't gone."

And just like that, they've circled back around again. This time, they've gone all the way back to the start. Caution creeps into Asher's eyes. "I don't want to have this fight with you right now."

"It's not a fight, Asher, it's a fact. My mom's heart is still beating, which means she isn't gone. And neither are any of those people."

"Those *people* would rip your throat out without a second thought. Why do you think they exterminate entire towns if one of them gets loose? Why do you think we go in and wipe the whole place? How do you think the Rot spreads, Parker? Huh?"

"I don't know," she admits.

"Your dad never told you, did he?" Asher rolls up the map, his expression grim. "He never explained what exactly happened in Highbush. Do you even know how it started?"

"It started with a woman named Rose Darnell," says Poppy quietly. "She ingested untreated water from a pump by her house. The neighbors found her in the kitchen, eating her husband's intestines. They put her down and thought that was the end of it. But once it mutates, it spreads through the bite. It's almost impossible to contain an outbreak. The only effective way has been mass quarantine."

"Or death," adds Lys. "It's cheaper."

Shea's stomach pits. "I didn't know that."

"Because you live in a bubble," says Asher. "Your parents cushioned you from everything. You don't have the first idea what things are really like out here. If you did, you'd never have gone into the Gravewood in the first place."

"That's not fair," whispers Shea, but Asher isn't done.

"You want to feel bad for the hollows? Fine. But watch them rip someone apart in front of you first and then tell me how you feel."

The quiet shuts up around them. She has never felt smaller than this, caught in Asher's crosshairs, her naivete on full display.

"And that's why it's too risky," says Lys, pulling Asher's focus. "If we go in close, we risk tangling with faulty wiring or a downed fence. I don't trust the camper to outpace a horde."

Asher unrolls the map. "Then we keep to the east—"

Shea doesn't hear any more. She slips out from the bathroom and into the hall beyond, the tile cool under her bare feet. No one notices when she goes. She is quiet and unobtrusive as a mouse. Little Shea Parker, no relevant skills. No helpful knowledge. No understanding of the way the world works outside her door.

Don't coddle her, Lys said. But that's what she is. Coddled. Clueless. Back in Mercy Ridge, Asher tried to talk Shea out of agreeing to Lys's terms. She'd thought, in that moment, that his insistence was born out of a lingering desire to protect her—leftovers from a childhood spent stepping in whenever there was trouble. She knows better now. He didn't want her because he knew how little she'd contribute.

At the end of the day, Shea Parker is nothing more than a liability. Trouble, down to her bones.

Her knapsack is in the camper, tucked away in a shallow cabinet above the bed. She pries it loose, rifling through the contents until she finds what she's looking for. The dress from Paris, red silk beneath black lace overlay.

Come to the revel. Alone.

The dress fits her like a glove, as if it's been tailored to her exact measurements. She slips it on in a hurry, keeping an eye on the house through the gaps in the blinds. No one has come after her. No one will. She is nonessential to the plan. They have everything they need to finish the job. Asher, the soldier. Lys, the prince. Poppy, the genius.

And then there's Shea Parker, the blood bag.

All she's good for is opening up a vein.

The silk clings to her curves, lace spilling down her figure like water. She's never worn anything so pretty in all her life. She doubts she ever will again. She's midway through stuffing Bugs back into her bag when the door swings shut. She turns, an excuse already building in her throat, and finds Poppy standing there, Kit in her arms. Several moments of silence unfold as Poppy looks her over.

"Shea," she says softly. "You can't."

"I'm just trying it on."

"Don't lie."

"He's the one who lied." Her eyes are hot with tears. "He promised me. He told me if I came with him, he'd get me a cure. He *lied*, Poppy. He lied about everything."

"He did," Poppy agrees. "He panicked, and he made a huge mistake—"

"Are you seriously defending him?"

"No." Poppy looks appalled. "*No*, I'm not defending him. I'm just saying that if you want to make him regret it, Shea, there are better ways."

"This isn't about Lys at all," she says, with more vehemence than she meant. "It's about my mom. It's about Ellie. You heard Asher in there—he doesn't even believe us. He won't listen, and I don't know why. Ellie is here. You *know* she's here. You feel it."

Poppy is quiet. "You really think Paris is going to help you?"

"I think he'd be willing to negotiate." She doesn't explain how, or why. She doesn't tell Poppy about the woman in the woods, or the promises she'd made. *Paris is a kingmaker. A dealbroker.* "The man at Van Haut's called me Keeling's 'singular obsession.' Do you remember? I can use that. I can work it to my advantage."

Poppy frowns. "I don't know, Shea. It feels like a bad idea."

"It's not. I'll go to the party. I'll introduce myself. I'll—I'll flirt."

Poppy makes a face. "Flirt?"

"Yes," insists Shea. "I can flirt."

"Shea, I've seen you flirt."

"No, you haven't."

"I have, too," Poppy counters. "I've watched you around Asher our whole lives. You panic. A-and your hands get sweaty. And, if I'm honest, you're a little bit rude."

"I don't have to be good at it, I just have to be there." She pushes her hands through her hair, casting another glance through the blinds. The house is still, the door shut. If she wants to leave without notice, it needs to be now. "Look, I'll wear the dress. I'll get close. I'll make a deal with Paris, whatever it is. I don't care about Lys's stupid little need for retribution. I don't care if Paris lives or dies. I care about my mom. I care about Ellie."

Poppy sinks onto the edge of the bed, frowning up at her. "Are you doing this because you think it's a good idea, or because Asher said you live in a bubble?"

The question jabs at her like a needle. "It's a good idea."

"You don't have to prove anything, Shea. It's not a condemnation of your character to have had people in your life who wanted to protect you as long as they could."

Shea thinks of her father, stacking spare change in the dead of night. Her mother, making broth out of nothing. Lying to her and lying to her to carve out a tiny little pocket of safety in the shadow of something sinister. What good had it done? She never knew things could be different until she woke up and found reality standing over her with fangs. This is her chance to set things right.

Come to the revel. Alone.

"I'm going," she says. "And I love you, Poppy, but nothing you say is going to change my mind. So, either help me get ready, or get out of my way."

TWENTY-FIVE

Shea

Leaving is easy.

It's the rest she miscalculated. Shea picks her way along the dunes, sweating already, her boots squishing in the sun-dried sand of a little inlet. Pink patches of muhly grass tickle her bare legs as she goes. The sky stretches on and on and on without end.

She's lost. And not a little bit lost, either—hopelessly. She ripped the map from the atlas before she left, following the route Asher marked in pen. She looks it over now, using her thumb and forefinger to try to measure out distance. It's futile. The road ahead is wide and flat and empty. Behind her is more of the same.

She walks a little faster. Poppy did something to her hair to make it feel like satin. It sits tucked behind her ears in a severe slash of gold. Her cross heats against her skin, Asher's spoon and Lys's gear clinking with each step. She should have chucked them both into the sea.

Beneath the dress, she wears a wooden stake strapped to her

thigh. Not a stunted bolt or a narrow palisade, but one with heft. White ash, whittled sharp.

At this point, she'd be better off falling on it herself.

There's no sign of life in any direction. She's hyperaware of the time, her eyes on the sun. Already, it's tipping out of the sky's midpoint. Any moment, Asher might wander out to the RV and find her gone. If he and Lys come after her now, she'll be outpaced within the hour. She can't think of anything more humiliating.

She walks a little faster, wicking sweat from her brow, and checks the map again.

There's a good possibility that she's grossly misjudged the distance.

She's gone another mile or so when she notices the car following her. She sees it along her periphery—a black jeep, windows tinted. It slows to a crawl without passing, tailing her at a snail's pace that raises the hair on the back of her neck.

She keeps going, waiting for it to move on. It doesn't. Instead, it pulls up beside her. Out of the corner of her eye, she sees the window roll down. A quick glance shows her the profile of a boy. He looks to be about her age, fair skin freckled by the sun, the wind ruffling a head of chestnut curls. His eyes are shaded behind a pair of dark sunglasses, but his grin is wide and bright and disarming.

"Need a ride?"

"No." She walks a little faster.

He matches her pace, the engine humming. "Where are you headed?"

"That's none of your business."

"You're right," he admits, grinning still. "But you're deep in

Keeling territory, and it's not too often you see a girl walking alone out here. At least not in the middle of the day. Are you going to the revel?"

She falters a step and then continues on. "That's also none of your business."

"That's a yes, then." He hits the brakes, sliding to a halt. "Just so you know—you're going the wrong direction."

She frowns down at the torn bit of road atlas. "That can't be right."

"Tragically true." He hooks his elbow out the window, keeping one hand on the wheel. Waiting as she turns the map this way, then that, grumbling all the while.

With a curse, she crushes the map into a ball. "I don't know how to read this."

"Let me give you a ride. Look, I've got— Hold on." He reaches into his glove compartment and comes up with a little black canister. "I've got pepper spray. If I do anything that makes you uncomfortable, you can *zzzt*"—he mimes spraying it—"spray it right in my eyes."

She looks at the road one more time. It veers out of sight up ahead, heat snapping against the asphalt. Her shoulders burn. Her feet ache. She's getting nowhere, fast.

"Fine," she says. "But only because I'm desperate."

He smiles as she rounds the front of the car, leaning across the passenger seat to push open the door. It's cool in the cabin. A fabricated chill envelops her the moment she climbs inside. The seats are leather, buttery and new. Everything in Little Hill is secondhand, rusted and reupholstered, and the newness of the interior strikes her momentarily numb.

"I'm Max," says the boy, when she's seated. "Hansen."

She reaches for her seat belt. "I'd say thanks for the ride, but I'm reserving that until you deliver me there alive."

"No thanks needed." Max glances over the top of his sunglasses. "I'd settle for a name, though."

Unease worms its way into her. She looks out the window, clinging to the pepper spray like it's a lifeline.

"Or," says Max, drawing it out, "we can sit here in friendly silence."

"Friendly silence, please."

"You got it."

They drive like that for a while, the wind ruffling in the windows as they cruise along the coast. When she finally garners the courage to glance his way, it's to see him eyeing her arms. Lys's half-moon bites constellate her bare skin, marking her from the base of her palms to the insides of her elbows. She draws her wrists in close, crossing her arms over her chest.

"I know, I know," he says, eyes back on the road. "None of my business."

The sunlit world slips past and past. To their left is the sea, oily and dark. The tide is out, and several algae-bitten yachts lie on their sides in the sucking mud. The beachfront is lined in a strip of mega-hotels, concrete gone discolored with mold.

It's full dusk by the time Max drops her off. He parks before a sprawling Southern mansion, pulling up behind a line of cars. The building's front is gridded in windows, every last pane painted black. Several sleek roman columns hold up a half-circle balcony, over which spills vibrant red caladium. Towering palm trees girdled in yellow fairy lights line the paver-clad roadway. Everything is soft and lovely and welcoming—glittering gold and draped in splendor.

It's nothing at all like Lys's ice-clad kingdom in the north.

"Are you coming?" she asks Max, halfway out of the car.

"Er, no." His eyes dart from the building and back to her. He seems suddenly apprehensive. "I'm not on the guest list. I was just in the area."

Wariness builds into a blister. "Doing what?"

"That's a good question." He drums a thumb on the wheel. "Really good. Let's just say I was protecting an investment of mine."

"Is that a polite way of saying it's none of my business?"

His smile is faint. "Something like that, yeah."

"Perfect." She shuts the door, bending down to address him through the open window. "Thanks for the ride. For what it's worth, I'm really grateful you didn't try to kill me."

He tugs his sunglasses down his nose. His eyes are a rich, warm brown. "Is that a regular occurrence for you?"

"You have no idea."

"I might have some," she thinks she hears him say.

"What?"

"No, nothing. You, uh—look really nice in that dress, by the way. I'm glad you wore it."

She straightens in surprise just as he puts the car in reverse. By the time she's gathered her sense enough to ask him what he means, he's gone, backing out into the lot and taking off down the road. She watches his jeep until it's out of sight, certain she'd heard him incorrectly.

Overhead, the sky is the exact color of a bruise.

Bracing herself, she turns to go in and stops.

Someone is standing beneath the overhang. A boy, or perhaps a man. He's tall and tapered, dressed in a gray vest and pleated slacks, the white sleeves of his shirt cuffed at the elbows. His hair, so black it looks almost blue, has been combed back from his face, revealing pale, angular features.

"You look lost," he says, coming closer.

She clears her throat. "Do I?"

"Very much so." He looks older up close. There's the slightest bit of silver at his temples. "Paris Keeling's parties are famously invite-only."

"I *was* invited. Paris asked me here himself."

He angles his head to the side, searching her face. "Did he?"

"Yes."

"Interesting."

Somewhere inside, music is playing. It thuds in her feet. Hums in her core. All she can hear is the rush of the ocean. The man is still studying her, an achingly familiar look of introspection in his eyes.

"You're awfully pretty," he notes. "I don't suppose you'll tell me your name."

"It's Shea," she says. "Parker."

The man's smile is startling—a razor-sharp smirk that sets off warning bells in her head.

"You're absolutely right. I *did* ask for you."

It takes her brain a moment to catch up. Her mind does a frantic cartwheel, doing whatever it can to integrate all that she knows about the infamous Paris Keeling with this man in front of her. All this time, she'd been picturing him as a boy Lys's age, or close to it. Eighteen years old and ruthless. The kind of monster who would use the life of a girl as collateral in a game.

This man is none of those things. Not at first glance. He's unsettlingly lovely, his smile alluring. His eyes are a cool, clear blue. They glimmer, sapphiric, as he offers his arm.

"Would you like to accompany me inside?" asks Paris Keeling.

She's come all this way. The plan hasn't changed, just because he's different from how she expected him to be. She slips her fingers in the crook of his elbow and lets him lead her up the steps and into the building.

Mercy Ridge is all cut timber and stacked stone—a building meant for weathering trouble. Immediately, Shea can see that the Keeling mansion is the lodge's opposite in every way. The moment they cross the threshold, she's greeted by the sight of an open ballroom, sprawling in scope and equally resplendent.

It takes her a minute to absorb every vast, glittering thing. A dazzling old-world chandelier hangs overhead, throwing light into the ornate stained glass, its colors jewel dark. A sprawling main staircase descends into the middle of the room, carpeted steps flush with bodies. Everything glimmers and churns and throbs. Beneath it all, raising the hairs along the back of her neck, is the coppery smack of blood.

"Do you like it?" asks Paris, directly into her ear. She leans back to read his lips, struggling to pick out the lines of him in the swirling lights. "The party—are you impressed?"

"I guess so," she says, and shrugs. "I've seen better."

His smile stretches wider. He's just like Lys, delighted by the push—captivated by the possibility of a chase. "Don't tell me you prefer it up north in Oliver's chilly little lodge."

"I do. It's quieter there."

He regards her over the thin bridge of his nose. "I can bring you someplace quiet, if that's what you'd prefer. We could discuss your mother. Would you like that?"

The warning bells scream louder. "I wouldn't like that, no."

"Oh, you're afraid." Paris's eyes crinkle at the corners. "You don't want to be alone with me. Let me reassure you—your instinct is misguided. Do you think I need to usher you away somewhere quiet to hurt you? That I couldn't do whatever I wanted to you right here, right now?" He steps behind her, his chest at her back, his mouth at her ear. She strains to hear him above the noise. "Look around. I could drain you of every drop right now, and no one in this room would bat an eye. And it isn't because they're occupied. It's not because they're distracted. It's because I own everyone here, body and soul."

"You won't do it." Her bravery is a facade. She's certain he can hear her heart hammering.

"You sound very sure of yourself."

"I am."

"And why is that?"

She turns to face him head-on in the swirling miasma. "Because the only audience you care about isn't even here."

His eyes glitter. He looks like a cat with a bird trapped between its paws. "Is that so?"

"There's no point in killing me if Lys isn't around to see you do it."

"Oh, you're clever. I can see why he's drawn to you."

"I hold my own."

"I'll bet you do." He's watching her a touch too closely, and it makes her skin crawl. "You remind me very much of a girl I fancied myself in love with, once upon a time. She was human, just like you. Did Oliver ever tell you that sordid little tale?"

"He doesn't talk about you at all, actually," says Shea.

She'd meant for it to hurt. Instead, Paris's smile sharpens. "The two of you must not talk about very much, since you seem to have no idea what it is we're doing here this evening. Tell me honestly—do you not have a single clue what all this pageantry is for?"

"It's the hunter's revel," guesses Shea, taking a desperate stab at an answer. "You're celebrating the full moon."

Paris lets out a laugh, loud and full-bodied. "The *full moon*? How pagan. Is that really what you think?"

She scrambles for something to say. Something witty, like Lys. Something clever, like Poppy. Something brave, like Asher.

She comes up empty.

"I can hear you panicking," says Paris. He tucks her hand back into the crook of his arm, tapping his fingers in time to the tempo of her pulse. "It's such a pretty sound. An aphrodisiac. Has Oliver ever told you so?"

"He hasn't mentioned it," she lies.

Paris cuts her a pitying glance. "He's behaved very poorly, then. It's unsporting, to keep you in the dark. This is a birthday party. A very special one."

Through a slit in the paint, a Scorpio moon leers in at her.

A coincidence, Lys called it. Fear cramps her stomach.

"Enough small talk." Paris guides her out of the crowd and up the stairs. "I have someone here that's been waiting for you. Another young woman who stumbled into my path at a most fortuitous time."

Just as he says it, Shea becomes aware of a girl standing at the top of the stairs. She's dressed in a gown of poured gold, her platinum hair falling in waves down her back. At the sight of her, a sick trepidation slithers into Shea's chest.

It isn't because it's Camellia Thorley. It's because of the look on her face. There's hunger there, the Rot weaving just beneath her skin in pale blue fibers. The hazel of her eyes is slightly off-color, her pupils blown. A thousand memories of Camellia cycle through Shea's head. Camellia under a starry sprawl. Camellia passing her a note in the back of class. Camellia in the bathroom, her cheeks wet with tears.

"Camellia?" Her voice is smoke. *"Ellie."*

"You're here." Camellia's voice is remote. A moon knocked out of orbit. "I was hoping you wouldn't come."

"She *finally* made it," booms Paris, beckoning Camellia closer. "Isn't it fantastic? Looks like your big brother kept his promise after all."

"I left you a note," whispers Camellia. "I told you to stay away."

Shea barely hears her. She's looking at Paris, a wordless something imploding horribly inside her chest. "What promise? What are you talking about?"

"Answer a question for me first," says Paris, tapping a finger to his lip. "I'd like to parse out if you're truly as clever as you pretend. How do you think it is that Asher Thorley knew to come looking for you after his sister's tragic disappearance?"

Lys's voice wings through her: *I think Thorley is hiding something.*

"He needed help," coaxes Paris. "He tracked *you* down. Why?"

Shea cuts a glance toward Camellia and finds her staring at her feet. Skeins of blue fracture across her throat, her jaw, her cheeks. Bloodlust, endless and all-consuming.

"Because I'm her best friend," Shea whispers. Even as she says it, she knows it's wrong.

Thorley is hiding something. Thorley is hiding something.

"I'll tell you why he did it," says Paris. "Because *I* told him to."

The world shifts beneath her, the ground crumbling out from underfoot. She grabs hold of the railing, knuckles white against the sleek varnish. It was right in front of her nose. She saw it, and she ignored it. Lys saw it, and she called him a liar.

"Come on now," goads Paris. "Did you *really* think a first-year ranger came up with the brilliant idea to assassinate me all on his own?"

"I don't understand. Why would you put out a hit on yourself?"

Paris's laugh rings out like a bell. Several heads turn their way, a dozen hungry eyes glittering in the light. "At no point in any of this did Asher Thorley intend to hurt me. He was, however, doing whatever I told him to do in order to rescue his poor sister from my clutches. Isn't that right, Camellia?"

A single tear tracks down Camellia's cheek. She doesn't look at Shea at all.

"This whole thing was a trap," says Shea, understanding nearly knocking her off her feet. "You used Asher to lure Lys away from Mercy Ridge so you could kill him."

"*Kill* him?" Paris looks genuinely aghast. "How appalling.

Contrary to what Oliver might have told you, I think very highly of him. I'd never harm one raven hair on that beautiful boy's head."

"Then what?" Her voice wrings out of her, hoarse. "What was the point of all this?"

"Why, *you*, of course," says Paris, as though it should have been obvious. "You are a wrecking ball, Shea Parker. You smashed your way into Oliver's life. You blew up his infuriating little idiosyncracies in a way that I've never quite been able to do. And now, you have one last role to play. The festivities are about to begin. Asher Thorley's job was to make sure you didn't miss even a minute of the party."

A coincidence, pulses Lys's voice in her head. *A coincidence.*

Suspicion crawls into her, cold and skittering. "Whose birthday is it?"

Paris's smile is heartrendingly familiar. "Why, my son's, of course."

In the distance, the music clicks off. A hush falls over the crowd. It's as if someone placed a glass jar over a living flame—everything snuffs out all at once. In the open door stands a devil in a three-piece suit, his dark hair slicked into a hard part. Oliver Lysander, the night falling in around him.

"He prefers to go by his middle name these days," says Paris. "But I have always called him the name his mother gave him, the day he was born."

Understanding is a fist around her throat. "And what name is that?"

"Oliver," he says. "Oliver Keeling."

TWENTY-SIX

Lysander

It's been nearly four years since Lysander last laid eyes on his father.

Even after all this time, it still feels like looking into a mirror. Lit by the chandelier, the too-familiar lines of Paris Keeling's face are thrown into stark relief. The crowd parts around him like water as he descends the steps, crossing the ballroom to meet Lysander where he stands.

He's flanked by two figures. Shea, and a girl Lysander doesn't recognize. Blonde hair. Hazel eyes. A face gridded in hunger. It doesn't take a genius to figure out who she is—Camellia Thorley, transformed. Another pawn in his father's endless schemes.

With a bitter pang, the last of his suspicions click into place: Asher Thorley has led him to a slaughter.

There's nothing he can do about it now. The plan is in motion. He keeps his eyes trained on his father as they approach. He doesn't look at Shea. He can't. Not in that red fucking dress. Not when she left without a word. Not when he deserved it.

"You seem on edge, Oliver," notes Paris.

His molars grind hard enough to hurt. "I'm fine."

Out of the corner of his eye, he sees Shea glancing from person to person. Her mouth tight, she studies the motionless faces in the crowd, taking in the room's nightmare silence, the preternatural stillness of it all. She has no idea what's coming.

But he does. He was born for it, after all.

"I must say, Oliver," says Paris, "I'm alarmed at how little she knows. You've kept her well and truly in the dark."

"I didn't want her to be a part of this."

Paris looks disappointed. "What have I told you about playing a role? You can't do it forever. Eventually, the mask slips. Have you even told her what you are?"

"Look at me," he snarls. "She knows."

"Not all of it," says Paris. "Not the whole, sordid truth. You were afraid she wouldn't find you worthy of her, if she knew. But the truth, Oliver, is that she is not worthy of you."

This time, Lysander can't help but look. And there she stands—a liar in a red dress. A traitor in combat boots. A cataclysm. He knows, sure as he draws breath, that only one of them will make it out of this night alive.

"You asked me what we're celebrating," says Paris, speaking directly in Shea's ear. He doesn't bother standing where she can see his face. He doesn't understand anything about her at all. "For most, Turning is a metamorphosis. For Oliver, it was a nativity. He was born in the dark, the very first of his kind. His birth was meant to herald in a new world order. Tonight, it will."

Paris snaps his fingers. To his great shame, Lysander knows what's coming.

The lights twist in, pinning him in a spotlight. He's rendered blind, one hand thrown up against the glare. A woman materializes, acrobat lithe and clutching a coronet of hammered brass. It's a small bit of pageantry to entertain the masses. Humiliating and showy, just the way his father likes it. He wants to shove the woman away—to flinch back like an animal. But he has learned, over the years, that to do anything but cooperate will earn a punishment.

Not for him. Never for him.

The coronet is set atop his head. It tips to the side, clinking awfully against his horns.

There's a flicker of movement, the sound of laughter, and Shea is shoved unceremoniously into the circle of light before him. Someone has jammed a similar coronet on her head, only where his is brass, hers is bone. A slender weaving of antler sheds, bleached white. Hunter and prey. God and human. She peers up at him, blinking furiously.

"You didn't tell her."

Paris's voice drifts in from behind. From the side. He's circling them like a shark, a silhouette of Lysander's worst nightmare come to life.

"You didn't tell her the reason she is so priceless to you is that you've never been able to hunt. Not like the others. Not without carving away another little sliver of humanity with each kill. And you have held on to your humanity for quite a long time, haven't you, Oliver? In spite of my efforts, you have rebelled against me at every turn. You let yourself starve, drinking filthy pig's blood. Ignoring your baser instincts. Hobbling yourself. Until her."

Shea hasn't taken her eyes off him. He stares right back.

"How many times have you killed for her, Oliver?" asks Paris. "How many times did she make you bend your precious code? How many nights have you carved yourself up to keep her?"

He shuts his eyes. When he opens them again, Shea is watching him still. For the first time ever, her eyes are full of stars. Tears glimmer, spotlit, in her lower lids.

"I did this to you," she whispers.

He shakes his head. "No."

"I did. It's my fault."

"It's not. It's mine." He takes her face in his hands, ignoring the cheer that goes up from the crowd. Someone whistles, sharp. He pretends he can't hear it, catching starlight on his thumb. His skin comes away wet. "Listen to me. When I tell you to run, you run."

"With you?"

He smiles down at her. Everything hurts. Everything ends. "I won't be leaving this ballroom."

"Then I'm not leaving, either."

He searches her face. Memorizing it. It feels like he's reaching in and ripping out his own heart. And in a way, he is. He always knew this was where it would end. He knew, and he ignored it. He is what he is. What he's always been. Selfish and impulsive.

Quietly, he says, "Do you remember when I told you I don't have a soul?"

"Yes."

"I was wrong. It's you."

"Lys—"

He doesn't let her finish. "You want to keep it intact?"

"Yes," she breathes.

"Then run."

All around them, the crowd has begun to chant. Their voices rise and fall in a repeated benediction. It's the same cry he's heard all his life—an apostle's prayer, etched into the walls of his childhood bedroom.

"—from the fount of the forest comes the age of the beast. From the fount of the forest comes the age of the beast—"

Oliver Lysander Keeling has always been very careful with his humanity. His mother raised him to be. She taught him how to cling to it. How to keep it. How to hold fast to the beating heart of whatever made him feel alive. In a few minutes' time, he'll carve it all away.

The chanting grows louder. The room thunders with it. In the melee, Shea's eyes dart to his. He thinks of her in springtime, blood on her hands and determination in her eyes. He thinks he loved her right then. Isn't that the way all tragedies begin?

"Any minute now," he says. "Don't stop for anyone. Don't look back. Not until the sun comes up, do you understand?"

TWENTY-SEVEN

Shea

As quickly as the chanting began, it stops.

Silence settles in after it, like an unseen conductor has just brought an orchestral piece to a close. Lys and Shea are left standing face-to-face in the quiet, blinking like voles. He looks devastating beneath the broad white light, a crown of brass gleaming at his temples.

Ridiculously, she thinks this is how he was meant to look all along. Like royalty.

A shadow appears at the edge of the circle. Slowly, it coalesces into the tapering figure of a man. Into Paris, wearing Lys's smile. Looking out of Lys's eyes. Seeing them like this—side by side—she wonders how it's possible that she didn't see the resemblance right away. He clasps Lys on the shoulder, his smile paternal. Lys holds himself still, but she can see the flinch behind his eyes.

"I know you're angry, Oliver," says Paris, "but this is what you were bred to do. You're destined for so much more than what you've become. All that drivel your mother put into your head in her efforts to manufacture you a conscience—it's done nothing but plague you. Yoke you."

"I'm not yoked to anything," snarls Lys in a voice Shea has never heard him use.

"You won't be, before long," agrees Paris. "Look at you—the change has already begun. Tonight, we put an end to your suffering. We cast off your mortal coil. Set you free."

Lys's jaw wires tight. He watches Shea like he's memorizing her.

Beneath her chest, her heart punches into her bones.

"You'll see it my way once it's over," says Paris. "Every single person in this room has been given the order to hunt and kill Shea Parker. If you don't want that to happen, you'll have to bring them to heel yourself."

Lys doesn't look surprised to hear it. He doesn't look anything at all. He is as rigid as a statue. As unblinking as an effigy.

"You can't possibly save her," says Paris, "but, oh, you'll try. You'll break yourself with the trying. By the time the sun rises, this pretty little distraction of yours will be among the myriad dead. You won't even remember her name."

Lys's stare burns clean through her. She feels like a rabbit must feel, frozen in the crosshairs of a wolf.

"A head start would be sporting, I think," says Paris. "Don't you?"

Lys doesn't appear to have heard his father. He tilts his head, listening. All around them, so do the others. Paris stills, frowning. Shea listens, too. She hears nothing at all. Nothing but the harsh saw of her own breathing.

And then, beneath it, comes the roar of a motorcycle engine.

"Always with the big fucking entrances," mutters Lys. His eyes slide to hers. "Run."

She doesn't hesitate. She turns, racing out of the spotlight and into the crowd, urged on by the way they break and surge, calling after her. They mock and jeer, clutching at her dress and whistling in her direction, but they don't give chase. Not yet—not without an order from Paris.

At the far side of the ballroom, the doors slam open. There, bracketed in moonlight, stands Asher Thorley, his shotgun at the ready. Streaming in behind him is a horde of hollows. They climb one over the other in a thoughtless swarm, snapping their teeth at anyone unfortunate enough to be in their way.

The cheers throttle, turning to screams. The crowd shoves and pushes, chaos bleeding into carnage. Tripping over her dress, Shea fumbles up the stairs and bursts onto the balcony, searching this way and that for Camellia. A hand grips her by the collar and she topples backward, slamming into the railing hard enough to bruise her spine. A man's round face appears in her field of view, his fangs gleaming ivory in the light.

"Should have been faster, Princess," he snarls.

She thrashes, shoving at him as best she can—trying and failing to reach for the stake beneath her dress. She's just managed to grab hold of it when, with a yelp, he's gone. There's a heavy thud, the sound of a body crashing against the floor. Lys is there, crouching over her attacker with claws extended.

In his face is the final death rattle of his humanity.

His talons sing through the air. Skin splits. Blood spatters, violet dark, against the wall.

Shea doesn't stick around to watch. She runs. Fast as she can, pulling open the first door she sees and slamming it shut behind her. She's in an empty salon, the air thick with dust. The windows here are similarly blacked out, no moon at all to see by. Enveloped in the pitch dark, she feels her way to the windows, searching for a latch. As she does, she hears the warning knell of dying batteries. There's a single, damning beep, and silence falls.

Not now, she thinks desperately. *Not now.*

She spins out, pinning herself flat against the wall. Back home in Little Hill, the silence was a balm. Here, in the bloodthirsty dark of the Keeling mansion, it's a bane. In the newly fallen quiet, she feels the creak of the floor under her feet. The shifting pressure of a body, moving just outside. A shadow pulls along the bottom of the door. She clasps her hand over her mouth, silencing her breathing as best she can. Waiting—begging—for the owner of the shadow to move on.

Eventually, it does. She waits another minute. She waits two, deaf to the anarchy raging just outside the door. Cut off from everyone, trapped in her little dark corner.

She can't stay there forever, and she knows it. Eventually, she'll be found. In the middle of the room is a chair, tipped on its side. There's no way to gauge the volume outside the door. No way to tell whether or not the sound of shattering glass will draw a predator. She hefts it up anyway, swinging it at the window as hard as she can. Glass fractures in an explosion of color, raining to her feet.

She climbs through quickly, her dress snagging on the window's jagged remains as she crawls out onto the second-story balcony. The terrace is hemmed in by a stony balustrade, pilasters overgrown with pink begonias. The air is thick with the sweet-smelling blooms. She leans over the top, hoping it's enough to mask her scent as she scans the dark.

Below, the revel has begun to pour out into the street, partygoers desperate to get free of the hollows. It's a stampede, the ground shaking as everyone flees in each direction. Blanketed in the silence, she feels apart from it all. Detached, as though she's a ghost, floating far above the scene. Untouchable, the way she is impervious to the Gravewood in the silence.

In the dark, it's impossible to distinguish between hollow and hunter. She tries anyway, searching the melee for Lys.

She finds him right away. He's standing in the road out front, watching the building with an unearthly calm. The black of his eyes bleeds into his face in swollen tributaries. His hands hang, sheathed in gore, at his sides. A cluster of hollows breaks free of the crowd, moving as one, their sallow faces peeled back in snarls.

Lys doesn't move.

The hollows race around him as though he's little more than an obstruction someone has plunked in their path. They don't see him. They don't touch him. The night pulses, the air shifting around the turmoil of fleeing bodies, the sky thick with the smell of blood.

Only Oliver Lysander remains apart from it all. Removed, the way she's removed, as if both of them have stepped outside the fabric of time and into a silent little pocket of their own. His eyes lift, searching. His gaze settles on hers. He doesn't move, and neither does she. She knows what it feels like to be hunted.

Slowly, his mouth tips into a chilling smile.

A cataclysm, Van Haut called her. All around her, the night is in violent upheaval. Because of her. Because she couldn't save herself. Because she didn't know how. Because she knocked Oliver Keeling so far out of alignment, he came all apart.

Everything has an end, he told her.

The wind picks up, turning choppy. It whips her hair into her eyes, plucks the petals from the begonias. Pink swirls through the dark in a fluttering maelstrom as she peers overhead. At first, it feels like she's seeing stars. Dozens upon dozens of them, spanning the sky in ruby-red constellations. Slowly, a helicopter coalesces out of the dark. It hovers, lights blinking, rotors spinning. She watches, arrested, as something is dropped into the carnage. It hits the ground with a bang she feels in her chest. There's a spark, firecracker bright, and a heavy smoke pours out into the street. Shea throws herself down on the balcony, covering her mouth and nose with her hands.

She doesn't know how long she lies there, exposed and afraid, before the helicopter moves on. The bladed hum of it goes out of the stone. The wind dies down. For a long time afterward, there is nothing at all. She lies flat, blanketed in petals, and waits for the air to clear. Carefully, she crawls on her hands and knees to the edge of the balustrade and peers over.

The stars have gone white again, pale in comparison with the wide face of the hunter's moon. The street below is empty. A sickly sweet smell clings to the air. It slips down her throat, turning her breaths papery. She coughs into her fist, searching for any sign at all of Lys.

He's gone. Disappeared, along with the rest of the crowd. A lone figure walks down the road. She's dressed all in colors, a possum cradled in her arms.

"Poppy," hisses Shea, waving her hands over her head. "Poppy, I'm up here!"

Poppy spots Shea and smiles, her mouth moving. Shea's too far to read her lips. Her words are lost to the dark, soundless and adrift.

"Hold on," Shea calls. "I'm coming down."

Hiking up her dress, she eases herself over the railing, clinging to the begonia vines as she feels her way slowly to a pilaster. The way is fraught, and there are precious few handholds. She makes it partway before she falls, landing hard in a bloodred swath of burning bush.

"Ow."

Poppy appears in her field of vision, talking still as she helps Shea up.

"I can't hear anything," she explains, brushing petals from her dress. "My batteries died in the middle of the attack."

Poppy asks something else. It looks like, *Didn't you bring any spares?*

"I've been busy." The begonias were thorny, and her palms are gridded in scrapes. "Plus, this dress doesn't have any pockets."

Poppy holds up a finger, silently signaling for her to wait. Fishing through the bib of her overalls, she pries loose a half-empty blister packet, the remaining cells winking silver. The very last of Lys's stock. Shea rushes to replace the old batteries with the new, taking a breath as sound comes rushing in on a dizzying wave.

"I could kiss you," she tells Poppy. "Did anyone ever tell you you're the best person in the world?"

"It's been said," says Poppy. "Are you okay?"

"Not really." The smoke is gone, but the odor lingers, pungent and sweet. "Where'd everyone go?"

"I'm not sure. Those smoke grenades sent them running. It smells a little bit like the hawthorn trees behind the schoolyard. Did you notice? Whenever the wind blew through the blooms, I always thought it smelled like fish."

"Why would that make them run?"

Poppy considers as they walk, edging carefully around each subsequent corner. Every alleyway is empty. Every road is deserted. There's no one in sight for miles. "Maybe it's trimethylamine. The smell, I mean. It's the same chemical emitted by a dead body as it decomposes. I bet they don't like it. The Rot needs a living host."

Shea falters, glancing over at her. "Where do you even learn something like that?"

"At school," says Poppy patiently. "You just never did the reading. Is there a reason you're wearing a crown?"

"Oh." Shea pulls off the circlet of bone and grips it tight in her hands. She doesn't know how to tell Poppy how sideways everything has gone. "Poppy I—" Her voice sticks in her throat. She tries again. "I have to tell you something. It's about Ellie."

"She's here." Poppy's eyes are bright in the dark. "We were right, weren't we?"

Shea swallows sharply. "Yes, but it's not that simple—"

"I knew it." Poppy's smile turns hopeful. "I knew we'd find her. Is she—she's okay? Has Asher seen her yet?"

Shea shuts her eyes. She feels as though she's splintering into a thousand pieces. "About Asher—"

The sudden clap of a bell pours through the dark, silencing her. It rings and it rings, pealing out in a clarion call. A brassy convocation, low and deep. Over the tops of the buildings, Shea can just make out a red-capped cathedral, narrow campanile lit from beneath.

A ward against evil, or else a summons. *Come kneel at my feet.*

"That's him. It's Lys."

Poppy doesn't look so sure. "Are we positive?"

"Yes, I'm sure. It has to be." She breaks into a run, dragging Poppy behind her. "Come on. If we hurry, maybe we can get there before Paris does."

TWENTY-EIGHT

Shea

The church sits on the opposite side of a narrow river, over a segmented bridge with the pavement gone efflorescent and down a thin side street set with squat residentials devoured in pokeweed. Only the house of worship stands intact. It rises out from behind a wall of leafy dog fennel, two towering palms flanking the entrance like sentinels.

Inside, the sanctuary is carpeted in a hush. A fountain sits behind the pews, dark with varnish. Inside the lower basin is a pool of standing water, the surface sponged in fairy moss. The cathedral's sole source of light pours in from overhead, moonlight raining down through a hole in the roof.

Just before the altar stands a boy. He's discarded his jacket, and his forearms are violet with blood. His head is bowed, eyes downturned. In his talon-sharp claws, he clutches a book. He looks almost like himself this way. Quiet. Contemplative—the way he looked the first night she came upon him at Mercy Ridge, crimson pooling in her palm.

"*Lys,*" she calls.

His head darts up at the sound of his name. Blood paints his throat in Rot-dark spatters, thick as oil. The book slips out of his hand, toppling to his feet. Moonlight limns the curve of his horns. He reminds her of the Minotaur, shut away in the labyrinth of his own mind.

Waiting to give chase.

The wrongness of it all strikes her cold.

"I wouldn't approach him if I were you." In the dark of the sanctuary, Paris Keeling rises from a pew. He tugs Camellia up after him, hauling her onto her feet. Next to Shea, Poppy gasps.

"Ellie?"

Camellia's eyes lift, horrified. Her voice is fractured, full of teeth. "You're not supposed to be here."

"I came to find you," says Poppy. "We all did."

Camellia looks as furious as Shea has ever seen her. "I didn't ask you to do that. I don't *want you here*, Poppy. You should have stayed in Little Hill."

Poppy flinches back as if she's been struck.

"Easy now," says Paris soothingly. "There's no need to lash out. Your friends have been worried about you, that's all." He smiles over at them, unfazed. "You'll have to be patient with Camellia. She, like Oliver, is undergoing a bit of a personal reckoning."

"A reckoning," echoes Shea. "You destroyed him."

"On the contrary," counters Paris. "I had very little to do with his deconstruction. It was all you. And—might I add—you did it beautifully. All Oliver's life, I have worked to nudge him into greatness—to trigger the snap in him, so that he'd realize his full potential. I did terrible things. Necessary things. Nothing worked.

Nothing took. Not until you. You gave him something worth unmaking himself for, and look at him now."

In the little chancel, Lys hardly seems aware of them. His attention is focused on a warped milk crate someone has set atop the altar. It's piled high with books, the bright covers and paperboard corners boasting dancing bears and humanoid trains and floppy rabbits. Children's books. Dozens of them. He lifts one of them from the pile. It's a thin book of poems, leather bound, the pages dog-eared.

"He was born with the forest beating in his blood," says Paris. "I have always seen him for what he is. A messiah. His mother didn't agree. From the start, she dampened his flame. She filled his head with stories. She fabricated for him a soul, taught him how to play at boyhood. And in doing so, she made him weak."

Without a word, Lys rips a page from the book. A poem flutters to the floor. A second follows. A third. Papers flutter every which way, until finally the book is empty. Tossed aside, it lands spine-up atop its innards.

"You've done my family a great service," says Paris. "I'd like to repay you for what you've done to preserve the Keeling name."

Shea's eyes blur with tears. "Stop saying it like I did you a favor."

"Oh, but you have. I meant what I said before. You're not worthy of my son. But you could be."

She breaks her gaze from Lys, surprised. Paris's smile is patient as he gestures toward the fountain, its finials packed with leafy cascades. "We have our very own fount of holy water. It was brought here from a spring-fed stream, deep in the heart of the forest. All you have to do is take a sip."

"What happens if I say no?"

"I let you walk away, and my debt to you is cleared."

The quiet stings. Lys stands predator still, listening to every word.

Paris watches her wrestle with her indecision, his smile unwavering. "I feel it's paramount to remind you that Oliver called you here, not I. It was quite a thing to behold. One ring of the bell, and you appeared. He has you very well trained."

"What are you saying?"

"Only that I might be willing to let you leave, but I'm not sure I can say the same for him."

He drew her out. He brought her here. And she fell for it, thinking it meant there was something of him remaining. When she peers back at the altar, Lys is smiling over at her, his canines sharp, his chin dark with blood. Here, at last, is the wolf he wished for when he was small. There is nothing human left in his stare.

Tell me how to fix this, he begged her.

There's no fixing any of this. The damage is done.

"The decision is yours," says Paris. "Die in the street, or live like a queen."

The back of her neck prickles with a sudden awareness. The air shifts, pressure changing, and a shadow breaks free of the rest.

"You forgot the third option," she says.

Paris's eyes glimmer. "And what's that?"

"You can go to hell."

There's a whistle, sharp. The unmistakable *thwack* of a missile finding its mark. Paris staggers back, black widening in a circle over his heart. From his chest protrudes a thin wooden stake. White oak, whittled by hand. For a moment, he wavers where he stands, staring down at his body like he can't quite understand what he's seeing. And then, with a silent cry, he drops to his knees.

From out of the dark steps Asher. The crossbow hangs slack at his side.

"We had a deal," gasps out Paris. "We had *a deal*."

"We did," agrees Asher. "You broke it. You promised me—you *swore*—that you would keep my sister safe if I did what you told me to do."

"And I did. Look at her. She's stronger than ever—"

"You killed her," says Asher, silencing him. "I did everything you asked, and you killed her."

His quiet anger reverberates through the dark cathedral. The very air seems to shudder with it. He doesn't spare a glance toward Camellia. She hovers in the dark of a shallow niche, her eyes wide and flat. Poppy starts for her, but Shea catches her by the wrist, shaking her head.

Wedging himself between them, Asher crouches down in front of the kneeling Paris. "All that work. All that planning. Everything you did—it was for nothing. The Keeling legacy will die with you."

"You're already too late," gasps Paris. "You can't stop what's coming, you—"

Paris's head lolls back the instant Asher pries the stake loose. His eyes go flat, his chest still. Rising to his feet, Asher casts the weapon aside. It clatters onto the floor, rolling noisily along the aisle before coming to a stop at the toe of Lys's boot. Lys leans down and picks it up, turning it over for inspection.

"A thank-you would be nice," gripes Asher.

Lys is silent, pressing a finger to the stake's bloodied point.

"I'd also accept an apology from Parker," adds Asher, rounding on her. "I mean, what the hell were you thinking—"

"Asher," says Poppy, "let it go."

"Why?" His gaze lands on Lys and lingers, assessing. "What's wrong with him?"

No one answers. The sanctuary is gripped in a graveyard hush. Slowly, Lys drags his eyes to Shea's. She feels like a little girl again, staring up at the forest. Wishing for it. She sees it in him, plain as day—the same dendroid grip. The same eldritch pulse.

There is nothing left of Lys behind his eyes.

He makes his careful way down the aisle, moving like a predator. Silent. Sure. Asher is the only one who doesn't step aside at his approach. He plants himself in the center aisle like a wall, obstructing Lys's exit.

"What the hell is your problem?"

Lys stares dead ahead, cold and intractable.

"Snap out of it," he orders. "It's over."

"Asher," whispers Poppy.

"Did you hear me?" Asher cuffs Lys's collar, drawing his gaze. "Pull it together, asshole."

"Asher, stop," says Poppy. "It's no use."

Asher ignores her. "I know you hear me."

Lys checks him hard, his strength unnatural, sending Asher flying into the nearest pew. Camellia rushes forward with a cry, skidding to a stop as Lys brushes past her.

He doesn't spare another look in Shea's direction. Not once. Not even a glance. He heads, instead, for the wide double doors that lead out into the night. The first pale glimmers of dawn shine through the stained glass, turning the sanctuary murky with light. She feels like she's drowning in it.

She rounds on Asher the moment Lys is gone. He's busy pulling himself from the pew, his hands clutched protectively over his ribs.

"What the hell was that?" His gaze cuts to hers. "You didn't want to weigh in?"

The confusion in his eyes breaks the dam. Shea charges, slamming a fist into his chest, knocking him back against the pew with less force than Lys had managed but with double the fury. Asher does what he can to shield himself as she rains blow after blow against his ribs.

"This is *your* fault," she cries. "You're a traitor. None of this would have happened if it wasn't for you. We trusted you. *He* trusted you."

"I won't apologize," says Asher, catching her wrists against his chest. "I had it under control."

"Yeah?" She tears herself out from his grasp. "Does this feel like control to you? Is this a victory?"

His jaw tightens. "I handled it."

"No. I don't accept that. You should have told me what was happening. We could have figured it out together. That was what we promised."

"That promise was broken the second you set foot in the Gravewood."

And there it is. His anger has claws. It snatches the breath clean from her lungs.

"You were gone," she whispers. "I did what I had to do to protect my family."

"Yeah? Well, so did I."

She can't stand the sight of his face. She turns away from him, stomach sick. When she starts down the aisle, he follows.

"It's over," he tells her. "It's done. Whatever happens next, we'll be okay. We'll figure it—"

"Don't." She rounds on him so fast, he flinches. "Don't say another word. Not one more. I never want to speak to you again."

Asher looks as though he's the one with the stake in his chest. All the blood drains from his face, leaving him white as a sheet. Behind her, Camellia is crying openly.

"Shea, wait a minute." Poppy's touch alights on her arm. "Let's think this through."

"Don't touch me." She shakes Poppy off, launching up onto her toes in an effort to get right in Asher's face. "You've ruined everything, do you understand that? Lys was all I had left."

Asher's eyes flash. "You had me. You've always had me."

"Not anymore." Her voice shakes. "You're *dead* to me, Asher Thorley."

"Shea!"

She ignores Poppy, pushing past Camellia and shoving out into the fledgling dawn.

Where she slams directly into Oliver Keeling, waiting on the topmost step.

TWENTY-NINE

Shea

Lys doesn't react to the impact.

He's a steel wall, cold and unyielding, his back to her. He's staring out at something in the street, and it doesn't take her long to understand what has caught his eye. A barricade of unmarked vans lines the road before them. Outside the vans stands a small arsenal of armed militia, each of them wielding weapons retrofitted with wooden bullets.

Soldiers of the watch, here to collect.

Shea thought she was afraid before. Now her heart stops cold. Because standing at their helm is Egor van Haut. He smiles at the sight of them, tugging loose his glasses to clean the lenses.

"You never asked me." He says it conversationally, as though they're still at tea in his living room. "You never asked me why the perimeters of my farm are off-limits. Why I live alone, in the middle of nowhere. You never asked what sort of work I'm doing."

"I don't care," grits out Shea.

"You should," says Egor, unruffled. "I am on the cusp of a groundbreaking discovery. A cure, Shea. A *cure*. For Nel. For others like him. The trouble is, I cannot do the work that I do for free. Surely, you understand—I'm told your mother is very ill."

The door behind Shea opens. Asher emerges, flanked by Poppy and Camellia. He draws up short at the sight of the heavily armed presence.

"Oh shit."

Egor replaces his glasses. "It's a very big bounty, Private Thorley."

"Asher Thorley," calls a uniformed man standing beside Egor. "You are being apprehended and placed under arrest for abandoning your post. You will be transported back to base, where you will be tried and hanged for desertion."

"Asher," whispers Camellia, distraught.

Asher says nothing at all. He stands at attention, his gaze shuttered.

"You have the right to remain silent," continues the man. "Any statement made may be used as evidence against you in a trial by court-martial."

Egor smiles wanly at Shea. "I am so close to cracking the genome. You must understand—my motivations are good."

Shea's heart flies into her throat. "Asher—"

He doesn't meet her eyes. "Looks like you'll get what you wanted."

"Asher, wait—" Her voice cracks. "Wait."

There's no chance for an apology. No space to take back what she said. To undo it and undo it. An order is given and two members of the watch ascend the steps, forcing Asher's hands behind his back. He's shoved forward, stumbling as he goes.

Still in the shadow of the cathedral, Camellia makes a strangled sound. "Asher?"

"It's okay," he calls back to her. "It's just a formality. Stick together, all right?"

His head is pressed down, and he's loaded into the back of the van.

"Wait!" Camellia surges forward. "Please, wait. That's my brother. Please, I didn't even get to say goodbye."

The door to the van rattles shut with a slam. On the bottom step, Camellia is met with the jagged end of a wooden bayonet.

"That's far enough," someone barks. "One more step, and you're dust."

"Easy," chides Egor. "There's no need to resort to violence. Especially not on Keeling territory. Surely you can understand why she's upset."

The engine kicks over. The van departs, careening around the corner and out of sight. Shea feels like half her heart has gone with it.

Beside her, Lys is a statue. Solid as an oak. Rooted as a maple. Rotted as a hawthorn. He takes everything in without a word, watching the van disappear into the gray, gray dawn. The moment it's out of sight, he turns his attention to Egor.

"I'm curious to know how you saw this going," he says, and his voice is an entire register too low. A creature's voice, not a boy's. "Is one of those vans for me? Will you cart me back to Pennsylvania? Keep me in a barn, like your sad little son? Feed me from a blood bag and stick me full of needles, like the good old days?"

"I think," says Egor, "that you'll be happily compliant, no matter what I ask of you."

"Compliant," echoes Lys, his lip curling.

"Yes," says Egor. "Because you're going to want a cure."

There's a pronounced pause. Then, "I'm listening."

"I've done some digging into Shea Parker," says Egor. "Into her family. Genes like that, well, they tend to be hereditary. It would be a shame, wouldn't it? To lose her that way? After everything you've sacrificed to keep her intact?"

An excruciating silence follows. Lys smiles his most alluring smile. An aggressive mimicry of a boy.

"You seem to be operating under the misconception that you can hold Shea Parker over my head. That you can use her to manipulate me. To bring me to heel."

Something in his voice makes the watch creep closer.

"My father made the same mistake," says Lys mildly.

Without warning, he pulls Shea to him. Her back slams into his chest. His fingers close around her neck. She struggles, fighting against him, as his hold tightens enough to hurt.

"One was the claw," he mutters into her cheek. "The other one the will."

His bite clamps down around the soft underside of her throat.

There's a blister of pain, more familiar than it has any right to be. The kiss of venom ribbons through her, sugar sweet and ambrosia warm. Her mind continues to fight, even as her arms go slack. Distantly, she's aware of pandemonium—the sounds of shouting, wordless and far away: *Don't shoot! Don't shoot him, goddamn it!*

And then it's quiet in her head, too.

She blinks and sees her mother in the kitchen, clear-eyed and dressed in yellow, her apron full of wild bergamot. Her father in his armchair, his hands dancing through the candlelit dark. Poppy and

Camellia in the bottom branches of an old oak, laughing into the sky. Asher in the surf, the sky falling around him as he leaned in and kissed her.

And then, at the end of it all, is Oliver Keeling, his hair in his eyes, the crooked slash of his smile bright in the dark. His mouth at her throat. His heart in her hands: *I'm so gone for you.*

Gone.

I'm gone.

There's a violent impact, and the image shatters. She drops to her knees on warm concrete. Someone is shouting. A man, his voice twisted in fury. There's the sound of running feet. A rush of bodies. A hand around her wrist. Someone is urging her to get up. To move. To run.

In front of her kneels Oliver Lysander Keeling. The Gravewood Devil, brought to heel. His mouth hangs slack. Her blood paints his chin, runs in red, red rivers down his throat. His cheeks are flush with color. His eyes are clear and bright and blue.

From his chest protrudes a wooden stake. It takes her a moment to recognize her own trembling hand wrapped around it. She lets go, toppling back. Gingerly, he pokes at it. A circle of dark spreads like oil along his shirt. His eyes lift to hers. Everything is slow, slow, slow, like they're both underwater. And then, with a terrible, icy surfacing, all sense comes rushing back. Sound slams into her as the world tips back into motion.

"The sun is in your eyes," he whispers.

"Get him up," bellows Egor, somewhere out of sight. "Help him up! Do it now!"

Lys is wrenched onto his feet, disappearing from her field of view.

Boots hammer on the ground. A door slams. An engine turns over.

"Move," shouts a voice. "Let's go!"

Tires screech against pavement, loud at first and then quiet. Shea's knees are scraped open. Her palms gashed. There's blood everywhere. Hers. His. It gathers in violet pools along the concrete.

"Get up," cries Poppy. "Please, get up."

The sun is bleeding, too. It leaks through the buildings in a wide, red swath of brilliance, flooding the space with light.

"Get *up*, Shea," cries Poppy. "We have to go."

The wind intensifies. It buffets Shea in a steady *chop, chop, chop*, turning the saltwater tug of a breeze to a roar that shuts out all other sound. Her hair whips into her face. Her vision tunnels.

When her head hits the ground, she doesn't feel anything at all.

...OF THE END.

Shea Parker's missing poster is the same as all the others.

The girl in the photograph is small and unsmiling, her hair in braids. The image is old. A Polaroid her father snapped, the Christmas before he left. She stares at it for a long time before she flips it over, setting it face down on the table.

"I want to see my friends," she says, for the fourth time in as many minutes.

Across from her sits a woman, her hair slicked back in a sleek red bun. She's dressed in a suit, neat and crisp, her features angular.

"I'm sure you do, but I need you to answer the question first."

They're in an old classroom, complete with linoleum floors and yellow blinds, a chalkboard on one wall. Snow gathers on the windowsill. She can feel the cold press of it through the glass.

"I forgot the question," she says.

The woman raises a brow. "Again?"

"I hit my head pretty hard."

The woman's smile stretches thin. Shea stares across the table. She waits. Her neck is bound in gauze. Every bone in her body aches. They've been sitting here for an hour. Maybe more.

The clock on the wall doesn't work.

At first, the woman was chatty. Open. She told Shea how Oliver

Keeling took out an entire transport somewhere north of the Flatwood. How they found the caravan going up in smoke, no tracks, no trace. No survivors.

She explained that they were somewhere along the northernmost terminus. The first watch, deep in the mountains of Maine, situated along the mouth of the Gravewood, dark as Tartarus. They'd been watching Shea for a while. Tracking her movements. Monitoring her—aware that she wasn't just another missing girl from Little Hill.

After that, she'd been close-lipped.

"We can make our own inferences, of course," she says. "But we'd rather you tell us your version of things directly."

Shea bites her tongue. She says nothing.

With a sigh, the woman flips open the manila file in front of her. She spends some time shuffling through a short ream of papers before prying one loose. "This says here that you suffer from sensorineural hearing loss. A childhood illness, was it?"

"Scarlet fever," says Shea.

"That's a shame."

"I manage just fine."

"I'm sure you do. You've had to be clever, though, haven't you? Our rangers say Keeling was getting you batteries from a shuttered shipping facility down in Nashua. It was a lucky find on his part. Most of them have been torched. Even still, he was pulling from a finite supply. I'm curious—what would you have done when he ran out?"

"That's your question?" asks Shea. "A hypothetical?"

The woman lets the file fall shut. "We can get you batteries, if that's what you need. We can get you in front of an audiologist. We can have you assessed by a surgeon. You want it? All you have to do is ask."

"I'm waiting for the catch," says Shea.

"Don't play dumb. It's a waste of both of our time. You already know what I want."

"You want Lys," guesses Shea. "Why?"

"He's a threat that needs to be neutralized. His father played by the rules. He stayed within the agreed upon lines. But Oliver?" The woman sits back, hooking an elbow over the back of her chair. "People will die, Ms. Parker. Good people. Oliver Keeling is a contagion risk. He's not in control of himself."

Shea regards the woman sideways. "Are you with the watch?"

"What do you think?"

"I think you don't look like a soldier."

Eyes narrowing, the woman sits forward. "Why don't you let me ask the questions, and you just focus on getting better?"

"Why?" asks Shea. "So I can help you kill him?"

"If that's what it takes."

"No, thank you."

The woman's smile flickers. She taps her fingers together in a loose steeple. "The pattern of the bites on your wrist seem to denote a parasitic symbiotic relationship with Keeling, while the bite at your throat is analogous with an attack. Now, our team doesn't have access to what transpired inside St. Mary's Church, but we can guess. He's dangerous. And I think you know it."

"What about Asher?"

The woman's mouth tightens. "Asher Thorley is not our concern."

"Well, he's mine," says Shea.

"Ms. Parker—"

"You said if I want something, to ask for it. This is me asking. I want Asher."

"He's not on the table."

"Then neither am I." Shea pushes the poster toward her. "I'd like to see my friends."

There's a knock at the door, soft. The woman's eye twitches.

"Excuse me a moment."

Her chair scrapes back and she crosses the classroom, heels clicking across the linoleum. Shutting her eyes, Shea tips back in her chair and waits as the woman speaks with someone out in the hall. She can't make out what it is they're saying, but she can hear the tension in it. Whatever it is, it doesn't seem friendly. Cracking one eye open, she peers over at the door. A boy stands there, startlingly familiar.

His name skids into her in a burst of awareness. Max Hansen.

His chestnut curls have been combed flat and his sunglasses are gone, but there's no mistaking his face—it's the same boy who gave her a ride to the revel. She feels a tiny stab of treason as his eyes flick to hers. If he's surprised to see her, he doesn't show it. Instead, he flashes her a smile, small and secretive, and ducks out of the room without a word. The door shuts. The woman returns, looking harried.

"I'm being called into a meeting," she says, gathering up her papers. "We'll continue this later."

When she's gone, a pair of unsmiling rangers escort Shea back to the infirmary where she's been kept in recovery. It's a glorified nurse's room, cots thin and blankets thinner, posters about sexual health plastered across the concrete walls. The windows have been slung with blankets, stifling the sun. Poppy sits at a cluttered desk, rifling through an old medical textbook. On the cot farthest from the light sits Camellia, her knees hugged to her chest and Poppy's scarf looped thrice around her throat. She doesn't look up when Shea enters.

"Are you okay?" asks Poppy, the moment the door is shut.

"I'm fine," says Shea, though she feels anything but. "Has she said anything yet?"

Poppy glances at Camellia. "No."

"Has she fed?"

Poppy shakes her head.

"She can't starve forever. She'll come around."

"Maybe." The hollows of Poppy's eyes are pronounced, dark with bruises. She hasn't slept in days. Neither of them has. "What did she want? That woman?"

"She wants Lys."

Even saying his name hurts, like sticking a finger into an open wound. She's been struggling to come back to herself, in the days since St. Mary's. His venom is a fever she can't flush out. She sees him, sometimes, as if he's standing right there. Her own personal ghost, stalking her through her waking hours.

He's there now, standing beneath the window, the dark bending oddly around him. He doesn't speak. He doesn't move. He only stares, his face gaunt and his eyes hollow. A silent, spectral version of himself. She tries not to look at him.

She tries, but sometimes he's all she sees.

"What are you going to do?" asks Poppy.

She forces herself to look away from her ghost. "I'm going to negotiate. If I play my cards right, maybe they can help us with Asher."

At the mention of Asher, Poppy casts a worried glance toward Camellia. She stares at the wall, showing no sign at all of having heard. Leaning in close, Poppy drops her voice to a whisper. "I overheard some of the rangers talking at breakfast this morning. They're saying his trial is in two months. Some of them are even planning on going down to New York for it, like it's some sort of festival."

"Two months means we have time," says Shea.

"To do what? We can't exactly break him out of a military prison."

"Yet."

"Shea—"

"We'll figure it out."

"How?" Poppy looks as frustrated as Shea has ever seen her. She's treading water. They all are. "Even if we knew what we were doing, it's a mess out there. Lysander's been emptying out the Gravewood for weeks. Yesterday I heard someone say there's been a surge in outbreaks. The watchtowers are empty. The Rot is in everything. How can we possibly help?"

Sometimes, when Shea is lying awake at night in her cot, she hears Lys's voice in her head.

Tell me how to fix this.

"It's my fault he's like this. That makes it my mess to clean up."

"That's not fair," says Poppy. "Shea, you can't do that to yourself. It's not all on you."

It feels like it is. It keeps her up at night, the guilt. The understanding that if she'd known more, done more, been more, she could have prevented this. She doesn't know how to make things right. Not yet. But she'll find a way. She's always fought best when she's backed into a corner.

"They'll cave," she says. "They'll get me Asher. They want Lys dead, and they need me."

Poppy doesn't look convinced. "They need you as bait. It's Paris all over again."

"It's not. We'll be better this time. We'll be ready. We'll figure out a way to get Asher, and then we'll find Lys. We'll bring him back."

"And what if we can't?" asks Poppy. "What if he's too far gone?"

Shea shuts her eyes. She pictures his face on the steps of the church. His eyes had been clear and blue and bright. His hands around hers shook, blood ribboning through their fingers. In that singular moment, on the cusp of death, she'd felt it. Their hearts, beating in tandem. Twin flames, forever each other's inverse.

When she opens her eyes, he's standing right in front of her.

Tell me how to fix this, she wills him.

He says nothing, because it isn't up to him. It's up to her. Oliver Lysander Keeling is a monster of her creation. She'll find a way to fix the damage they've done, or she'll end it.

"If we can't reach him," she says, "if he's really gone, I'll hunt him down and put a stake through his heart myself."

ACKNOWLEDGMENTS

This book was a long time in the making, which means the list of people I have to thank is even longer. You'd think, after four books, I'd have nailed down a process. Instead, what I've learned is this: Some projects come together quickly and some are a slow burn. This one was one of the slowest. I've been fortunate to work with so many lovely people along the way.

First and foremost, I'd like to thank my spouse, who first encouraged me to chase this idea and see where it led. I chased it right to New York, where I stumbled into what has become this whole wild publishing journey. For that, and everything else, I will always be thankful.

To my parents, thank you for continuing to step in and take care of the girls when I'm on a deadline crunch. They're getting so much extra time at Grandma and Papa's these days, and they're all the better for it.

To my daughters, you two are the reason I write. Thank you for your joy and your curiosity and for always cheering me on.

To my agent, Josh, thanks for being a constant champion of my stories, and for always getting them into the right hands. It's been a dream working with you.

To my editor, Mallory, thank you for letting me work plot tangles out in my own oddball way, and for always being willing to hop on the phone and talk me through the little details. I am so thankful you gave this story a chance.

To Maya, you are a superstar. You stepped into the editing process right in the middle of my madness and picked up seamlessly where Mallory left off.

To my UK editor, Rachel, it has been so wonderful being back with you again, and I'm thrilled we are getting the opportunity to work together a second time, and on something so exciting.

To my production editor, Janell, thank you for your keen eye and your constant patience. I couldn't make these final drafts shine without your attention to detail.

To my publicist, Tessa, I'm thrilled to be here marketing another book with you. I'm a bit of a chaos gremlin, and you keep the trains running on time.

To everyone else at Scholastic, thank you for all that you do to get my books into the hands of readers. Every time I get to come back and write another one, I know it is because of all your hard work.

Years ago, when I first started playing with this story, there was a litany of people who were cheering me on (and encouraging me to make Lys even worse). Thank you to Lindsay Bilgram, Zoulfa Katouh, Jordan Gray, Hannah Whitten, Allison Saft, Reba Adler, Abigail Carlson, Lyndall Clipstone, and Clementine Fraser for the constant feedback in our various writing chats, and for reading and loving this book in some of its earliest, ugliest iterations.

Thank you to Hafsah Faizal, who let me slide this book into her DMs many years ago now, and who has walked me through several parts of the process.

Thank you to Jen Carnelian and M. K. Lobb, who have read nearly every draft of this book and who are polite enough to gasp at the plot twists every single time.

Thank you to De Elizabeth for the early-morning writing chats and for always listening to my unsolicited voice notes.

Thank you to Anna Munger, for cheering me on through every word and for helping me unravel so many plot tangles.

Thank you to Kamilah Cole, for reading an early draft and for helping to keep me sane through the last few rounds of edits while I was putting out another book.

Thank you to Henry, my faithful canine sidekick, who has just turned twelve. When I first jotted Shea Parker's name down in my writing journal, he was two years old and still chewing the spines off my books. He has sat beside me in the writing of every book since.

And finally, to you—the reader—thank you for reading. It's because of all of you that I get to keep doing this, and for that I am full of gratitude.

ABOUT THE AUTHOR

Kelly Andrew lost her hearing when she was four years old and she's been dreaming up stories in the silence ever since. Andrew lives in New England with her husband and their two daughters (and a very grouchy Boston terrier). She has a BSW but received her Masters in English & Creative Writing. When she's not writing, she enjoys obsessing over a good book, scouring flea markets for treasure, and getting intentionally lost in the woods. Andrew is the *New York Times* bestselling author of *Your Blood, My Bones*, as well as two interconnected horrors, *The Whispering Dark* and *I Am Made of Death*.

You can find her online at @KayAyDrew.